The Lawyer

Originally published as *The Scribe*.

Also by A.A. Chaudhuri

KRAMER AND CARVER
Book 1: The Lawyer
Book 2: The Abduction

THE LAWYER

A.A. CHAUDHURI

LUME BOOKS
A JOFFE BOOKS COMPANY

Revised edition 2024
Lume Books, London
A Joffe Books Company
www.lumebooks.co.uk

First published by Lume Books in 2019

Please note this book was previously published as *The Scribe.*

This paperback edition first published in Great Britain 2024

We love to hear from our readers!
Please email any feedback you have to: feedback@joffebooks.com

Cover design by Imogen Buchanan

ISBN: 978-1-83901-591-5

Chapter One

Tuesday 28 October 2014, 2 a.m.

Her sixth sense told her she was not alone.

There, muffled noises from behind, a faint footstep, a quiet intake of breath, the soft sound of a door sweeping the plush carpet beneath it…and then a voice breaking the pin-drop silence – soft, husky, self-assured. An all-too-memorable voice, one she hadn't heard in a long time – one that froze her in her tracks.

'Hello, Sarah. Did I startle you? I'm sorry, I didn't mean to.'

It was a patent lie, spoken with a sinister calmness that only served to underline its fiction. The speaker knew it, and so did Sarah who, startled by the sudden intrusion, unwittingly dropped the wodge of papers she'd just spent the last ten minutes assembling in date order.

Not least because she hadn't been expecting company, let alone this unwelcome blast from the past, at just gone 2 a.m. She'd realised half an hour ago, when she'd sleepwalked to the kitchen to make her tenth black coffee of the day, that she was the only one left on the soulless conference room floor. And only moments ago, Frank – the security guard on reception – had called to confirm they were the only two left in the building.

This hadn't surprised her; she shouldn't have been there herself. But tomorrow, the deal she and the rest of her team had been busting a gut on was closing, and she needed to ensure that everything was shipshape for signature. Despite the partner in charge telling her to make tracks several hours ago and come in early tomorrow instead. But as usual, she'd wanted to stand out, make an impression, prove her worth and commitment to the firm, and, above all, bag that coveted associate's spot in one of the City's most celebrated legal banking departments.

And yet here they were alone together. The other not a part of the firm, nor, to her knowledge, a client, and yet, not a stranger to her; their last exchange laced with anger, bitterness and spite.

'No, I mean yes, kind of,' she replied twitchily, hastily gathering up the unruly pile of papers, yet trying her best to conceal her alarm. 'I'm just surprised to see you. It's been a long time, and it's late. I'm amazed Frank let you up, to be honest. You're not a client as far as I know, and we're certainly not friends.' She paused, incredulity swathing her face. 'Is that what you told him? How you got past security?' It wasn't a straightforward question. Her tone was mocking, sarcastic.

Maddening.

She hadn't changed. Still the same snotty-nosed conceited bitch. She was by far the worst of them. The one who most deserved what was coming to her.

'Your confusion is perfectly understandable.' Underneath the outward civility, the affable banter, the genial smile, there was a definite edge to the intruder's voice. An underlying frostiness. A hidden agenda.

This wasn't right. None of it felt right. She sensed danger. *Where the hell is Frank?*

'I have this problem, Sarah. I've had it for some time, in fact, and it's really starting to niggle me. So much so, I can't sleep, I can't eat. It needs sorting out before I go quite insane.'

Sarah fiddled nervously with the papers between her fingertips, her eyes flitting every now and again to the door which was blocked but tantalisingly ajar, her mind desperately trying to devise an escape plan. *Get out, get out*, she screamed inside.

The intruder closed the door, then began to walk towards her. Her only means of escape was gone. Her only lifeline severed in the briefest of moments.

Her natural eye for detail took in the long leather trench coat, the black leather gloves, the perfectly groomed hair scraped back and set firm. *Is it hairspray? Gel?* Not one strand hung loose. And then she saw the shoes – shiny black Nike trainers. Not what she'd expected. They looked brand new.

'I'm sorry to hear that. Were you hoping I might be of assistance?' She tried to remain calm, but she heard the crack in her voice, felt weak-legged, her bowels suddenly loose. *Why didn't I go home like Jefferson told me to?*

She saw the steely determination in the intruder's eyes, realised what this was all about, and sensed her time was up.

'Yes, I was.'

It was all too quick for her to grasp what was happening, to put up any kind of a fight. The gun seemed to appear from nowhere, and there was no means of avoiding its fire.

The killer watched the silent bullet invade the girl's stomach, like a meteorite assaulting the Earth's atmosphere, before allowing a self-satisfied smile to take hold when it became obvious that she wasn't dead.

That had always been the plan. Death by gunshot wound alone was too good for the filthy whore. Too kind. There was a lot more work to be done. Creative, artistic work. The most enjoyable part of the plan.

Sarah's knees buckled, her eyes wide with horror as she tumbled to the floor, hitting the ground hard. She lay there, paralysed by fear, not yet unconscious, although pain and shock rendered her speechless. She instinctively pressed her trembling hands over her gaping wound in a bid to stem the bleeding. But it was futile; her fingers – which, along with the rest of her body, were gradually becoming colder – soon enveloped in a claret-coloured sticky mass.

And then she heard music. Soft, classical music. Beethoven's *Moonlight Sonata*. One of her favourites. Reminiscent of happier, carefree times. Ordinarily, she would have welcomed its soothing lilt and beautiful inflection. But the gentle sound – symbolic of the killer's disturbing poise – chilled her to the bone. She managed to raise her head a few millimetres to her left and noticed the red MP3 player positioned on the edge of the conference table.

Her killer smiled, then knelt over her, like a hunter admiring his kill. Her heart jabbed with terror as she watched the leather gloves being removed, revealing long, lean fingers, smooth and well groomed, just as she'd remembered them to be; a feature that had always surprised her. The sturdy gloves were replaced with a pair of latex ones, and she couldn't help wincing at the screeching sound they made while being pulled on with meticulous precision. Like an experienced surgeon prepping for the operating table.

She felt a rubbery finger trace the skin between her breasts, then watched in panic as the gleaming blade bore down upon her, her killer's eyes mad with elation, revenge and triumph.

Monday 7 September 2009

The professor surveyed the room. Full of zealous, fresh-faced postgrads. The new batch. Young, driven, but sorely naive. An incessant whirr of vibrant chatter and carefree laughter buzzed in his eardrums like animated cicadas on a balmy summer's evening. He allowed himself a moment to assimilate the buoyant mood, breathe in the hormones, the anticipation of youth. Using the room's energy to bolster his imminent introduction to Contract Law.

Despite years of practice, it was always a little daunting resuming the routine after the summer break. But as the saying went: old habits die hard. And, like riding a bike, once he got going, he never looked back. By the middle of his first lecture, he knew it would seem like he'd never been away.

Casting his eyes once more over the mixed crowd, three especially pretty students captured his gaze. He could always guarantee one or two stunners. It was what he looked forward to at the start of the new academic year, the prospect of which had excited him to the point of orgasm that morning, when he'd got out of bed and headed straight to the bathroom to masturbate, Classic FM turned up to the max so that Elizabeth, his wife of fifteen years, wouldn't hear the frantic jerking of his slippery penis.

Although he guessed she'd suspected. Just as he was almost sure she knew about his affairs. She wasn't stupid, despite never raising the subject openly. He could see the suspicion in her eyes, hear the mistrust in her voice. But she wasn't the type to make a scene. Which was partly what aggravated him, drove him away into the arms of hot-blooded young women, wet between the loins and not afraid to express themselves, in and out of bed.

That, along with the painful secret he and Elizabeth shared, of course.

The professor instinctively straightened his tie, felt the adrenaline rush up in him as he cleared his throat. 'Good morning. My name is Professor James Stirling. Welcome to the Bloomsbury Academy of Law. Being supremely smart individuals, I am certain none of you harbour any illusions that learning a three-year law degree in ten months is going to be a piece of cake. Because it isn't, and at times it'll feel like hell on Earth. But I can assure you that, so long as you fully commit yourselves to the next ten months, it will be worth it, and the satisfaction you feel when you hold up that diploma will be worth all the blood, sweat and tears.' He paused, resisting the urge to chuckle at the newly petrified montage of faces. Mute, glum-faced, the unnatural silence more deafening than the previous chatter. 'So, before I begin, can anyone tell me the elements required to form a contract?'

A hand shot up from the row he'd glued his eyes on only minutes before. It belonged to a sultry brunette. Her large brown eyes sparkled with excitement, desperate for that first brownie point. She was drop-dead hot. He was grateful for the podium.

'Yes?' He gave her a wolfish smile.

'Offer, consideration and acceptance.' There wasn't a trace of doubt in her voice, and it made her hotter. He noticed the striking blonde to her left scowl. He liked the look of her too. And the mixed-race beauty to her right. Clearly, rivalries were already forming. That was good. Inter-female competition was such a turn-on. A few seats along from the brunette sat a dark-haired young man. Handsome, yet with a quiet look about him. He seemed to sense the professor's gaze, and immediately looked away.

'Very good, and your name is?'

'Sarah,' the girl replied. 'Sarah Morrell.'

'Excellent, Sarah. So, as Sarah said…'

As the professor continued his lecture, he smiled smugly inside. Mindful of his magnetism, of the hold he had over his impressionable young students. Many of them quick to develop crushes on the academy's most fuckable tutor. Only just forty. Handsome, strong, broad-shouldered, with a toned, manly physique, yet not too muscular. He had thick, jet-black hair highlighted with a few streaks of grey, dreamy ebony eyes, and a ravishingly rich, guttural voice that drew in his audience like moths to a flame. He was also supremely intelligent and well respected in his field. More mature than the average college boy, but not so old that his flirting could be termed creepy.

At least, he didn't think so.

Yes, he could tell that this was going to be a good year. So much optimism, so much potential, so much beauty.

He was really going to enjoy himself.

So long as they played ball.

Chapter Two

Tuesday 28 October 2014, 6.30 a.m.

'Victim's name?'

'Sarah Morrell, sir. Twenty-five. Fourth-seat trainee.'

'Fourth seat?' DCI Jake Carver frowned. 'That means nothing to me, Detective. Speak to me in English for Christ's sake.'

Having been woken abruptly less than an hour ago by Sergeant Matthews at Bishopsgate police station, Carver's routinely low tolerance level was running even nearer to the ground.

He'd had an argument with Rachel, his ex-wife, last night. Daniel, his six-year-old son, had started calling Rachel's dull but irritatingly dependable boyfriend Carl "Dad", at "Dad's" insistence, and it was *really* pissing him off. She'd refused to ask Carl to tone it down, or even see her ex's point of view. As a result, he'd spent the rest of the evening pummelling the punchball he kept in his bedroom before downing several whiskies.

Which was unlike him. When he and Rachel split, Carver had refused to become a cliché. That well-worn formula for glossy American novels and Hollywood blockbusters. The embittered divorced police officer, who drowns his sorrows in booze and loose women as a means of coping with his shitty personal life. In fact, he'd been celibate for nearly two years now – although sometimes it killed him – and had substituted boxing down the local gym for booze at his "local". Channelling his anger and miserable personal life into carefully controlled punches which never did anyone any real harm but kept him sane and sober.

But last night, he'd slipped. And despite knocking back some Nurofen with a large Americano en route to the crime scene, his head pounded and his body ached not from the punches, but from too much booze and too little sleep. He hated himself for it and vowed not to let it happen again. It wasn't good for him, and it certainly wasn't good for his son.

Detective Constable Ben Drake looked down at his notes. 'Trainee lawyers typically work in four to six departments, known as "seats", over their two-year training period, sir, before choosing where to specialise on qualification. At Channing & Barton they do four six-month seats.'

'Hmm, I see,' Carver nodded disinterestedly. 'And what *seat* had this poor girl been *sitting* in?'

'Banking, sir. She started her training in March 2013 and was due to qualify in five months' time.'

'Have the parents been notified?'

'The firm's senior partner, William Coleridge, has that unfortunate task, sir. I spoke to him around twenty minutes ago. Shocked, of course. Said he'd be right over once he'd spoken to the victims' families and informed his staff.'

'He'll tell them to stay put, I hope? The staff I mean.'

'Yes. Although he did ask when they'd be able to return to work.'

Carver grimaced. Working class born and bred, he was suddenly acutely aware of his surroundings. A far cry from his upbringing, spent watching his conscientious parents struggle daily. Looking around, he saw plush furnishings, a well-stocked fridge, state-of-the-art air con, a whopping great plasma screen built into the wall. It reeked of money, it lacked soul, and Carver felt sorely out of place.

'Typical,' he sneered. 'Business can't afford to flag even if there's been a double murder on site. Just keep the cheques rolling in.' His tone was bitter, sarcastic, but the comment didn't appear to warrant an answer, so Drake kept tight-lipped. 'We can't give him an answer until forensics give their initial assessment.'

'No, of course not, sir.'

'I want every shred of evidence captured, and if that means closing off the whole shebang for however long, Coleridge'll have to lump it and make alternative arrangements for his staff.'

'Yes, sir.'

Carver, decked out in protective clothing from head to toe, rustled as he knelt over the body and examined the message engraved across the girl's chest. Her face, neck and shoulders were ghostly pale, evidence of rigor mortis having set in and a stark contrast to the once-spotless cream carpet surrounding her, now stained ruby red. "*C-o-n-t-r-a-c-t.*" He'd seen some nasty sights since joining the Homicide and Serious Crime Command three years ago, but this was something else.

'Any ideas, Drake?' Carver looked back over his shoulder, his cast iron glare making it clear a response wasn't optional.

Recently posted to Bishopsgate police station, Drake had been processing yet another tedious missing persons' report when the call had come through at 5.15 a.m. He could scarcely believe his luck when Sergeant Matthews had appeared at his desk telling him to get over quick sharp to a suspected murder scene on Camomile Street, a short walk from Liverpool Street station. The body of Frank Jones, the overnight security guard, had been found by Mike Evans, his replacement, at 5 a.m. By the time Drake reached Camomile Street, Mike had also found Sarah's.

Fear and excitement had pulsed through him all the way. He was young, bright, eager to learn, eager to shine, yet desperate not to screw up. A shaken Mike, barely able to speak, had had the sense not to touch either corpse. Frank was still lying on his back in reception, his forehead a mess from where the bullet had struck, the shiny marble floor surrounding him sprayed with blood, like a quirky piece of modern art. Together, they'd erected a makeshift cordon around the body, awaiting the arrival of Dominic Avery – the crime-scene manager – and his team.

Mike had taken the initiative and already reviewed the CCTV. Unfortunately, it didn't help. Between 1.30-3.30 a.m. the tape was blank. Somehow, someone – the killer presumably – had disabled the device before entering the building. No sign of an intruder, and no video evidence of the murder taking place.

Drake had been greeted by a pool of vomit outside conference room four, where the body of Sarah Morrell lay. On the plus side, Mike had held on long enough to throw up outside the room, thereby avoiding further cross-contamination. After a cursory examination of the scene, Drake sent an initial report back to the Chief Superintendent. Soon after, Carver arrived, along with Avery and his team.

Carver was whip-smart, with ox-like stamina and a rock under pressure. He was one of the best at solving tough cases, but his hard upbringing meant he had little patience for laziness or indecision. A fair, modest man at heart, his outward bluster was often mistaken for arrogance. This, coupled with his short temper, meant he wasn't the sort who made or retained friends easily. The last thing Drake wanted was to get off on the wrong foot with his new boss.

'Well, sir, I'm guessing it's something to do with law.'

This earned him a wide-eyed look of disbelief. 'No shit, Sherlock. You think?'

So much for not getting off on the wrong foot. Luckily, Drake was a calm sort, and it took a lot to rattle him. He told himself to hold it together and not let Carver's cutting remark distract his train of thought. 'And I would imagine, sir, I mean, I'm just speculating, that in the Banking department of large City law firms, it's all about doing deals and drafting contracts. So maybe that's what the killer was getting at here. I mean, look at all those papers.' He pointed to the table, littered with crisp, fat documents, as well as the pile of dishevelled papers on the floor, each one labelled "Monicrom". 'The victim must have been working on these when the killer showed up. Presumably she dropped some when he surprised her?'

Carver raised himself up and made space for the crime-scene photographer who'd just arrived. But his animated eyes remained glued to the corpse. 'Yes, but why, Drake, why? Why's the killer trying to make this point?' His voice sounded breathless, while Drake could almost hear the frantic ticking of his brain. He took a step back so that he was facing the girl's feet. 'It looks as if he shot her in the stomach first…' he spun round, took several steps back, as if mimicking the girl's last movements, '…causing her to fall to the ground, before finishing her off. Very precise, painstakingly thought-through.'

Carver rested his chin between his index finger and thumb. Thinking, speculating. The case had already locked him in, clearing his headache in a way no number of painkillers could. 'Why did the killer choose this method, why? And what was it about this girl?'

This time, the question sounded more rhetorical. Even so, Drake racked his brain for an answer. But Carver's next question stopped him mid-thought. 'When's the pathologist and his team arriving?'

'Any time now, sir.'

'Good. We'll see what he has to say. In the meantime, don't you, or anyone…' he gave the photographer an icy stare, '…touch the body or anything else in this room.'

'Yes, sir.'

The photographer nodded, then widened his eyes at Drake when Carver wasn't looking. He knew the drill and was insulted by Carver's insinuation that he didn't.

'I'd like you to video the scene before the pathologist arrives.' Carver twisted round, catching the photographer off guard. He nearly jumped out of his skin, while his face turned cherry red. 'Close-ups of the girl, the bloodstains on the carpet, the table, walls – everything in the room, in as much detail as possible, please.'

'Yes, sir.'

'Drake, the day's going to get very busy indeed. Horrendously so. Are you ready for that?' Carver narrowed his eyes at Drake, already testing his rookie, needing to know that he'd make the cut.

Drake didn't hesitate. 'Yes, sir.'

'Good. After we've spoken to Coleridge and the pathologist, I expect I'll have to go and make a brief statement to the press. So, before the party starts, take a note of what I want you to do.'

Drake shot to attention. Pen poised, ears pricked, his heart beating double time.

'Get the girl's full history.' Carver's delivery was fast and furious, and Drake was thankful for shorthand. 'Everything from the year dot to the present. Where she grew up, family, likes, dislikes, hobbies, schooling, boyfriends, girlfriends, et cetera. Check out her home, get it swept for prints, hairs, fibres, every kind of bodily fluid. Talk to her family, friends, neighbours. Find out if she travelled as a student, and where. We'll need to interview all Channing & Barton staff, from the partners to the cleaners.'

'Do you think it's someone who worked here, sir?'

'I can't comment on that yet. We may know more once forensics are through. What I'm ninety per cent sure of, from the way she died, is that she was the end game – it's way too calculated, too precise – while the unfortunate guard just got in the way.' Carver gazed back down at the body. 'But somehow, don't ask me why, I've got a horrible feeling we've not heard the last of her killer.'

7 a.m.

'I would say she's been dead less than five hours.'

Carver watched Dr Charles Grayson, the pathologist, steadily slide the thermometer out of Sarah's rectum. He was a short, rotund man, with beefy fingers and very little sign of a neck. He also had a shiny bald head and small suspicious eyes concealed behind thick tortoiseshell glasses, while his portly appearance made his velvety James Bond drawl doubly surprising. They had worked together several times before, although Carver was woefully unaware that his brusqueness wound Grayson up.

Grayson had stripped the girl naked. Her lower half was dark purple, her top half as pale as snow.

'Why's that?'

'Because there's still some movement in her lower legs.' Grayson demonstrated. 'And her body temperature's thirty-one degrees. A dead body loses 1.5 degrees per hour until reaching the ambient temperature. Assuming she wasn't unwell, or especially cold, she'd have had a temperature of around 37.7 degrees while still alive.'

'Okay, what else?' Carver asked impatiently.

Grayson flinched at Carver's tone, but told himself he should be used to it by now. He swallowed his irritation. 'Rigor mortis normally sets in two hours after death. But as I said, so far, it's only affected her top and middle half. This suggests she's been dead more than two hours but less than six. Lastly, see these purple splotches over her legs and feet?'

'Yes.'

'It's what we call "lividity". It kicks off once the body's had contact with a firm surface – in this case the floor – for a period of time. As you can see, it hasn't reached her top half yet, which is still pale.' He paused. 'But now look at this.'

Grayson hauled the body onto its side. The purple colouring immediately began to dispel.

'Why's that happening?' Drake blurted out. Unlike some of his more squeamish peers, forensic pathology fascinated him.

'Because her blood's not set yet,' Carver answered for Grayson. 'It's realigned in the new position of gravity.' He gave a surprised Drake a wry smile. 'I've seen a fair few dead bodies.'

'The blood remains liquid for the first four to six hours after death,' Grayson explained. 'It's only after six to eight hours that it becomes relatively fixed in position, and the blood vessels will have begun to break down within the body.'

Carver cut to the chase. 'Can you put an estimated time on death?'

Grayson stood up, gazed down at the body. 'I would say between 2.30 a.m. and 3 a.m.' He looked back up at both men. 'But there's still a lot of work to be done. We'll need to take various samples and go much wider than the girl and this room. Assuming the killer came in the front?'

'We think so. That's roughly where the security guard was shot dead. I agree about widening the parameters. The killer may have tried a number of rooms and/or floors first before finding the victim. We don't know how he got up here. There are six lifts, as well as the stairs. Whoever it was must have been certain Sarah was in the building.'

'How?' Drake asked.

'If it's an inside job, that's a no-brainer. Otherwise, he could have been stalking the place all day, waiting for her to leave. Then, when she didn't, decided to take a chance and go inside. Could have been a friend or acquaintance who knew she'd been working late or heard as much from someone else. There are so many ifs and buts, Drake, and we just don't have enough to go on at this stage.'

'I'll need to perform a post-mortem to determine the exact physiological time and manner of death,' Grayson said.

Carver nodded. 'Agreed. Just be sure to extract as much evidence as you can from the body and surrounding area first before you move her. Anything that might have been in contact with the killer, however brief.'

'Of course.' Grayson contemplated the body again. 'Having taken a perfunctory look, it doesn't look like she was sexually assaulted. For one, she was fully clothed, aside from her blouse being torn apart. Even so—'

'Even so,' Carver interrupted, 'we must rule it out for certain, so a thorough examination must be done. Semen, saliva, you know the drill. Be sure to make a detailed written record of your findings. I don't want any claims of post-mortem injury being made.'

Grayson felt his blood pressure rise at Carver's needless remark. 'I will,' he said through gritted teeth.

There was a knock on the door. Drake opened it to see a distinguished-looking man standing there. He was smartly dressed, with hair as white as whipped cream. Worry imprinted his face, deeply lined by the trials of life. Drake wondered whether his hair colour was the result of advancing age or stress.

'Mr Coleridge?'

'Yes.' His voice was clear, yet soft. Perhaps he was still in shock.

Carver went over and introduced himself. He didn't want Coleridge going any further. He couldn't risk another vomiting episode contaminating the scene.

'Is Sarah…is Sarah still in there?'

'She is, Mr Coleridge. It's a very distressing sight, and I think it's best if we talk somewhere else. Another conference room perhaps?'

'Yes, yes of course,' Coleridge nodded with obvious relief.

Carver looked back over his shoulder at Grayson. 'I won't be long.'

'Right you are,' Grayson replied without looking up, deep in conversation with one of his team.

'I'm still finding it rather hard to come to terms with,' Coleridge admitted, sitting across from Carver and Drake in one of the smaller meeting rooms. He fiddled distractedly with his collar. 'I just can't think why anyone would want to murder Frank or Sarah.'

'We believe Ms Morrell was the target,' Carver explained, 'while Mr Jones was just a means to an end I'm sorry to say. Unfortunately, your CCTV, normally an invaluable source of evidence, had been disabled. Presumably by the killer.'

'How?'

Carver shrugged his shoulders. 'May have hacked in, switched it off remotely. It's something we need to look into. Clearly, we're dealing with someone who's as smart as they are dangerous.' Carver's gaze fixed on Coleridge. 'Ms Morrell was the victim of cold, premeditated murder, and it's therefore essential that we secure all of the available evidence to give us the best chance of catching her killer.'

Coleridge sighed heavily. Rubbed his glassy blue eyes in frustration. 'I'm assuming you can't do that with my staff around?'

'No, we can't. Presupposing the killer came in the front, we'll need to sweep the entire building. We don't know what route he took to get to Sarah, and we can't risk missing anything.'

'DCI Carver, I have a law firm to run, and several thousand clients to keep happy. I need my offices back as soon as is humanly possible. As it is, I fear I'm going to lose clients after what's happened.'

Carver's patience was wearing thin. He tried not to lose his temper. 'I understand. But I'm running a very different show here, Mr Coleridge. A *murder* investigation. And I'm sure you'll want to do everything *humanly* possible to assist me in catching this lunatic. Because until then, I don't think you, or any of your staff, are going to sleep easy at night.'

Coleridge couldn't argue with that. His resigned face said as much. He gave another heavy sigh. 'Okay, Chief Inspector, I understand. Just urge your team to work as fast as they can.'

'I will. Meantime, can you get me an up-to-date list of employees, support staff included. I'll need to question everyone once forensics are done.'

'Yes, of course. You'll have it before midday.'

Carver thanked him, then leaned back in his chair, glancing at Drake. A signal to pick up his pen.

'Did you know Ms Morrell well?'

'Not well, no. As the firm's senior partner, much of my work is on the administrative and marketing side. I have very little day-to-day contact with the more junior staff, although I was aware Sarah was in her last seat, and due to qualify next March. In fact, only last week we had a partners' meeting to discuss which trainees were going to be offered jobs and where, and her name came up.'

'Her fate had already been decided?'

'Sarah had been an exceptional trainee. Although she'd only been with him a month, Mark Warren, the head of Banking, saw how good she was. Plus, she'd made it clear from the outset that Banking was her first choice. He was keen to offer her a permanent position on his team.'

'The competition for jobs must be fierce,' Carver said. 'I imagine trainees would do anything to get a position in today's unpredictable climate?'

Coleridge looked visibly affronted. 'If you're insinuating that any of my trainees would be prepared to murder for the sake of a job, I'm sure you're very much mistaken.'

Carver smiled inside, amazed at people's naivety, their trust in human nature, especially where "well-educated, respectable types" were concerned. Everyone had a dark side. Everyone was capable of murder. But most were able to tame their urges. 'I have to consider all possibilities, Mr Coleridge. Nothing surprises me after twenty years on the force.'

Coleridge leaned in, his hands clasped together. 'Still, that doesn't explain Frank's death, does it? Surely, if it was one of my staff, they could have just walked in through the front door without having to kill him first.'

He has a point. 'Maybe.' Carver changed tack. 'Was Sarah popular? Among her peers, I mean?'

'I really can't answer that. You'd have to ask them. All I know is that she was smart and dedicated and had a promising future ahead of her.'

The ensuing silence was shattered by the telephone.

Coleridge shot up to answer it. 'Yes?' A pause. 'It's for you.'

Carver took the phone, listened. 'Okay, I'll be down shortly.'

He rang off, turned to Drake. 'The media are here. I need to go down and make a statement.'

'Do I need to be there?' Coleridge asked nervously.

'No, not for this. They'll want a comment from you at some point today, though, so be prepared. All I'm going to do now is make a brief statement. There'll be a full press conference later.'

Coleridge looked relieved once again.

Despite his contempt for the money-making mentality of the City, Carver felt some sympathy for the man. In less than a day, his celebrated law firm had become the site of a double murder. A news story for all the wrong reasons, and a huge burden for him to bear.

It wasn't going to be good for morale, and it wasn't going to be good for business, because the simple truth was, until the killer was caught, who in their right mind would want to walk through the doors of Channing & Barton?

If Coleridge wanted to save his firm, he had no choice but to cooperate.

And the same went for his staff.

Chapter Three

Tuesday 28 October 2014, 8.15 a.m.

'Maddy, quick, come here. You need to see this.'

Madeline Kramer angrily spat out the frothy mass of toothpaste she'd hastily been slathering over her teeth, conscious of the fact that – yet again – she was running late for work. Why was it, no matter how early she set the alarm, no matter how quickly she got through the bathroom before shovelling some breakfast down her throat, she never seemed to leave the flat on time? And she hadn't even had the chance to check her emails since hauling herself out of bed. There was probably a string of them lined up, waiting to be answered, each one as important as the next.

Maddy, who'd recently turned twenty-six, was blessed with both brains and beauty. She had light caramel skin, wide-set eyes a person might get lost in, and straight, shiny black hair cascading just past her shoulders. Her body was naturally lithe and toned, although working out helped, while her brain worked quicker than most. Orphaned at nine – her parents David and Alisha had been killed in a car crash coming home from the theatre one night – she'd been raised into womanhood by her widowed grandmother, who'd showered her with more love than some children get from two parents. As a result, Maddy grew up content and secure. She had no trouble making friends or showing affection in her platonic relationships. She was caring, approachable, empathetic, and yet an astute judge of character. No one ran rings around Maddy, except maybe Paul, her flatmate, whom she adored.

He was her weakness. Along with red wine, chocolate and tear-jerker movies. But she constantly reminded herself the first two were good for the heart, the third for the soul.

The only kind of relationships Maddy found herself backing away from were those of a romantic nature. She rarely let a man get too close, her longest relationship having lasted six months back when she was an English undergraduate at King's College, London. He'd wanted to take the next step, move in together, but that had scared her. What if she did, and they got married, had kids, were blissfully happy, and then boom! Just like that, something dreadful happened, and it was all taken away from her, or, even worse, her children were robbed of their parents in the blink of an eye? Bursting their perfect bubble of happiness and security. She couldn't risk that happening again. Not to her, and certainly not to her children. She'd been lucky. Her grandmother, Rose, was special, one in a million. She'd held her hand through those initial dark months, when she'd woken up, night after night, screaming for her mother. She'd kept her strong, made sure she didn't retreat into her shell, too scared to face the big bad world, let alone make her mark in it. But Maddy had no mother to protect any future bereaved child of hers, and right now she couldn't imagine her son or daughter suffering in the way she might have, had it not been for Rose. In any case, now was not the right time to be tied down. She was still so young, with no shortage of friends, and a job that ensured a serious relationship could never be on the cards.

Maddy was a one-year-qualified litigation associate at Channing & Barton. City law demanded a sharp mind and a thick skin, and Maddy was cut from the right cloth. But despite being popular among the partners she worked her butt off for, she'd sensed her head of department giving her the evil eye when she'd darted past his office at 9.35 a.m. yesterday morning. And not for the first time. Okay, so she rarely left the office before 8 p.m., frequently worked weekends, bank holidays, and even during her annual leave, but it was still a written rule that all staff were to be in by 9.30 a.m. at the latest, and if she didn't watch out, she'd find herself being summoned for a terse ticking-off and a stern warning that she'd better get her act together pronto or face being replaced by some equally ambitious associate, only too eager to relinquish any sort of life for none at all.

'Maddy, did you hear me? Come and look at the news. I don't think you'll be going into work today.'

Maddy rolled her eyes at Atticus, her beloved white Persian cat, who'd just come into the bathroom and was gazing at her sympathetically with his brilliant copper eyes. She gave him a weary smile. *He has it good. Not a care in the world, aside from his next saucer of milk, and regular nap schedule.* Sometimes, she wished she could trade places with him, or at least slow down a bit and make some time for herself.

She hurriedly wiped away the white moustache that had developed above her top lip. What's he on about now, she thought crossly as she adjusted the belt on her pencil skirt. It was him, Paul King, her best friend from law school. *He* was the one responsible for her habitual tardiness. Always talking, always distracting her with something on the telly, the latest gossip, daily updates on his complicated love life involving men he fancied but who didn't fancy him back. She loved Paul to bits; she owed him everything after he'd saved her one night from a couple of thugs out on the prowl for a pretty college girl.

He was kind, considerate and thoughtful, and loved nothing more than curling up on the sofa in front of a soppy romcom with a *Cosmo* and a tub of Ben & Jerry's. But in terms of looks, Paul was a man's man. Tall, dark-haired, powerfully built; physically speaking, he wasn't someone you'd want to mess with. One look at him, and Maddy's weedier assailants had scarpered. She often wondered what might have happened if he hadn't appeared in the nick of time, bravely warning them to get lost. He was her knight in shining armour. If only he was straight. Then he would have been perfect.

They'd moved in together at the end of their first year at the Bloomsbury Academy of Law. But after finishing there, their lives had taken very different paths. Maddy had landed a training contract with Channing & Barton before starting at the academy. All she had to do was pass the Graduate Diploma in Law along with the Legal Practice Course to secure her place. She ended up with a distinction in both.

In contrast, one year on, Paul had passed his exams but failed to secure a training contract, working a series of dead-end day jobs to pay the rent, still partying hard like a student at night, while Maddy kept her nose to the grindstone.

Not that it seemed to bother Paul. One night, over a skinful, he'd confessed to Maddy that he'd never much liked law. It was too dull, and his heart wasn't in it; a sentiment that probably came across at interview.

Paul's father – George King, a rich City lawyer himself – had pushed his only child into law, considering it, along with medicine and accounting, to be a credible, worthy profession, and one that would perhaps make up for his son's sexuality, something he could never accept, even when it was just him and Paul alone together.

Unlike his self-absorbed mother, Evelyn, who'd palmed him off to nannies the moment she'd pushed him out into the world, and had numerous affairs, Paul had worshipped his father. Which made the hurt on his face when Paul had revealed his homosexuality almost too much to bear. Desperate to win back his father's favour, Paul had suppressed his dreams of becoming a writer, and gone to law school. But his world came crashing down when George died of a massive heart attack during his first year at the academy. Evelyn, now free to spend the substantial proceeds of her dead husband's estate to her heart's content, didn't much care what Paul did with his life. Which, ironically, was good for Paul. He'd always lacked the confidence to stand his ground, and so her indifference made his decision easier for him. He finished the course out of respect for his father, but now there was no one to stop him from following his heart, which was to write. Maddy had been happy for him. He'd already written two novels, which he'd self-published on Amazon, but for an unknown like him, securing a publisher was akin to winning the lottery. Which was why he worked nights in an East End bar to pay the rent, coming home in the small hours to the two-bedroom flat they shared a few minutes' walk from Bow Road Tube station.

'Paul, I'm running late again. I really have to go.' Maddy came racing into the living room in search of her favourite suit jacket which had gone AWOL, Atticus following leisurely behind.

'Looking for this?' Paul offered up the missing item.

'Oh, yeah, thanks.' She seized it off him, missing his sober expression. As she swivelled round, desperate to make a quick exit, something on the TV caught her eye. A photo of someone she knew well, but whose face she'd never expected to see on BBC News at 8.20 a.m. As she turned around slowly to face the screen square on, her surprise turned to disbelief, then fear.

The words "Double murder at top City law firm" appeared on the rolling caption at the foot of the screen.

'*And now some breaking news just in…*' the newscaster was saying, '*… we're getting reports that the body of Sarah Morrell, a second-year trainee at top City law firm Channing & Barton, was found around 5.30 a.m. this morning by security guard Michael Evans. The body of Frank Jones, another security guard at the firm who had been working the night shift, was found by Evans around thirty minutes before. We understand that the police have launched an official murder investigation. Forensics are currently at the scene trying to gather as much evidence as possible…*'

'This can't be happening,' Maddy murmured. 'Frank, Sarah…dead?' It felt like time had stopped; that she was trapped in some bizarre parallel world that was surely playing a sick joke on her.

As reality kicked in, her legs turned to jelly. She felt her knees buckle, but Paul was quick to reach out and steady her, before gently sitting her down on the sofa as if she was made of glass.

'*…And now we're able to take you live to the offices of Channing & Barton for a brief statement from the officer in charge of the investigation…*'

The footage switched to outside Channing & Barton's offices. A man appeared on screen. The caption at the bottom revealed him to be Detective Chief Inspector Jake Carver.

'*…DCI Carver, as the senior investigating officer for the case, what can you tell us at this time…?*'

Despite her woozy state, Maddy took in Carver's face. It was ruggedly handsome, with a strong square jaw etched with a series of prominent lines which zigzagged all the way up his cheeks to his forehead like a rough dirt track. Visible signs of a hard life, a life that had seen and endured a lot, and which continued to take its toll. His walnut-brown hair was cut short, his unusual pale grey eyes open and honest. The camera zoomed in close, and she could just about decipher a scar on his chin. *Acquired in the line of duty, or a boyhood tumble?* She could tell he was a tough, pragmatic type, and before he spoke, she imagined his voice to be deep and gravelly.

She imagined right.

'…*Michael Evans, a security guard at City law firm Channing & Barton, arrived for his shift at 5 a.m. this morning. Upon arrival, he found the body of Frank Jones, the security guard who had been working the night shift, in the reception area of the building. Mr Jones had been killed with a single gunshot wound to his forehead…*'

Maddy covered her mouth in shock. She vaguely felt Paul rub her back, and was grateful for his familiar touch.

'…*Half an hour later, having called the police, Mr Evans found the body of Sarah Morrell, a trainee at the firm who, as we understand things, had been working late the previous night, and had not yet signed out in accordance with firm procedure…*'

'The Monicrom deal…' Maddy whispered. 'Remember I mentioned it's been running the Banking team ragged? It was about to close, I think.'

'…*in one of the larger meeting rooms on the twelfth floor of the building…*'

'Can I get you some water?' Paul asked.

Maddy's eyes remained fixed on Carver. 'No, I'm fine.'

'…*Are you able to give us any further details as to how Ms Morrell died?* the reporter enquired.

Carver's expression became grave. '*Not at this time. The circumstances of Ms Morrell's death are extremely distressing, and our sympathies go out to the families and loved ones of both victims. We're waiting for forensics to confirm the exact nature and timing of Ms Morrell's death, but at present it doesn't look like the attack was sexually motivated …*'

Maddy shook her head slowly. Clutched her mid-riff tight. 'I feel sick. This can't be happening.'

'I know, it's bloody awful. I'll get you some water.' Maddy kept her gaze on the TV as Paul made for the kitchen.

'*...Do you have any leads on the killer's identity?*' the reporter asked.

'*Not at present,*' Carver replied. '*What I can say for certain is that we are dealing with a very dangerous individual, who killed both victims in cold blood. It is therefore of the utmost importance for anyone who believes they may have seen or heard anything suspicious which may be connected to these shocking murders, to come forward. I'll be saying more at a formal press conference later today. Thank you.*'

Before the reporter could get another word in, Carver turned away and the footage switched back to the newsreader in the studio.

Paul returned with a glass of water. Maddy put it to her mouth, but hardly noticed the liquid moisten her lips. She felt numb, her frantic urgency to leave the flat shot down in flames by the ghastly news.

She wasn't shy to admit that she and Sarah had never seen eye to eye. From day one at law school, they had clashed, sharing a fair number of heated exchanges. Like Sarah, Maddy was bright, ambitious and beautiful, but that was where any similarity ended. Unlike Sarah, she didn't flaunt her beauty to get what she wanted or take her ambition to unhealthy extremes. Sarah always had an angle, a hidden agenda. She had to be first, had to be the best, and resented anyone who dared to challenge her.

And she'd identified Maddy as a threat from their first lecture together in front of James Stirling, the Head of Contract. Consequently, she'd alienated Maddy and most of the other female students with whom she might have bonded.

Including Paige Summers, another of Maddy's best friends from law school. A pretty, warm-hearted blonde, who was now a barrister at Inner Temple chambers.

Only a month into their first year, a rumour had spread that Sarah was sleeping with Stirling. Earning her a reputation for using her looks to get ahead. Still, in fairness to Sarah, Maddy knew she wasn't the only girl in the year Stirling had taken a fancy to, having been propositioned by him herself. It was common knowledge that he couldn't keep his dick in his trousers when it came to pretty girls, and she was almost certain he'd slept with at least one other student by the end of her first year. Even now, she wondered how he got away with it. She'd even had her suspicions about Paige but had never worked up the courage to confront her. It was clear from early on that Paige had developed a serious crush on Stirling. From the way her eyes had lingered on him in lectures, the way she'd frequently drop his name into conversations, the way she'd put on extra make-up for his tutorials, yet never bothering for other tutors.

Stirling hadn't fooled Maddy. She'd seen right through him and was far too proud to become just another notch on his belt. Still, she understood why girls fell for him. Intelligent, handsome, wealthy; he was the complete package in many ways. Plus, with connections at some notable firms, having practised briefly himself, a good word from him might seal entry into one of them. Cynical as it sounded, Maddy was almost certain this was how Sarah had got the job at Channings.

Training contracts were like gold dust, and like Paul and countless others, Sarah had arrived at the academy without one. But by some miracle, only a few months into the course, Sarah had secured a position at Channings, causing tongues to wag as to whether spreading her legs for Stirling had paid off for her.

'We never got along, you know that.' Maddy looked directly at Paul, pushing her raven-black hair away from her face. 'But I would never in a million years have wished this on her. I mean, I know she was a bit of a bitch, but I can't imagine who would have wanted her dead. And poor Frank, he was such a sweetheart.'

'I never much liked Sarah either,' Paul said. 'Although for me it was less of an issue, you know, being gay. I wasn't direct competition as far as she was concerned. But like you said, she didn't deserve this. Was she getting on okay at work?'

'I assume so. Our paths rarely crossed. Even when she did her litigation seat, she sat with a partner and worked almost exclusively for him. All in all, we barely said two words to each other all the time she was there…'

She didn't know why she was lying to Paul. There was no reason to lie, particularly to him. But there didn't seem any point in bringing up her row with Sarah last Friday. She regretted – now she couldn't make things right – the things she'd said, the hurtful words she'd thrown at her. Accusing her of blind ambition, of using sex as a weapon to get what she wanted. But then again, Sarah had driven her to it. She'd been equally spiteful, insinuating that Maddy had only got the job because she fulfilled the ethnic quota, being from mixed-race parentage. She'd also accused her of being a hypocrite in that she didn't seem to mind being best friends with Paige despite knowing for a fact that she'd slept with Stirling. It had been late, and Maddy didn't think anyone had overheard them. But still, what if someone had?

'…I did hear she was rooting for Banking. She was smart and committed. I'm pretty sure she was going to be offered a permanent position.'

Paul shook his head. 'What a waste.' No one spoke. Shock still stalked the air like a heavy fog that wouldn't shift. 'So, I guess it's going to be pretty weird at work for a while?'

'Weird? That's one word for it, I guess. I think it's going to be a whole bunch of things. Manic, grim, completely alien. I expect the police will be permanent residents for a while.'

Maddy inspected her watch. 8.45 a.m. Ordinarily, she'd have been well and truly screwed by now. *But surely no one will be going in today?* Pondering this, she realised she still hadn't checked her messages, too wrapped up in the news to give a second's thought to anything else. *Maybe Coleridge has sent an email.* She sprinted across the room and fished out her iPhone from her bag.

He had. All staff were to work from home until further notice. Client meetings would be held by conference call, and time should still be recorded as usual. Even murder didn't get in the way of racking up billable hours.

'I'm going to be working from home until the police are done going over our offices.' Maddy looked up at Paul. 'I bet Coleridge is pissed. Pissed and stressed as hell.'

'What does he expect? Surely, he can't expect things to pick up as normal without some interruption. It's a bloody murder investigation, not some petty burglary.'

'I get your point, but he's running a business. The responsibilities that come with that are huge. This'll be a massive dent in our reputation.'

'Why? It's not like the firm's messed up, or done anything dodgy.'

'True, but it's only natural for people to wonder, for clients to wonder, whether it's an inside job, whether there's a murderer loose within the walls of their lawyers' offices. Even if they don't, they'll worry about the firm not being up to the job and may decide to take their business elsewhere.'

Paul nodded. 'My father would have thought the same way. But how Coleridge expects any of you to focus on work today, I don't know. He could at least give you twenty-four hours to process what's happened.'

Atticus came up and nuzzled the side of his face against Maddy's leg. She bent down and stroked the top of his silky soft head, then looked up at Paul. 'It's going to be tough. But maybe work's exactly what we need to take our minds off all this.'

Paul eyed Maddy as if she was from a different planet. 'Whatever you say, Mads. But I'm worried for you. Make sure you carry your pepper spray with you everywhere. Don't walk down any dark alleys, keep to main roads, and always take a black cab. Do you hear me?'

'Yes, Dad,' she smiled, planting a quick kiss on Paul's cheek. She glanced back down at her iPhone.

'Coleridge says he hopes the police will be done within a couple of days. After that, we'll be able to return to the office and carry on as normal.'

'Carry on as normal,' Paul mocked. 'They're like machines, these people. Glad I never got sucked into that world.' He got up. 'I'm gonna take a shower. You'll be okay for a while?'

'I'll be fine. Although I may need your help accessing my remote working. It's been playing up recently, and you know I'm hopeless with all that geeky stuff.'

'No problem, just give us a shout.'

Maddy smiled gratefully. She didn't know what she'd do without

Paul. Being able to use Word and navigate the internet was about as technical as she got. But Paul was an IT wizard, frequently saving her sanity when her laptop seemed to acquire a mind of its own.

No matter how much Coleridge tried to convince everyone to carry on as normal, she knew Paul was right: until the murderer was caught, anyone who'd known Sarah, or, in fact, had any connection with Channing & Barton, was going to be living in fear.

Until then, no day was going to be just a "regular day" at the office.

Every day was going to be filled with questions and marred by suspicion.

Chapter Four

Friday 20 November 2009

James Stirling gazed up at the ravishing beauty straddling his torso, her gyrating hips grinding his penis so deliciously, so expertly, it was a struggle to stop himself from coming there and then. But he willed himself to hold on, despite being stupidly turned on by her smooth, flat stomach and large breasts, her hands teasingly fondling them as if to enhance her own, as well as his, arousal. He wanted to prove that he could stand the test of time, that he had the stamina to fulfil her needs as well as his own.

'Louder,' he commanded, slyly glancing at the camcorder he'd secretly positioned in the corner of the room, filming every second of their fornication. Just like he did with all of them. Home-made porno movies in which he had one of the starring roles, saved on a memory stick he kept under lock and key in his office drawer at work. Dangerous, some might say, but far less risky than keeping it at home, where Elizabeth might find it. 'I want to hear you, I want to hear you scream my name,' he commanded again.

He delighted in the sound of her panting, gradually becoming more rapid, her Bambi eyes wide with pleasure, her bee-stung lips slightly parted, her chocolate-brown hair hanging loose and untamed across her shoulders. And then his own panting became increasingly frantic as their mutual state of arousal rose to unbearable heights, before she gasped out loud – 'Oh James, you're so fucking good, I'm coming so bad' – confirmation of her imminent orgasm driving his to even headier levels as he climaxed with an unbridled groan of ecstasy.

Each of them sighed with contentment as Sarah lightly kissed her lover's chest, before tumbling over onto her back beside him.

Stirling reached for the pack of Marlboro Reds lying on the bedside table to his left. He took one out, offered it to Sarah. 'Cigarette?'

'Definitely.' She popped it straight between her lips, waited for Stirling to light it for her. 'I fancy some music,' she announced, before taking her first drag. 'Put on some Beethoven, will you? I know you have it on your MP3 player.'

'My favourite. But of course.'

As they both lay there, top to toe relaxed by sex, cigarettes and the soporific intonations of the *Moonlight Sonata*, the morning sun gradually filtering light into the hotel room they'd surreptitiously acquired for the night, Stirling wondered whether Elizabeth had bought his tale about going to visit his sick mother (suddenly struck down with the flu) in Hampton.

He doubted it. Aside from the fact that she was a tough old bird who, despite not being much of a mother to him when he was a boy, had no other family and was therefore bound to leave everything to him, she'd fallen sick with some ailment or other countless times before, and not once had her darling son packed an overnight bag and come running. No, it was just one more thread in a web of lies he'd spun over the years at the expense of his long-suffering wife.

Deep down, he knew it was wrong. But he'd managed to push any guilt he felt so far back in his mind that he felt able to live with himself. And the fact remained, he was addicted. Addicted to his young, pretty students; addicted to luring them in and fucking them senseless; addicted to the thrill of hearing them call out his name when he made them come.

Nothing gave him greater pleasure than seeking and acquiring sexual dominance over them. Of showing them who was boss. The only downside was the crushing sense of loss, of disappointment, of emasculation he felt when they moved on with their lives, both professional and personal.

That was hard to take. He liked his affairs to end on his terms, not theirs.

'Penny for your thoughts?' Sarah turned to him, her mocha eyes invading his.

On the verge of revealing his Achilles heel, Stirling quickly stopped himself. *Never reveal your limitations*, he reminded himself. *You are the dominator, not them.*

He couldn't allow word to get out. There would be many more fish to draw into his net – for one, the honey blonde named Paige had been giving him the eye since week two of the course, so he doubted it would take much effort on his part to score there. Any sign of weakness could prove detrimental to his design.

Although, he had to admit, he'd become especially fond of Sarah. She was different to the others. Not so clingy, not so desperate. She was so self-confident, and he found that particularly sexy. He wasn't sure how he was going to be able to move on from her.

'Nothing, it's nothing,' he replied. Quickly followed by a suggestive grin. 'Now put that out, will you? I think it's my turn to go on top.'

Thursday 30 October 2014

There was something different about the place.

Nearly fifty hours had passed since she'd seen Sarah's face on TV, and as Maddy stepped through Channing & Barton's revolving doors, there was a marked chill in the air. Gone was the palpable buzz, the supercilious sense of invincibility. In its place was a haunting gloom that felt alien to her.

For one, two policemen – who almost made her feel like a suspect herself when they demanded to see her pass before letting her through – hovered outside the entrance to the building, still cordoned off with a barrier marked "Police line – do not cross"; and two, half of reception was barricaded with a similar sign. Although, if it wasn't for the sign, it would have been hard to imagine that poor Frank's lifeless body had once lain there, the pristine marble floor shone so bright.

But she'd been prepared for the scene that awaited her. On her way into work, sitting among the hordes of grim-faced commuters, she'd reread the email Coleridge had sent the previous night, confirming that forensics had worked tirelessly over the last two days to complete their trawl of the building, and now all staff were expected to return to work in the morning. On-site client meetings would not resume until the following week as police would be using the firm's conference rooms to interview employees over the next forty-eight hours. He'd stressed that security had been stepped up with a permanent police presence, and therefore staff had nothing to fear, and every reason to feel safe.

Easier said than done.

At 6 p.m. on Tuesday, Maddy and Paul had sat mutely in front of the TV, watching a live press conference led by Carver. Coleridge, Sarah's parents, and Frank's widow were also present. Although there'd been no love lost between her and Sarah and she'd barely known Frank, one look at their loved ones' grief-stricken faces, and she'd been unable to stop the tears from flowing. She'd even noticed Paul's eyes water and took his offer to make her a second coffee in less than half an hour as an excuse to leave the room. But she'd sat transfixed as Carver had explained how there was no evidence of sexual assault or a struggle between Sarah and her killer, and so far, no helpful DNA to go on. The killer had been smart and scrupulous.

As she rode the lift to the Litigation department ten floors up, Maddy checked her emails. There was one from Cara, her best friend from King's, now a journalist. It was copied to Paige. Both had called as soon as they'd heard the news, wanting to know how Maddy was holding up. She'd appreciated their concern, but with all three leading such busy lives, they'd only been able to chat briefly.

But now, with the week drawing to a close, Cara had suggested meeting for a drink tomorrow, Friday, to talk properly. The question put to her, Maddy realised she could do with some female company, and they agreed to meet at a bar in Paternoster Square, next to St Paul's Cathedral. Paige was assisting with a trial nearby at the Old Bailey, so the location made sense for her.

The same sombre mood permeated the air on the tenth floor. The secretarial booths and sprawling corridors, usually a hubbub of noise, were eerily quiet, shock and distress paralysing the most industrious, draining the most sanguine.

'You okay, Margaret?' Maddy asked her PA.

Margaret looked up from her station, her eyes fractious. 'It's not really sunk in.' She was a sparrow-like, 58-year-old widow, who worked hard and never complained. Unlike some of her younger, lazier, more demanding colleagues.

Having grown quite fond of her PA, Maddy didn't like seeing her look so upset. 'It's just so horrendous. I mean, why Frank, why Sarah? What on God's good Earth could they have done to deserve such treatment?'

Margaret was a devout Christian, attending church every Sunday without fail, always wearing the same silver cross around her neck. Her unflinching belief astounded Maddy. It was a world she could never believe in, robbed of her parents one month short of her tenth birthday. In her head she felt like grasping Margaret by her shoulders and shaking some sense into her, telling her: 'This Earth is far from good, there is no God, and even if there is, he's one hell of an arsehole for allowing all the pain, suffering and heartache that good, innocent people are made to endure,' but instead, her hand resting on Margaret's shoulder, she replied, 'Nothing. We just can't make sense of these things. The world is full of crazy, wicked people, and kindness or reason just don't come into play as far as they're concerned.'

Margaret looked around cagily, her smoker's mouth quivering with nerves. 'Do you think the killer will strike again? Here, I mean? Are we safe continuing to work here?'

'The police are going to be watching this building 24/7, Margaret. The killer must know that. He might be a raving psycho, but I'm sure he's not stupid.'

'Is it true the police are going to question all of us?'

'Yes. It's their job to make sure every angle's covered, and if it helps bring the monster responsible to justice, I'm all for it.'

So long as they don't find out about my argument with Sarah. That won't look good even if I'd never have wished her dead.

Maddy gave Margaret a reassuring smile, then quickly scanned her watch – 10.15. Coleridge was speaking to the litigation team at midday, and she had a chunky witness statement to review before then. She made for her office and as she opened the door, Jeff Sanders, the senior associate she shared a room with, looked up from his computer. 'Hey Maddy.' Jeff was a larger-than-life Kiwi, who'd married an English girl and made London his home. A dead-set for partnership, he was one of the nicest guys she knew. She only hoped partnership didn't change him, as was often the case.

'Morning, Jeff.' Maddy sat down at her desk, her face serious. 'You okay?'

'Still in shock. How about you?' Gone was the usual morning banter, wide grin.

'The same. I mean, you hear all sorts of terrible things on the news, but when it happens to someone you know, it's hard to believe it's true.'

'Tell me about it.' Jeff shook his head. 'I'll admit I've been having trouble focussing on anything since it happened. But we need to try and get on with life, with work, as best we can. Hopefully, the cops will find the bastard soon.'

'Hopefully,' Maddy said softly.

'So, enough of my talking. I would now like to introduce Detective Chief Inspector Jake Carver, a senior investigating officer with the Homicide and Serious Crime Command unit of the Metropolitan Police. DCI Carver is leading the investigation, and it's imperative that each of you fully cooperates with him and his team so that we can all help bring the perpetrator to justice.'

12.15. Maddy and her team had just listened to Coleridge deliver a speech on how tragic the recent deaths were, that Sarah and Frank would be sorely missed, but that they must all carry on as best as possible, and not let the killer win by getting under their skin. They had a job to do, and life must go on. Counselling was, however, being offered to anyone who felt in need of it. Later in the day, around 5.00, there would be a minute's silence as a mark of respect for their dead colleagues.

But now they'd come to the interesting bit. It was as if an electric current had shot through the room. Maddy noticed her colleagues lean forward as Carver stood up to say his piece. Eyes focussed, ears pricked, hearts thumping with anticipation. He was an engaging speaker and, having seen him twice on screen, she found herself equally keen to hear what he had to say.

'Good afternoon, everyone,' he began in that same gravelly tone she'd heard on the television. He was dressed in a charcoal-grey suit and navy tie, his hair parted to one side. She suspected he didn't always look so smart and had made a special effort for the occasion. Perhaps in his early to mid-forties, he was taller than she'd expected, maybe around six-four, but the formidable presence he'd generated on screen was even more prevalent in the flesh. Not only in the way he spoke, but in the way he surveyed the room, making eye contact with each of them, making it known that he was in charge and that if any one of them messed with him, there'd be trouble.

'I understand how hard this must be for all of you. Murder is never a pleasant affair, not least when it occurs in your place of work, when it happens to someone you know. Some of you will have known Sarah well, some of you may never even have spoken to her. All of you, I am sure, will have spoken to Frank at some point, if only briefly. Whatever your relationship with either victim, you will all be questioned over the next few days about their murders. We have a very dangerous killer out there, and I'm certain you will want him caught as soon as possible so that we can all stop looking over our shoulders.'

Carver probed the sea of rapt faces, wanting to make sure he'd got his point across. He had. Every single head, Maddy's included, bobbed up and down, hypnotised by him and the still-surreal turn of events.

'Good. Once we've spoken to each department as a whole, we'll begin questioning individuals team by team, starting with Banking. That includes all secretarial staff. We'll then move on to other support staff.'

A hand shot up. It belonged to Jeremy Ashcroft, a poncey public schoolboy who loved the sound of his own voice. Maddy despised him. He was a litigator, five years qualified, but acted like he was running the show. He belonged in Corporate, not Litigation, and would no doubt make senior partner one day.

'It's been a couple of days now. Don't you have any leads yet? Any idea at all why the killer targeted Sarah?'

Carver flexed his jaw, clearly irritated by Ashcroft's smart-arse tone. Maddy rolled her eyes at Jeff and received a raised eyebrow in return.

'No. It's far too early to say, particularly due to the lack of DNA evidence or CCTV images. That's why we need to start questioning all staff as soon as possible.'

Ashcroft nodded smugly, clearly pleased with himself for asking the question. *Thank goodness I never went to law school with him*, thought Maddy.

'Before I let you go,' Carver continued, 'I'd remind you all to think carefully about whether there is anything you know, or may have seen or heard, that could be relevant to Sarah's or Frank's murders, in advance of your interviews. Please do not hold back, even if it means implicating a friend or colleague. The smallest detail could prove crucial to finding the murderer.'

Another intense stare, grinding his warning into them, making it known that he couldn't care less that they were hotshot lawyers with brains the size of a planet and a bank balance to match. 'The truth will come to light,' he warned, 'and it will not reflect well on anyone who withholds information that hampers or damages our investigation.'

More robotic nodding of heads.

'Excellent. Well, I have nothing further to say.' Carver turned to Coleridge, who instructed his staff to return to their desks and wait to be questioned.

'He seems like a no-nonsense kind of guy,' Jeff whispered into Maddy's ear as they left the room. 'The type who'd see through any shit like cellophane.'

'As eloquent as ever, Jeff,' Maddy smiled.

But he was right. In fact, Carver was way more intimidating in person than on screen. If she didn't own up about her row with Sarah – as inconsequential as it was – Maddy was pretty sure he'd find out.

So she'd come clean and clear her name before anyone had the chance to point the finger.

Chapter Five

Saturday 3 April 2010

'I think we've run our course.'

Flabbergasted, a butt-naked Stirling bolted out of bed. 'What's that supposed to mean? I thought we were still having fun?'

They'd just had one of their marathon sex sessions. One of their best. Or so he'd thought.

What is she playing at?

Don't act so desperate, he rebuked himself. *This is so unlike you. Usually, you have your fun, then move on.* But this one had got to him. He'd even restrained himself with two other potential conquests.

'We were, we did. But now we're through.'

It was her cool, detached tone that infuriated him more than anything. Stirling clenched his fist tight; so tight the veins on the back of his hand protruded through his skin. 'You've found yourself some fresh-faced college boy to fuck?'

'Oh, for Christ's sake, don't tell me you're jealous? Grow up, will you? No, it's nothing like that. I've got exams coming up, and I just think we should cool it.'

Although Sarah was worried about the examining board getting wind of their affair, the truth was she had set her sights on a particularly gorgeous LPC student who'd been giving her the eye the week before at a house party. She'd had her fill of Stirling. It had been fun, but she was much like a man when it came to relationships: she relished the chase but was easily bored. It was time to move on to the next bit of eye candy.

And this time she was going for someone more her own age.

But there was no point in upsetting the professor further. He'd been good to her, and she owed him for putting in a good word with the partners at Channing & Barton.

'You think your reputation's not already in tatters?' he bit back.

Then again…

She might have been grateful to him, but that didn't mean she had to take that kind of abuse. She wasn't the sort to let anyone walk all over her. No matter who they were.

'My reputation? Ha!' Sarah's eyes bristled with scorn. 'That's a bit rich coming from you. You think you're this…' she did the quotation mark sign with her fingers, '…supposedly whiter-than-white law professor, but you don't really believe you're beyond reproach, do you? I mean, if anyone should worry about their reputation, it should be you. It's only because of your wealth and contacts that you've kept your job. If word got out what you're really like, you'd be finished.'

Anger bubbled up in Stirling. His ego badly dented, her catty remarks having veered closer to the truth than he'd have liked to admit, he darted back onto the bed and struck the back of his hand across the side of Sarah's face.

He'd never been violent towards her before. Unlike Suzanne, who was weak and clingy, who got on his nerves and pushed him to the limit repeatedly.

Sarah doubled back in horror, her right cheek – bright red with the force of the blow – throbbing. But she quickly regained her composure, her gaze full of contempt and revulsion. 'You miserable, pathetic bastard,' she said coldly, scrambling off the bed, and sweeping up her clothes which had been lying in a crumpled heap on the floor. 'I can't believe I ever fancied you. You're fucking crazy.'

'Sarah, look, I'm sorry,' Stirling started to apologise. 'I don't know what came over me.'

'Save it,' she snarled, zipping up the back of her dress. 'And don't you even think about screwing with my job at Channings.' Her eyes were hard and meant business. 'If you so much as say one word to jeopardise my career, I'll send you and your career to the cleaners. Your wife, your employers, the whole fucking world will know about your fetish for screwing your innocent pupils. What's more, I'll bring an action for assault. Got it?'

Stirling nodded, still seething inside.

Friday 31 October 2014

'What did you find at her flat?'

It was 8 a.m. and Carver and Drake were sitting in a twenty-four-hour café opposite Liverpool Street station. It looked and felt like an upmarket greasy spoon, with a menu offering standard British fare but consisting of posher ingredients served with Michelin-star finesse. The air smelt of crisp bacon and roasted ground coffee, and the clientele was a mix of businessmen, tourists and blue-collar workers, all tucked into cosy padded booths set against cream-tiled walls.

Carver sipped black coffee, his nose buried in a copy of the *Guardian*, while Drake dug into a classic fry-up. He hadn't eaten much to speak of in the last forty-eight hours and, with another taxing day of interviews ahead of him, he took the chance to recharge his batteries with something hearty.

Carver, on the other hand, seemed able to live on air and black coffee. That morning, he'd already spoken to his technical expert who'd confirmed that the CCTV camera at Channing & Barton had been installed with remote internet access enabled by default, together with weak password security which failed to lock out a user after several wrong guesses – a classic recipe for security failure that would have allowed the killer to remotely tap into video feeds and control the direction and zoom of the camera. Carver had been amazed to hear that this was commonplace and that three of the most popular brands of CCTV cameras on the market were sold with remote internet access.

'Not much to speak of, sir.' Drake plunged his fork into a sausage. 'No sign of intrusion, nothing out of the ordinary. She lived alone.

We found some family photographs, but she didn't appear to have a boyfriend. At least, not a regular one.'

'Have her parents confirmed that?'

'They have, sir.' Drake recalled the horrendous conversation he'd had with Sarah's distraught parents. They'd just arrived home from a fortnight in the Caribbean when the devastating news of their daughter's murder was given to them. The mother could barely speak between sobs, while the father, although it was clear he was trying to be brave and answer Drake's questions without breaking down, couldn't conceal his grief.

No, their daughter didn't have a boyfriend as far as they knew; she'd been enjoying her training too much to have time for a relationship, and she'd been looking forward to qualifying and making a name for herself. They'd given Drake the names of a few friends – non-lawyers – who Sarah occasionally socialised with, and confirmed the timeline of her all-too-brief life to date.

They'd been looking forward to having their daughter and son over for a family dinner at the weekend.

But instead they had their youngest child's funeral to plan.

'Anything else?'

'It appears she was something of a workaholic. Routinely stayed late at the office. Not many friends to speak of.'

'So? Some of us like it that way.' Carver's attempt at humour was accompanied by a light chuckle. Drake wasn't sure whether this was his cue to laugh back. He played it safe and gave his boss a friendly half-smile.

'Of course, sir, and there may be nothing in it, but I just wondered if her ambition possibly rubbed colleagues up the wrong way? She was bright and very attractive. It seems a bit strange that she didn't have a boyfriend or many friends. Plus, when we spoke with Mark Warren yesterday, he said she'd made it clear that she'd do anything to qualify into his department. Also that she didn't appear to be especially friendly with her fellow trainees.'

'It's a theory, Drake, I'll give you that,' Carver nodded, 'but still too early to say. The trainees we've spoken to so far have been rather non-committal. Not a bad word to say about her between them. Which doesn't add up with Warren's comments.' He sipped his coffee. 'But we may have a better idea of whether you're on to something there once we've spoken to everyone.'

'Yes, sir.'

Carver looked back down at his paper. 'But well done for thinking laterally,' he murmured, eyes locked on the print.

Drake felt his heart swell with pride. It was only a passing comment, muttered under his boss's breath, but it was a start. Maybe there was a soft centre within that hard exterior of Carver's after all.

'How are you bearing up?'

The question wasn't asked out of love or concern. It was born from contempt and stained with malice.

'What do you mean?' James Stirling lowered his copy of *The Lawyer* and looked across the dining table at his wife, who was absent-mindedly pushing the cereal in her bowl back and forth with a spoon. She was staring at him in that cold, irritatingly poised way of hers.

Once, he'd found it sexy. Now it just made him hate her more.

'She was one of your students, as we all know. Or should I say one of your little floozies? You must be devastated.' She paused, then said quietly, provocatively, 'Or maybe you're not?'

'I don't know what you're talking about, Elizabeth,' Stirling snapped. 'Have you stopped taking your medication?'

Elizabeth rolled her eyes, made a tutting sound. 'Oh please, don't play that card with me. I saw you with her, remember? Arriving at one of your shady little hotels. I watched her leave alone, after she'd cut you loose; before you moved on to another tramp like her. What a way to meet her Maker. Or maybe it's not her Maker she's gone to meet, the little bitch.'

Stirling regarded his wife with a mixture of pity and loathing. It wasn't like her to get verbally aggressive. Even when she was mad about something, she rarely raised her voice, despite the anger being evident in her gritty tone. Sometimes, he wished she was dead. That way he could be rid of her without the public scandal of a messy divorce. He couldn't take the chance she wouldn't broadcast his extracurricular activities to all and sundry if he left her.

There was scarcely anything left of the woman who'd once put a check on his roving eye and made an honest man out of him. She'd been exquisitely beautiful when he'd first met her at Oxford in the third year of his law degree. With her feline eyes, slim build, long dark hair, low rasping voice, there had been something almost ethereal about her, drawing him in under her spell.

And then there was her ability to send you to heaven when she played the piano or the cello, her every performance overflowing with such passion, such heart. Oh, how he remembered the first time he'd watched her on stage performing the *Moonlight Sonata*, one of his all-time favourites. He'd sat in the audience, enchanted. As if only he and she had existed in the room, and everything else was immaterial.

But deep down, she'd always been a cold fish, and what she'd put into her music, she'd failed to put into her sex life, her marriage.

They'd married a year after finishing at Oxford, and for a while, were happy. But then, having discovered she was unable to have children two years into the marriage, Elizabeth slowly drifted into her shell. More and more detached with every passing month. As if she had no more purpose in life, as if sex with her husband was now pointless. As if their love was cursed. She became nothing more than an anorexic husk of a wife, who spent much of her day crafting inane ceramics at her pottery wheel upstairs in her windowless studio. Taking her pain and self-loathing out on her husband and sending him back to what he'd always been: a womaniser, an adulterer, a sex addict.

And a man who lashed out when his anger got the better of him. Just like his father before him.

He'd fooled himself into imagining Elizabeth would never confront him about his affairs. That maybe she preferred a life of frigidity and was even relieved that he got his kicks elsewhere. But it was as if something had snapped in her. She'd followed him and Sarah that unseasonably frosty evening in April 2010. To the same cheap hotel in Ealing they always used.

She'd parked right next to his BMW, sorely tempted to stick something sharp in its tyres. And there she had remained all night, waiting for them to reappear.

Like a murderess lying in wait for her victims.

A glut of emotions had raged through her tiny frame as she'd waited. Anger, hurt, betrayal, humiliation. She just couldn't sit back, go home, turn a blind eye. She had to confront them. See what the filthy slut and the cheating rat had to say. And a little after 10 a.m. the next day, having dozed off for a couple of hours, she'd stirred just in time to see the girl – so beautiful, so fresh – surface from the hotel entrance. She'd looked uptight, her face twisted into an ugly grimace, flushed with tension rather than love. This had given Elizabeth some gratification. But not as much pleasure as seeing the look on her husband's face when he'd emerged looking equally fraught thirty minutes later and she'd sprung out of her car and surprised him. Challenged him before he'd even had the chance to open his door.

Of course, he'd denied it. Made up some cock-and-bull story which only served to make his lies more pathetic and intensify her wrath. And from then on, things between them had got worse. Her life was one long treadmill of self-hate and misery, and she saw no way of getting off it.

Until now.

'They're bound to find out,' she said snidely as the carriage clock on the mantelpiece chimed the hour, piercing the sombre silence. 'Bound to question you. You know as well as I do that you weren't home that night.'

'Let them.' Stirling stood up, thrashed the magazine down on the table. 'I have nothing to be sorry for.'

'If that's what you think,' Elizabeth muttered as she watched him leave the room, 'then you're more of a fool than I thought.'

She knew he was still cheating on her with his students. And Suzanne, of course. That wretched woman he went back to when there was nothing better on offer. When his fat ego needed massaging. She should never have married him. Her mother, God rest her soul, had warned her not to fall for his charms. But she hadn't listened. She hadn't wanted to listen. He'd been handsome, witty, clever, just like her father whom she'd adored, but who had broken her mother's heart and drank himself into oblivion.

Facing up to him that day had done nothing to stem his compulsion. She should have just left him. But since then, she'd decided that was far too easy. That was letting him off the hook lightly, and she'd be damned if she let him escape scot-free the way her father had.

She had something much bigger in mind. A plan she'd recently set in motion.

A plan designed to make him pay.

Maddy took a moment to collect her thoughts before knocking on the door. She felt her pulse accelerate, unable to recall the last time she'd been this nervous. She'd yet to meet Carver personally, but having seen him in action, she found the prospect daunting. Several of her colleagues who'd already had the pleasure had made it clear the experience wasn't going to be a walk in the park.

The core of her apprehension lay in revealing her history with Sarah, particularly their recent argument, for fear of opening a can of worms she wouldn't be able to contain. But she knew that if she said nothing, and Carver discovered down the line that she hadn't been completely honest with him, she might be making things a whole lot worse for herself. No, it was much better to be candid from the start.

'Okay, here goes,' Maddy said under her breath before knocking.

She was told to enter, and as she did so Carver and Drake instantly stood up. Drake gave her a warm smile. He looked about her age. With his clean-shaven skin and tidy chestnut-brown hair, he looked so wholesome, so presentable, in stark contrast to his boss, donning a face that said it had been through the wars, and didn't enjoy a great deal of sleep.

Conference room twelve was the smallest of the firm's fifteen meeting rooms. Carver and Drake were standing behind a small rectangular desk positioned in the centre of the room, the larger round conference table having been pushed to one side against the wall.

'I don't feel comfortable conducting my interviews at such a large table,' Carver explained, having noticed Maddy eyeing the new arrangement. She felt herself blush, having thought she was being subtle. *Clearly, he doesn't miss a thing.* 'It creates too much of a barrier, and I like things to be a bit more informal. I'm here to solve a murder after all, not negotiate a business transaction.'

Drake gave Maddy another smile, as if to offer her encouragement. *Classic good cop, bad cop*, she thought. Client meetings suddenly seemed like a piece of cake, and she found herself wishing she was in one right now.

'Yes, thank you. I can understand that,' she replied calmly, although her guts were churning. The room was like an igloo. She tried not to shiver. It was late October and winter was looming, but it felt like it had already arrived within those four walls. Carver had the air con on full blast. Perhaps it was designed to keep his interviewees awake and on the ball. She wished she hadn't left her suit jacket on the back of her chair.

'Take a seat, Ms Kramer.'

She did as instructed.

'So, you're a one-year-qualified litigation associate?'

'That's right.'

'You trained here?'

'Yes.'

'And how well did you know Ms Morrell?'

Straight to the point. *Okay, this is it, be honest.*

'Quite well actually.'

Carver's attention was caught. He leaned forward like a runner at the blocks, heightening Maddy's nerves.

'We didn't train together. I knew her before she came to Channings. We were in the same year at the Bloomsbury Academy of Law.'

'Where's that?'

'Just off Bloomsbury Square, near Tottenham Court Road. Like me, Sarah didn't read law as her first degree. We both had to pass the Graduate Diploma in Law before being able to take the Legal Practice Course like other law graduates.'

Drake took notes as Carver led the interview, his gaze never leaving Maddy for a second.

'I see. But you qualified ahead of Ms Morrell, despite being in the same academic year?'

'Yes, that's right. Sarah took a year out. I was offered a training contract before starting law school, so there was a place waiting for me as soon as I finished the LPC. Sarah landed hers with Channings around six months into our first year at the academy, but they could only offer her a place in the next intake, which, if I remember correctly, was March 2013.'

'I see. These training contracts are hard to come by?'

'Yes,' Maddy nodded, feeling marginally more relaxed, 'incredibly. There are just so many applicants for so few places.'

'Sounds tough.'

'It is.'

Silence. Maddy's discomfort returned. She wondered what was coming next.

'And were you and Sarah good friends?'

She knew he'd ask this. Even so, her stomach flipped again. *What will he read from my answer, my hesitation?* No one got on with everyone; that wasn't how the world worked. But that didn't mean they went around killing each other. She had nothing to hide.

'No, we weren't.'

She felt the tension levels rise. Drake instantly looked up from his notepad. Observed her with a new-found degree of suspicion.

'I see,' Carver said coolly. 'Can you elaborate, please?'

'Sarah had a habit of getting on the wrong side of people. Especially her peers.' Maddy paused. 'Especially her *female* peers. Right from the beginning, she made it clear that she wanted to excel and be the best, and seemed to resent anyone else doing well, or at least, doing better than her. Always shooting her hand up to answer, always wanting to get the upper hand. And I guess because I'm reasonably intelligent, and okay-looking…' she knew she was more than that – she was extraordinarily bright, and exceptionally beautiful, but unlike Sarah, she wasn't the bragging type '…Sarah viewed me as a threat to her dominance. She was the same with all the other attractive, intelligent girls on the course. Much less so with the men, and the plainer girls. Although she could be spiteful about them too.'

'How so?'

'She'd look down on them. Make it clear she considered them inferior to her.'

Carver found himself liking the victim less and less. Quite frankly, she sounded like a nasty piece of work. But it wasn't his job to like or dislike his murder victims. Feelings didn't come into it. It was his job to find their killer. Plain and simple. 'And did your relationship remain frosty when she came to work here at Channing & Barton?'

Frosty. That was a harsh word. It set Maddy on edge. She wriggled awkwardly in her seat, wanting the interrogation to be over.

'I think *frosty* is a little extreme. It's a large building and we were in different departments most of the time. Even when she did her six months in litigation, she sat with a partner and I had very little contact with her. He used her almost exclusively.'

'Is that normal?'

'It happens a lot, but largely depends on the partner and their workload.'

'And was she good at her job? Well thought of, respected?'

'Sarah was a good lawyer. And from what I understand, the partners thought a lot of her. I'd have been very surprised if she hadn't been kept on.' Maddy took a breather, working up the courage to continue.

'But?' Carver urged, his eyes narrowing. 'There is a "but" coming, isn't there?'

'But, from what I heard, she didn't make a lot of friends here. She alienated her fellow trainees, just like she did at law school. She didn't socialise much, except when it was a client event.'

'That's not a crime, is it?'

'No, of course not. It's her, I mean, it *was* her life. But Channings is a very sociable firm, and the trainees and assistants go out a lot. For drinks after work, and such like.'

'I'm surprised there's time for socialising considering the hours you put in. That's why you all get paid so much, right? Burning the midnight oil day after day.'

Sarcasm underscored Carver's question, and Maddy saw the resentment in his eyes. It irritated her, because who was he to judge? But she told herself to let it go. She didn't know his background, plus he probably thought himself seriously underpaid considering the sick, twisted crap he had to deal with day in, day out.

'Yes, we do put in very long hours, and that's precisely why, when we do have the chance to let off some steam, it's usually with our colleagues. Friends outside law get fed up of being let down time after time. They don't understand that we have no choice.'

'When was the last time you spoke to Sarah?'

In a split second, Maddy's mouth went dry. The room suddenly wasn't cool enough.

'Can I have a glass of water, please?' she asked, her mind frantically trying to prepare a response. It was the wrong time to ask for water, a sure sign of her nerves; as if she had something to hide. But she needed a bit of breathing space and had acted on impulse. It was too late to backtrack.

'Of course. Drake, please pour Ms Kramer some water.'

Drake did as he was told and offered the glass to Maddy.

She took it with thanks, managed a small sip, her hand not quite as steady as she'd have liked it to be. 'Sorry, that's better.'

'When was the last time you spoke to Sarah?' Carver repeated.

'Last Friday.'

'What did you talk about?'

'A fraud case I'm working on. Last week, I asked Mark Warren to get one of his trainees to prepare a research memo on insider trading. He asked Sarah. The memo she produced was good but needed a bit more detail. So, on Friday afternoon, I asked her to pop round to my office, so I could explain exactly what I wanted her to do.' Maddy paused, then said, 'Let's just say she made it obvious that she resented me being her superior. I think it was too much for her ego.'

'Did you argue?'

Maddy filled her lungs, and despite being a committed atheist, found herself saying a silent prayer that she wasn't about to land herself in even deeper shit.

'Yes.'

'What about?'

'She accused me of deliberately making more work for her, just so I could play the I-am-your-boss card. I said she was being ridiculous, that ever since I've known her, she's always had a chip on her shoulder, that she needed to stop acting like a diva and grow up.'

Carver raised his eyebrows and suppressed a smile. This girl was no pushover. He found himself liking her, and not because of her beauty. Although that certainly hadn't escaped him. She had personality, guts. Intuition bred from a blend of talent and experience told him she wasn't a suspect, but he needed to hear her out all the same. 'And how did she respond?'

'She said I only got the job because the partners took pity on me, because I'm an orphan and because I fit the ethnic criteria, being half Asian.'

Drake and Carver exchanged a brief look. 'Harsh words,' Carver said. His eyes drilled through her once more. 'That must have been hard to hear.' A pause. 'Hard to digest.' Another pause. 'Hard to forget.'

'It didn't make me want to murder her, though,' Maddy blurted out without thinking. Realising what she'd said, she felt herself redden. *Stupid idiot way to go, Mads.*

'I never said it did,' Carver replied. 'But tell me, how did you respond?'

'Rather childishly, I'm afraid. I told her she was blinded by ambition and had used her looks to get where she was.'

Carver leaned forward slightly. 'Her looks? Are you saying she slept around?'

The conversation had steered into dangerous territory. She couldn't back-pedal from what she'd started, but she feared she'd be making life very difficult for others.

Maddy swallowed hard. 'Yes. Sarah was a stunning girl and she attracted a lot of male attention.'

'At law school?'

'Yes.'

'From other students her age, or did she aim a little higher?'

Fuck. Now she was wading in mud. If she revealed his name, who knew what the implications might be for his reputation, his career, his marriage? But this was a police investigation, and there was no room for holding anything back. Besides, she was a terrible liar.

'Both.'

'Can you give me some names?'

Maddy squirmed in her seat, hating herself for exposing him, but again realising she had no choice. Reluctantly, she said, 'It was pretty much common knowledge among our year that Sarah had a relationship with one of the professors.'

'A sexual relationship?'

'Yes.'

'With who?'

She hesitated. 'Professor James Stirling. He taught Contract. Still does as far as I know.'

A look of recognition passed between Carver and Drake. Clearly this last piece of information had struck a chord. Once more, Carver shifted his body weight forward, like a tiger smelling its kill. 'Contract, you say?'

'Yes. Is that relevant?'

'Ms Kramer, I'd like to show you some photographs now. But I want you to prepare yourself for what you're about to see. They are extremely unpleasant.'

She didn't need him to spell it out. She knew what was coming. From nowhere, it felt like a lump the size of an orange had lodged itself in her throat. She tried to swallow it away, at the same time drawing in oxygen as if it was in short supply, preparing herself for the worst.

'Okay,' she nodded.

Until now, she hadn't really noticed the large brown envelope lying to one side of the desk. Carver picked it up, pulled out several photographs, then slid them across to her. Her hands shook as she scooped them up. For a second, she didn't dare look down. But then she told herself to be strong and went for it. As she looked through them, one by one, nausea surged through her. It was the most harrowing sight she'd ever seen, made worse by the fact that she'd known the victim. She inhaled deeply to stop herself from gagging.

'Take your time,' Carver said gently. 'I know it's upsetting. But I need you to think carefully and see if what's written across Ms Morrell's chest makes any sense to you.'

Maddy knew the circumstances of Sarah's death from news reports, but only now, by seeing the ghastly images with her own eyes, was she able to grasp what had stoked the fire in Carver and Drake.

She looked at both men in turn. 'Just because the killer inscribed "Contract" doesn't mean it's Professor Stirling.'

'No, you're right, it doesn't, but it's interesting, don't you think?'

Maddy shrugged her shoulders. 'I guess you could call it that. But I can't believe it of Professor Stirling. I just can't.'

'Was he your lover too?'

'No, certainly not! I'm not like that.'

'Not cheap, you mean? Like Sarah?'

The room was suddenly a pressure cooker. *Has the air con stopped working?* She felt like a witness under cross-examination, hit with quick-fire questions designed to catch her off guard, expose holes in her story.

'Like I said, she took her ambition to unhealthy extremes. And there were rumours that—'

'Rumours that what?'

'Rumours that she used Stirling to get a training contract. He's got a lot of clout in the City, including with this firm.'

'Coleridge?'

'I really don't know,' Maddy shook her head truthfully.

'Do you know how long their relationship lasted?'

'Maybe around six, seven months, I'm not sure, that's my guess. I know she saw this other guy for a while. He was in the second year when we started.'

'Name?'

'Connor something or other. I genuinely can't remember his surname.'

It dawned on Maddy that she'd probably gone and incriminated another perfectly innocent guy. But a brief glance down at the photos told her it was the right thing to do. As much as she'd disliked Sarah, she hadn't deserved this.

'Okay, that's fine. We'll look into it. Do you know if Sarah and Stirling's relationship ended mutually?'

'Again, I don't. We weren't exactly in the habit of having heart-to-hearts.'

'Do you know if Stirling had relationships with other female students? Whether he made a habit out of it?'

'I don't know if he made a habit out of it as such. But I am pretty sure he slept with another student in my year.'

She'd fudged the truth there. She was almost certain Paige had slept with Stirling too, but she wasn't about to land one of her best friends in it. If Carver was as good as he appeared to be, he'd find out soon enough.

'What was her name?'

'Lisa Ryland.'

'Where is she now?'

'A firm called Blackfields Symes, near Tower Bridge. She's a property lawyer.'

'Is Professor Stirling married?'

'He was when I was at the academy. Still is as far as I know.'

'Have you ever met his wife?'

'No, I know very little about her, except that she used to be a concert cellist.'

'Is he musical too?'

What the hell does that have to do with anything? What is this, the Spanish Inquisition? Has he gone on this long with my colleagues?

'I believe he plays the piano. I remember him being very keen on classical music. He'd urge us to listen to Beethoven as we revised. Said it would calm us down, focus our minds. How is that relevant?'

'And what was your impression of Professor Stirling?' Carver asked, ignoring her question. 'You said you never slept with him, but did he ever proposition you?'

Again, she had no choice but to be truthful.

'Once, at the Christmas party, during my second year. He was pretty drunk, asked if I fancied going on somewhere after for a drink. I declined, and he backed off.'

'Did he seem angry?'

'No, not angry. His pride may have been a little wounded, but he certainly didn't become aggressive, or treat me any differently going forward because I said no.'

'Why did you reject him?'

'He's married, he was my tutor, he wasn't my type. Is that enough for you?'

She hadn't meant to get aggressive, but the question had really pissed her off. It was insulting, and seemed pointless.

Carver looked taken aback. 'Sorry, I didn't mean to offend you. Let me put it another way. If he hadn't been your tutor, or married, would you maybe have found him attractive?'

'He's a handsome man, and very intelligent. I can see why women find him attractive.'

'But not you?'

'No. As I said, he wasn't my type.' Maddy paused, debating in her mind whether to continue. Carver sensed her hesitation.

'There's something else, isn't there?'

'Okay, so maybe I found him a little smarmy.'

There was a brief lull as Carver weighed this up. To Maddy, it felt like hours.

'Can I just ask something?' She eventually broke the excruciating hush.

'Of course.'

'Have you been this thorough with everyone else you've interviewed so far? I mean, you've gone into a lot of detail with me, asked me a lot of personal questions.'

Her determined gaze demanded an honest response.

'Look, Ms Kramer, the last thing I want to do is upset or offend you. But the fact is, you're the only one at the firm I've interviewed so far who attended law school with Ms Morrell. And as is often the way with police investigations, your answers to some of my questions have posed new questions which demand answers.'

He was right, she saw that. It wasn't his fault. He was doing his job and had asked all the right questions. Questions raised by her responses, like he said.

'Just a few more questions, Ms Kramer, if you don't mind, and then we're done.'

'Okay.' She took another sip of water, suddenly feeling wilted. It had been a long, arduous week. She couldn't wait to escape the firm and find sanctuary with her friends.

'Was Sarah seeing anyone at Channings to your knowledge?'

'No, not to my knowledge. As I said, I had far less to do with her here than when we were at the academy together.'

'Okay, I understand.' A pause, then, 'I know it's difficult, but I want you to take another look at this photo.'

Maddy's heart sank. She'd been hoping that was a one-time thing. But apparently not. Reluctantly, she glanced down at the photo Carver slid once more in front of her.

'What comes to mind when you look at this? Aside from the obvious, I mean. Tell me what you see.'

'I see the word "Contract" engraved across her chest.'

'And what does the word "Contract" mean to you?'

What kind of a question is that? She gave him a puzzled look, as if to emphasise its ridiculous nature.

'I know it might seem like a stupid question, Ms Kramer, but sometimes, to solve an investigation, we need to break things down. Make things as simple as possible to find the answer.'

Put that way, Maddy sort of understood. 'It means an agreement made between two or more parties where there is offer, acceptance and consideration. Something that crops up in all areas of life, something which would have formed the basis of the matter Sarah had been working on the night she was murdered. Something core to Banking Law, a fundamental area of law we study at law school, and which all aspiring lawyers must master.'

Carver appeared bowled over by the breadth of Maddy's response. 'Okay, that's really helpful, Ms Kramer. I have one last question.'

'Yes?' She could almost taste the red wine she planned on glugging in a few hours' time.

It was the obvious question. One that everybody on Channing & Barton's payroll would be asked.

'Where were you the night Ms Morrell was murdered?'

She didn't hesitate. 'I was at home.'

'Can anyone vouch for you?'

'No, I was alone,' she replied boldly. 'You'll just have to take my word for it.'

'You live alone?'

'No, I live with my flatmate, Paul. He's a writer, but works nights in a bar. I was in bed by the time he got home.'

'Okay, Ms Kramer, thank you. You've been most cooperative. We're done for now.'

'For now?' she repeated.

'Because of what you've told us this afternoon, particularly your history with Ms Morrell at law school, we may need your help with our investigation going forward. That's all.'

What could she say to that? She knew what he meant. He was referring to Professor Stirling and that Connor guy, poor sod. And goodness knows who else Sarah had got her claws into at the academy.

At least she'd been level with him about her row with Sarah. It felt good to get that off her chest. He didn't give much away, but she didn't think Carver considered her a suspect.

For now, she could go back to her office and try her best to ignore the fear and suspicion blackening her firm.

'What do you think, sir?' Drake asked after Maddy had left.

'She's not a suspect,' Carver said with conviction. 'As far as I could tell, she wasn't holding anything back. And she's given us some very useful leads.'

Carver had so far found himself riddled with frustration. He liked to move quickly, make progress. But not one of the ninety members of staff he'd interviewed so far had given him much to chew on. Like Kramer had confirmed, Sarah hadn't socialised much with her peers, seemingly wedded to her work, to impressing the partners. And because no one at the firm, aside from Kramer, appeared to have known Sarah before she came to Channing & Barton, extracting any useful information about her life before Channings had been a dead end.

But Maddy Kramer had given him something meaty to sink his teeth into. He turned to Drake. 'Ring the Bloomsbury Academy of Law and get hold of a list of Sarah Morrell's classmates for both academic years she attended, 2009 to 2011. Also her tutors. Then arrange a time for us to go in and speak to Professor Stirling. Keep it low-key. Whatever you do, don't make it seem like he's a suspect. Just say we're pursuing all lines of enquiry, trying to paint a picture of Sarah's life before Channings, and would appreciate a moment of his time.'

'Yes, sir. Do you think he's a suspect?'

'Too early to say, Drake. Right now, all we have is hearsay. But he definitely has a lot of explaining to do.'

Chapter Six

'Hi, girls, sorry I'm late, my interview pushed me behind schedule.'

Having fought her way through the hot, heaving bar, chock-a-block with stressed City suits celebrating the weekend by knocking back booze like it was going out of fashion, Maddy had finally spotted Paige and Cara perched on a couple of stools at a table in the corner. They'd opened a bottle of red, and no sooner had she spied the empty glass reserved for her than she'd poured herself a large measure before she'd even sat down. It was Halloween and the bar had entered into the spirit of things. Flawlessly carved freaky-eyed pumpkins were dotted around the room, along with thin, whispery cobwebs clinging to the ceiling, and rubbery bats hanging from the walls. Thankfully, the music was chilled-out soul, rather than cheesy ghoulish tunes. Maddy was in no mood for the latter and would probably have walked out in protest.

'Tough day?' Cara – an elfin ash-blonde with an eternally sunny disposition – asked.

'You could say that.' Maddy threw back her wine. She felt herself relax a little as the velvety Merlot trickled down her throat and entered her bloodstream. Her nerves were shot. She'd found the interview gruelling – worse than any of her job interviews and they'd been bad enough – and she had a strong hunch her part in Carver's investigation wasn't over yet, just as he'd intimated. Even in death, Sarah was going to make her life difficult.

'I still can't believe it,' Paige said, shaking her head. 'I mean, I didn't much like Sarah, but no one deserves to die like that.'

'Do you know if the police have any leads yet?' Cara asked.

Never off duty, Maddy sensed the cogs in Cara's journalist brain turning at breakneck speed.

'No,' she lied, not wanting to reveal her conversation with Carver about Stirling. Maddy loved Cara to bits, but she was a journalist, and like any journalist, she couldn't keep her mouth shut when it came to a potential scoop. The fact was she knew people, and people talked. She also suspected Paige still harboured feelings for Stirling, despite having a boyfriend. She didn't want her warning Stirling that he might be in trouble before the police had a chance to question him. Although he hadn't said as much, and it wasn't the same as the strict rule of privilege between lawyers and their clients, Maddy didn't think Carver would take kindly to her revealing intimate details of their conversation to her friends. The last thing she wanted was to get into his bad books.

'Who would do such a thing?' Paige asked.

Maddy shrugged. 'That's the million-dollar question. Sarah wasn't popular. It could have been anyone.'

'Anyone we know? I mean, from the academy?'

Maybe she's thinking about Stirling even if she doesn't say it out loud.

Maddy deliberately kept her answer vague. 'I don't think we can rule it out.'

'The fact that the killer wrote "Contract" across her chest would suggest it's someone connected with law, don't you think?' Paige said.

'Why? Anyone can read up on the basic elements of law from a text book. I don't need to be a doctor to know that all aspiring medics must study "anatomy". People make contracts all the time, in all areas of life. I mean, you hand over money to a cashier in a supermarket in exchange for a loaf of bread and you've made a contract. Anyone acquainted with Sarah would have known what she did for a living, what her job roughly entailed.'

'Maybe she'd made a contract with the killer?' Paige suggested. 'Some sort of deal she didn't keep to?'

'It's possible. I should point that out to Carver.'

'What's he like?' Cara asked, her eyes twinkling.

'DCI Carver?'

'Yep.'

Cara's sudden change in topic caught Maddy by surprise. The full-bodied wine on an empty stomach had already made her feel a little heady. She gave an impish smile. 'Quite fit actually.' She thought about his earlier questioning; the rich tone of his voice, the scar on his chin. She liked them like that. Perfectly imperfect. Maybe because she hadn't had the perfect upbringing. She was afraid of perfection. Perfection didn't exist. Perfection scared her.

'Really?' both girls said in unison, leaning in closer.

'Forget the murder investigation; this is far more interesting,' Cara grinned.

'More information, please,' Paige demanded.

'Well, he must be in his early to mid-forties, but he's got this rough-and-tough look and manner about him. Comes across as a bit arrogant, but also the sort you can rely on to cut the crap.'

'Exactly Ms Kramer's type then,' Cara tittered. 'You were never into the soft, smooth-talking Romeos, were you? Even at uni, you always went for the straight-talking guys. Greg was like that. And yet you dumped him, poor bloke.'

'I ended things with Greg because he wanted more than I was prepared to give. I was too young to be tied down; I still am. As for the smooth-talkers, yes, you're right. I don't like all the show, the buttering up. I like what-you-see-is-what-you-get. Unlike Ms Summers here, who's a sucker for a charming Casanova.'

'Nothing wrong with that,' Paige retorted. 'I like a man to open doors, pay the bill, and treat me like the lady I am. What's wrong with that?'

'Does Ben do that?' Cara asked.

'Not as much as I'd like,' Paige sighed. 'In fact, I'm not sure I want to carry on seeing him. It's all become very dull, very predictable.'

'But he's such a nice guy,' Maddy said.

'That's partly the problem. Too nice. Boring, some might say. Right now, he's in Frankfurt on business, and I can't say I miss him.'

'I know what it is,' Cara said, giving Maddy a nudge. 'It's that professor bloke, isn't it? You never got over him, that's the problem.'

Paige was lucky the wine and warmth of the bar had already caused her cheeks to colour. Even so, she betrayed her embarrassment by fidgeting in her seat. 'I…I don't know what you mean.'

'Yes, you do.' Cara turned to Maddy. 'What was his name? Didn't all the girls like him? In fact, didn't Sarah have a bit of a fling with him? And there was that Lisa friend of yours, wasn't there?'

Having just started to relax, Maddy felt her body tense. Cara's memory was second to none.

'Er,' she replied, picking up her glass, 'you mean Professor Stirling?' She noticed Paige lower her eyes to the floor.

'Yes, that's the one.'

'Yeah, there were rumours that he and Sarah had an affair. He was a flirt, for sure.' She glanced at Paige, wondering if this was the moment when she'd finally reveal whether there'd ever been anything between her and Stirling. But she kept her head down, which kind of said it all.

Maddy took it as a sign not to probe further. Before Cara could say another word, she downed the rest of her wine, then raised her empty glass. 'Another bottle?'

'Thought you'd never ask.' Paige finally looked up and smiled.

'Great, my round.' Maddy got down from her stool and practically sprinted to the bar.

Paige chaotically fished around in her bag for her umbrella as she stumbled right down a quiet side alley in Paternoster Square towards St Paul's Churchyard. The bar had thinned out early, and no sooner had she stepped outside than she realised why. Not only was it belting with rain, it was bloody freezing. She could barely feel her toes in her sheer tights as she teetered along. She felt smashed after nearly a bottle of red on a few measly bar snacks. She cursed the crap British weather for being so bloody inconsiderate.

At times like this, she wished she lived east like Cara and Maddy. But when she awoke in her Sloane Square flat in the sober light of day, she knew she'd feel differently. She'd always been a south-west London girl – inherited wealth had secured Paige her own flat off the King's

Road – and she knew she'd never feel comfortable, or safe for that matter, slumming it in the East End.

Having said goodbye outside the bar, Maddy and Cara had headed straight for St Paul's underground to jump on the Central Line. Although they'd offered to accompany Paige to Mansion House Tube, where the District or Circle line would take her straight to Sloane Square, she'd told them not to worry. She didn't want to put them out on such a horrendous night, and she was more than capable of managing the short walk alone. She'd also wanted to avoid Cara asking her more uncomfortable questions. Cara was a good friend, but she was so bloody nosy! Paige had never divulged her feelings for Professor Stirling out loud, and she wasn't about to start now – four years after their brief affair.

Even now she still thought about him, wondered how he was doing. She knew he couldn't be trusted. That he had seduced her, like he had seduced so many others before, and no doubt continued to do so. She hated the thought of him being with other women, despite knowing he could never be hers.

And it had been her pathetic clinginess, begging him not to see other girls, asking him to leave his wife, that had made him lose interest. She'd been shocked when he'd grabbed her by the wrists, and then by the neck, telling her to get out. That if she didn't stop bothering him, he'd see to it that she never got a pupillage.

So, she'd backed off, done as he'd commanded. Unlike Sarah, she wasn't the type to fight back, to make counter-threats. She still recalled the mad look in his eyes as he'd hauled her to the door like she was dirt. He'd been so charming, so tender, initially. His switch from Jekyll to Hyde had shocked her.

But there was still something about him – his film star looks, his intellect, the way he'd made love to her – that had lit a fire inside her that no man before or since had managed to achieve. And her inability to get over him continued to hinder her chances of ever making a proper go of it with another man. Including Ben, who she knew, deep down, she was lucky to have.

When sober, Paige knew the quickest, safest route to Mansion House underground like the back of her hand: straight through Paternoster Square towards New Change, turn right and follow the main road around the edge of St Paul's Churchyard towards the Tube. But she wasn't thinking clearly. No sooner had she staggered left out of the bar, she'd stumbled right, hitting St Paul's Churchyard, and the left flank of Sir Christopher Wren's masterpiece.

If she hadn't been so plastered, she might have felt a little nervous veering off the main street, tottering left into the empty, dark churchyard; more aware of her solitariness, her vulnerability, the darkness encasing her. Especially tonight, Halloween. But the alcohol had warped her usually cautious temperament.

She wobbled her way through the ebony spike-topped gates of the north-east churchyard, the cathedral's vast waxen columns to her immediate right seeming larger and more daunting through her glazed eyes. She carried on walking, across a wide paved area leading onto a narrower pathway, edged on either side by sodden grass and lofty trees, naked and bereft of colour, their sprawling, gnarled branches resembling thin, withered fingers.

She swerved her way around the imposing column mounted with a gilded statue of St Paul, and right onto a paved area decorated with a plaque marking the location of St Paul's Cross, lined on either side with several drenched wooden benches.

It was a spot which, in the height of summer, would be buzzing with activity.

But not tonight. Tonight, there was no one about, despite it being an iconic spot and relatively early by Friday night London standards. Paige wasn't surprised. It was sheeting down with rain. Rebounding off the ground with unforgiving brutality. Why would anyone be out walking in such horrendous weather?

But there was someone there. Footsteps approaching from behind... just about audible under the hammering rain...gaining time on her sluggish, more erratic pace, her gait slowed not only by her intoxication, but by the four-inch stilettos she'd been wearing all day in court.

Her senses suddenly more alert, sobered up by the knowledge that she had unexpected company, Paige tried to quicken her pace. At the same time, she reached inside her bag for her mobile phone, an exercise made more difficult by the fact that she was still holding her umbrella with her other hand. The wind had picked up. Any minute her brolly was going to turn inside out. It was no use. She stopped for a second to close it. But just as she did, a gloved hand grabbed her neck from behind. Fear impaled her, like a poisoned arrow rendering her muscles numb, her voice mute.

She should have taken up Cara and Maddy's offer to escort her to the station. *Why the hell hadn't she?*

She couldn't speak, both from terror and because her attacker's hand was wrapped so tightly around her neck. Whoever it was, was strong, and Paige was no match. Her eyes frantically darted all around for a friendlier human presence, but she was very much alone. The trees and the shadows were no friend to her. They were the allies of her attacker. Rain lashed down on her, blinding her vision, saturating her hair, her face, her skin, through her wringing wet clothes.

Was that leather she could smell? Her legs like blancmange, her head spinning with booze and fear, she realised she'd come to the end of the line. And then her mouth was suddenly being covered with something. A cloth or rag. Distinctive, sweet-smelling.

Before she knew it, she'd fallen unconscious.

A blessing in disguise, although Paige would never know that.

Because she wouldn't have wanted to be conscious for the next stage.

She was one of the lucky ones.

Chapter Seven

Saturday 1 November 2014, 8.30 a.m.

'Christ, not another one. Not so soon.'

Carver stood stock-still as he studied the bloody scrawl imprinted on the girl's chest, trying to make sense of what the killer was getting at. '*C-r-i-m-e,*' he muttered. He wasn't surprised the killer had struck again. But the timing surprised him. A second kill just three days after the first. Was the killer trying to send a particular message, or just playing with them for the hell of it? Was he involved with law, or completely unconnected? What had these girls done to deserve such violent deaths?

The body of Paige Summers had been spotted by an early morning jogger within a dense cluster of trees and shrubbery at the back of St Paul's Cathedral in the north-east side of the churchyard. Sprawled across a bed of sodden leaves, her clothes had been caked with a thin layer of mud, a couple of bramble cuts to her face. But it was nothing compared to the gelatinous mess vandalising her chest like obscene graffiti.

'Looks like the same killer, sir.'

'Do we have an ID?'

Drake looked down at his notepad. 'Yes, sir, the victim's bag was lying by her body when the jogger found her. There was a driver's licence in her purse, along with various credit cards and her work ID. Paige Summers, twenty-five. A barrister at Inner Temple chambers.'

'Another lawyer. And the same age as the last. On the bright side, we seem to have a pattern emerging. Although she wasn't shot like Morrell. Nor do there appear to be any signs of strangulation.'

'Maybe smothered to death?'

'Maybe, Drake. Or maybe she died from her injuries.'

'Yes, sir, but surely the killer would have had to have incapacitated her in some way before being able to carve so neatly into her chest. I mean, it's such a clean job. Just like with Morrell. As if the killer had all the time in the world. Maybe she was drugged first?'

'Good point, Drake.'

It was a good point. An obvious point he should have thought of. But Carver was distracted and feeling more pissed off with the world than usual.

He wasn't meant to be there. He was meant to be taking Daniel to Saturday morning football practice. But like so many times before, he'd had to bail on his little boy. Now Carl would be cheering Daniel on from the sidelines, and now Rachel would have another reason to get pissy and bitch about him to her equally bitchy friends. A poor excuse for a father. Devoted to the job more than his boy.

He needed to make it up to him. But for now, that would have to wait.

'We need to trace her last movements,' Carver said. 'Who was the last person to see her? Visit her chambers, find out what cases she'd been working on and where. Whether she prosecuted or defended, or both. Who she's put away or got off in the past, and who might bear a grudge as a result. For all we know, that could be what the killer's getting at.'

'That she's committed a crime by either helping someone go free, or putting them away, sir?'

'Precisely, Drake. Just a theory, but we need to consider everything. Do all the usual background checks. Find out where she studied law – she's about the same age as Maddy Kramer – although I realise there are a lot of law schools out there, so it's a long shot they knew one another.' He paused to reflect. 'I'm guessing she was either heading home from the pub, or from work. Once Grayson's performed the post-mortem, we'll have a better idea of whether she'd been drinking, and how exactly she died.'

Something in the distance, behind Carver's shoulder, caught Drake's eye. 'Speak of the devil.' Carver spun round to see Grayson coming along the path towards them. As he approached, he flashed his ID card at two officers guarding the cordon. They let him through.

'So, what have we here?' Grayson asked after they'd said their good mornings and he'd suited up.

'Looks like the same killer,' Carver said. 'Another lawyer, another legal term scrawled across her chest. But unlike Morrell, she wasn't shot.'

Grayson bent down over the body. Although it had stopped raining, the ground around them was still wet, the sky overhead a dreary battleship grey.

'Chloroform,' he announced, glancing back at Carver and Drake. 'Unmistakable.'

'It seems you were right, Drake.' Carver turned to his charge. The boy was good. Sharper than the average new kid on the block. Confident enough to offer his opinion, humble enough to want to learn.

Drake felt his cheeks colour. 'Just a hunch, sir.'

'Don't be coy about it, Drake.'

'No, sir, sorry, sir.'

Drake caught Grayson rolling his eyes at this exchange. He suppressed a grin but couldn't help smiling inside.

'Drake also thinks the girl may have been suffocated to death before she was cut.'

'It's possible, yes. We'll do some bloods to check for levels of CO_2. Usually, with asphyxiation cases, the deceased's eyes will be bloodshot and there's often bruising around the mouth and cheeks.'

'But if the girl was drugged first, her eyes would have been closed,' Drake said. 'Plus, the killer wouldn't have needed to hold her down with as much force. It would have been easy.'

'That's true,' Grayson nodded. 'And it explains why there are no visible signs of a struggle.'

'Interesting,' Carver mumbled.

'What, sir?' Drake asked.

'Well, it's almost as if the killer was being, dare I say it, "kinder" to this victim. Drugging and suffocating her first, before getting down to the gruesome stuff. Whereas with Morrell, it seems like he wanted her to be in pain till the end.'

'I see what you mean, sir. The manner of the killings isn't entirely consistent.'

'But there is a pattern emerging all the same. Two female lawyers, both twenty-five, both of whom had legal jargon inscribed across their chests.' He paused, as if thinking this over, then looked at Grayson. 'We'll let you and your team get on with your work.'

Carver and Drake walked away. 'Let's head back to the station, Drake. I need to speak to the Chief about getting a few more bodies on the team. We may be dealing with a serial killer, and we need to get ahead of the game before this sicko strikes again.'

The killer carefully washed down the blade. Scrupulously cleansing it of the girl's blood. Another defenceless victim, doubtless believing her beauty, youth and intelligence would protect her from the murkier side of life.

Beauty was such a blessing. Just like music. Nothing brought the killer more pleasure than beautiful music. Mozart, Handel, Beethoven especially; they were all such masters of their calling, having created works of perfection.

Yes, beauty was such an exquisite thing to behold, to treasure. But underneath a thing of beauty, there was often such ugliness. And that was exasperating beyond belief. The cruellest of deceptions that needed to be drawn out and eradicated.

Despite the late hour and abysmal weather, it had been risky pulling her comatose body under the sprawling fir tree, placing the polythene bag over her head, watching and waiting for her to draw her last breath. But there had been no choice. The killer hadn't planned to kill her so soon, but a chance had presented itself and it had to be grabbed. And the powerful timbres of Beethoven's *Symphony No. 5* playing softly in the killer's ears had provided added resolve to get the job done.

But this one hadn't been as satisfying as the last. She'd been naive, desperate, weak; not arrogant, bitchy and wilful like Sarah. Which is why drugging and suffocating her first, before getting down to the most creative part, had been the kinder option. It wouldn't have been right to make her suffer the way Sarah had suffered.

But she was still a whore, still a two-faced bitch. Still someone who'd deserved what was coming to her. And still arrogant enough to walk through St Paul's Churchyard at night, thinking she was immune from danger. Perhaps because she'd only been minutes away from the largest criminal court in the land.

How wrong she'd been.

'Oh, God, no.'

Paul stood motionless, his face a picture of shock.

'May we come in?' Carver asked. It was midday on Saturday. Having discovered through their enquiries that Paige Summers and Maddy Kramer had, as chance would have it, been in the same year at the same law school, Carver and Drake had made a beeline for Maddy and Paul's flat. Disappointed to learn Maddy was out, Carver had just broken the news of Paige's death to Paul.

'Yes, yes of course,' Paul responded weakly.

He led Carver and Drake into the living room. An inviting aroma of coffee, eggs and toast hung in the air. The telly was showing some US comedy, while the remnants of Paul's breakfast lay on the coffee table, piled high on one side with women's magazines and the latest edition of *GQ*. Paul made a quick attempt at tidying up, then removed a displeased-looking Atticus from the sofa. He gestured for his guests to take a seat. 'As I said, Maddy's popped out for a swim. It's kind of her Saturday morning ritual, but she should be back soon.'

'We don't mind waiting.'

Paul made coffee, then pulled up a chair opposite Carver and Drake. Carver gave Atticus a guarded look. He wasn't too fond of cats, principally because he was prone to allergies, and their natural shedding process didn't agree with him. Atticus seemed to sense this and gave Carver an equally wary look in return.

'How long have you and Ms Kramer been living together?' Carver asked, avoiding further eye contact with his furry foe.

'Since our second year at the academy. So just over four years.'

'You also studied there?'

'Yes, for my sins.' Paul shook his head ruefully. 'But law wasn't for me. I write full-time now.'

'Ah yes, Ms Kramer mentioned that. Anything I might have heard of?'

'No,' Paul sighed. 'If you had, I wouldn't have to work nights in a bar to pay the rent.'

Carver gave a sympathetic half-smile, then asked, 'Were Ms Kramer and Ms Summers close?'

'Very. Paige was an amazing girl. Gentle, kind. Everyone loved her. I just can't believe it. First Sarah, now Paige. I'm scared for Maddy.' He leaned in, looked at Carver earnestly. 'Do you think she's in danger?'

'I don't know. But you're right to be scared. There's no way of knowing when the killer will strike again, or against whom. So far, we've got the impression that Ms Morrell wasn't too popular among her peers. Would you say that's true?'

'Yes. She was very ambitious. Which is all well and good, but not when you take it to extremes.'

'You weren't friends with her I take it?'

'No, I wasn't. But there was no bad blood between us. I just stayed out of her way, and she stayed out of mine. She was more bothered by the female competition.'

'Because of Professor Stirling?'

Paul looked surprised, but his response was deflected by the sound of the front door being opened. Atticus immediately scampered out of the room. 'Oh, fuck.' Paul stood up, breathed deeply, as if bracing himself for Maddy's reaction.

'Hiya,' came her bright and breezy voice from the hallway. 'Boy, that was good. Hangover's practically gone.' They listened to the sound of keys being thrown on the hall table, jacket unzipped, shoes removed and flung to one side.

'Hello, sweetheart,' they heard her say to Atticus.

She came skipping into the living room, cradling Atticus in her arms. Full of life and cheerful weekend spirit. But she stopped dead in her tracks on spotting Carver and Drake. Her eyes flitted between them. She sensed from their expressions that this was more than just a follow-up visit. Something major had happened.

'DCI Carver, DC Drake,' she said, 'has there been a development in the case?' She lightly placed Atticus on the floor.

Paul went up and put his arm around her shoulder, then guided her towards the other sofa. He sat her down gently, took her hand, and clasped it tight. She looked at him fearfully. 'What is it? You're scaring me.'

'Maddy…' Paul began. But Carver beat him to it.

'Ms Kramer, I'm afraid I have some bad news. This morning, your friend Paige Summers was found dead in St Paul's Churchyard. We believe it was the same killer.'

Years on the job had taught Carver to be direct when relaying news of a loved one's death. One could say it sympathetically, but there was little point in beating around the bush. Even though a quick glance told him he'd seriously pissed off the flatmate.

As Carver waited for Maddy's reaction, he took in her appearance. She looked so different from yesterday, when she'd been dressed in a sleek black suit, hair straight and smooth, flawless make-up, killer heels. Now she was dressed in joggers and a baggy sweatshirt, bare-faced, her hair roughly tied up in a bun. Now she looked unaffected and rather cute. He told himself to focus on the job.

Maddy could barely breathe, let alone speak. Her lips were suddenly anesthetised, her ears plugged with cotton wool. *Did I hear right?* It seemed impossible. She'd only seen Paige last night. Talked with her, laughed with her. *And now…now she's gone?*

'It can't be true,' she finally whispered. She clutched Paul closer. He stroked her hair, kissed her forehead. 'It is, hon, it is. I don't want to believe it either.'

'How was she found?' Maddy asked, her heart racing. It was a question she did, and yet didn't, want to know the answer to.

Drake explained. 'Forensics have yet to confirm, but we believe she was drugged first, then smothered to death. She had the word "Crime" inscribed across her chest. We're pretty sure the killer did this after killing her.'

Maddy wanted to throw up. She'd swum hard on little breakfast and felt faint. She turned to Paul. 'Can you get me some water, with a little sugar in it.'

Paul dashed out of the room and was back in a flash. Carver saw how close they were. Not like lovers. Like brother and sister.

Maddy took baby sips of the syrupy mixture, finding it hard to swallow.

'When was the last time you saw Ms Summers?' Carver asked.

'Last night.' Maddy's voice was scarcely audible.

Carver's pulse quickened. 'Where and when?'

Maddy explained how she and Cara had parted from Paige outside the bar, after she'd rejected their offer to accompany her to Mansion House Tube station. Jesus, how she wished she could turn back time, convince Paige to let them walk with her. She should have insisted. Why the fuck hadn't she?

'How did she seem?'

'Fine.' Maddy blinked back tears. Tried to answer Carver's question without breaking down. 'We drank a bit too much. But it was Friday night and we'd all had a tough week.' *Why Paige, why Paige?* The words kept spinning around in her head. 'She'd been assisting with a murder trial at the Old Bailey all week and needed to let off some steam.'

'Prosecuting or defending?'

'Prosecuting, I think. I don't know much more than that; you'll have to ask her chambers.'

'Was Paige seeing anyone?'

'Yes. A guy named Ben. He's a chartered accountant. Lovely guy.'

'Serious?'

'He was keener than her, I think.' Maddy narrowed her eyes at Carver. 'There's no way he could have done this. For one, he's been away on business.'

'We can't rule anything out at this stage, Ms Kramer.'

'But you think it's the same killer, right? I mean, it must be. It's too similar.'

'More than likely,' Carver said. 'You and Ms Summers were at law school together. How did she get on there? Make any enemies? Love interests?'

Maddy hesitated. She knew where this was going. Paige's sex life. 'She was very popular. Bright, conscientious, passed her exams with flying colours.'

'That's the academic side covered. What about her personal life? Boyfriends?'

'Not really.' She heard her voice. It wasn't convincing.

'That's a bit cryptic. Ms Kramer, I understand how hard this must be for you, but if you know or even suspect anything that may help us, you need to tell us. You owe it to your friend.'

Maddy was still struggling with the news. For so long, she'd imagined the milestones she and Paige would share. Marriage, motherhood, the vagaries of the menopause. Now she would have none of those memories to look forward to. Every major event in her life would be tarnished by the loss of her friend, as it had been with the loss of her parents.

A friend who, like Sarah, had slept with Stirling.

She recalled the uncomfortable look on Paige's face in the bar, the way she'd bowed her head when Cara had broached the subject of her feelings for Stirling. She hadn't needed a signed, sealed confession to know what had gone on.

Something *had* gone on between them, she was sure of it.

'She never dated anyone on the course. But I know she liked someone, and I have my suspicions that something went on with the man in question.'

'The man?'

Maddy chewed her lip nervously, glancing at Paul as if seeking his approval that she was doing the right thing.

'Say it, Maddy,' Paul urged. 'Like DCI Carver said, you owe it to Paige to try and help bring this arsehole to justice. And Sarah for that matter.'

He was right. She did owe it to both women. To herself. Who knew who was next on the killer's list? Why should she consider herself immune? It would be crazy, downright arrogant, to assume she was.

'Professor Stirling.'

Carver glanced at Drake. 'Just so we're clear,' he said, 'the same Professor Stirling who had an affair with Ms Morrell?'

Maddy nodded. 'It was obvious. But she never told me to my face. Never admitted that she liked him, let alone had an affair with him.' She paused, then quickly covered herself. 'That's why I didn't mention it yesterday.'

Carver let this slide. 'Did you ever notice Professor Stirling paying Ms Summers special attention?'

'Not especially. He was nice to everyone, especially the girls.'

'I see.' Carver sat back. 'Why do you think the killer wrote "Crime" across Ms Summers' chest?'

Maddy shrugged her shoulders limply, her eyes filling again. 'Because she's...sorry, she *was* a criminal barrister.'

'No other reason? You don't know if she ever wronged anyone? Offended, hurt them in some way? Helped put someone away where the evidence was weak? Committed a crime herself?'

Rage motored through Maddy. She looked at Carver as if he was mad. Too emotional to see that he was just doing his job, exploring all avenues for the greater good.

'Her being a criminal barrister seems a pretty good reason to me. Paige would never intentionally hurt anyone, let alone commit a crime. The idea's unthinkable. As for prosecuting someone where the evidence was weak, again, you'll have to speak to her chambers.'

Maddy felt drained. She wanted Carver and Drake to leave her in peace; allow her time to grieve.

Carver saw this. 'I can see you need some time alone, Ms Kramer.' He got up, thanked Paul for the coffee. 'We'll be going now.'

'She's obviously pretty shaken up by Ms Summers' death,' Carver said to Paul at the front door. 'Keep a close eye on her over the weekend.'

'Thanks, I will,' Paul said.

Back in the living room, he wrapped Maddy up in his arms while she sobbed like a child, unable to believe that she would never set eyes on Paige again.

'We need to question this Professor Stirling.' Adrenaline shot through Carver as he turned on the ignition of his Vauxhall Astra.

'Sir, you know we have a meeting already set up for Monday morning?'

'It can't wait till then, Drake. We're going to his house. Now.'

Chapter Eight

An hour later, Maddy stared at the television, watching Carver, standing in front of St Paul's Churchyard earlier that morning, announce Paige's death. *Has it really only been four days since he announced Sarah's?*

Two young, bright, beautiful women, dead within days of each other. The thought of who could be next on the list spooked her.

As soon as Carver and Drake had left, she'd called her grandmother. Although it didn't ease the pain, it was comforting to hear her steady voice. A voice that had been through it all with her. Rose didn't have a miracle cure for her pain. Only time could heal that. But she'd assured her granddaughter of two things: that she was strong enough to get through it; and that she wouldn't feel like this forever.

It gave Maddy courage. She didn't want to feel or live like this – constantly looking over her shoulder, wary of every turn she took, every stranger she passed, every look, gesture, fleeting glance. She had no clue who the killer was, but he was already impacting on her life, threatening to stop it in its tracks.

She couldn't have him dictating her every move. Whoever it was had to be stopped. As she continued to watch Carver on screen, Maddy told herself, *No more.* She needed to swallow her self-pity, and draw strength from the same dogged determination that had got her this far in life.

She leapt up from the sofa and dashed to her bedroom. In the corner was a small oak bookcase. Maddy was a hoarder when it came to her career and her studies. She never threw anything away for fear she might need it somewhere down the line. It was a fear partly born from common sense, but more from superstition. Below the shelf lined up with assorted legal textbooks were various lever-arch files containing her notes from law school. She ran her finger across them, as if seeking inspiration as to the killer's motive.

As she'd explained to Carver, as non-law undergraduates, she and her peers had had to study and pass exams in seven legal areas during their first year.

She traced her finger across the labelled files. "Equity", "Land", "European", "Tort", "Public", "Contract", "Crime".

As she mouthed these last two out loud, it hit her. 'That's it!'

'What's it?'

Maddy spun round to see Paul standing in the doorway.

'I think I know what the killer's doing.'

'You do?'

'Yes, he's following the syllabus. Contract, Crime. They're two of the subjects we studied in our first year. See for yourself.'

Paul came into the room, crouched down on his knees next to Maddy, and scanned the files. When he'd finished, he looked at her, astonished. 'Bloody hell, Mads, you could be on to something there. Can't believe you kept all your notes.'

'You know me, can't throw anything away.' She allowed herself a half-smile. 'After law school, Paige became a criminal barrister, which is probably why the killer wrote "Crime" across her chest, while Sarah hoped to qualify into Banking, an area of law governed by "Contracts".'

Paul looked perplexed. 'But we studied five other areas.' He skimmed his index finger across the first five files. 'Equity, Land, European, Tort and Public.'

Maddy nodded grimly. 'If I'm right, the killer's planning five more murders. And I'm betting each of the targets qualified into a department connected to one of those areas.'

Paul swallowed hard. 'Christ. Litigation could be any of those.' He was trying to remain calm, but Maddy saw the look in his eyes. He was afraid for her.

'Yeah, I know; I could be next. That's why I need to speak to Carver.'

Her voice was almost breathless. She dashed to the hallway, her heart racing as she picked up the handheld, then dug out Carver's card from her coat pocket. She dialled the number, but it went straight to voicemail. She shot Paul an exasperated look, before leaving a message, asking Carver to call her back ASAP.

'Do you have any idea who might be next?' Paul asked.

'No, but I'm guessing it's someone who attended the academy. Has to be.'

'What you need is a list of everyone in our year, then find out who went on to practise and where.'

'Exactly my thinking.' Maddy looked down at the handset she was still holding. 'Come on, Carver, where are you? Call me back.'

Saturday 1 November 2014, 1.30 p.m.

'Please, come through to the living room and take a seat. James is upstairs in his study. I'll go fetch him.'

Carver and Drake watched Elizabeth Stirling leave the room as they sat down on a swish cream leather sofa opposite the fireplace. The first thing Carver thought as she'd opened the front door and he and Drake had stepped into the large entrance hall, was that the man they'd come to question had done all right for himself.

The couple lived in a Grade II-listed, four-storey detached house just off Gray's Inn Road in central London, close to King's Cross Station and nearby Bloomsbury, where Stirling worked. It was a beautiful period property, with vast amounts of space. The one thing it was missing, though, thought Carver, was the chaos of children.

Once he was sure Elizabeth was out of earshot, Drake turned to Carver and said under his breath, 'This is going to be tricky, asking questions with the wife around.'

'Hmm, I wonder if she suspects,' Carver mused. 'If things get too awkward, we'll just have to concoct a reason for her to leave the room.'

After a few minutes, James Stirling appeared, Elizabeth at his side. Carver immediately saw the appeal. He was a handsome man. Dark hair, dark eyes, a strong physique. That, coupled with his intellect, would make many a college girl a sure thing.

'How can I help?' Stirling shook hands with both men and gave them a warm, relaxed smile. *He certainly doesn't look like a killer*, thought Carver. But then, who did? It was often the most charming, polite, impeccably dressed individuals who turned out to be the most psychotic. Who blended in, and looked like twenty other men, hiding behind a carefully constructed veneer of normality.

Carver introduced himself and Drake, then got down to business.

'I presume you're aware that one of your former students, Sarah Morrell, was murdered in the early hours of last Tuesday morning?'

He observed Stirling closely, studying his face for a reaction, any sign of guilt.

'Yes, of course, a shocking business.' Stirling shook his head gravely. 'She was an excellent student, and it's hard to imagine who might have wanted to do this to her.'

'I'm not sure if you've seen the news, but there's been another murder. Of a similar nature.' Carver's gaze lingered on Stirling. *Is that a slight twitching of the mouth? Tensing of shoulders?* 'Early this morning, the body of Paige Summers, another former student of yours, was found in St Paul's Churchyard. We're waiting for forensics to confirm, but we believe Ms Summers was drugged, then smothered to death. The killer then inscribed the word "Crime" across her chest.'

Stirling turned pale. He glanced at his wife, who remained impassive. Eerily so. Awkward, to say the least.

Was he imagining it, or was she taking some sort of pleasure in this news? thought Carver. *Maybe she does know about her husband's affairs.*

'My God, you think it was the same killer?'

'More than likely, yes. Judging by the inscriptions.'

'Why do you think he's targeting my ex-students?'

'That's something we were hoping you could shed some light on.'

Stirling's eyes flickered with apprehension. Elizabeth remained poker-faced. All except her eyes, which, unlike her husband's, looked animated rather than anxious.

'And how might that be?' Stirling's mellifluous voice was suddenly croaky. 'Both girls graduated, well, it must be at least a couple of years ago now. No, make that three. Surely, it's their families and colleagues you should be questioning? Their clients?'

'Don't worry, we've got that covered.' Carver shifted his gaze to Elizabeth, flashed her his best smile. 'Mrs Stirling, may my colleague and I trouble you for a cup of coffee? We've been up since the crack of dawn and could do with the caffeine hit.'

He saw it in her eyes. She knew why he wanted her out of the room. But to her credit, she played along all the same. 'Of course.' She glanced slyly at her husband. 'I'll be back as quickly as I can.'

Carver noticed the way Stirling deliberately avoided her gaze, the atmosphere chilly as she left the room. Clearly theirs was not a happy marriage. He wondered what secrets they harboured.

'Why don't you sit down?' he said to Stirling.

Stirling had barely settled himself when Carver hit him with a bigger bombshell. 'Professor Stirling, is it true that you once had a sexual relationship with Ms Morrell?'

Stirling's face reddened. 'What?' he said, looking aghast. 'Where did you hear such nonsense? That's preposterous.'

Carver stared at him coldly. 'May I remind you, Professor Stirling, that I am conducting an official murder investigation here. It's vital that you tell the truth from the outset. As an ex-lawyer, I needn't remind you of the penalties for perjury and obstructing a police investigation.'

Stirling wavered. He looked over his shoulder, presumably for any sign of his wife, before responding. 'Okay, okay, yes, I had a brief affair with Sarah, but it can't get out. I have my job, my reputation to think of.'

Carver was already starting to dislike the man. To take advantage of his young, impressionable students, and then expect his reputation to remain intact was arrogant beyond belief. He had to fight to keep his cool. 'Is it also true that you had an affair with Ms Summers?'

Now Stirling looked like he wanted to disappear into oblivion. He switched his gaze to Drake, as if for support, even though he was a stranger. But Drake's face was blank. Equally appalled by Stirling's hypocrisy.

'That was nothing,' Stirling said dismissively. 'With Sarah, it was different. We saw each other for around six months. I developed feelings for her, while Paige was a minor dalliance. I know it sounds conceited, but the girl was infatuated with me.'

'And you took advantage of that? A respected, married academic.' Carver's eyes drilled through Stirling's, trying to catch him out.

'Look, I'm not proud of cheating on my wife, but you have to understand, we don't exactly have a happy marriage.'

'You're not exactly giving that a fair chance by sleeping with your students,' Carver said.

'Look, Chief Inspector, you know nothing about my wife or our marriage. It's complicated.'

'Okay,' Carver said, 'but coming back to Sarah and Paige, how did those affairs end? You say you had feelings for Ms Morrell. What happened?'

'It just came to a natural end. I wasn't going to leave my wife, and it wasn't fair on Sarah. We decided to call it a day.'

His explanation lacked conviction. He was lying, Carver was certain. But he pressed on.

'When was the last time you saw Ms Morrell?'

'Three years ago, after she passed the Legal Practice Course. And the same goes for Ms Summers.'

'Besides academically, how did both women get on at the academy? Did they strike up any strong friendships? Form any rivalries?'

Stirling let out a heavy sigh. 'Sarah was a difficult one. She was crazily ambitious, to the point she put people's backs up. She didn't make a lot of friends as far as I know.'

'And Paige?'

'Paige was different. Driven, but not to the point of obsession. She was extremely popular with her peers. One girl particularly. Madeline Kramer, I believe her name was. Another bright young woman. The two of them became inseparable from what I can recall.'

'Was Ms Kramer friendly with Sarah?'

'No, not especially. She was popular, though, like Paige.'

'Professor Stirling, where were you in the early hours of last Tuesday morning?'

Carver's questioning had switched from the general to the specific in the blink of an eye. It caught Stirling by surprise. He faltered for a second, then said, 'I was at home, in bed.'

'Your wife can attest to that?'

'I can.' Elizabeth reappeared holding a trayful of coffee and biscuits. 'James and I went to bed around the same time. In the middle of the night, I got up to fetch a glass of water. James was fast asleep.'

Stirling appeared to swallow hard. As if he'd been gasping for air but was finally able to breathe again. Carver was sure she was lying.

'I see. And last night? Where were you, Professor Stirling?'

'I was at a staff function.'

'Where?'

Stirling dithered.

'Have you forgotten?' Carver questioned.

'No.'

'So, where were you?'

'The Saint bar.'

'Where's that?'

More dithering. Then, 'Paternoster Square.'

Carver jolted in his seat. Glanced at Drake. Their apparent collusion further unnerved Stirling, who shifted uneasily.

'Listen,' he said, looking at both men, 'I know what you must be thinking. That I was only a stone's throw away from where Paige was murdered. But I can assure you that I was home by midnight.'

'We don't know the exact timing of Ms Summers' death yet,' Carver said, 'but we do know that she'd been drinking with friends in Paternoster Square before she was murdered.'

Stirling flinched, fidgeted again. Carver turned to Elizabeth. 'Mrs Stirling, can you vouch for your husband's whereabouts?'

Elizabeth glanced Stirling's way through slitty eyes, then back at

Carver. 'No, I'm afraid I was away last night, staying over at a friend's. I only came home this morning.' Her tone was calm, almost smug.

Stirling grew visibly distressed. 'Look, I have to say this is well and truly out of order. You have no right to come questioning me on a Saturday afternoon, all because I once taught both victims, and happened to be in the vicinity of where one of them died.'

Carver raised his tall frame up in his seat. 'Professor Stirling, I have a right to conduct my investigation as I see fit. And in view of your *history* with both girls...' he stole a look at Elizabeth, '...it is perfectly reasonable that I should want to question you.' Stirling didn't speak. 'How did you get home?'

'Cab.'

'Alone?'

'Yes.'

'Did anyone you know see you get in the cab?'

'No, not that I'm aware of. I walked to Newgate Street from the bar and hailed a cab halfway down.'

'Did you get a receipt?'

'No.'

For a few seconds Carver said nothing. He looked around the room, glancing at the piano and cello nestled in the corner. They'd caught his eye the minute he'd sat down.

'Who's the musician?'

'Both of us,' Stirling replied, looking somewhat puzzled by Carver's swift shift to the prosaic.

'I used to be a concert cellist,' Elizabeth explained. 'James is really the pianist.' She smiled at Stirling; a little too sweetly. 'It's what drew us together, isn't it, darling?'

Her husband wriggled in his chair. 'Er, yes, a *classical* romance, you might say.' He followed this up with an uneasy chuckle. 'But Elizabeth's the pro. I just play for pleasure.'

'That's true,' Elizabeth muttered.

Carver widened his eyes at Drake, then stood up. 'Well, thank you both for your time. That'll be all. For now.'

Stirling looked relieved that the interrogation was over. He and his wife stood up and saw Carver and Drake to the door.

'Don't disappear, will you, Professor?' Carver said as Stirling held the door open. 'I expect I'll be popping by your office soon.'

'No problem,' Stirling said artificially.

They left. Stirling closed the door and exhaled loudly with relief.

He was walking a fine line. He'd have to be more careful in future.

Back in the car, Drake drove while Carver rode shotgun. He listened to Maddy's voicemail, then pressed the hash key.

After a few seconds, Maddy picked up. 'DCI Carver, thanks for calling me back. I think I know what the killer's doing.'

Carver straightened. 'You do?'

'Yes. He's following the syllabus from the Graduate Diploma in Law. The GDL. What we studied in our first year at the academy. I'm almost positive.'

'What makes you think that?'

'Crime and Contract are two of the core subjects non-law undergrads must study on the GDL.'

'How many subjects are there?'

'Seven.'

'Jesus. So you're telling me the killer's planning five more murders?'

'If I'm right, then yes, I'm afraid so.'

'Any idea why the killer chose those particular subjects for Morrell and Summers?'

Maddy explained her theory. 'It's the only logical explanation I can think of.'

'It makes sense, I'll grant you that. Thanks, Ms Kramer.'

Carver glanced at Drake, who had one ear on the conversation, one eye on driving – a risky arrangement in Saturday afternoon London traffic. 'So how are we going to pre-empt the next victims?'

Carver had an idea himself but wanted Maddy's take on it. She was bright, as expected from a City lawyer. But it wasn't just her intellect that interested him. He could tell she had good sense and sound judgement;

not like most of the other suits he'd interviewed at Channings, sealed in their own corporate bubbles, blind to reality. He guessed he shouldn't be surprised. If all you did was work long hours within the same four walls, with the same people, day after day, dealing with impossibly rich clients and their impossible demands, you *would* start to lose touch with reality.

'If the killer is specifically targeting my year, we need to get hold of a list of everyone who attended the academy from 2009 to 2011, then find out whether they went on to practise, and if so, where and in what field.'

'Thanks, I'll get Drake on it.'

'No problem. I want to do anything I can to help catch this animal.'

Carver smiled at her spirit. 'Watch your back, Ms Kramer. Stay around people as much as possible. Take well-lit routes at night. Trust no one.'

'Thanks for the warning, but I'll be fine.'

That's what they all say, thought Carver. 'I'll be in touch.' He hung up, filled Drake in on Maddy's theory.

'She's a smart cookie, isn't she?' Drake observed. Carver said nothing, just smiled to himself. 'As soon as we get back to the station,' Drake continued, 'I'll give the academy a call. Get them to email the list ASAP. What did you make of Stirling and his wife?'

'They were both holding back. And she covered for him, though Lord knows why. She clearly knows he's been cheating on her left, right and centre. We need to keep a close eye on him. Whether he's our man I can't say, but there's something not right about him. Or her for that matter.'

'I'm going over to Gran's this evening.' Later that same Saturday, Maddy walked into the living room with two mugs of tea. She handed one to Paul, then sat down beside him, Atticus purring contentedly at her feet. Rose lived alone in Barnes, an affluent suburb of south-west London. She was eighty-five, but remained as bright as a button. She was Maddy's anchor, and right now, her granddaughter needed her.

'She okay?'

'Yeah, she's fine. Worried sick about me, though.'

'She's not the only one.'

'It was good to speak to her on the phone. But I feel like I need to see her.'

'What time will you be back?'

Maddy curled her legs to one side and blew on her tea. 'I think I'm going to stay over. It takes forever trekking back from west London. Plus, I don't fancy coming back in the dark the way things are.'

'Understandable. In fact, I was going to suggest you stay over. Much safer.' Paul smiled cheekily. 'I have an ulterior motive, of course.'

Maddy looked puzzled. Then, as she studied his face, the penny dropped. 'You've met someone?'

'Yep. His name's Justin. It's early days, but he came into the bar, we started chatting and kind of hit it off. He's twenty-six, a graphic designer. Smart *and* hot. I'm planning on dinner and a movie. What do you reckon?'

Maddy affectionately patted Paul's knee. 'That's great, I'm really pleased for you.'

Had the circumstances been different, she would have squealed with excitement at his news. Cracked open some red, begged him to please tell her more, and when could she meet him?

She'd been on at Paul about getting his romantic life sorted for ages. More than anyone, he deserved to be happy. But Paige's death was still painfully fresh. After speaking to Carver, she'd felt shattered and dozed off; dreamed of a holiday she and Paige had taken together in Spain. The most fun she'd ever had. It had felt so real, as if Paige was still alive. The realisation when she woke up that she was gone forever had almost been unbearable. What's more, the photos of Sarah continued to plague her, knowing that Paige had met a similar fate. All she could think about was the sheer terror and helplessness she must have felt. How her poor parents must be in hell right now. She'd thought about calling them but had stopped herself. It was too soon, and in any case, she wasn't sure what she'd say besides the obvious, which, out loud, sounded lame.

'Sorry, Mads, I suddenly feel like a bit of a twat bringing up my love life after what's happened. It was inconsiderate of me. I know how close you and Paige were.'

'Don't be silly,' Maddy said. 'I'm happy for you. And I'm glad to be out of your hair tonight.'

They hugged tenderly, then Paul broke away. 'I just pray Carver catches this maniac. I mean, if he's targeting our year, any one of us could be next.'

'True. But my gut tells me he's only targeting female students who went on to practise. And it must be someone we knew at the time. I find it hard to believe a stranger would target our intake out of the blue.'

'Do you think Stirling's capable of such a thing?'

Maddy shook her head. 'You never know what a person's like behind closed doors. I'm just thankful I never let the creep take advantage of me.'

Paul brushed his index finger across the tip of Maddy's nose. 'You're not the average girl, you're in a different class.'

She smiled at him gratefully, a warm, fuzzy feeling filling her insides. At least she still had Paul, even if Paige was gone. He, along with Rose, would help her through this. 'Thanks. I don't know what I'd do without you.'

Chapter Nine

Sunday 2 November 2014

'Here's the list, sir.'

Sunday, 9 p.m. Carver was in his office, set apart from the main station floor, but with large windows allowing him to keep tabs on his team. He hovered from one foot to the other as he studied the flow chart he'd scrawled on one of several whiteboards dotted around the room. A victimology analysis. It hadn't really told him anything new, but it was good to get it down in writing. It helped him think better, often inspired ideas lodged at the back of his brain but which had yet to come to the fore.

He looked up, took the list from Drake, and quickly ran his eyes over it. 'There's a helluva lot of names here. Get someone to highlight every female, then find out what happened to each of them after finishing at the academy. I want to know who went on to practise, and where.'

'Will do, sir.'

'We also need to start questioning all academy personnel. Particularly those who worked there from 2009 to 2011. Surely, one of them must know or remember something helpful.'

But they didn't.

Having spent much of the next day interviewing tutors other than Stirling who'd taught at the academy from 2009 to 2011, some of whom were still there, it transpired that none of them remembered seeing or teaching anyone suspicious at the time. And all of them had rock-hard alibis for both murders.

Later, back at the station, Drake darted into Carver's office. It was 7 p.m.

'Here's the amended list, sir,' he said, handing it over.

'About bloody time.'

'There were 130 females in the victims' years. Two-thirds went on to practise law, and I've highlighted these in blue. The highlighted names with a tick and a comment next to them are those students who went on to specialise in areas associated with the subjects Maddy Kramer has suggested the killer might inscribe next. Thirty in total. For example, you'll see that by Jennifer Madley's name, I've written "Public", because she became a government lawyer. Likewise, Stella Parker went on to become a medical negligence lawyer, so I've written "Tort" next to her.'

'What's Tort?'

'It's a civil action, concerned with remedying wrongs committed by one person against another. For example, if someone, say, a doctor, is negligent.'

Carver smiled. 'Have you been reading up on the syllabus, Drake?'

Drake coloured slightly. 'Yes, sir.'

'Nice work. But you need to get Kramer to confirm all this. I notice you've ticked her name.'

'Yes. She's a litigator, and litigation can relate to any of the four remaining subjects.'

'That's a worry. Go and see Kramer first thing in the morning. I've got a meeting with the Chief at 9 a.m. Report back to me when you're done.'

Chapter Ten

Tuesday 4 November 2014

'DC Drake is downstairs, Maddy.'

9.15 a.m. Maddy was trying to focus on a brief to Counsel, but she was preoccupied; consumed by thoughts of Paige, and what evidence, if any, the police had found. She looked up and saw Margaret peeping her head around the door. 'Okay, thanks, Margaret. I'll be right down.'

She glanced at Jeff, who was eyeing her with concern. Or was it suspicion? He was a lawyer after all. 'What does he want with you again?'

'Don't worry, it's nothing terrible,' Maddy said, eager to set the record straight that she wasn't a suspect. 'I've just had a bit of a theory about the murders, and I suspect DC Drake's here about that.'

Jeff's doubtful expression switched to one of amusement. 'Well, well, looks like we've got our very own on-site Nancy Drew. Don't let them turn you into a P.I. full-time. You're too good a lawyer to lose.'

Despite her low mood, Maddy laughed, secretly buoyed by the compliment. 'Don't worry, there's no chance of that. Police work's far too grisly a business for me.'

Five minutes later, she was sitting on one side of a conference table with Drake, studying the list.

'What do you think?' he asked keenly.

'You've matched them up well,' Maddy said. 'But I'm sorry to say that aside from Lisa Ryland, I don't remember any of them. The academy was so large, they split us into small tutor groups, so I only ever mixed with my group. Which included Sarah, Paige and Lisa, plus Lisa's friend – Marcia Devereux. She left after the first year and never became a lawyer as far as I know. And the others in my group were all blokes.'

Drake tried to conceal his disappointment. 'Okay, don't worry.' Just then, something occurred to him. 'So, leaving the possible victims aside, do you have any ideas where the killer might strike? What I mean is, for contract, he chose a boardroom; and for crime, it was near the Old Bailey.' The same keen look. Maddy could feel the hope, the determination to succeed, radiating off him. She wanted to help, but she couldn't very well magic a solution from thin air.

She gave him a sympathetic smile. He was kind of cute, but too wholesome for her. She liked them a little rougher around the edges. Just then, an image of Carver popped into her head. She instantly scolded herself for thinking such frivolous thoughts at a time like this. *Snap out of it.* She pinched her temples, willing herself to think. Then she picked up her pen and began to draw a table on the pad in front of her:

Equity	Public	Tort	EU	Land
Family court (Royal Courts of Justice (RCJ))	Houses of Parliament/ Supreme Court	Hospital	Any UK Court sitting as a Court of First Instance	Business premises
Wills & Probate Office	Government building	Home	The European Court of Justice	Residential premises

Chancery Court	Court of Human Rights	Anywhere where an accident might occur? E.g., the road	Any foreign office of the victim's firm	Land Registry

When she'd finished, she put her pen down, slid the pad towards Drake.

'That's a pretty wide list,' he said, raising his eyebrows. 'How the hell are we going to second-guess any of those?' He gave Maddy another hopeful look. As if she had the answer.

But she didn't. His guess was as good as hers. 'We can't,' she said. 'This is pure guesswork. Really and truly I don't know where the killer might strike next.'

Friday 7 November 2014

Maddy clutched Paul's hand as they sat near the front of the church, watching Graham Summers, Paige's father, try not to break down as he eulogised his daughter's brief life. Despair clouded his face, and to Maddy, he looked like he'd aged about ten years since her death. The same went for his wife, seated on the front row, her other children's arms wrapped around either side of her as her back juddered up and down. Maddy couldn't begin to imagine what they were going through. It was every parent's worst nightmare to lose a child, and their lives would never be the same.

It was a drab, drizzly day, fittingly symbolic of what Paige's death represented. Maddy, dressed in a demure black skirt suit, tried her best not to lose it as she listened to Graham praise his daughter's kindness, spirit and intelligence.

Ben, Paige's boyfriend, was seated in the second row. His head bowed, every now and again he pinched his temples, as if trying to rouse himself from a nightmare. He'd been eliminated as a suspect. As Maddy had told Carver, he'd been away on business in Germany the night Paige was murdered, and this had been confirmed by the clients he'd been having dinner with at the time.

They'd had to wait for the post-mortem to be performed before being able to bury Paige. Unfortunately, it hadn't revealed anything particularly useful, only confirming that she'd been sedated with chloroform, then suffocated. No DNA had been found at the immediate scene. The only thing they had to go on was a set of footprints found near her body: Nike LunarGlides, Carver had explained to Maddy over the phone. In contrast to the first murder, where the killer had left no outsole impression. The obvious explanation there was that he'd worn brand new trainers or shoe covers.

All in all, the police had so far drawn a blank.

Later, at the wake, Maddy approached Ben, who was drinking his wine rather too quickly. 'Hi, Ben, how are you?'

In truth, he looked ghastly. He wasn't strikingly handsome, but he was attractive enough. His voice was flat as he answered Maddy. 'Holding up.' He gave her a forced smile. 'You?'

'The same.'

'I still can't believe it,' he said, shaking his head. 'I keep thinking, what if I hadn't gone away?'

'No, stop that.' Maddy put her hand on his. 'There's nothing you could have done. Whoever it was must have been planning it for some time. It wasn't some random murder. And neither was Sarah's.'

'What the fuck are the police doing, Maddy?' Ben blinked back tears.

'All they can.' She leaned in closer. 'Ben, did Paige ever talk about her days at law school? Did she ever mention anyone she liked? Romantically, I mean. Or, on the flip side, anyone she didn't get on with?'

'You mean that slimeball Stirling?' Ben's eyes became hard and filled with hate.

His response surprised Maddy. 'She mentioned him to you?'

'Not in so many words. Paige sleep-talked. Every now and again, she'd call out his name.'

'Did you confront her?'

'Yes, of course. But she brushed it off. Said it was nothing, in my imagination. But then one time, after we'd argued and she'd had too much to drink, she accused me of being a disappointment, that the love of her life had got away, and that I'd never match up to him. I knew it was Stirling.'

Maddy was shocked. She'd never have thought Paige capable of saying something so hurtful. But love could do that to a person, she supposed.

'I'm sorry to hear that, Ben,' she said. 'But I'm sure she loved you. You have to believe that.'

Ben gave a limp smile. Maddy could tell he didn't really believe it but appreciated her saying it all the same.

Chapter Eleven

Saturday 15 November 2014

It had just gone 9 p.m. and Lisa Ryland was glad to be indoors. A savage wind rammed her kitchen window, rattling the pane violently as she poured herself a glass of Shiraz and brought it through to the living room.

She should have been at a house party. But that afternoon, the hostess – Marcia Devereux, a good friend from law school – had called it off. There'd been no development in the hunt for Sarah and Paige's killer, and so Marcia had had no urge to party. Neither had Lisa. Somehow, having known both victims, it didn't seem right. They'd agreed to meet up and catch a movie the following day.

Lisa hadn't been close to Sarah or Paige. And since leaving law school, they'd lost touch completely. But she remembered them well. They'd had lectures and tutorials together, been on the same moot team. She also shared another common factor with them, but she refused to believe that *he* was the killer. *Surely, he isn't that insane? Surely, he has too much to lose?*

Even so, these common factors, frighteningly close to home, had been enough to unnerve Lisa. Especially when she'd received a call from a DC Drake, asking her if she remembered anyone suspicious at the academy, and warning her to be vigilant with the killer still at large. He'd also asked if she'd been involved with anyone there. She'd flatly denied it, of course. Couldn't risk the truth being aired, ruining the reputation she'd worked so hard to build at the firm.

Still, she shuddered at the thought of a possible serial killer, whoever it was, being out there, targeting young female lawyers like her.

At times like this, she wished she had a flatmate. She usually craved her space; a free spirit who never committed herself to a relationship, flitting from one romance to the next, never short of male admirers. She knew her good looks made her irresistible to men. It was how she'd snared the professor that night. That one and only night they'd had sex. That night had been enough for her, even though he'd taken her teasing to mean something else.

No, the ability to do whatever she liked, whenever she wanted, with whom she wanted, was how Lisa liked it. And it had been one of the best days of her life when she'd been handed the keys to her first flat.

As a property associate at Blackfields Symes, Lisa had been involved with countless property transactions, but nothing matched the feeling of securing her own place in Camden Town. She'd always loved the area, with its diverse music venues, quirky markets and alternative culture. There was never a dull moment; no time to miss having a roommate. She was always too busy, either at work or socialising in the neighbourhood, to feel lonely.

Even so, right now she could have done with some company. The vile weather only seemed to intensify the creaks and shadows that came alive at night.

She switched on the television, tucked her legs underneath her on the sofa and flicked from one channel to the other. Nothing caught her interest; in fact, there was sod all on apart from inane reality shows, which she loathed. She decided to run a bath instead, taking her wine and a magazine into the bathroom with her. She worked so hard, she rarely had time for such luxuries, and it was high time she indulged herself.

Ten minutes later, she switched on Capital FM, then sunk down into the tub, allowing the lavender-scented bubbles to cocoon her body and relax her mind. Warm, soft, sensual. She reached for her glass, took a drawn-out sip of wine, then laid her head back, closing her eyes and enjoying a rare moment of tranquillity after yet another hectic week at the office.

When she opened them, two eyes were looking at her. She knew those eyes. Black, like opals. She knew that face. It was unforgettable. But she was too shocked to scream. Even if she had been capable of screaming, she wasn't given the chance. Before she knew it, her head was being plunged beneath the bubbles. Overcome with fear and panic, she held her breath, frantically grabbing the sides of the bath, thrashing her legs about wildly, water spilling over the edge and onto the bathroom floor, in a bid to extricate herself from the killer's control. But it was futile. The killer was strong. The killer had the advantage.

The killer didn't let her come up for air.

Until her lungs, clogged with water, were no longer capable of taking in air, and the fight went out of her.

When she eventually resurfaced, the killer turned up the radio and switched stations from Capital to Classic FM.

Then Lisa's killer got down to business.

Sunday 16 November 2014

'The press is going to have a field day.'

5 p.m. Carver had just bitten into a burger when he got the call. A big, fat mother of all burgers. The Big Tasty. He hadn't even had the chance to chew the disgustingly delicious mixture of meat, cheese and relish. Savour the sensation of flavours on his tongue, the satisfaction of grease in his belly. He and Daniel had seen a movie in Leicester Square, and having managed to demolish a mammoth tub of popcorn between them, they'd been looking forward to ingesting yet more junk at the golden arches nearby. Daniel had barely reacted as he heard his father tell Drake, 'I can be there within the hour.' Accepting with good grace that he had no choice but to cut short their long overdue day together and drive him back home to his mother's in Swiss Cottage. Happy Meal untouched, save for the plastic toy on top, which he'd excitedly ripped out of its packet as soon as they'd sat down. Carver thought how fortunate he was to have a son like him. But although Daniel's gracious acceptance made him love his son more, it also made him feel worse about himself.

As did Daniel's mother, whose look might have turned her ex to stone had her head been infested with a mass of writhing asps.

'Details, Drake.' Carver tried to ignore the hole in his belly. On hearing the news, he'd lost his appetite and binned the junk. But now, despite the sight in front of him, it was making a comeback.

'Property lawyer at Blackfields Symes. Firm near Tower Bridge, Sir. Lisa Ryland…'

'Ryland?' Carver cut in, his interest elevated. 'Why does that ring a bell?'

'She was one of the women I highlighted on the list I showed Kramer. Kramer mentioned Ryland when we interviewed her. They were in the same tutor group, and she thought she'd had a fling with Stirling. I only spoke to her on the phone last week.'

Carver massaged his chin. He hadn't shaved for a few days, and the stubble was already thick and coarse. And very tempting to scratch. 'She denied having an affair with Stirling?'

'Yes, sir.'

'Kramer's theory is looking more and more plausible.'

'She was twenty-six,' Drake continued. 'Lived alone and was supposed to be meeting a girlfriend – Marcia Devereux – at the cinema earlier this afternoon. When she didn't show up, or answer her phone, the friend got worried and popped round. She's got a key, apparently, and lives close by in Chalk Farm.'

Carver stepped back as the photographer did his job. It was clear she'd been dead for some time. Stiff, white-faced, her lips lavender blue. "Land" carved into her chest.

There was a strong stench in the air, the bathwater in which she lay contaminated with her urine and faeces as well as her blood. Clearly, she'd lost all bladder and bowel control on death.

'Looks like the killer drowned her first, then started cutting,' Drake observed.

'In which case, it'll be trickier estimating time of death based on rigor mortis.'

Carver noted Drake's puzzled expression and explained. 'Rigor mortis can set in immediately in drowning cases where a victim struggled hard against their attacker. As Ryland struggled, her muscles would have gone rigid.'

Drake nodded, inwardly hoping that one day he'd be a fountain of knowledge like his boss.

'Where's the friend?'

'Being treated for shock. She did say that when she arrived, Classic FM was playing loudly on the radio.'

'Did she mention whether the victim was a fan?'

'She said she was surprised because Ryland hated classical music.'

'Which indicates it was the killer's choice.'

'Yes, sir. The friend also studied with Ryland and Kramer at the academy. But she dropped out after the first year and became a clinical psychologist.'

'She's probably safe from the killer's clutches then. I'll call Kramer later from the office. Once the friend's calmed down, question her thoroughly. Same drill. How well she knew Ryland, as well as the other two. Was Ryland popular, did she make any enemies?' Carver sighed heavily. 'The public are going to get fidgety, Drake. We need a breakthrough. We should pay Stirling another visit. Pin him down on whether he did sleep with Ryland, and where he was last night. The wife too. There's something not quite right about her. Something that sets me on edge.'

Drake offered Marcia Devereux a clean handkerchief. They were seated in a discreet corner of a small coffee house on Camden Road. Forensics were all over Lisa's flat, and it was not the right environment for questioning. Besides, she was still in quite a state. The last thing she needed was to be in the same place where her dead friend's body lay. It was early Sunday evening, and the café was quiet.

'You sure?' she asked.

'Yes, keep it.' Drake smiled kindly.

Marcia blew her rather large nose with some force. With few people about, the noise seemed to echo around the room, only some innocuous background music and the intermittent whirr of the coffee machine breaking the silence. Drake felt sorry for her. He could see she was still in shock. She was a tall, ungainly woman, with dark brown pixie-cut hair, and a face that appeared older than her twenty-six years. Her eyes were small and out of proportion to her nose, while her flat top lip looked odd compared to her fuller lower one, almost like she was upside down. He watched her dab the corners of her eyes, quickly replaced by fresh tears.

'You and Lisa were close?'

'Very,' Marcia replied between sniffs. Her voice was low and hoarse. Probably all the hysterical crying, thought Drake. 'From the first, we were inseparable. It didn't matter that we went on to pursue different careers, we still saw each other regularly. And despite her hours, she always made time for me. I can't believe she's gone. She was my best friend. I keep seeing her in that grim pool of water.' She shuddered, blew her nose again. 'What a way to die.'

'Marcia, we suspect Lisa was killed by the same person who killed Sarah Morrell and Paige Summers.'

'Because of the inscriptions on their chests?'

'Yes. All three studied at the academy. A crucial link. Did you know Sarah and Paige well?'

Marcia shook her head. 'Not well, no. I mean, Sarah and Paige were in my tutor group, but I wasn't particularly good friends with either of them. Not like I was with Lisa. Sarah could be a bit standoffish, but as far as I can remember, Paige was a nice girl, and popular with the boys.'

Her answer was consistent with everything they'd learned so far. 'I see,' Drake said. 'Even so, can you think of anyone who would want to hurt these women? Being in the same tutor group as them, you must have seen them daily, noticed who they talked to, were close to? Maybe they fell out with someone? Someone who might therefore bear a grudge against them?'

'I was only there a year but…' Marcia took a moment, her large brow furrowing as she pondered the question. 'I can think of one person.' She bit her lip nervously and sipped from her mug which was now empty, but an obvious means of distraction.

'Who?'

'Professor James Stirling.' Drake's interest immediately cranked up a level. 'He taught Contract. He was our tutor group leader.'

'Why him?'

Again, Marcia appeared to struggle to reply. She looked around the café twitchily, even though it was practically empty.

'It's okay,' Drake urged, 'you can tell me. You have to tell me, for the sake of other women who might be in danger.'

Marcia nodded. 'He had a fling with Sarah; that was common knowledge. And I'm pretty certain he slept with Paige, at least once.'

'Why?'

'Because of the way she looked at him.' *Exactly Kramer's point.* 'And because one time, during a tutorial, I noticed the way they looked at each other. It was a look of lust, unmistakable. And…'

'And what?'

'Lisa had sex with Stirling at the summer party.' She blurted this out as if it was a difficult truth she needed to say, and the best thing was just to go for it. But then hesitated again.

'And?' Drake asked, still processing this latest revelation.

'I don't know about Sarah and Paige, but he threatened Lisa when she joked about telling his wife.'

'She joked about that?'

'Yes. That was just Lisa. She was a bit of a flirt, a bit of a tease, definitely not the commitment sort. But she wasn't malicious.' She sniffed and dabbed her eyes again. 'Just messed around sometimes. Wound people up for the fun of it.'

'How do you know Stirling threatened her?'

'Lisa told me. Like I said, we were best friends. We told each other everything.' She blew her nose once more, folded the hankie over, then wiped her bloodshot eyes. 'And now I've lost her.' Her face became hard. 'Find this maniac, DC Drake. Find him and make sure he pays for what he's done.'

Chapter Twelve

The killer looked down at the list of possibilities. Four more to go, and only one marked as a definite. The oldest, least attractive. And the largest. *She has way more insulation than the others. It will take longer for her flesh to stiffen.* Thinking about it, she should be last. She was the neediest one of all. She, who after all these years, still clung to some desperate fantasy, too deluded to realise it could never come true.

But which other three ought it to be? And in what order? It didn't really matter. There were several options, and whichever three were chosen would suffer the same fate. Although these would require more planning.

Still, it was getting too easy. It was time to accelerate the plan, have a little fun.

The killer picked up the phone, dialled a number and listened to it ring. Finally, the person at the other end picked up.

'It's me. I need you to do something. I need you to write a letter to Detective Chief Inspector Jake Carver.'

Elizabeth Stirling sat at her pottery wheel, moulding the clay into the face of a beautiful young woman. A Christmas present for her "beloved" husband. As she gently swayed her head, she allowed her mind to get lost in the accompanying music: Handel's *Hallelujah Chorus* – spectacular, moving, triumphant; a fitting accompaniment to her current work.

She loved the sensation of using her hands for some artistic purpose, whether that be playing an instrument, or sculpting a piece of art. Or anything really…

It was the only time she felt alive…free…happy.

She glanced at the photograph lying to the side of the wheel. The first victim had been so beautiful. Elizabeth recalled the day she'd confronted Sarah in front of the beefcake she'd moved on to. *Connor? Yes, that was his name.* She'd denied it, of course. Even after Elizabeth had explained how she'd followed them that weekend and confronted her husband in the car park. The bitch had been so smug. Made Elizabeth feel pathetic, desperate, no better than a shrivelled-up prune of a woman. Elizabeth would have been tempted to kill her there and then if it hadn't been for the boy. It had taken all the will she could muster to walk away.

But now who was having the last laugh?

She understood why her husband had fallen for Sarah. Beautiful, smart, feisty. But the others? What was it about them? Pretty, yes, but not exceptional. Why had he needed to stray so many times? She hadn't been a bad lover. Was it purely because she couldn't bear him children that he'd grown so cold towards her? She was the way she was because of him. He'd turned her into a vengeful, hard-hearted machine.

And because of that, she'd make him suffer.

As she worked her fingers into Sarah's eyes, imagining them to be real, Elizabeth hoped her husband would appreciate her last gift to him. Because before long, he'd be inside, and this sculpture would be the closest thing he got to female company.

9.05 p.m. Maddy looked over her shoulder as she turned left off Whitechapel Road onto her street. Only a few minutes' walk from Bow Road underground. She'd gone to see her grandmother again after a particularly stressful week. Paige's funeral had drained her, plus she was feeling frustrated with the lack of leads and her inability to foretell where and against whom the killer might strike next – despite reason telling her it was an impossible task.

Recently, she'd been having nightmares, similar to the ones she'd had as a little girl. Seeing her parents' faces, at first smiling at her with such love, it took her breath away. And then suddenly, they became sad, almost terrified, edging backwards, further and further away from her, into a dark abyss, before disappearing altogether. Now Paige was appearing in her dreams. Taking the same ominous route into the unknown. Twice she'd woken in a cold sweat; once she'd screamed out loud and Paul had come rushing in, reassured her it was just a bad dream and that she'd be okay. Rose had done the same over the weekend, and having had every intention of making tracks before it was dark, Maddy had been reluctant to leave. Rose was the one person, aside from Paul, who made her feel safe.

Eventually, just before eight, she'd decided she'd better head off. There was no avoiding work in the morning. Plus her grandmother was getting anxious about the time, and Maddy didn't want to inflame her anxieties. She may have been in her eighties, but she watched the news and read the papers. She knew who the killer was targeting, and that her granddaughter could easily be next.

A car door slammed, and Maddy nearly jumped out of her skin. A stray cat scurried across her pathway, pausing to shine its luminous eyes at her before moving on. It seemed like the night was trying its best to unsettle her; making her aware of every noise, every shadow, every unexpected movement.

Maddy's natural confidence was waning. And tonight's news had made things worse. She could scarcely believe it when Carver had called as she'd sat on the train from Barnes to Waterloo, informing her of Lisa Ryland's death. He'd wanted to know if she remembered a girl from law school called Marcia Devereux. Maddy did. She'd been on Drake's list. She hadn't been especially good friends with her, but she remembered Lisa had been, and wasn't surprised to hear they'd remained close.

Lisa. Another female victim from her year at the academy. Again, Maddy wondered if she was next. Whether it was only a matter of time?

Her street was quiet and dimly lit, no human soul about. Maddy's heart kicked as she turned the key in the door and stepped inside her building. She shut it quickly, almost as if death was chasing her, and let out a sigh of relief. Relieved to have made it back in one piece. Relieved to be safely home.

Still, Lisa must have thought she'd been safe inside her flat. But there was nowhere guaranteed safe. Not until the killer was found and got off the streets.

'Hello,' she called out as she entered her hallway. The temperature was warm and toasty, a stark contrast to the outside. All at once, she felt calmer. She removed her coat, placed her keys on the ledge. Atticus was suddenly there at her feet, welcoming her home with a soft meow. Maddy picked him up. 'Hello, my favourite little man. Have you been good?' She kissed the side of his face and received a contented purr in return, then placed him back down on the floor.

'Thank God you're home.' Paul suddenly appeared in the hallway. He gave Maddy a fierce hug. Then stepped back, his eyes awash with sadness. 'You heard about Lisa?'

'Yes, Carver called me. How do you know?'

'It's been on the news. I can't believe there's been another one. It's almost as if it's too easy. What the hell are the police doing?'

'It's not that simple. The killer's obviously very smart, as well as being a complete psycho. On the plus side, we can safely say he's killing to a pattern, and therefore try to predict who's next. Judging by the syllabus, we can expect four more murders to make it complete, corresponding with the four remaining subjects: Equity, Public, Tort and EU.'

'Yes, but second-guessing who the victims are, or where they'll be killed is like finding a needle in a haystack.'

He'd voiced her own misgivings. 'I know, that's the worrying bit.'

Paul's face grew serious. 'You're wondering if you're one of the needles, aren't you?'

'Yes, I can't help it. That's why we need to keep trying. We need to break things down logically. It's the only way. For example, I'm thinking with Equity – which, as you know, is all about making wills, establishing trust funds, et cetera – the killer might target a probate or trusts lawyer. And then, in the case of Tort – which, as you also know, concerns a civil wrong that unfairly causes someone else to suffer loss or harm resulting in legal liability – the victim could be a litigator. Like me.'

Paul raised his eyebrows in awe. 'The police are lucky to have you on their side. Seems to me like you're the one coming up with all the ideas.' His expression became solemn again. 'Your gran must be worried sick.'

'That's an understatement.' Maddy gave Paul a faint smile, but it quickly faded away. 'So am I, if I'm being honest. For the first time since Mum and Dad died, I'm scared.' As she said this, her heart thumped hard in her chest. She couldn't help imagining the worst-case scenario.

Paul pulled Maddy towards him, burying her head in his chest. 'Don't worry, Mads. I know you'll be okay. You have to be okay. I won't let anything happen to you.'

Friday 25 June 2010

He'd had a few. Not enough to lose control of his senses. But just enough to work up the courage to make his move. He'd fancied her for some time. Particularly since he'd called it a day with Paige.

Paige had been the brief interlude he'd needed after Sarah. Patently gagging for it, he'd swiftly rebounded into her, and his badly deflated ego had been pumped back to its full capacity. But he'd quickly grown bored with her. She was pretty, but not exciting like Sarah, and after a couple of months, it had been time to move on.

And right now his next catch was standing in full view.

Wearing a low-back scarlet dress which traced every curve of her shapely frame, she was a sight for sore eyes. But he knew he also looked good. Dressed in a slick black tux for the academy's end-of-year party, his confidence was flying high. He was on fire.

He grabbed another glass of champagne from a circling waiter and went up to the bar. She was standing there with Marcia Devereux, probably the most unattractive girl in the year. Fat, geeky and as plain as they come, she was also incredibly shy; a trait which didn't bode well for her future career as a lawyer, although he hadn't had the heart to say it to her face. Hopefully, she'd realise of her own accord and move on. Marcia smiled shyly at him, but he didn't want to send the wrong signal and returned the gesture with a grim-faced nod.

'Having a good time?' He directed his question at the hot one, not giving Marcia a second look. She recoiled with humiliation, but he didn't notice.

Lisa Ryland turned to Stirling and smiled. She was smashed. He could tell from her eyes. 'Yes, thank you, Professor Stirling. It's a relief to let loose after such an intense few weeks. I've never studied so hard in my life. It's going to be torture waiting for the results.' She glanced at her friend, while he took in her tempting neck, prominent cheekbones, fulsome breasts teasing him from under her halter-neck bodice. 'Isn't it, Marcia?'

A far soberer Marcia nodded, looking both embarrassed and put out. Feeling like a giant gooseberry, she said, 'I need the loo. Be back in a sec.'

Thank God, thought Stirling. With Marcia out of the way, he leaned back against the bar next to Lisa, their bodies almost touching, the air fizzing with wanton desire. 'You did well in the mocks. I have no doubt you'll be fine.'

She flashed him a smile, her glazed eyes lingering on his. Shameless. Lustful.

He read her mind. He'd triumphed again. She was his for the night.

They didn't make it out of the hotel. Highly dangerous, but goddamn electrifying all the same.

Getting the lift. Pressing the emergency button. Hitching her dress up high above her waist. Sliding his hand inside her thong, pulling it down, then launching himself between her legs, desperate to be inside her. So exciting, so delicious. Breathing heavily, he ground himself into her, hard and furious, grunting as he came, delighting in her panting, her gasps of ecstasy, in his own triumph and release. A world away from his stifled home life and passionless marriage. She was like his whore, so dirty, so filthy. But not illegal. And she didn't cost him a penny. Life didn't get any better.

But then she surprised him. Put her index finger over his mouth and said with a grin, 'Why, Professor Stirling, that was quite something. What would the board of governors say? What would your wife say?'

She'd said it in jest, because that was how Lisa was. But it had enraged him all the same. He placed his hand around her neck, their bodies still pressed up against each other. Hot, sticky.

'They won't say anything, because no one's going to tell them. Right?' He grinned at her, but his eyes weren't laughing.

She chuckled uneasily, felt his hot champagne breath, smelled herself on his fingers, saw the venom in his eyes. 'Please remove your hand. I was only joking.'

He slowly released his grip, then smiled. 'Make yourself decent. We should get back to the party before anyone gets suspicious.'

Chapter Thirteen

Monday 17 November 2014

'Sir, I've got something.'

8.30 a.m. Carver had slept badly. His head hurt, and his muscles felt tight. His chief was piling on the pressure. Demanding to know what his team were up to, whether Carver had any frigging clue who was behind the murders. The press was also closing in for the kill. Ready to take a bite, place blame, stoke up public hysteria and resentment.

'On Ryland?' Carver looked up at Drake, an impatient look on his face. Drake was holding a plastic evidence bag at his side, although Carver couldn't quite make out what was in it.

He was growing quite fond of the boy: hard-working, proactive, respectful. And, in the last few weeks he had proved he had the mettle for the job. He'd go far, so long as he didn't get too big for his boots.

'Still waiting on that. But this was found at Summers' flat.' Drake unsealed the bag and removed the contents. 'Her diary for 2014. It was tucked inside the fold of a suitcase.' Carver's spirits lifted at the sight of the pale blue leather-bound journal. 'Please tell me some good news.'

'Look at Wednesday, 29 October, sir.'

Carver took the diary from Drake, opened it up at 29 October, and read the neat scrawl:

Feel guilty for not caring Sarah's dead. She was the reason James could never love me. When he was making love to me, she was always there. I can't help wondering how he's feeling. Whether I should give him a call. I can't get that last night with him out of my head. All I ever wanted to do was love him. I never thought he'd hurt me the way he did. I close my eyes and can still feel his hands around my neck. Was it just me? Or is he like that with all of them? With his wife?

Carver shot up from his desk, recalling Drake's report of his conversation with Marcia Devereux. She'd said Stirling had behaved aggressively towards Ryland, and now they had proof from the horse's mouth that he'd been violent towards Summers. 'Let's go see Professor Stirling.'

Stirling had just finished delivering a lecture when Carver and Drake arrived at the Bloomsbury Academy of Law. It was a large, expansive edifice, overrun with droves of wannabe lawyers who looked at Carver and Drake as if they'd arrived from Mars as they waited for Stirling in reception.

It wasn't long before Stirling appeared. He looked harassed, his eyes darting all around – presumably fearful of drawing attention to himself – as he ushered them into his office. *Is it a guilty conscience, or merely a question of his professional reputation?* Carver didn't know.

Stirling shut the door, sat behind his desk and gestured for Carver and Drake to take a seat opposite. Carver's eyes scoped out the room. A person's desk spoke volumes about its owner in Carver's mind. His own desk wasn't so overrun with clutter that he couldn't see the wood for the trees, but neither was it all shipshape. A bit like his personal life; it wasn't the best – there was certainly room for improvement – but his son ensured it wasn't a lost cause.

Stirling's desk, however, was meticulous. Every item, every bit of stationery neatly arranged in separate compartments. The man was scrupulous. Clearly not one for mess. Carver noticed the framed photo of Elizabeth on his desk. *There for show, or because he wants it there?* His cynical side plumped for the former. The bookshelf set against the wall to Carver's right was stacked with various legal textbooks, lever-arch files and interestingly, classical music CDs. He noticed a CD player in the corner of the room to the left of Stirling's desk.

'You really are into your classical music, aren't you, Professor Stirling?' Carver gave Drake a quick nod of the head to fish out his notepad.

'Yes, yes, I am.' Stirling was obviously unsettled, despite his efforts not to show it. 'It calms me down, allows me to think.'

'Maybe I should try it,' Carver half-smiled.

'What can I do for you, Chief Inspector?' Stirling was done with the small talk.

'You've heard about Lisa Ryland?'

'Yes. Another tragedy. And only a couple of weeks since the last. Do you have any leads?'

'Hard to say,' Carver replied cryptically. He studied Stirling's face, trying to read his mindset. 'We did find this, however, at Ms Summers' flat.' He threw Paige's diary on the desk in front of Stirling.

'What's this?' Stirling asked nervously.

'Ms Summers' diary for this year. Take a look at 29 October.'

Stirling's fingers quivered as he turned to the relevant date. As he began to read, his face turned ashen. Eventually, he looked up, gave an uneasy chuckle. 'But this is preposterous. I don't know what Paige was thinking. She was clearly a little unbalanced. Always struck me as a bit unhinged, come to think of it.'

'Is that right?'

'Yes. You see, Chief Inspector, as much as it embarrasses me to say so, Paige was obsessed with me. She was a bright, attractive girl, but we had our fun, and when I ended things, she took it badly. Between you and me, I don't think her father gave her much time as a child. Rich as hell and work-obsessed. She was looking for a sugar daddy, and that just wasn't me, I'm afraid.'

Carver wasn't buying it. The man was talking shit to save his skin. 'This is Ms Summers' diary,' he said, glowering at Stirling. 'Why would she make things up in her own diary? People don't intend for others to see their diaries. It's a vehicle for their own personal thoughts and feelings.' He raised himself up to full height, a tactic designed to put Stirling on the back foot. It worked. Stirling sat back in his chair, at the same time briefly glancing at Drake, the good cop. But Drake was learning fast. He stared back at him suspiciously.

'Did you, or did you not, put your hands around Ms Summers' neck?' Carver demanded.

'No, of course not!' Stirling's response was too quick, his voice catching. 'I would never do a thing like that. As I said, it's ridiculous. Paige was clearly deluded.'

'Yes, you've mentioned that.' Carver could see Stirling wasn't about to change his story, so he moved on. 'Did you have an affair with Lisa Ryland?'

'No,' Stirling said firmly. But his eyes said otherwise.

'You never had sex with Lisa Ryland, or threatened her in any way?'

'No.' Carver saw the sheen developing across Stirling's brow. He changed course. 'Where were you on Saturday night, between the hours of 7 p.m. and midnight?'

Stirling hesitated for a split second, then said, 'I…I was having a drink with an old friend.'

'Male or female?'

'Female.'

Carver raised an eyebrow. 'Another one of your conquests?'

'No, nothing like that. We read law together at Oxford. She's now a named partner at a firm in Putney.'

'I see. Can I have a name?'

'Is that necessary?'

'Yes.'

'Okay. It's Suzanne Carroll.'

'Thank you. And the firm?'

'Bryson Carroll. Will that be all? I have a lot to be getting on with, I'm afraid.'

Like making a quick call to Carroll? Carver wasn't convinced by Stirling's alibi.

'Just one more thing. Did anyone who attended the academy from 2009 to 2011 ever strike you as suspicious? Unbalanced?' He paused, then said with a trace of sarcasm. 'Aside from Paige, of course.'

Stirling appeared to consider this for a while. Carver couldn't figure out whether he was genuinely making an effort to think, whether he was trying to concoct some lie, or whether he was considering whether or not to be truthful. Finally, he said, 'No, not that I noticed. But you may want to question the other tutors. I'm not the only one who taught at the time, you know.'

Yes, but you do seem to be the only one who banged half the intake, thought Carver.

'We've got that covered, thanks.'

They said their goodbyes, then Carver and Drake left.

Stirling exhaled with relief. But the tension was still there, and it was taking its toll.

He was a suspect; that much was clear. He picked up the phone, dialled a number and waited. 'Suzanne, it's me. Listen, I need you to do me a favour. If some policemen come knocking asking whether I was with you on Saturday night, say yes. Say we were having a drink at the Durell Arms on the Fulham Road.' A pause. 'I can't explain why. But yes, I'll come and see you. I promise I will if you do this for me.' Stirling allowed himself a smile as he got the answer he wanted. 'You're my rock. I'll see you tomorrow night.'

He hung up. He couldn't see Suzanne tonight. He had other plans, but no one could know. Not Suzanne. Not his wife. And certainly not the police.

Carver tapped his dashboard restlessly. He was parked just off Putney High Street, waiting for Drake to emerge from Costa Coffee. They'd left the academy and headed straight for Bryson Carroll Solicitors at the top of Putney High Street, making a quick pit stop for sustenance along the way.

He'd already knocked back five Americanos that day. Small wonder his heart was going like the clappers. What he really needed was to hit the gym and throw some punches, just to release the adrenaline whizzing round him. But time to himself wasn't a luxury he could afford right now. The killer was making sure of that.

That morning, the Chief had bumped up Carver's team from four to eight. Normally, he avoided big teams. He preferred to keep things tight. Often, with big teams, lines of communication went haywire and things got missed. But this case was posing too many lines of enquiry (not to mention the usual nut-job callers) for Carver and Drake to pursue single-handedly, and time was ticking.

Two of Carver's bumped-up team had already spoken to Lisa Ryland's distraught parents and brother, all of whom had alibis and no idea who might have wanted to murder Lisa. And in the last fifteen minutes, Carver had instructed the same two to question those tutors (other than Stirling) who'd taught at the academy from 2009 to 2011, as to where they'd been on Saturday night. He suspected they'd all have alibis, and so the exercise was unlikely to prove fruitful. But it was a necessary one all the same.

Carver looked down at his iPhone and reread the forensics report on Lisa which Grayson had emailed through to him. Estimated time of death between 8-9 p.m. Drowned. No surprise there. Again, no signs of sexual assault, or, more frustratingly, any unknown DNA.

What was the killer's motive, if not sexual? Just pure crazy? A crime of passion, or revenge?

The way things stood, the common thread between all three women was law, the academy and screwing Stirling.

Perhaps it was time to drop in on Elizabeth Stirling again. But first, Carroll.

'What can I do for you, gentlemen?'

Suzanne Carroll was an imposing woman. Tall, neither slim nor fat – statuesque was the right word. She had straight dark hair that fell just below her shoulders, tiny black liquorice eyes, a prominent Roman nose and wide, stretched lips which, when moved, emitted a raspy lilt. She also wore a look as if to say, *Don't mess with me if you know what's good for you.*

But she didn't intimidate Carver. He'd dealt with all kinds of characters over the years, and he had an uncanny habit of unnerving even the most serene of individuals. He and Drake sat facing Suzanne in her office. It was a world away from the glitzy world of Channing & Barton, almost like something out of a Dickens novel – a small, dark, wood-panelled room, with a tired, musty smell and way too much stuff in it.

Drake got out his notepad and waited for his boss to begin.

'You're a trusts lawyer?' Carver said.

'A trusts *partner*,' Suzanne corrected with a disdainful look. 'I also do a bit of probate and estate planning.' She gave Carver a knowing smile. 'I'm sure that sounds very dull to you, Chief Inspector.'

'Not at all,' Carver lied. 'I assume you've heard about the recent spate of murders involving young female lawyers?'

'Yes, I have. Who hasn't? It's shocking.'

'We're in the process of following up various leads.'

'I see.' Suzanne's lips twitched ever so slightly. This was followed by an equally twitchy half-smile. 'I'm not sure how I can be of any help, but you're clearly here because you think I can.'

'Did you meet Professor James Stirling for a drink on Saturday evening?'

'Surely, you don't think James is involved in some way?' she responded with almost a snigger. And quickly. Way too quickly. It felt rehearsed.

Carver gave nothing away. 'As I said, we're following up several leads. Please answer the question.'

Suzanne didn't hesitate. Raising her chin, she gave an assertive, 'Yes.'

'Where?'

'The Durell Arms on the Fulham Road.'

'And when did you part company?'

'I should say around 11-ish. I can't quite remember, but I do know it was well before the last Tube.'

'He's a good friend of yours?'

'Yes. We go way back. Read law together at Oxford.'

'And you've kept in touch ever since?'

'Yes.'

'How friendly are you with Mrs Stirling?'

It was a swift change of subject, hitting her out of the blue. Her mouth flapped again, her eyes betraying a glint of apprehension. Or was it malice? 'I know Elizabeth fairly well. Through James, of course. But we're not close, if I can put it like that.'

'Is there some sort of rivalry for the professor's affections going on there?' Carver kept his tone light, but all three knew what he was getting at. Before she could answer, he carried on. 'Have you ever had a sexual relationship with Professor Stirling?' His eyes lasered through her.

'No, certainly not,' Suzanne replied, laughing a little too heartily. 'We're just good friends. Like brother and sister really. But Elizabeth and I are very different species.'

'How so?'

'Elizabeth's an introvert, I'm an extrovert. I tend to show my emotions, while Elizabeth keeps them in. Chalk and cheese.'

'I see.' Carver said. 'Are you aware that Professor Stirling has had a number of affairs with his students over the years?'

Suzanne flinched. He'd found her weak spot, his way in.

'That's absurd. And quite an accusation. I should watch your step, DCI Carver. You don't want to go accusing an ex-lawyer and top law professor of such things before you've got your facts right.'

'My facts are from the man in question. Professor Stirling has admitted to the affairs.' Carver's eyes bore through Suzanne's again. 'Not in public, but to me.'

She hadn't expected that. 'So, what of it?' she stumbled. 'Does that make him a killer?'

'No, but it makes him a suspect. Particularly as we have good reason to believe he's behaved violently towards his lovers in the past.' Silence, then, 'So tell me, Ms Carroll, did you really meet Professor Stirling for a drink on Saturday night? It's vital that we know the truth.'

Again, she didn't falter. 'Yes. I was with him.'

Carver dropped back in his seat, his gaze still locked on Suzanne. She shifted awkwardly in her own, fiddling with her hair the way people do when they have something to hide. Finally, Carver stood up. 'Well, thank you, Ms Carroll, you've been most helpful. We won't take up any more of your time.'

He saw the relief on her face as she stood up and walked them to the door.

'Do you have any *plausible* leads on the killer, DCI Carver?' Having regained her composure, Suzanne's tone was deliberately condescending.

'No, not yet. Whoever it is covers his tracks very well.'

Once Carver and Drake had gone, Suzanne didn't waste any time in picking up the phone. 'They were just here, as you predicted.' A pause. 'Yes, I told them I was with you. James, should I be concerned about you?' Another pause. 'Okay. So I'll see you tomorrow night?' Pause. 'Great, please be careful, darling.'

She rang off, feeling slightly calmer. But still with an uneasy feeling in the pit of her stomach.

And still racked with jealousy having learned of Stirling's disclosure. It wasn't news to her. But it was still something that made her skin crawl every time she heard it out loud.

Chapter Fourteen

Tuesday 18 November 2014

'Where were you last night?'

'I told you. I was meeting Guy for a drink. Jill's run off with someone, and he needed a sounding board.'

Bollocks, thought Elizabeth as she watched her husband struggle to fix his tie. 'How kind of you, dear,' she said sarcastically.

She went up and fixed it for him. Securing the knot a little too tightly around his neck.

She knew his explanation was bullshit. Not just because she'd long stopped believing anything that came out of the lying cheat's mouth. But because an old friend of hers – who'd never liked him and was always on at her to leave "the fuckwit" – had watched him chat up an attractive young woman all night in Duke's Hotel, one of Mayfair's most chic hotspots. Stirling had been so engrossed in the girl, he hadn't spotted the friend, who'd been having a drink with a work colleague. Elizabeth's friend knew all about Stirling's sex addiction, and she'd surreptitiously taken a few snaps of the couple with her phone before sending them to Elizabeth.

She'd heard her husband stumble in around 12.30, no doubt half-cut and revelling in his latest conquest. She couldn't help but smile to herself, picturing the look on his face when he realised what was missing from his office drawer.

And later, when he discovered who Elizabeth had sent the missing item to.

* * *

The doorbell rang, and her heart leapt, her insides charged with the anticipation of seeing him again after what seemed like an eternity. She'd blow-dried her hair straight and smooth, enhanced her eyes with black mascara and eyeliner, but left her lips nude and glossy – the way he liked it. She'd swapped her staid black suit for a figure-hugging red dress, beneath which he'd soon discover her red lace underwear and matching stockings.

Her hands trembling with excitement, she undid the latch and opened the door of her swish Fulham flat.

'Hello, Suzanne.' He was looking as gorgeous as ever, dressed in a tan leather jacket and dark blue jeans, smooth-shaven, and wearing his favourite designer glasses. And, judging by the smell of him, his favourite Paul Smith cologne. His dreamy dark eyes, which creased up at the sides as he smiled, delved into her, and she thought she might melt on the spot.

He handed her a bouquet of roses. 'For you.'

She blushed like a shy schoolgirl. The successful trusts partner of a prominent family law firm no longer visible. 'Thank you, James. Come in.'

He'd always had the ability to reduce her to a tongue-tied teenager. Right from when she'd first set eyes on him at Oxford. He'd caught her eye, held her gaze until she'd turned crimson. And from that moment she'd become his. After chatting her up in the student union, he'd taken her back to his digs and shagged her senseless. It was the best sex she'd ever had.

Suzanne knew she wasn't the most beautiful of women. She was big-boned, with hips that bordered on cumbersome, rather than curvy. Her eyes were small, her lips, though wide, were too thin for her liking, while her nose seemed to overshadow the rest of her face.

But Stirling made her feel irresistible. And when she was with him, she forgot about her insecurities. The fact that growing up, she'd always been the plain one. The one men made their sister, rather than their lover. The one they turned to for advice on how to make a move on her hotter, skinnier friends.

She was only too aware of Stirling's kinky fetishes; the fact that he'd slept with most of the girls in their first year at Oxford and continued to screw his pretty female students at the academy. Although it wasn't easy, she'd accepted it. Accepted that she could only have him on his terms, when he wanted to see her. She was the one he always came back to when another of his steamy affairs fizzled out. It made her feel special, rather than sad. She was the one he'd never cut loose. She would always have a part of him. Until the day she died.

But the one person who had always, and who continued to drive her crazy, was Stirling's wife. She loathed Elizabeth. What was it about her that was so special he'd put a ring on her finger? She, with her fucking classical music and ice-queen act.

Sometimes, she wanted to kill the bitch. Her only comfort was knowing how abysmally unhappy Elizabeth made her true love. And that the cold fish no longer shared his bed.

Stirling closed the door. He kissed Suzanne on the mouth and handed her the wine he was holding in his free hand. After she'd poured two glasses, he beckoned for her to join him on the sofa. 'Thank you for covering for me,' he said, his gaze intense.

Suzanne sipped her wine. She knew him better than most. But he still made her feel nervous, even after all these years. He was just so intoxicating, so masterful in bed. She needed the alcohol to loosen her inhibitions, wanting more than anything to please him.

'Of course, James. You know I'd do anything for you.' She hesitated. 'But what, if you don't mind me asking, is it all about? Why do they seem to be treating you as a suspect for those girls' murders?'

'Because they have nothing else to go on, that's why!' Stirling angrily threw back his wine. 'All three were my students.'

'Who you slept with?' Again, Suzanne spoke tentatively, nervous of his reaction. Her jealous side also dreaded his answer.

'Yes.' Stirling grinned. The grin became a smirk. 'You're not jealous, are you, Suzanne? We've always had a good arrangement. You know I have my needs.'

There were times when an almost insane look flickered through her lover's eyes. Now was one of them.

'I know,' she said apprehensively. 'But can't you tell me where you were that night?'

Stirling leaned in closer, his familiar cologne invading her nostrils. 'I was with another woman, if you must know.'

His tone was cruel. Mocking. He knew it would hurt her. It felt like he'd wanted to hurt her. She felt small, pitiful. Every fibre in her body bristled with pain, rage and jealousy. She should have been relieved. Relieved that he'd answered her truthfully. Not given her cause to wonder whether the police had good reason to suspect him.

But her pain was raw, envy eating away at her like acid. 'Another one of your students, James? Tell me, what do you see in those brainless bimbos? It's a wonder you don't get fired. One phone call, and that's you out.' She chuckled to herself, clicked her fingers as she said this – not anticipating Stirling's next move. His hand was suddenly around her neck, not tight enough to suck the air out of her, but enough to make breathing difficult. Fear gripped her, her eyes awash with alarm as she stared into his – almost homicidal.

'Don't you even think about blackmailing me, Suzanne!'

'I…I didn't mean…' she spluttered, but he cut her off sharply.

'Don't play games with me, you pathetic moose of a woman.'

Of all the hurtful things he'd said to her, this wounded her the most. He'd never, in all their years together, had a dig at her plainness. Why was he doing it now? What had got into him?

He loosened his hold on her. Got up, grabbed his jacket and made for the door.

'James, don't go,' she begged. 'I need you.' Even as she said the words, she could hear how pitiful she sounded. But she couldn't help herself. Driven by her crazy obsession for a man she knew didn't love her back – a man who used her for his own devices when he saw fit. She went after him, attempted to grab his hand.

'Get off me,' he snarled, yanking his hand away. He eyed her with contempt. 'You've achieved a first tonight, Suzanne. You've reduced my sex drive to a flat zero. Guess you'll be reaching inside your bedside cabinet when I'm gone. Like I imagine you do most evenings.'

Suzanne felt the tears gather. His words wrenched at her heart, echoed in her mind. Before she could respond, he was gone, slamming the door behind him.

She sank down to her knees, buried her head in her hands, and cried like a baby. And then she got up, reached for her wine glass, and hurled it across the living room, watching it smash to smithereens against the far wall, shards of glass littering the cashmere rug beneath it, where she and Stirling had once made love.

Stirling walked purposefully towards Parsons Green Tube station.

He shouldn't have let his temper get the better of him. Suzanne was his ally; his only *reliable* ally whom he could trust to cover for him. But he was still smarting from last night.

He was losing his touch. Natasha Coleridge had been giving him the eye all term. She'd agreed to meet him for a drink last night at Duke's Hotel in Mayfair. He'd thought they'd had a good time, but at the end of the night, she'd rejected him outside Green Park Tube station. It infuriated him that she'd led him on, made him think she was interested. Made him rack up a seventy-quid cocktail bill, but then failed to follow through with her "come-to-bed" eyes.

He wouldn't let her get away with playing him for a fool like that. The girl deserved a lesson in life. He didn't care who her father was.

She'd made a grave mistake in turning him down.

Chapter Fifteen

Tuesday 25 November 2014

4 p.m. Carver was headed for his office when Sergeant Matthews stopped him. 'This came for you.'

Carver examined the brown envelope Matthews was holding. It had a sticky label with his name typed on it, but no address. 'Who brought this in?' he asked Matthews, taking the item off him.

'I dunno. Was put through the door with no explanation. One of the boys picked it up. Very unusual.'

'I'll say,' Carver muttered as he turned on his heel.

Inside his office, he shut the door, sat down and used a letter opener to carefully unseal the envelope. Inside was a one-page typed note. A4-sized. He recognised the font as Times New Roman eleven point, and it looked like 1.5 line spacing. As he began to read it through, his back went rigid.

Dear DCI Carver,

I hope my note finds you well, and that you aren't feeling too frustrated. I know that you've spoken to many people lately, but with little to show for it. So, as a goodwill gesture, I'm going to give you a little help with my next victim. For one, it's been too easy for me so far, and I could do with the challenge. Killing is much more fun when it's preceded by a little game of cat and mouse. So here goes, pay attention to this famous saying which holds a deep personal resonance for me:

"The supreme art of war is to subdue the enemy without fighting."

And here's another parting quote for you, Chief Inspector:

"The most important asset of any library goes home at night."

Until next time. Good luck.

'What the…?' Carver hissed. Was he going to kill a librarian? If so, it didn't fit the pattern so far.

'Sir?'

Lost in his thoughts, Carver looked up to see Drake eyeing him curiously. He'd been so engrossed in the note, he hadn't heard him walk in. He passed it to him. Drake's face spoke volumes as he read it through.

'Bloody hell, sir.'

'Exactly. Any ideas? Allegedly, the first quote's famous.'

'I'll Google them, sir. See if I can come up with anything.'

'Good. I'll call Maddy Kramer. See if she's got any clue what this headcase is getting at. It's got to have some legal connection.' He pounded his desk in frustration. 'We need to think fast, Drake. I've got a feeling this fucker's gonna strike again soon.'

To add to Carver's frustration, Maddy wasn't picking up. He left a message for her to call him ASAP.

It had just gone 5.30 when Maddy finally got back to her desk and saw the red light flashing. Hearing the urgency in Carver's voice, she called him immediately. 'DCI Carver, I've been tied up in court. Has there been a development?'

'Yes, of sorts. The killer sent me a typed note, claiming to offer a clue as to the next murder.'

Maddy's stomach frothed with both terror and excitement. 'What sort of clue?'

'A riddle. I've scanned you a copy of the note. Check your emails, have a look, and get back to me as soon as you can. I don't think we've got long.'

Maddy hung up, found Carver's email and clicked on it, itching to see what the note said.

As she read it through, the killer was suddenly more formidable. Not content with murdering in cold blood, he was prepared to indulge in some sick game, and in doing so, risk exposure. It was cocky beyond belief.

She was about to Google the quotes when the phone rang. *Damn!* Her team was convening for a meeting in exactly two minutes. "Be late and expect to face the music" was the gist of the message.

As much as it irked her, she had no choice. This was her career, her bread and butter. For now, it had to take priority. She closed Carver's email, promising herself she'd get back to it as soon as her meeting was over.

'The first quote's by Sun Tzu, sir…' Drake came rushing up to Carver's desk, notebook clutched in his hand, '…a Chinese military general and philosopher who wrote *The Art of War*.'

'Okay, and how does that help us?' Carver asked anxiously.

'Not sure, sir.'

'Damn it, Drake!' Carver pummelled his desk for the second time that day. 'I could have found that out myself, but it's of no use to me if I don't know what the fucker means!'

Maddy had yet to get back to them. She struck Carver as the conscientious type. He even thought he'd detected a drop of excitement in her voice when he'd told her about the note. The kind of excitement he felt when faced with a challenge in the shape of a cold-blooded killer.

He knew her work was demanding. But all the same, the delay was frustrating. He looked at Drake, saw the offence in his eyes.

'Sorry, Drake, that was unfair. I realise you're trying your best. Sit down. Let's put our heads together on this.'

Drake's expression softened. He took a seat across from Carver, who turned the killer's note on its side, so they could both read it.

'Who's the second quote by?'

Drake referred to his notebook. 'The Reverend Timothy S. Healy, a Jesuit priest, who was once in charge of the New York Public Library.'

Carver scratched his head. 'Jesus. So *is* he going to strike at a library? He's certainly well read. Your average Joe Bloggs wouldn't have come up with something like this.'

'Points to Stirling again, doesn't it, sir?'

'Not necessarily, Drake. There's a lot of smart people out there.'

They examined the note again. 'There must be a key word in here. Is it "art"?'

'Could be, sir. Maybe he plans on striking at a museum. We've certainly got plenty of them in London.'

'Fair point.' Carver smoothed the hair on his chin, now a proper beard. Cases like this, the sort that consumed him, made him superstitious. He was scared to pick up a razor until it was solved. 'But where's the legal connection? That's the crucial element we're missing. Or is all this talk of librarians just a red herring to throw us off guard?'

The phone rang and Carver jumped to pick it up. As he listened to what Maddy had to say, his face brightened. 'Thank you, Ms Kramer. Sit tight. I'll be in touch.'

He hung up, looked at Drake. 'Let's get going.' His voice sounded energised.

'Where, sir?'

'The Supreme Court, Parliament Square.'

Chapter Sixteen

Maddy's meeting had lasted over an hour. As she'd sat there, trying her best to pay attention, she couldn't stop her mind from wandering. Desperate to get back to her desk and have a crack at solving the killer's riddle. When she'd eventually escaped, she'd locked herself inside her office and stared long and hard at the note, highlighting the key words, willing herself to come up with an answer. And then, when she'd fished out the table she'd sketched in front of Drake, it came to her.

The killer talked about subduing the enemy without fighting. That had to mean through words, diplomacy, strategy. *And where and in what context does that happen? Through negotiation, reasoned argument and debate. In court cases.* And then, as she'd continued to stare at the first quote, the key word had jumped out in front of her. *Supreme.* She was almost sure that "Supreme" referred to the UK Supreme Court, based in Parliament Square in the heart of Westminster.

Under the Constitutional Reform Act 2005, it had replaced the House of Lords as the highest court in the land, hearing civil cases from all over the UK, and criminal cases from England, Wales and Northern Ireland. On the GDL course, they'd studied constitutional law, among other areas, under the guise of "Public Law". She was therefore certain that this was the subject the killer planned on inscribing next.

As the riddle implied, the Supreme Court was a place where battles were resolved through articulate legal arguments in a setting conducive to reasoned debate, and not through bloody physical combat on the battlefield.

The second quote had puzzled her more. She'd swigged more coffee as she'd scribbled down notes. The killer seemed to be implying that the next victim was a librarian. *Is she therefore one at the Supreme Court?* Maddy knew it housed an impressive law library, which she'd toured herself as a trainee. But if that was the case, her theory about all the victims having gone on to practise in a field related to one of the GDL subjects was blown apart. As was Drake's list. It meant the killer wasn't only targeting qualified lawyers – which made ex-students like Marcia Devereux a possible target.

Maddy had been lucky enough to sit in on a live trial at the Supreme Court. And now, desperate to be right that the killer planned on striking at this formidable bastion of British society, she felt strangely exhilarated.

She just prayed she wasn't too late.

7.30 p.m.

The UK Supreme Court is housed in a Grade II-listed building resting on a site closely linked with justice and law for nearly a thousand years. Westminster Abbey stands to one side of it. The Houses of Parliament and Big Ben are directly opposite. Open daily to the public, in winter the court closes at 4.30. So, by the time Carver and Drake stood facing its magnificent doors a little over three hours later, both staff and visitors had long gone. It had been a grey, dull day, and the night had fallen more quickly than usual. As the two men circled its path, they didn't notice anyone suspicious. In fact, there was hardly anyone about, such was the inhospitable weather.

'I'll call for a team of officers to keep guard overnight,' Carver said to Drake, delving his frozen hand into his pocket for his mobile. 'We'll keep an eye out till then.'

Two hours earlier

Emma Marsden stepped out of the Supreme Court into the chilly early evening air a little after 5.30, glad of her knitted scarf, thick coat and knee-high boots. Without them, the cold would be murderous to her slim build.

She stood there for a moment, surveying the scene – a scene she never tired of. Parliament Square was still thrumming with activity: a few tourists milling about, taking selfies; workers marching towards Westminster Tube station, their faces making it clear they were on a mission and anyone who got in their way did so at their own peril; activists standing opposite Parliament making the usual worthy but unrewarded protests. And surrounding it, a conveyor belt of incessant traffic.

Emma wasn't heading home just yet. She was meeting a friend for a drink at Fortnum & Mason on Piccadilly at six, and instead of bothering with the Tube, she decided to walk and cut through St James's Park. It was cold, but at least it was dry, and she fancied stretching her legs after sitting virtually all day.

Her mother often berated her for walking alone in the dark. 'It's too dangerous,' she would chide. 'You never know what lunatic's lurking in the shadows.' But Emma paid no attention. London's glorious royal parks were one of the things she loved most about the capital – a feature that set it apart from other cities. She counted herself lucky to be working so close to the one she considered the prettiest, and she'd damn well make the most of it.

Five thirty was a decent time to leave, Emma smiled to herself as she turned left, walked the short distance along Little George Street until she hit Great George Street and again turned left in the direction of the park. Not like some of her friends who, after finishing at the academy, had started their training contracts at high-powered law firms and never saw the light of day; working every other weekend, iPhones glued to their hands like a part of their anatomy, sometimes never leaving the office before midnight months on the trot, on the verge of collapse, no time for a life.

Emma had enjoyed studying law. But by the end of her second year, she was certain she didn't want to be a lawyer. Two internships had seen to that. It was too stressful, too punishing for her liking. She'd never been that ambitious or money-oriented, and she enjoyed her social life too much to be a slave to the hard-nosed ethos of the City.

Working in the library of the highest court in the land suited Emma fine. She'd already spent a good portion of her life with her nose buried in books, and wasn't afraid to admit that the academic side of law had fascinated her far more than practising it.

It was something her former law professor had picked up on. Something that had drawn him to her. Aside from her fiery red locks and hourglass figure, of course. It had been nearly two years to the day since they'd shared their first kiss. In his office of all places. So exciting, so dangerous. Right from the start of the course, she'd caught him glancing her way every now and again as he'd delivered his lectures. And when he'd summoned her to his office to go over a paper, she'd found herself fantasising about him sweeping her up in his arms, throwing her across his desk, making love to her on the spot. She'd known he had a roving eye. But she didn't care. Not about that, or the fact that he was married. There was just something about him that was too attractive to fend off or ignore. She'd always been a sucker for the older man, especially when they were as smart and as handsome as Professor Stirling.

He'd sat down beside her as he went through her case study, their shoulders brushing, the air thick with sexual tension. And when she'd turned to him to answer a question, she'd stared into his eyes, seeing the hunger and desire in them. And that's when she'd kissed him. At first softly, unsure of his reaction. But then he'd reciprocated, only more forcefully, pulling her towards him, making her heady.

Their affair had lasted four months; quickies in his office, or at her flat. She didn't have a flatmate, so Stirling had no reservations about meeting her there. And then, predictably, he'd grown tired of her, moved on to the next best thing.

She'd been hurt, confused, made to feel like a fool. And when she'd confronted him one evening as he was about to leave work, threatening to go to his wife if he didn't take her back, he'd pushed her up against the wall, his fingers locked around her throat.

'Don't you dare threaten me, Emma.' His eyes had been rabid. 'I have the power to make or break your career, and I won't hesitate to break it if you so much as breathe a word to anyone.'

At the time she'd not even finished her first year, and like everyone else, was desperate for a training contract. She'd seen the look in his eyes, realised he was serious, and promised to keep quiet.

But that was all water under the bridge. She was over him. She had a good life and a steady boyfriend. The past was the past.

Emma saw the odd person as she made her way along Horse Guard's Road around the edge of the park, clutching her scarf tighter around her neck. But no one looked dodgy or caused her to pick up speed. It was cold and dark, and she hadn't expected to see many people about. A short way along, she hit the entrance to the park on her left and went in boldly. Straight ahead she saw the lake, vaguely made out the stunning Tiffany Fountain in the middle but saw no sign of the park's famous pelicans.

Emma turned right, the lake now on her left. She carried on walking in the direction of the Mall, past Duck Island Cottage, until she reached a fork in the path. There was a sign pointing left towards the park café, playground and Buckingham Palace. Emma carried on straight, this being the most direct route to Piccadilly, Horse Guard's Parade visible to her right, several sorry-looking flower beds to her left. But no human life.

She was just passing some public toilets when she heard a faint whimpering sound, almost like someone was in pain. It was hard to tell whether the person was male or female, the voice was so muffled, but as it was coming from the Ladies' toilets – a small brick building concealed within tightly packed shrubbery – she assumed it was a woman. Emma was a good person. A little reckless maybe, but not someone to ignore a cry for help. Thinking whoever it was might be sick or badly injured, she turned off the path and walked through a small green gate towards the Ladies.

'Hello,' she called out, 'is someone there? Are you hurt?' She stepped into the chilly toilets, cold and stark and reeking of damp and urine. It was spookily quiet; only the monotonous drip of a tap that hadn't quite been turned off breaking the silence. 'Hello?' she said again, this time more nervously. And then, out of nowhere, she heard classical music coming from one of the cubicles; the third cubicle to her left, she thought. She should have run then. But she'd come this far, and it was almost as if her feet were rooted to the spot. She edged forward, the sound of her heels on the tiled floor echoing in the air as she did so. She stopped, pushed the cubicle door open, and saw a red MP3 player resting on the cistern. She recognised the music: Beethoven's *Silencio.*

Something wasn't right. The whimpering had stopped. She should run. She should get out.

Before she had time to turn around, she felt a rubbery hand around her neck, wrenching her scarf off. Then a sharp, cold blade across her throat.

Then…

Emma never saw her killer. But even if she had, it would have made no difference. Emma had been a goner from the moment she'd first kissed Professor Stirling.

Chapter Seventeen

Maddy stared at the flow chart she'd pinned to her bedroom wall. She should have been working, but the murders hounded her, and it was all she could focus on.

Solving the case was now an addiction for her – an addiction that could only be cracked with the killer's capture. It wouldn't bring Paige back, but it would get her justice.

On the flow chart, she'd listed the victims' common traits, but above all, it was Stirling who stood out like a sore thumb.

He'd always struck Maddy as a bit seedy. But was he capable of something so ghastly? And, if so, why? Maddy wished Paul was around so that she could pick his brain. Not just because she was a typical lawyer, big on brainstorming, but because Paul had known all the victims. And Stirling.

But he was working an extra shift and wouldn't be home till gone midnight. It had never bothered her before, but Maddy was suddenly nervous about going to bed before he got back. Before she could put the chain on the door.

She'd sleep with a knife under her pillow tonight. If, that is, she slept at all.

After a team of officers arrived in Parliament Square to relieve Carver and Drake, Drake had returned to the station to revisit the list of women he'd gone over with Maddy, hoping for inspiration as to who the next victim might be. But he got none.

It was now gone midnight, and he had yet to finish his report for the day. Realising he needed caffeine badly, he headed for the vending machine. As he stood there, waiting for it to churn out something resembling coffee, Carver came rushing up. He looked livid. Drake nearly had a heart attack, having thought his boss had long gone home.

'You won't frigging believe this. A body's been found in one of the Ladies' loos in St James's Park.' Drake's face fell. 'One of the attendants was about to lock up for the night, when he stumbled on a woman sprawled in one of the cubicles. Throat slashed. "Public" sliced into her chest.'

'Who was she?'

'Don't know yet. The bastard misled us. Made us think we had a fighting chance of saving her before he struck. We need to get Maddy Kramer over there.'

'What, now, sir? She's a civilian. Can we bother her at this time of night?'

Carver didn't budge. 'I don't care, Drake. She's the closest thing we've got to cracking this thing. I want her to see the body if she's got the stomach for it. She might know the girl, spot something at the scene we're missing. Because so far, we're coming up with jack shit, and the Chief is *this* close to having my head on a stick. Grayson and his team are on their way, so let's go. We'll call Kramer en route and, assuming she's up for it, send a car to pick her up.'

Still riding high on the thrill of the kill, the killer smiled and pretended to listen to the woman, a friend, sitting opposite in the jam-packed bar; all the time thinking about the events of roughly six hours ago and fighting a burning urge to boast about it to the friend, knowing that this would be fatal to the plan.

A couple of stiff drinks was just what was needed to unwind. As with Paige, it hadn't been as exhilarating as it had been with Sarah and Lisa. They'd never shared eye contact, and so Emma hadn't seen the hatred in the killer's eyes. Likewise, the killer had been denied the pleasure of seeing the sheer terror in Emma's when she'd realised she was toast.

Even so, having received the signal that Marsden had left the Supreme Court and was heading for the park, it had been exciting waiting for her in the grim park toilets. Murmuring like an injured cat, luring her into the trap like a frail little mouse; showing her who was boss, and that brains always outshone beauty.

Even more thrilling was the thought that once again, the police had been too late, despite being forewarned. Okay, so they'd been slightly misled – a little cheeky – but giving Carver too big a head start was far too risky. And the satisfaction of outwitting him, of making him realise that he was so near and yet so far, had been far more arousing than any sexual conquest.

The killer flashed a smile at the woman sitting opposite, secretly looking forward to outsmarting Jake Carver once again with victim number five.

Maddy thought she must be dreaming when her mobile started ringing.

After staring at the flow chart another thirty minutes, she'd spent a couple of hours working before calling it a night at 11.30. She'd been shattered, and despite feeling nervous about going to bed alone in the flat, had fallen into a deep sleep almost as soon as her head hit the pillow – albeit with a knife tucked under it.

She turned on her bedside lamp and fumbled around for her phone. 'Hello?' she croaked, her eyes still adjusting to the light.

'I'm sorry to disturb you, Ms Kramer, but it's DC Drake. There's been another murder. At St James's Park.'

Maddy sat up, suddenly wide awake. 'You're kidding me? That's just behind the Supreme Court. Was no one guarding the area?'

She'd uttered the words without really thinking, but almost as soon as she'd said them, realised how patronising she must have sounded.

'After your call, we had men surround the Supreme Court all night,' Drake put her straight.

Maddy's cheeks burned. He was perfectly entitled to be short with her. There had been no reason to think that the killer would strike in St James's Park when the riddle had indicated nothing to that effect.

She certainly hadn't thought of it. What's more, she was the one who told them to monitor the court.

She quickly apologised.

'It's fine, Ms Kramer,' Drake said. 'I'm calling because DCI Carver would appreciate your assistance. If we sent a car, would you be willing to attend the crime scene? I appreciate it's a lot to ask, given the hour and the circumstances. But he thinks you might be able to offer some useful input.'

She hadn't seen that coming; was both amazed and flattered by Carver's faith in her. And although she was scared, the photos of Sarah flying through her mind, she realised she couldn't say no. She was already in too deep, and she had to be strong, in memory of those who had died and for the sake of future victims. Including, potentially, herself.

'Yes, I'll come. I can be ready in five minutes.'

After hanging up, Maddy got out of bed, slung on some clothes, then raced to the bathroom and splashed her face with ice-cold water.

She didn't know why – for Christ's sake, she was about to attend a grisly murder scene – but she felt compelled to put on some make-up. Checking her appearance in the mirror, she felt the butterflies in her stomach. Was it Carver? Something about him that stirred an urge to impress him? It was bloody ridiculous. *Get your priorities right*, she told herself. *Stop acting like some shallow adolescent.*

As she stood at the living room window, curtain pulled back, looking out for the police car, she heard a key turn in the front door.

It was Paul. He looked dead beat.

'Hi,' he said, looking surprised. 'What are you doing up?' He gave her the once-over. Grinned. 'Going out for a jog?'

His light-hearted remark was understandable. But Maddy had no urge to smile.

'There's been another murder, Paul.'

'You've got to be joking.' Paul tossed his rucksack on the floor, then joined Maddy at the window. 'When? Where? How do you know?'

'I don't know when, but a body was found in St James's Park. DC Drake just called with the news.'

'Jesus. Who was she?'

'Don't know. But the police want my input at the crime scene.'

'What the fuck!' Paul was fuming. 'What the hell for? They shouldn't be putting you in danger like this, Mads. It's unacceptable. You're a lawyer, not bloody Miss Marple. Leave them to fight their own battles.' He pointed to his watch. 'Have you seen the time, for pity's sake?'

Paul rarely got angry. It dawned on Maddy just how much he cared for her; how lucky she was to have him.

'Calm down,' she begged. She massaged his shoulder, willing him to come round. 'I want to do this, Paul, I have to; for Paige's sake, if nothing else. I spoke to her mum earlier, just to see how she was coping. She could barely speak, poor woman. I need to feel like I'm helping.'

'But why do the police think you can help them? I don't understand.' Paul's face was creased with exasperation.

'Wait there a sec.' Maddy raced out of the living room and was back in less than thirty seconds. She handed Paul the killer's riddle. 'I solved it, Paul. Well, sort of. I was close.'

As she watched Paul read, she recalled the excitement she'd felt trying to unscramble the riddle. She'd always had a talent for problem-solving. It was something that set her apart, made her an exceptional lawyer, rather than a mediocre one. 'I told the police the murder would take place at the Supreme Court, and that the next legal subject the killer planned on inscribing would be—'

'"Public",' Paul cut in.

'Yes.'

'He's one hell of a sick bastard.'

The door buzzed. Maddy glanced out the window and saw a car. Its registration matched the one Drake had texted her. 'The police are here. I'd better go.'

She made to leave, but Paul stopped her, hugged her fiercely. His heart was thumping as wildly as hers. 'Please be careful, Mads. I love you. Christ, I'd marry you if I didn't bat for the other side.'

His comment brought a smile to Maddy's face. 'That's the most romantic thing anyone's ever said to me.'

'I'm just worried you're getting too involved. This monster's too slick. What if he realises you're helping the police? Who's to say he won't go for you next?'

'You're right, and I'm not gonna lie, I'm scared shitless. But I'd rather risk my life trying to help the police catch him, than stand by and let him carry on mutilating innocent women. Life's too precious to treat it with contempt, as this killer appears to. My parents' deaths taught me that.'

'Okay,' Paul said wearily, 'you win. Just watch your back. And don't be a hero.' He kissed her lightly on the forehead, then watched her disappear from sight.

Carver was standing behind a police cordon surrounding the Ladies' toilets in St James's Park when Maddy arrived. It was minus two, and as she ducked her head under the tape, she cursed herself for foolishly forgetting her gloves. Her hands were like ice, while the biting air knifed her slender frame.

'Thank you for coming, Ms Kramer.' They shook hands. Like everyone else at the scene, Carver was dressed in protective clothing. For a moment, they said nothing, eyes lingering on the other a little longer than necessary. Maddy saw the dark shadows under his eyes, the frustration enveloping his bearded face, the worry lines traversing his brow deeper than ever. It made her realise that although her job was highly pressured, when it boiled down to it, she operated in a world where it was only ever money at stake – not people's lives; not the safety of the public. This was what Carver faced, day in, day out, and she couldn't begin to imagine the strain it put on him. And with this latest psychopath on the loose, Carver was facing pressure on a whole other scale; pressure that made the company disputes she was asked to assist on seem inconsequential.

'It's no problem,' she said.

The area buzzed with activity. Maddy watched, her eyes agog, hardly able to believe she was witnessing a world she'd only ever had a taste of from crime novels and TV shows.

Carver handed her a set of protective clothing identical to his. She hastily put it on, thankful for the extra warmth.

As he led the way towards the entrance, her insides were suddenly doing somersaults. She knew what was coming, but the anticipation almost made things worse.

As if sensing her fear, Carver stopped, turned to face her. 'I just want to make sure you're ready for this.' She was standing so close, he could smell her perfume – fruity, feminine, sophisticated. He was trained to pick up on such things, but only as an observation, not a feeling, as it was in this instance. It took him by surprise. 'You're strong, Ms Kramer, I can tell. So far, you've been of immense help to our investigation, and my instinct tells me your help going forward will be invaluable.'

His words lifted her. Law was her forte, solving crimes was his. But he needed her, and that helped her brave the next step.

'Thank you,' she said, 'I'm ready.' She followed Carver into the toilets, a pungent smell assaulting her nostrils as she did so. He walked on, then came to a stop in front of the third cubicle to her left. Maddy lingered behind, having noticed a thin trail of dried blood running from the floor of the cubicle to the central aisle. It gave her goose pimples. Carver stepped aside, allowing her space to edge forward. Realising this was the moment, she took the plunge and looked in.

She wished she hadn't. She recoiled in horror as her eyes fixed on the dead girl's body, slumped on the floor against the toilet bowl. Her head was flopped to one side like a ragdoll, her slashed neck infused with curdled blood. Blood had trickled down and saturated her clothes, as well as the floor surrounding her. She was still wearing her coat, but it had been unbuttoned all the way down, as had her suit jacket beneath it.

As had her white silk blouse beneath that, also drenched with blood, her lacerated chest fully exposed and inscribed with "PUBLIC".

Maddy felt bile in her throat and was suddenly seeing stars. Without thinking, she spun round and buried her head in Carver's chest. He felt a brief rush of excitement, then tilted her chin up with the tip of his finger. Looked at her with calm, steady eyes. 'It's okay, Ms Kramer, your reaction is perfectly normal. Take deep breaths.'

He demonstrated this for her, filling his lungs to the brim, then exhaling. Slowly, rhythmically. Just watching his chest heave up and down made her feel calmer, her vision clearer. Then, embarrassed, she smiled shyly and stood back, inhaled large chunks of air herself – air that had been soured by the smell of death.

'Do you recognise her?' Carver asked, once he was sure she'd recovered.

'No, I'm afraid not. There were around two hundred students in my year. And as I explained to DC Drake, I only ever knew the students in my tutor and lecture groups. The entire year was split into morning and afternoon sessions. I did mornings, so I wouldn't have known anyone who did afternoons.'

'I see,' Carver sighed. 'Well, it seems you were right about the inscription, but the killer's displaced one of our theories.'

Maddy had a hunch what was coming.

'The victim was a librarian at the Supreme Court. They close at 4.30, so it's likely she'd been dead for some time when the park attendant found her. She might have decided to cut through the park on her way home. So, you were right about the court being connected to the murder, but not about it being the exact location; or the fact that the killer is only targeting qualified practising lawyers.'

Maddy was suddenly furious. Furious with herself for not spotting this possibility, for thinking too narrowly. And furious with the killer for intentionally misleading them. 'No,' she muttered, 'it seems not. But did she study law? At the academy, I mean?'

'Drake's finding that out.'

'She had to have studied there,' Maddy said in despair. 'Otherwise, the first three murders make no sense. It completely destroys the pattern.'

'I agree.'

'Sir!' A young officer came running into the toilets.

'What is it?'

'We may have an eyewitness.' *A glimmer of light.* 'Of sorts.'

Carver frowned. 'What do you mean, *of sorts*?'

'A tramp claims to have been passing by when he saw the victim enter the toilets. He said he'd decided to hover outside for a while, intent on scrounging some money off her when she reappeared. But when she didn't emerge after some time, he grew bored and buggered off.'

'He didn't come back this way? Catch a glimpse of the killer leaving?'

'No. He said that while he was waiting, he heard strange noises, almost like feet shuffling, decided something fishy was going on and bolted.'

Carver sighed jadedly. 'So how does this help us?'

'He also claims to have heard classical music playing inside.'

Maddy and Carver exchanged looks, wondering if the other was thinking the same thing.

Wondering what the hell Professor Stirling had been up to several hours earlier.

Chapter Eighteen

Paul's bedroom door was closed when Maddy got home around 2.30 a.m. Carver and Drake had dropped her off. Told her they'd be in touch once they had more information on Marsden, along with the pathologist's report.

Maddy felt wired. There was no chance of her sleeping just yet. She kept seeing Marsden's body, while the smell of death still lingered in her nostrils. She made herself some cocoa as Atticus slept peacefully in his basket. Took that, along with a brandy, into the living room, curled up on the sofa and tried to calm herself down.

She knew the police still weren't any closer to finding the killer. Yes, Stirling was a suspect, but only in the loosest sense. Only because he'd taught and had affairs with the first three victims. It didn't make him their killer, and whether he'd had a relationship with Marsden remained to be seen.

The fact was, there was nothing to physically connect him to the murders. Whoever it was had planned each one with meticulous precision, making sure he'd cleaned up after himself every time.

But the tramp's claim to have heard classical music playing inside the toilets was interesting, not least because the radio in Lisa Ryland's flat had been tuned to Classic FM when her body was found by Marcia Devereux. Surely, that was too much of a coincidence?

Was this part of the process with every murder? Maddy wondered. If so, were they looking at a classical music fan, or even a trained musician? Or was the killer just playing with them?

It was common knowledge that both Stirling and his wife were classical music enthusiasts. But if one of them was the murderer, would he or she really have been so blazon about it? It seemed completely illogical.

Maddy knocked back her brandy. It took the edge off, at least for tonight.

She lay back, closed her eyes, and dozed off within seconds.

Wednesday 26 November 2014

Carver rolled over in bed and looked at the time on his alarm clock: 6.30 a.m. After he'd eventually made it home to his flat in Hoxton, he'd barely slept. There were so many questions, so many ifs and buts going over in his mind, he'd been unable to shut his brain down, riled by a killer who'd outsmarted him, and remained as elusive as ever.

He and Rachel had moved to the East End when they were both young, and head over heels in love. It was a time when neither could put a foot wrong in the other's eyes. Before real life got in the way.

Hoxton was still as hip as it was back then. Perhaps more so. Hoxton Square was the heart of the area's arts and media scene, with a host of bars, restaurants and clubs he and Rachel had once frequented.

But Carver's life was very different now. For him, that scene was a thing of the past. His home was where he slept, and really, he could have been anywhere. Other than his son, he had no life. Work was his life, and his happy, carefree days were a distant memory.

He rubbed his tired eyes, hauled himself up and off the bed. He was just contemplating a quick shower when the phone rang. It was Drake. The boy was keen, no arguments there.

'Sir, I have some information on Marsden.'

'Tell me.' Carver opened a drawer, pulled out some fresh underwear, phone tucked under his chin.

'She studied law at the academy, but not in the same year as the other victims. She was two intakes later, 2011 to 2013.'

'Bang goes our theory that the killer's only targeting Kramer's year.' Carver slammed the drawer shut.

'Seems so, sir. She passed both the GDL and the LPC but started working at the Supreme Court library six months after she left the academy.'

Carver slumped back down on the bed. 'We need to start again, widen the net. The list you marked up is too narrow.'

'Sir, working out the next victim's identity is going to be impossible.'

He wasn't far wrong. 'We should question Marsden's intake. See if she got friendly with Stirling at any point.'

'He's our strongest suspect, sir.'

'He's our only bloody suspect, Drake.'

Wednesday, 1 p.m. Jeff was in Paris interviewing a witness, so Maddy had their office to herself. She was glad of it. She was struggling to keep her eyes open; something her eagle-eyed roommate would have no doubt demanded an explanation for.

As she sat at her desk munching a sandwich, she clicked on the BBC News website and watched footage of Carver's earlier press conference on Marsden's murder. Her eyes filled as Marsden's parents, clinging to each other like superglue, made an impassioned plea to anyone who might have information leading to the capture of their precious daughter's killer. Carver sat to the mother's left. Solemn-faced. Maddy didn't know how he did it. Having to deliver the worst news any parent could receive. Bearing witness to their pain and suffering. Forced to question them at a time when all they wanted was to be left alone. She realised again that although her job could be stressful, it was a damn sight easier than Carver's.

'Unfortunately,' Carver explained to a bunch of reporters and photographers once the parents had finished, 'although our forensic team has worked non-stop throughout the night and all morning, they were unable to turn up any evidence which might help us identify the killer. Our only possible lead is a member of the public who claims to have watched Ms Marsden enter the park toilets, and heard classical music coming from inside. We may therefore be looking at someone with a penchant for classical music, or a musician themselves, who chooses to accompany the crimes with this type of music. But at present, this is purely speculative.'

There was a knock on the door. It was the postboy. He handed Maddy some mail – two she recognised as work-related and a slim brown envelope she did not. She couldn't think what it could be. She put the other mail to one side and unsealed it. Inside, was a single A4-sized typed letter, with no sender address. She recognised the font as Times New Roman. She also noticed a series of faint lines running across the page. As if there'd been something wrong with the printer.

But as she started to read and realisation hit, fear overcame her. She flopped back in her chair, staring at the words over and over.

Dear Ms Kramer,

I hope I find you well. You have always been an exceptionally bright, talented young woman. I spotted that from the start. But lately, you have got ahead of yourself, allowed yourself to step out of your comfort zone which, let's be honest, is being a lawyer. I do not take kindly to you meddling with DCI Carver's investigation. It is a game I intend to play with him and him alone, and if you continue to jeopardise my mission to rid this world of some of the ungrateful whores who pollute it, I shall have no choice but to add you to my list.

You rejected me once, something I didn't take kindly to at the time, and which I will never forget. If you don't do as I say, you may lose the only family you have left in this world.

I'm sure you wouldn't want anything to happen to your beloved grandmother. Or your friend, Paul.

Stick to law, Ms Kramer. You were always good at it. You are good at it.

And don't breathe a word to anyone about this note.

Maddy's sandwich repeated on her. The killer must have been watching her last night. Watching her with Carver. And if he knew about her grandmother, about Paul, he no doubt knew where she lived.

She thought for a moment about the men she'd rejected in the past. None had seemed to take particular offence, while she and Greg, her longest relationship, had parted amicably.

She stood up and paced the room, forced herself to think harder. And then Stirling sprang to mind. She'd rejected his offer of a drink politely, but firmly. And just as she'd told Carver, he hadn't seemed angry, hadn't treated her any differently after that.

But he was the one man out of all the men she'd rejected over the years who could credibly be connected to the murders.

She looked down at the words again.

> *...You have always been an exceptionally bright, talented young woman. I spotted that from the start...*
>
> *You rejected me once, something I didn't take kindly to at the time, and which I will never forget.*
>
> *Stick to law, Ms Kramer. You were always good at it. You are good at it.*

Stirling could easily be the author. But would he really risk his identity being blown by threatening her? All because of her interference in the case? Then again, who knew what went on in the minds of psychopaths, if that's what Stirling was?

Maddy was faced with a dangerous choice. Her grandmother and Paul were everything to her. The thought of losing them was unbearable.

But the killer had to be stopped, and she was determined not to let his intimidation get the better of her.

It was too risky to meet with Carver in person from now on. Even email was chancy. They'd have to communicate by mobile alone. She dialled Carver's number, and when he answered, she told him everything.

Chapter Nineteen

Monday 1 December 2014

8.30 p.m. Five days later. Carver looked around the table at his bleary-eyed team. They'd been working round the clock since Sarah's murder. Strangers to their families. Existing on junk, caffeine and snippets of sleep. Gripped by a serial killer who continued to outwit and elude them. Expecting another strike, yet not knowing when or where that might be.

It had been slow progress tracking down and interviewing past academy students from Emma Marsden's intake. And of those they had managed to locate and interview so far, either they didn't remember Emma, or if they did, had no recollection of an affair between her and Stirling. On that basis, with no witnesses, or even a jot of hearsay to attest to a relationship between them, Carver had no leverage to put Stirling on the spot.

All eyes fixed on Carver. None of them strangers to his strict work ethic, they made sure they listened to his every word, the fear of being caught out and humiliated in front of their colleagues far surpassing the urge to daydream or catnap.

They were gathered in one of the breakout rooms. Carver swivelled his chair round to face the whiteboard behind him. On it, he'd drawn a spider diagram. The middle point read "Bloomsbury Academy of Law", the seven branches sprawling from it representing each of the legal subjects taught on the GDL.

Next to Contract, Crime, Land and Public, he'd written the dead girls' names. Question marks accompanied the remaining subjects: Tort, EU and Equity. Simply because Carver had no idea who was next on the killer's list.

He'd drawn another arrow out of the middle point, at the tip of which he'd written Stirling's name with a question mark. Scribbled at the top in the left-hand corner, he'd written "Classical music" and "Letter to Maddy Kramer: from Stirling, or not?"

There was no magic to what he'd written, but it focussed everyone's minds on what they were dealing with and who they were facing.

He turned his attention to the killer's letter to Maddy.

'Ms Kramer is adamant Stirling never resented her for turning him down.'

'But, sir,' Drake said, 'how do we know that's true? He might harbour a secret grudge.'

'He might, Drake, and we need to bear that in mind.' He scanned the room again. 'The thing about serial killers is that they're often the most unlikely suspects: normal, popular, respectable folk who pay their bills and never put a foot wrong as far as the outside world is concerned.

'From the way in which these murders have been carried out so far, none appear to be random. Careful planning has gone into each murder, and it is likely that this, along with the resulting notoriety, has given the killer almost as much gratification as the act of killing itself.' He turned over the sheet of paper to reveal a fresh, unmarked one.

At the top, he scribbled "Stirling", then wrote several points underneath his prime suspect's name:

- *Well-liked, respected member of the community*
- *Law professor, hence versed in the legal subjects the killer inscribes on his victims' chests*
- *Highly intelligent, but is he technically proficient? E.g. hacking into Channing & Barton's security system and disabling the CCTV*
- *Unhappy marriage – seeks gratification elsewhere?*
- *Has affairs with students, including the victims*

- *Enjoys classical music (heard at the scene of Emma Marsden's murder plus Lisa Ryland's radio tuned to Classic FM when body found)*
- *Rejected by Maddy Kramer once, therefore possibly bears a grudge against MK and sent a letter warning her to back off?*

Once again, Carver's gaze zoned in on his disciples. Willing his words to ignite some spark of ingenuity.

'Sir.' A young officer named Sandra Keel raised her hand.

'Yes?'

'Do we know anything about Stirling's childhood?'

'Good thinking, Keel. I was just coming to that.'

Keel beamed inside at Carver's compliment. She looked down at her notepad and pretended to write something. 'We need to look into Stirling's background. Find out if his parents are still alive, and if so, question them. Find out where he lived, went to school. Question old neighbours, teachers, friends. If he's our man, there's got to be something that's driven him to this. Serial killers often kill as a means of striking out against things that have happened to them in the past. Against people who have hurt them. It's a means of gaining control, recognition and revenge. This killer is focussing on young, attractive law graduates. A small fraction of society. Why? Who or what has angered the killer in the past to lead him to this?' Carver bent over to whisper into Drake's ear. 'We should question the wife again. Their marriage may not be a bed of roses, but no one knows a man better than his wife.' He paused, then added: 'Aside from his mother, of course.'

It had been a longer journey than anticipated, unexpected signal failure halting the Tube train abruptly between stations, and finding the killer stuck underground among a carriage load of tetchy commuters; with their filthy, bedraggled *Metro*s, vile germs and hostile faces. The killer surveyed the mixed bunch: bookworms buried in novels they only ever found time to read to and from the office; sickly lovers engrossed in each other; moronic students; desperate singletons; raucous groups out on Christmas jollies; earphone junkies locked in their own reclusive worlds, deaf to their surroundings.

The killer had hoped to be at the hideout by now. Sipping a hard drink to the soothing lilt of Beethoven. Laptop whirring, the creative juices flowing, brain contemplating another letter to DCI Carver.

But it seemed that would have to wait.

The killer sat back, head resting between clasped hands, legs outstretched, eyes closed, mind imagining: imagining the look on Carver's face when he received another riddle he'd be incapable of solving in time, even with Kramer's help; imagining the next victim who, right now, believed the world was her oyster, revelling in her beauty and youth, her ability to cast men off with callous regard, yet blissfully ignorant that on Thursday she would die a horrible death; imagining the sense of deep satisfaction when her perfect body had been butchered like the others, and this ugly, twisted world was rid of yet another selfish bitch who believed she had the right to ruin lives at others' expense. They – the others – were life's real victims, not her.

The killer felt aroused just thinking about it.

Natasha Coleridge was so wrong in thinking she could treat people the way she did. Just as women who failed their children were so wrong. Not least the woman who'd failed the killer, her only child.

The killer smiled at the prospect of another kill and forgot about being stuck fifty metres below street level.

Chapter Twenty

Thursday 4 December 2014

Feet swung over his desk, Carver hurled the stress ball he'd received in last year's Secret Santa at the wall to his right. It was only 7 a.m but he'd been in the office since 5 a.m., unable to sleep.

Despite the little evidence they had to go on pointing to Stirling being their man, a persistent doubt lurked at the back of his mind. Besides, there was also something not quite right about his wife, something sinister, almost as if she was planning something nasty. As soon as Drake showed up, and the clock hit a reasonable hour, they'd go pay her another visit.

There was a knock at the door, and the postboy walked in. He dumped a pile of mail on Carver's desk and left. Hidden within it was a slim brown envelope. It looked very much like the one he'd received from the killer. There was no postmark, only a sticky white label with Carver's name printed on it.

Carver dashed outside and spotted the postboy at the end of the corridor. 'Hey,' he yelled, rushing towards him. The boy looked alarmed, only too aware of Carver's reputation.

'Any idea who brought this in?' Carver waved the envelope at him.

The boy shook his head. 'Sorry, sir, I've no idea.'

'Hmm. No matter.' Carver turned away and headed back to his office.

Dread took hold of him as he opened the envelope and unfolded the single sheet of A4 paper. Sure enough, it was from the killer, the font and spacing identical to the one before.

Dear DCI Carver,

I hope I find you well, and not too frustrated. You made a brave attempt with my last riddle, but unfortunately you didn't quite make it. So here's another one for you to solve. Be quick, Chief Inspector, you don't have much time...

"If you prick us, do we not bleed? If you tickle us, do we not laugh? If you poison us, do we not die? And if you wrong us, shall we not take revenge?" (William Shakespeare)

And here's another clue to help you along...

She's not a lawyer, but she's the daughter of an eminent partner, a strong-willed warrior, a famous English poet. She lives alone. Her home is toxic.

She will die like an ant by this time tomorrow.

Trot along, Chief Inspector. The clock is ticking... tick-tock, tick-tock, tick-tock, tick-tock...

Mother of God! Was he going to poison her?

Carver hastily texted the riddle to Maddy, mindful of the killer's letter to her. The last thing he wanted was to place her in danger, or cause trouble with her firm.

But he needed her help. She had come so close to cracking the last riddle. He didn't have time to bring fresh blood in.

She was his best hope.

Maddy zipped up her skirt, then tucked her shirt into the waistband. She sat down at her dressing table and fixed her long dark hair into a neat bun, decorated her ears with the pearl studs her grandmother had given her for her twenty-first, and sprayed a touch of perfume either side of her neck. She had a meeting with a major client later that morning, and she wanted to look the part: polished, professional, in control; someone the firm's 55-year-old client – the CEO of a top investment bank – would believe capable of outsmarting the FCA officials who were suing his bank for fraud. She removed her jacket from the wardrobe and dashed into the kitchen, intent on throwing back a quick cup of coffee and anything edible she could get her hands on.

Paul wasn't up yet. He'd been out with Justin the night before and hadn't rolled in until the early hours. Maddy was dying to meet him. She was happy for Paul, but her instinct was to protect him, and she wanted to make sure she approved. She realised, what with recent events and work, that she hadn't made much time for her best friend lately. She'd text him later. See if he wanted to go for a drink, catch up. It couldn't be easy for him, having to pay the rent by waiting on others, when what he really craved was to earn his way in life through his writing. Still, she was sure he'd get there someday. He just needed that break.

Waiting for the kettle to boil, she checked her messages. Her pulse quickened when she saw a text from Carver. Too jittery to sit down, she rocked from one foot to the other as she tapped it open and read the letter – as disturbing as the last.

Paul was only a few doors away, but she couldn't help scrutinising her surroundings, as if she was being watched.

She told herself to get a grip, not let fear cloud her judgement. The killer had made it plain there wasn't much time. She glanced at her watch: 7.45. She needed to leave by eight. Her appetite gone, she hastily made a coffee, sat down at the table, and willed herself to crack the riddle before another innocent life was taken.

Carver watched Drake read the letter. When he'd finished, Drake looked up blankly.

'No ideas then?' He knew the answer to his question but desperation made him ask it all the same.

'All I can think of is poison, sir. But I haven't a clue about the victim.'

Carver shook his head. 'Me neither. I've sent it to Kramer. Let's hope she comes up with something. Meantime, get the entire team on it. We need to brainstorm.'

'What's wrong?' Paul appeared at the kitchen doorway as Maddy sat at the table, her head buried in her hands. She glanced up at him.

Barefoot, dressed in stripy pyjama bottoms, he seemed thinner of late. She hoped he wasn't running himself ragged, writing all day, working all night.

'The killer's sent Carver another riddle,' she explained. 'We have to act fast before he strikes again.'

Paul had seen that determined look before. 'Jesus, Mads, look what it's doing to you. How can you focus on work like this? It's not your job. It's Carver's and his team's.'

Maddy wasn't surprised by Paul's reaction. Which is why she hadn't told him about the killer's letter to her. He'd go ballistic if he knew.

'The killer's using legal terminology, but the police aren't lawyers, Paul. They don't know the subjects like me. I was so close to figuring out the last one.'

Seeing that same hell-bent look, Paul realised nothing he said was going to change her mind.

He made himself a coffee and sat down beside her. 'Can I take a look?'

Maddy smiled gratefully. 'Sure. Poison has to be the method of killing. I just can't decipher the crucial bit – the who and the where.' She passed him her phone, watched him stare at the riddle for a minute or two.

After a while, he looked up. 'I agree. Toxic must mean it's poison.'

'Yes. The riddle implies it'll happen at the victim's home. But *who* is the victim?'

Paul read the text out loud: '"Not a lawyer. The daughter of an eminent partner, a strong-willed warrior, a famous English poet." What the hell?' He shook his head in frustration, then glanced up at the clock. 'Mads, you do know it's nearly 8.15? You'll be late for work.'

'Shit!' She had a team meeting at 9.15 before the client arrived. The partner in charge would kill her if she missed it.

'I'll forward this to you,' she said, gesturing to her phone as she scraped back her chair. She gave Paul a quick kiss, threw down the last of her coffee – now almost cold – then raced out of the room.

'Yes, do,' Paul called after her. 'Have a good day.'

She didn't respond. Paul heard the door slam, then turned his attention to breakfast.

* * *

Maddy texted Carver her thoughts – which didn't amount to a whole lot more than what he'd already surmised himself – as she walked to Bow Road station. She then stared at the riddle all the way to work, wedged inside the oppressive Tube train so tightly she could scarcely draw breath.

How was poison related to one of the three legal subjects the killer had yet to inscribe? Maddy wondered.

EU? Equity? Tort?

She stared and stared and stared. Then suddenly…

'Yes!' she screamed. She felt herself turn pink and muttered a quick apology to her fellow passengers. She received a few smiles, several irritated scowls but then, the unexpected excitement over, everyone got back to their own business.

Maddy studied the killer's words again: "Trot along, Chief Inspector."

"Trot" was an anagram for tort, an area of law concerned with civil wrongs as opposed to criminal wrongs – wrongs like negligence, trespass, nuisance, product liability, in respect of which a claimant might try and claim compensation for the harm allegedly done to him or her.

Wrongs which also included: toxic torts.

A "toxic tort" was a type of personal injury lawsuit in which the claimant alleges that exposure to a chemical caused the claimant injury or disease. As a trainee, Maddy had spent the best part of her litigation seat assisting a partner with a mass toxic tort case involving a major pharmaceutical company. The action had centred on one of the company's products, the claimants alleging that it had induced heart attacks and other personal injuries in users of the product.

But if she and Paul were right about the killer's intention to poison his next victim, and "trot" was an anagram of tort, what kind of toxic tort did the killer have in mind?

Exposing the victim to a dangerous chemical in a public setting would endanger other lives as well as the victim's and was therefore far too risky. Plus, she felt sure this wasn't what the killer wanted. Carver had told her that serial killers usually targeted a specific type of victim, rather than carrying out some random killing spree against people they had no gripe with. Besides, the killer specifically said that the victim's "home" was toxic.

She looked down at the riddle again. Who was this girl? Who was her father? And why had the killer chosen her?

They were still underground. No signal. But Liverpool Street station was only two stops away. Once she was out in the open, she'd call Carver; texting took too long, and it was too important to delay getting the information to him a second longer.

Time wasn't on their side. Every second counted.

Chapter Twenty-One

Fifteen minutes later, Carver put down the phone, turned to Drake and explained Maddy's theory. 'She's got a meeting now she can't get out of. Doesn't expect to be free before one. Get the team to look into toxic torts. Particularly those that might occur in people's homes. The killer says the victim's not a lawyer, but Kramer thinks she must have some legal connection, else it doesn't fit the pattern.'

'Excuse me, sir, but isn't the father the connection? "An eminent partner".'

'Yes, Drake, but what if there's more to it than that? She may not be a lawyer, but that doesn't mean she's not studying law. Like all the others did. That, plus Stirling has been the common thread so far. Let's head for the academy. We need to find out if they've had any female students in at least the last five years whose fathers, or mothers for that matter, are partners at major law firms.'

Carver grabbed his coat from the back of his chair and made for the door. 'And we'll say hello to Professor Stirling while we're there.'

Maddy sat on one side of the conference table pretending to take notes, her mind only half there. She wanted to be in the library, researching toxic tort, trying to figure out which one the killer was likely to choose.

Next to her sat the lead partner on the matter, Jeremy Banner, plus a senior associate, and two trainees who looked like they might burst with eagerness. Sitting across from them was the CEO of the investment bank they represented, flanked on either side by his two underlings.

Dressed in dark suits, with deadpan expressions, they looked like a couple of villains from *The Matrix*.

'Maddy, what do you think?'

Maddy jolted to attention and glanced in surprise at Banner. He didn't look pleased. And neither did his clients. She didn't know what he was referring to, and everyone around the table knew it.

'Sorry, what was that?' She felt herself colour.

An hour later, the clients gone, for now appeased by Banner's damage-limitation tactics, Banner took Maddy aside. 'That was unacceptable. Completely unprofessional and, quite frankly, embarrassing.'

Maddy was mortified. She'd never messed up like that before. He was right. It *was* embarrassing, and she couldn't stand to come across as incompetent. But she had good reason. The last few weeks had changed things, thrown her and her ordered life out of sync.

'I'm sorry, Jeremy. It's been a tough few weeks, and I've not been sleeping well.'

Lame, lame, lame!

'I know it's been difficult, with everything that's gone on, and it can't be easy losing a good friend. But you have to get your act together. We're not in kindergarten playing dress-up. You work for a leading City law firm, representing the crème de la crème of clients. It's a time of huge change in the legal industry, and we can't afford to mess up. Even more so after what's happened.'

Maddy nodded. What he said was true. She'd said as much to Carver a few weeks back. Was it only a few weeks? It felt like six months, so much had happened.

'William Coleridge tells me you've been helping the police with their investigation.'

Another nod.

'We can't stop you assisting. That's the police's prerogative. But you cannot let it interfere with your work. You're held in high regard at the firm, Maddy. Don't do anything to jeopardise that.'

The law was Maddy's calling, her life. The thought of all those years of studying going down the drain was unthinkable.

'Understood. I won't.'

She meant it. She'd make damn sure she didn't slip up again. But she wasn't going to stop helping Carver. They were getting closer to finding the killer. She could feel it in her bones. And every time Paige's face appeared in her head, it strengthened her resolve.

Natasha Coleridge opened her front door, then tossed her keys in the bowl she'd reserved especially for them. Slim and petite, with long blonde hair and perfect features, Natasha attracted men wherever she went, lapping up the attention like a doted-on puppy and using her physical attractiveness to her advantage.

But she wasn't just a pretty face. She was also incredibly smart. And she was aiming high.

Natasha had been pleased with her decision to choose morning, rather than afternoon lectures at the academy. She'd always been a morning person and loved the fact that by 1 p.m., she'd already achieved so much. Her mind alert, buzzing with legal jargon, cases and concepts, she was ready to fortify what she'd learned with an afternoon of study.

Her father, William Coleridge, hadn't pushed her down the path he himself had taken. From the first, law was something that had fascinated her; not just the philosophical side of it, but the way it forced you to be creative. She couldn't wait to start practising in two years' time at the top-ten City firm where she'd been offered a training contract – hopefully due to her intellect and not because of who her father was. Where she would be constantly challenged to find new and inventive solutions to the most complex legal challenges clients faced, working with some of the world's most sophisticated businesses on groundbreaking transactions that altered the face of their industries, not to mention multi-million-pound disputes where reputations hung in the balance. And then there was getting a perverted kick out of the insane all-nighters and time-pressured deadlines that most people would balk at.

None of that scared her. She just had to make sure she passed her exams.

Although his temper had flared when she'd declined to take things further last week, and she'd sensed him giving her the cold treatment in tutorials, she didn't think Stirling would be so vicious or stupid as to tamper with her grades. And if he did, she'd go straight to her father. He was a powerful man in the City, and as much as she disliked the idea of confessing to him that she'd shamelessly flirted with her married professor twenty years her senior, she would if she had to. If push came to shove, she'd do whatever it took to follow in her father's footsteps. She had no doubt her father would make sure news of Stirling's escapades spread like wildfire, thereby putting an end to his career at the academy.

She'd been attracted to Stirling, she couldn't deny it. And flattered by his attention. It was exciting: the way he'd held her gaze, casually skimmed his hand across her knee as they'd gone over one of her papers in his office, the chemistry electric.

So when he'd slipped her a note, asking if she fancied meeting up for a quick drink to discuss her work further, she'd said what the hell.

Unlike most girls her age, struggling to make rent, Natasha lived the high life and had moved into her own three-bedroom flat in West Hampstead in her second year at uni.

By plying her with cocktails at one of London's most exclusive Mayfair hotels, Stirling had expected Natasha to be putty in his hands, free to mould to his desires. But she wasn't one to be so easily impressed. Born into money and glamour, it took a hell of a lot more than a swanky London hotel to get her between the sheets.

As Natasha removed her thick woollen coat and added it to the already chock-full stand of designer jackets, coats and scarves in her hallway, she grinned to herself as she remembered the look on Stirling's face when she'd turned him down.

The City was still very much a man's world, but it was funny to think how quickly women could reduce men to blithering idiots when it came to satisfying their innate carnal appetites. Sex was power as far as she was concerned, and she wielded such power expertly.

She'd set aside four hours of study before it was time to get ready for her parents' dinner party that evening. They held several during the holiday season, but she was particularly excited about tonight. The handsome son of one of her father's colleagues was going to be there. She'd wear her sexiest dress and style her hair in loose tumbling curls. She'd sit next to him, laugh at his jokes (funny or not), shower him with attention, preen her hair, flutter her eyelashes, purse her lips and make it clear she was his if he wanted her to be.

But first, lunch. She hadn't eaten since breakfast and her stomach felt raw. She went to the kitchen, grabbed a plate, knife and the fresh bread she'd picked up only yesterday from the bakery she adored on West End Lane, then set them aside on the work surface. She opened the fridge, fished out the cheese, tomatoes, some sunflower spread and her favourite apple juice. Seeing it, she realised she was thirsty. She poured a large glass and immediately slugged half of it. That was funny. It tasted bitter. It had only arrived with yesterday's home delivery. *So why does it taste bad?*

Shrugging it off, Natasha picked up the knife and began to spread some margarine on the bread. It was quiet, so she decided to liven up the atmosphere by switching on the radio. She pressed the button on top and it started playing classical music.

Strange. She peered at the dial. She always had it tuned to Kiss FM, but it was tuned to Classic FM. She was about to search for her favourite station when she started to feel unwell, her throat constricted, her breathing laboured. She'd only just had a drink, but her mouth was hit by an intense thirst. Clasping the sideboard for support, she turned the sink tap on and poured herself a glass of water, knocked it back in one. But she was still thirsty. And now, hot. Incredibly so. She was sweating profusely, as if she was trapped in a sauna. *What the hell is it?* She'd been fine one moment, and now it felt like she'd suffered a terrible allergic reaction to something. But she wasn't an allergy person; she didn't even get hay fever when everyone around her sneezed, itched and suffered all summer.

She grabbed a piece of kitchen towel and wiped the sweat from her brow. She gasped in oxygen, but every breath was a struggle and her chest hurt with the exertion. This was serious, she realised in alarm. She'd call 999 from her bedroom, then lie down on the bed, and pray for an ambulance to arrive in time.

She shuffled towards the bedroom, every step an effort, her stomach gripped with pain and nausea. She clutched her middle, realising she was going to be sick. She switched course and made for the bathroom, vomiting all over the floor and down her top before she was able to pull up the toilet seat lid and aim in the bowl. The sweating was getting worse now. Vomit dangled from her bottom lip and flooded her mouth. She was so incredibly hot. She bent her head over the sink, swished her mouth with water, then splashed her face. As she staggered to the bed, Natasha stripped off her clothes, now wet with perspiration. She lay down, and with every ounce of effort she could muster, reached over and grabbed the bedside phone, then pressed it to her ear.

What the fuck? Terror seized her. There was no dial tone. The line was dead. She needed her mobile but remembered she'd left it in her handbag in the hallway. She tried to force herself up, but then her muscles started to twitch. She tried to stop herself from shaking but it was no use. Her vision was becoming blurry, and she thought she must be hallucinating when she saw a figure standing over her, dressed in dark clothes and a balaclava. The stranger removed it – a stranger no more – then came closer, sat down on the bed next to her, and stared at her with cold eyes. Closer still, only a few inches separating them, as Natasha felt a leather-gloved hand stroke the side of her juddering face.

'Natasha, you have been so selfish – so wrong, so naive. You think all men are pawns in a female game of chess. But you cannot treat them like that – use them, toy with them, then cut them off like stray dogs as if they have no heart, no feelings of their own. As if they lack the ability to hurt, love and feel like any human being. What is it with women like you? Don't you understand psychology, Natasha, the way the human mind operates? We are all human. Men, women. But what marks us out is what's in our hearts. And you, Natasha, appear to have nothing in yours. You, Natasha, are empty.'

But Natasha did feel something – fear.

Her heart thudded with fear as she realised the intruder had poisoned her; that she was looking at the person who would send her to her

Maker. She was still lucid enough to remember the acrid taste of the apple juice, realising only now that it had been contaminated. *But with what?* It didn't matter. This was it: there would be no more dinner parties; no more swish restaurants; no more extortionately priced cocktails at glamorous bars; no more men to seduce, flatter, wrap around her delicate little finger; no more law school or dreams of following in her father's footsteps.

There would be no more Natasha Coleridge.

Chapter Twenty-Two

'I'm afraid Professor Stirling left around midday.'

'When will he be back?' a disappointed Carver asked the receptionist.

'Tomorrow.' She gave him a fake smile. Clearly, she wasn't about to offer any more information than that.

Irritating, but there it was. Earlier, they'd spoken to someone in the admissions department about obtaining a list of current and former female students whose fathers or mothers were partners at top City law firms.

Although Carver had stressed the urgency of the matter, he wasn't hopeful. The end of term was nearing, and the party season was already under way. So he'd settled for a list of every female who'd studied at the academy in the last five years. It would be up to Drake and the rest of the team to do the research and make the partner connection.

'Come on, let's go,' Carver said. 'Let's see if we have better luck finding Mrs Stirling.'

DC Sandra Keel turned onto the long shingle driveway leading up to Janis Stirling's five-bedroom house in the quaint Surrey village of East Molesey, the same house James Stirling grew up in. It was located on one of the area's most prestigious roads, and within walking distance of Hampton Court and the River Thames.

There were lovely areas of lawn to the front of the house with interspersed shrubs and trees, and the front facade itself was decorated with pretty climbing ivy and attractive bay windows.

Sandra parked her car in front of a detached garage to the left of the house, got out, and rang the doorbell. Having called ahead, she was expected. After about a minute, a willowy, white-haired woman, maybe in her late sixties, opened the door. It was hard to believe that this elderly lady still lived by herself in such a big house, although Sandra suspected she could easily afford hired help.

Mrs Stirling senior gave Sandra a faint smile. She had a mottled complexion, watery eyes and thin lips, made thinner by smoker's lines running all around her mouth. They looked like folds in crêpe paper.

Janis led her into a large reception room decorated with several expensive-looking pieces of art. The room smelt of fresh paint and cigarettes. Sandra was offered a seat and tea. She took up the first offer, declined the second.

'Excuse the smell, the house has only recently been redecorated,' Janis apologised. 'So, what can I do for you, Officer?' Her tone was affable, her eyes suspicious.

Sandra recounted what she had already explained on the phone: that she was part of a team investigating the murders of four females in central London within the last six weeks and was carrying out some routine enquiries.

'Is my son a suspect?' Janis narrowed her eyes at Sandra.

'No,' Sandra lied. 'But naturally we're questioning all staff at the academy because all four victims studied there.'

'I don't work there. Why are you questioning me?'

Sandra suddenly felt like she was the one being interviewed. She'd jumped at the chance to question Stirling's mother. But now she wondered if she was up to the challenge.

She could tell that underneath the polite, respectable facade, Janis was as tough as old boots.

'No, that's true, but you know your son better than anyone.'

'I thought you said he wasn't a suspect.' She was also as sharp as a tack.

'Please, Mrs Stirling, it's just routine. So we can rule your son out from our enquiries.'

Janis took a laborious breath, crossed her knees then sat back in her chair, her frail arms resting on either side like a queen. 'What would you like to know?'

Sandra inwardly sighed with relief that the old woman had come round, and that she wouldn't have to face Carver with her tail between her legs when she got back to the station.

'Do you see your son much?'

'Every now and then. It depends. He's very busy at work. I don't resent him for not visiting more regularly. He's a grown man.'

'Do you see anything of his wife?'

'Usually once a year. At Christmas.' Her tone was clipped.

'You don't like her?'

'That's an understatement.' She lit a cigarette, inhaled it like fresh sea air, the lines around her lips tightening like a closed umbrella. 'That woman was the worst thing that ever happened to my son. She's cold and selfish and doesn't deserve James.'

'Their marriage isn't a happy one?'

'No. She's barren. James wanted children more than anything, but she couldn't give them to him.'

Sandra thought about her own son. How she couldn't imagine life without him. Her heart suddenly bled for Elizabeth Stirling, and she resented Janis' spiteful attitude.

'Are you aware that your son has had several affairs over the years with his students?'

She saw slight trepidation in Janis' hazel eyes. Janis took another puff, exhaling in Sandra's direction.

'No. But I'm hardly surprised. Seeing as he doesn't get any at home.'

Sandra felt sickened by Janis' vulgar remark. It didn't sound right coming from the mouth of a "respectable" elderly lady. She decided to change the subject. She looked around the spacious room, and over Janis' shoulder to the bay window and rear garden beyond.

'Did your son grow up here? With you and your husband?'

'Yes. Although you should probably count the nanny too. James was an only child. I found pregnancy tiresome, and labour nothing short of sadistic torture. One was enough for me. Besides, I was far too busy playing tennis and bridge, and organising weekly coffee mornings.'

'And your husband? Was he around much?'

'No. My husband was a partner at Lovett Wardman, a top City firm. He was never home before ten and worked most weekends.'

'How did your son take that?'

'He didn't know any better, I suppose.' She pursed her lips into a crinkly mass. 'I doted on my son, still do. Though I'm not sure he realises it. But I wasn't what you call a "hands-on" mother. I didn't have the patience for bath times, nappy changing, eternal trips to the park and so forth. The nanny handled all that.'

'Do you think James resented that?' Sandra asked.

'No.' Janis said brusquely. 'James and I have a very acceptable relationship.'

Acceptable, thought Sandra. *That just about sums it up.*

'I can see you judging me, DC Keel. Don't. I had a lot to deal with.'

'How so?'

'Let's just say my husband had a temper, and a penchant for whisky. In large quantities. That's what killed him.'

'He was violent towards you? Towards James?'

'Never towards James. But yes, my husband would drink, and lash out at me. He had a highly stressful job, and I was his human punchbag.'

Sandra was shocked. Both by Janis' revelation and her apparent blunt acceptance of it. 'You didn't think about leaving him? Going to the police?'

'The late seventies, early eighties might not seem that long ago, but it was a very different world. Things have changed massively for women. They're much freer, with far more opportunities to make something of themselves, to be less dependent on their husbands. I didn't have those choices. I left school at eighteen in search of a rich husband. I had a child, and there was nowhere for me to go.'

There was no denying she was a bit of a battle-axe, but her eyes were sad, and Sandra found herself feeling sorry for Janis, despite her dismissive treatment of her daughter-in-law. Her husband had been a bastard, and she'd sought to escape the misery of her rotten marriage with tennis, bridge and coffee mornings.

Sandra again thought about her two-year-old son; the way she relished every moment spent with him.

If only Janis had realised that she needn't have looked further than her son to make up for the unhappiness in her marriage – for a sense of solace and purpose in her life. If only she'd recognised that tennis, bridge and coffee were meaningless trivialities that didn't come close to the bond shared between mother and son.

Then Sandra was sure that both Janis and her son would have had a much better chance of happiness in life.

'I have no idea where my husband is.' Elizabeth Stirling was a sylph-like woman and as she stood before him, Carver could understand why James Stirling had once fallen for her.

But he imagined she was now a shadow of the girl he'd married, no doubt driven to her current state by her husband's adultery. Carver wondered if they'd ever tried for children. Maybe Keel had got some answers from the elder Mrs Stirling.

'Are you aware of your husband's affairs, Mrs Stirling?' He didn't enjoy asking her the question, but it needed answering.

'Yes.' Her response was cool.

'It doesn't bother you?'

'I'd long suspected James was cheating on me, so I guess I shouldn't have been surprised. He had a reputation long before we got together at Oxford, but when I found out for certain I was still heartbroken. But heartache turned to anger, then resentment, then indifference. I channel my anger into my music, my sculpture.'

'Your sculpture?' Carver glanced at Drake.

'Yes, I have a studio upstairs. I've always enjoyed being creative. It's very calming. You should try it.'

'I'm afraid I'm not very creative,' Carver said with an uneasy chuckle. 'You've read about the way the murderer disfigures his victims? Do you think a person would necessarily have to be creative with their hands to do such a thing?'

Elizabeth smiled. 'I know where you're going with this, Chief Inspector. Just because I sculpt doesn't mean I carved up those girls.'

'But surely you resent them for sleeping with your husband? I assume you're pretty well versed in legal terminology, having been married to a law professor for nearly sixteen years.'

'I don't resent those girls. I resent *him*. There's a difference. If I was going to kill anyone, it would be him.'

Carver leaned forward. 'Do you consider your husband to be capable of murder, Mrs Stirling?'

A nail-biting pause, then Elizabeth said, 'I really can't say. One thing I can say for sure is that James has a temper.'

Progress. 'Has he ever hit you?'

'Yes.' She knew how much worse she was making things for her husband. But she didn't care. Despite what she'd told Carver, she wasn't indifferent. She was too riddled with hurt, spite and revenge to care about the consequences. This was her chance to get even with him.

'Frequently?'

'Not so much recently, but there was a period when he'd come home drunk every other night and take a swing at me. His father was the same apparently. I guess it's genetic.'

'Do you know if your husband has ever behaved violently towards any of his lovers?'

'No,' she lied, 'I don't.'

'Is he still sleeping with his students, Mrs Stirling?'

Elizabeth hesitated. Was it too soon to hasten her plan to destroy her husband? Should she wait? No, the urge was too great to resist. She got up and went over to the bureau in the corner of the room, removed a key from her trouser pocket and opened a drawer. From it, she pulled out a large brown manila envelope and handed it to Carver. He looked at it warily.

'What's this?'

'Open it and you'll see.'

The flap wasn't sealed. Carver pulled out several glossy prints of Stirling sitting in a bar with a young, attractive girl.

'When was this taken?' he asked.

'Last Monday evening.'

'You've been having your husband followed?'

'No. One of my girlfriends, who doesn't much care for James and was out drinking in the same bar that night, took the photos with her phone.'

'Do you know the girl?'

'She's one of his current students. Natasha Coleridge. Her father is William Coleridge. The senior partner of Channing & Barton.'

A look of alarm passed between Carver and Drake. They both shot up from the sofa. 'Excuse us, Mrs Stirling. Thank you so much for your time. We'll be leaving now.'

After she'd closed the door on her guests, Elizabeth sat down with her cello and started to play. As she caressed the strings like a long-lost lover, she thought back to Carver's question about whether she knew if her husband had ever behaved violently towards his lovers.

She'd almost been tempted to tell him what she knew, but it was far better for her sake that he received such information anonymously. After all, she didn't want to face criminal charges for breaking and entering. Or theft for that matter. He'd get the information soon, by post.

And then her wretched husband would really be in a bind.

Chapter Twenty-Three

Maddy put her phone on silent and moved stealthily across Channing & Barton's fourth-floor library towards the Tort section. She shouldn't have been in there. She should have been drafting an email to the client, making up for her earlier ineptitude.

But she couldn't help herself. Her client could wait a few hours. But the killer's next victim didn't have that luxury.

She cast her eyes along the dark-wood shelving, hoping the textbook she was after – one of the oldest, most respected authorities on Tort law – wasn't out on loan.

It wasn't. She grabbed it off the shelf and sat down at a table. Running her finger down the index, she found a section detailing different types of tort. There were lots. But the last category listed was "toxic tort". She turned to the relevant page and began to read.

A toxic tort was a legal claim for harm caused by exposure to a dangerous substance. Such claims often arose from occupational exposure, home exposure, consumer products and pharmaceutical drugs. The section listed some of the toxic substances shown to have caused significant injury to people.

Maddy thought for a while.

Those such as lead, asbestos, landfill waste and drugs were likely to cause injury from long-term, rather than short-term, use. She was sure that didn't apply here.

She read the paragraph on exposure in the home and consumer products. Under the former, examples such as mould, mildew and fungus were mentioned. Once again, these were torts generally arising from long-term exposure, and she suspected the killer, who had made it plain the next victim would die very soon, would use something sure to bring about instant death.

Maddy drew her finger down the paragraph until something interesting caught her eye. “Pesticides”. There were many types: herbicides; insecticides; fungicides.

The victim’s kitchen cupboard was likely to contain at least one of these, if not all three. She pulled up Carver’s text attaching the killer’s riddle: “Her home is toxic. She will die like an ant.”

Insecticide! The killer intended to poison the next victim with insecticide in her own home.

“The daughter of an eminent partner, a strong-willed warrior, a famous English poet.” She grabbed a pad and pencil from the centre of the table and bullet pointed key words. The sentence had to contain some hidden translation or meaning of the partner’s name, surely?

She fished out her iPhone, went to the internet, and typed in “strong-willed warrior”.

Bingo! The second entry down was a link to a baby-names website, explaining that “strong-willed warrior” was the literal translation of “William”. So, the father’s name was William.

Next, she typed in famous English poets. An image bar headed “Writers frequently mentioned on the web” appeared as the first result. She scrolled through the images, then froze as she read the fifteenth entry: Samuel Coleridge, a famous English poet.

She wrote down “William Samuel Coleridge” on her pad, then drew a line through “Samuel”.

How could she have been so slow?

Her senior partner’s daughter was the killer’s next victim.

Maddy burst into conference room eleven without knocking. She knew Coleridge would be irritated by the intrusion, but he’d thank her later.

‘What is the meaning of this, Madeline?’ Coleridge shot daggers at her. His eyes craftily skimmed the room, noting the displeasure on his clients' faces.

Maddy held her ground. 'Sir, it's a matter of urgency. I must speak with you now.'

'I'm sure it can wait, Ms Kramer.' He'd gone from first to second name terms just like that. She was in serious trouble. But that was irrelevant compared with what was at stake.

'It can't,' Maddy persisted. 'I believe your daughter is in grave danger, and you need to warn her. Now.'

'I can't get hold of Coleridge,' Drake said from the passenger seat as Carver wove his way down Grays Inn Road. 'The receptionist said he'd dashed out of his meeting to make an urgent call. I left a message for him to call me back immediately.'

'And Kramer?'

'She appears to be tied up too.'

'Okay, it can't be helped,' Carver said with a shrug. Although he couldn't be sure they'd drawn the right conclusion, it was one they couldn't sit on. He felt the rush of the chase, the feeling that they might be closing in on the killer. 'Ring the academy, find out where Natasha Coleridge lives and call for backup. The killer says her home is "toxic", so I'm guessing that's where she's meant to die. We need to head there before it's too late.'

'She's not answering her mobile, and when I try her landline, it says the number's not in use.' Coleridge's face was ashen. Until now, he'd seemed almost immortal to Maddy.

But now she saw that he was just another human being like her, like the rest of his firm: a husband and a father, with thoughts, vulnerabilities, fears of his own.

Seeing him look so helpless, Maddy didn't want to let on that she feared the worst. The kindest thing she could do for now was to keep moving and take control.

'We should go to her flat now.' She headed for the door.

Coleridge nodded, grabbed his coat off the hook, and obediently followed his associate out of the room. It was as if their roles had been reversed.

In the back of a black cab, battling heavy London traffic, Coleridge kept calling his daughter's mobile. But every time, it went to voicemail. He then tried his wife, not letting on why he needed to speak to Natasha so urgently for fear of upsetting her before they knew the facts. Unfortunately, she hadn't spoken to their daughter since the previous night.

It was one of the most uncomfortable thirty minutes of Maddy's life. Her mind beset with images of Sarah's and Emma's disfigured bodies, she couldn't help wondering whether she was about to come face-to-face with a third.

Finally, the cab turned onto West End Lane, the main road running through West Hampstead. A couple more turns and it came to a stop outside a four-storey Edwardian mansion block, converted into flats.

The cab fee was charged to the firm's account, so the driver sped off as soon as Maddy and Coleridge got out. Maddy waited nervously on the pavement as Coleridge rang the buzzer to his daughter's flat. No answer. He turned to her. 'Perhaps she stayed at the library to study. She does that sometimes. And it would explain her not answering her mobile.'

'Perhaps,' Maddy replied, not wanting to dent his optimism. 'But we should double-check all the same. Do you have a key?'

'I do.' Coleridge pulled out a key chain from his pocket, two keys dangling from it. 'Natasha gave it to us for emergencies.'

'This is an emergency,' Maddy said. She could tell he was dithering. 'Let's go in.'

She followed Coleridge up the stairs to the first floor. He knocked on his daughter's door, but there was no response. He waited another thirty seconds, then opened it, called out her name as they stepped into the hallway. Again, nothing.

'Her keys are in the bowl,' he noted.

Maddy heard classical music coming from somewhere. Had the killer beaten them to it?

'Wait here,' she instructed.

'Why?' Coleridge asked, his voice shaky.

'Please, just wait.'

Her heart in her mouth, Maddy started inspecting each room. The dining room was immaculate, as if it hadn't been touched in weeks. Nothing looked particularly out of place in the living room either. She kept going, spotting an open doorway ahead of her. It led her into the kitchen, where the music was coming from, turned up so loud it hurt her ears.

She used a piece of kitchen towel to turn it off, careful to avoid her fingerprints getting on the volume control. *Just in case...*

She noticed the lipstick-marked glass tumbler on the table, a third full of what looked like apple juice.

Then she saw two slices of bread laid out on a chopping board, buttered and ready to be filled with the cheese and tomatoes lying next to it.

Why had Natasha failed to make her sandwich? Had she received an urgent call and needed to dash off?

If only that were so.

Maddy had been right not to touch the radio – right not to touch anything with her bare hands.

Because the killer had been there. She'd suspected as much from the evidence before her.

But William Coleridge's grief-stricken cry confirmed her suspicions.

Chapter Twenty-Four

'She's not been dead long.' Grayson looked across the bed at Carver, Natasha lying between them. 'Body's only just starting to stiffen, and her temperature's just below normal.'

Carver and Drake had been on their way to Natasha's flat when Maddy's text had come through: "We were too late. My boss's daughter is dead. WC is with me. Distraught."

They'd arrived to find Maddy in the living room, sitting on the sofa beside a hysterical Coleridge, her arm wrapped around his quivering shoulder. He was sobbing like a child, his breathing erratic, his head buried in his hands, every now and again coming up for air and emitting a howl of pain. They'd immediately summoned a doctor, who'd administered a tranquilliser to calm him down. After he'd fallen asleep on the sofa, Drake had disappeared to break the news to his wife, busy getting ready for her dinner party.

Maddy stood at the foot of the bed, watching Carver and Grayson discuss the body as crime-scene officers and photographers moved busily around the room. Vomit trickled from Natasha's blue lips and onto the pillow she lay on. One of the CSOs took a sample and placed it in a clear plastic phial. They'd already taken samples from the bile on the bathroom floor Maddy had discovered earlier.

Other officers fished around in drawers and wardrobes, taking specimens of any liquids, pills or creams they came across.

Natasha's top half was naked – her bra and jumper lying inside out on the floor beside the bed – her chest inscribed with the word "Tort."

‘It looks like she was poisoned first,’ Grayson said. ‘From the vomit, and the blue tinge to her skin. See it?’

‘Yes,’ Carver nodded. ‘Any idea with what?’

‘My guess is some kind of household product or pesticide. It depends on the ingredients how quickly they react. Some are more lethal than others and require as little as a teaspoon to prove fatal. Hard to say definitively what we’re dealing with until we do the post-mortem and get the toxicology report. But that’s my gut feeling. It causes the victim to suffer severe stomach pains, nausea, headaches, sweating and eventually, if left untreated, seizures and death.’

‘There was a tumbler on the kitchen table,’ Maddy said. ‘About a third full of what looked like apple juice. But it didn’t smell like apple juice. It smelt sour.’

‘Yes, thank you, one of the CSOs saw it and has taken a sample. We’ll know soon enough.’

Carver turned to Maddy. ‘Ms Kramer, you beat us to it. I assume you know what the killer was getting at here?’

‘Yes. In a nutshell, tort law concerns injury a person has suffered because of another’s actions, for example through negligence or because of a faulty product. The person responsible will have had what’s known as a duty of care towards the injured party to ensure the injury didn’t happen.’ She took a breather. ‘In the past, pesticide poisoning has led to claims in tort. It’s what’s known as “toxic tort”. Especially in the States, where it’s been alleged that exposure to these types of chemicals has led people to become gravely ill, with all sorts of diseases.’

‘Like what?’

‘Blood cancer, aplastic anaemia. But I found a case where a perfectly healthy couple were discovered dead in a motel bedroom which had been sprayed with insecticide. Apparently, they died from breathing in the spray in mass quantities. It basically poisoned their bodies.’

‘I see.’ Carver felt deflated. He’d been so sure they’d get there in time.

‘I should get back to the office,’ Maddy said, eyeing her watch. For a few seconds, she and Carver stared at one another – a deliciously awkward moment. She saw the disappointment in his eyes, felt his frustration.

As for Carver, he marvelled at Maddy's strength. She was tougher than many young officers he'd trained over the years, and some older, more experienced ones. Most girls her age would have fainted or hurled on the spot. But she was different. Although he didn't want to admit it, he was attracted to this bright, spirited young woman. But he pushed the thought to the back of his mind. He was the senior investigating officer of a murder investigation, and their paths would never have crossed otherwise. They were poles apart – in age, outlook and lifestyle – and there could never be anything more between them, other than an underlying physical attraction.

'Of course. Thank you for your help once again, Ms Kramer. I know none of this is easy, and you're doing a fine job in keeping a level head.'

'Thanks, I'm just sorry for being too late to solve the riddle.' Maddy tried to shake off the torrid scene between her and Carver that was suddenly playing out in her mind. *How can I even think about such things at a time like this?* It was madness. But she couldn't help it. There was just something about him, something that had drawn her in from the moment she'd laid eyes on him that she couldn't quite put her finger on. Something that sent a wave of excitement through her every time they were in a room together.

'Don't be sorry,' he replied. 'We were all too late.'

'Natasha Coleridge is dead.'

Carver didn't take his eyes off Stirling, who was standing by his front door, about to unlock it.

After leaving the crime scene, Carver had met up with Drake and they'd headed straight for Stirling's house, arriving a little after 5.30 p.m.

Stirling appeared genuinely shocked. He also looked gaunt, sleep-deprived, as if something weighty was pressing on his mind. 'Oh my God,' he said in almost a whisper, his face suddenly drained of the little colour it had left in it.

'Her father found her poisoned in her flat. Her chest had been inscribed with the word "Tort".' He let his words sink in. 'Where were you all afternoon, Professor Stirling?'

The evidence against Stirling was getting stronger. He wondered what excuse he'd make up this time.

'Surely, you're not insinuating that I had anything to do with Natasha's death?' Stirling's expression was incredulous. Although his house was detached, and it was dark, he looked around guardedly, as if someone might overhear. 'Shall we go inside?'

They followed him into the house. Also dark, silent. 'My wife goes to Pilates every Thursday from five till six,' he explained.

He offered them coffee, but Carver declined, his tongue craving something stronger.

They all sat down in the living room, and Carver repeated his question. 'Where were you this afternoon, Professor Stirling? The girl on reception said you left around midday. Where did you go?'

'I'd rather not say.'

'I'm not sure you appreciate the seriousness of your situation. The law student daughter of a top City partner has been found murdered. And you were seen having a drink with her last Monday night, in Dukes Hotel.'

Stirling looked like he might be sick. He swallowed hard. No doubt urging himself inside to find a way out.

'Were you having an affair with Ms Coleridge?'

'No.'

'Were you trying to? Did she turn you down?'

Slight hesitation, then Stirling nodded. 'Yes, on both counts. She led me on all term. We drank cocktails all night, then went our separate ways.'

'Were you angry with her for turning you down?'

More hesitation. Carver had his answer.

'I was annoyed, rather than angry. I felt that she'd wasted my time.'

'Do you have a temper, Professor Stirling?'

'No, not really. I get angry once in a while. Like most people. But nothing out of the ordinary.'

'Really? That's not what we've heard.'

'Oh yes? From who? Someone who's obviously got it in for me and has been making up stories.'

'Have you ever hit your wife, Professor Stirling?'

A knowing smile as realisation hit. 'It's her, isn't it? My wife. You know she's a manic depressive? Pops pills like Smarties. She hates me, and now she's trying to get her revenge.'

'Revenge for your affairs? Or for abusing her? Or both?' Carver's questions came at Stirling like rapid gunfire.

The pressure was getting to him. Stirling sprung up from his seat, started manically pacing the room. He ran his hand down the back of his head in exasperation. 'I have never abused her per se…maybe slapped her across the cheek a few times. But that was a long time ago, when I was drinking too much, and I'm damn certain it happens between husbands and wives all the time. It doesn't make me a murderer by any stretch of the imagination.'

'You condone violence towards women?' Carver didn't let up. His tone was scathing.

Stirling shook his head, scrunching his eyes shut as he did so. 'No! That's not what I said. You're twisting things.'

'We have Paige Summers' diary. In it, she categorically states that you hit her. Are you saying she's a liar?'

Stirling raised his hands in the air, as if to emphasise his vexation. 'I've told you before, she was obsessed with me. She had a wild imagination. Who knows what other lies she invented?'

Carver shook his head in disgust, as if he didn't believe a word of what Stirling was saying.

'We've spoken to your mother. We know your father was abusive.'

'My father never abused me.'

'Maybe not you, but he hit your mother.'

'That's true. So what?'

'So, you know what they say, like father like son. Are you saying your father's violent behaviour towards your mother had no effect on you?'

Carver saw the desperation on Stirling's face. He was like a wild animal caught in a poacher's net struggling to free himself, but with no obvious means of doing so.

'None whatsoever,' he said. 'Naturally, it upset me. I certainly didn't condone it or feel moved to treat women in the same way.'

Carver was silent. Digesting Stirling's response. Making him sweat.

'Do you listen to classical music regularly, Professor Stirling?'

Stirling looked at Carver in surprise. 'Yes, you know I do. We only spoke the other day about my love for it. I find it relaxing. It helps me to deal with the stresses and strains of life.'

'Where do you listen to it?'

'At home, in the car, on the Tube.'

'You have an MP3 player, an iPod?'

'MP3 player. So what? What's this got to do with anything?'

'Just curious. Are you an artistic person, would you say?'

'Not particularly. Elizabeth's the arty one. Did she mention that she sculpts? She has her own studio upstairs.'

'She did. Can we take a look?'

Stirling wavered. 'I don't think my wife would take kindly to our snooping around her private things. She doesn't even allow me up there.'

'Please, Professor Stirling. It won't take a minute.'

Sensing that he didn't have a choice, Stirling reluctantly led Carver and Drake up two flights of stairs to the loft. The door was closed. Stirling tentatively opened it, almost as if his movements might telepathically alert his wife to their intrusion. It was pitch-black. He reached inside for the light and turned it on. The room was filled with paintings resting on easels and propped up against the walls, along with various sculptures set on plinths and sideboards. The air smelt of paint and clay, while the bare wooden floor was covered with a thick layer of dust.

Carver let his eyes wander around the room. In the corner, he spotted a large piece of tarpaulin covering something. Beside it, there was a stool, a stained green overall draped across it. 'Is that your wife's pottery wheel under there?'

'Yes.'

Carver walked over to it. He reached out his hand to remove the tarpaulin.

'I wouldn't do that.' Stirling stopped him in his stride.

'Too late for that,' Carver said as he uncovered the wheel.

For a while, all three men gawped at Elizabeth's latest work. A naked man and woman. The man was horizontal, the woman straddling his torso, a dagger in her right hand, bearing down into the man's heart.

Stirling's face was aghast.

'Christmas present perhaps?' Carver said sarcastically.

'Lately, Elizabeth's been spending more time up here than usual. I had no idea that this was what she was working on.'

'Do you think that might be you and her?'

'Good God, I hope not.' Stirling chuckled uneasily. But then his face grew long.

'What is it, Professor?'

'The woman looks like…'

'Yes?'

'She looks a bit like Sarah.'

Carver bent down over the sculpture. Noted the contempt on the woman's face, the sheer helplessness on the man's. 'You did say you think your wife's trying to take revenge on you.' He straightened. Looked directly at Stirling. 'Maybe you were right.'

Carver and Drake left Stirling before Elizabeth got home. In the car, Carver considered Stirling's reaction to his questions – and to his wife's artwork. All five murders had been committed by a highly intelligent, methodical person. But a cool, calm and collected approach would also have been required. Stirling was certainly clever and meticulous, but he hadn't come across as calm when questioned. He'd seemed genuinely flustered, his answers unrehearsed. Unless, of course, his dithering was merely an act to sway his interrogators from the possibility that he might be the killer?

Plus, Carver still didn't know where Stirling had been all afternoon.

Why had he been so reluctant to tell him? If he hadn't been out poisoning Natasha Coleridge, where the hell had he been?

And then Carver thought about Elizabeth's disdain for her husband, her graphic sculpture. Stirling had thought the woman holding the dagger was Sarah. Did this mean he'd also been violent towards her, as well as Paige, Lisa and Elizabeth? Did Elizabeth know this? If so, how?

Elizabeth had the motive to kill all five girls. *But does she have the capacity for murder? Is she so driven by revenge that she could be capable of such atrocities?* She wasn't a big woman either. Yes, she was smart, and good with her hands, but she was also paper-thin. Whether she had the physical strength to carry out the murders was debatable. Then again, the mind was an amazing tool. If a person was determined and driven enough, it was astonishing what they could achieve.

Carver prayed that this time round, the killer hadn't been so careful. That as his CSOs conducted their painstaking analysis of the crime scene, they'd find something, anything, that might lead them to the killer.

Chapter Twenty-Five

Friday 9 April 2010

'Can I help you?'

Sarah Morrell had been enjoying an intimate first date with hunky, rugby-playing LPC student Connor Dexter. With cheekbones you could cut glass on, dreamy blue eyes, kissable lips and a butt as pert as a peach, Sarah also suspected that underneath that slim-fit shirt of his he had a rock-hard six-pack. She was looking forward to finding out later if she was right.

The handsome couple were tucked away in a snug alcove of a popular Bloomsbury bar, nursing a bottle of Cabernet. The area was a hotspot for London university students and postgrads at the nearby Bloomsbury Academy of Law. But it was rarely frequented by the likes of the tall, elegant woman, dressed in a black cashmere overcoat, four-inch court shoes and wearing a massive rock on her ring finger, who'd just walked up to their table.

The woman glanced at Connor, cut him a dry smile. 'So, you're what she moved on to.' Her eyes ran over him. 'I can see why.'

Sarah's date looked dumbfounded. He said nothing, took a nervous sip of wine.

'Who the hell are you?' Sarah demanded.

Elizabeth Stirling picked up Sarah's wine glass, drained its contents, then placed it back down on the table. 'Elizabeth Stirling. Ring any bells?'

Sarah was a pro at keeping her cool. But Elizabeth saw apprehension in her almond-shaped eyes. She was rattled. Brilliant.

'Professor Stirling's wife?' Sarah said coolly. Just like that, the apprehension had evaporated, her expression inscrutable.

'Don't play innocent with me, you little home-wrecker. You know exactly who I am. And I know exactly what you've been getting up to with my husband over the last six months.' Elizabeth explained how she'd followed them to a hotel, watched them emerge separately the next morning, before challenging her startled husband in the car park.

Connor had gone from looking mildly uncomfortable to wanting the ground to swallow him up. 'Another bottle?' he asked Sarah hopefully.

'Don't move,' Elizabeth ordered.

'As far as I could tell, you don't have a home to wreck.' It was a cold, malign thing to say, but Sarah couldn't help herself. That was who she was. When anyone threatened or challenged her, she bit back. With interest. What's more, she was still furious with Stirling for striking her across the cheek the previous weekend, and for threatening her future with Channing & Barton.

Sarah was afraid of no one – certainly not Stirling or his psycho bitch wife.

She wanted Elizabeth to know that. So she kept going. Kept spouting her venom. 'Maybe if you weren't so cold, if you paid your husband a little more attention in the sex department, he wouldn't go looking for younger, hotter blood.' She cocked her head to one side, smiled smugly. 'Or maybe you've tried, but he's the one who's gone frigid because you can't give him kids.'

Elizabeth had come there to teach the little tart a lesson – to threaten her future hopes as a lawyer, to embarrass her in front of her new boyfriend. She hadn't imagined her to be so ruthless, so self-assured. Was that what had excited her husband?

The pain of not being able to have children was one that gnawed at Elizabeth every second of every day; like some ugly flesh-eating disease. Making her feel more and more abhorrent to the outside world as it devoured her. Making the simplest of tasks a chore. Making life almost unbearable. And now, to add to her suffering, she'd discovered that her husband, who, for all his despicable shortcomings, she'd never have believed capable of disclosing her most agonising secret to an outsider, had in fact revealed it to his shallow bit on the side. This beautiful, vicious young woman who'd used James for her own gratification and mercenary purposes, then cast him aside like yesterday's news, and now laughed in his wife's face as if her feelings meant nothing. As if she'd brought it on herself.

Sarah had made her feel so small, so pathetic, so worthless, Elizabeth didn't know what to say or where to look. She told herself to hold it together until she got out of there.

'Just stay away from my husband in future,' she warned, willing her voice not to falter. 'Or you'll live to regret it.'

She didn't allow Sarah the chance to respond; she turned on her heel and walked out of the bar, not noticing the individual sitting in a quiet corner sipping a beer, and who had been watching the show with interest from a discreet distance.

She didn't stop walking until she'd reached the end of the road and turned the corner.

At that moment, her body shaking with hurt and humiliation, Elizabeth saw that it was all her husband's fault that she'd been made to feel so useless, so unloved, so unattractive. If he'd stayed true, hadn't allowed his hands to wander like his father before him, none of this would have happened.

She'd give him one more chance. But if she discovered he still couldn't keep his flies zipped up, making a mockery of her and their marriage in the process, then she'd make him sorry.

She'd make him sorrier than he'd ever been.

Chapter Twenty-Six

Friday 12 December 2014

'So, you haven't told me. Are you going to your mother's for Christmas?'

Maddy sat opposite Paul in Jewel, a West End bar just off Regent Street. It was Friday night, and she'd managed to escape the office early, taking the opportunity to do a spot of Christmas shopping on Oxford Street before meeting Paul for a drink. The bar was rammed with an eclectic mix of shoppers, workers and tourists, while the ritzy decor was tasteful rather than garish.

Maddy usually loved central London at this time of the year: the streets lit up like a scene from a fairy tale; the buzz of stressed, excited shoppers; the delicious smell of roasted chestnuts hanging temptingly in the air; street stalls selling naff Santa hats and even naffer singing snowmen. There was an all-round aura of happiness, optimism and festive cheer.

But this year, it was lost on Maddy. Since Natasha's death, the office had felt like a morgue, everyone stunned by the senior partner's daughter's murder just weeks after Sarah's. More unsettling was the news that forensics had once again turned up nothing, other than confirming that the apple juice had been spiked with one of the most highly toxic insecticides on the market. This, together with the volume Natasha drank, had been a lethal combination.

Unsurprisingly, the firm's Christmas ball at the Dorchester Hotel had been cancelled as a mark of respect for Coleridge and his family, and the managing partner was holding the fort until Coleridge felt able to return to the helm.

Even as she'd battled her way through the masses on her way to meet Paul, Maddy couldn't help looking over her shoulder. Couldn't help wondering if the killer was behind her, tracking her every move, somehow aware that she was still helping Carver, waiting for the right moment to silence her for good.

But by the time she'd arrived at the bar on Glasshouse Street, only seconds away from seeing her best friend, she'd felt calmer, certain that the killer would never strike with Paul there at her side. Later, they'd take the Tube home together, and she'd be safe. For tonight at least.

'Not sure if I can stand it,' Paul said grimly. 'Philip will be there.' He rolled his eyes for effect.

'Her latest squeeze?'

'Uh-huh. He's more than that. They've been together for almost a year. He with the terrible toupee, Hitler moustache and donkey laugh.'

Maddy didn't know whether to laugh or cry. Her heart went out to Paul, forced to cope with his vacuous mother's soap opera love life, drifting from one man to another, forever putting her own needs above her son's. But the way Paul joked about her and her squeezes was also quite comical.

'Go on, laugh, I know you want to,' Paul said grumpily.

'I'm sorry,' Maddy giggled, twirling her straw between her thumb and index finger, 'it's just the way you describe them.'

'If I didn't make light of it, I'd go insane,' Paul laughed back. 'So, as I was saying, I'm not sure if I can be bothered. She hardly ever calls me to see how I'm doing, and I end up feeling like a giant gooseberry. Plus, I resent seeing some buffoon sitting at the head of the table. It was Dad's place, and all I can think is that he should be sitting there, not one of her idiot boyfriends.'

'Forget that, you should be sitting there. You're the head of the house.'

'It's because I'm gay,' Paul said. 'I'm not a real man as far as she's concerned.'

It was so unfair, Maddy thought. He didn't deserve to be treated so shoddily by his own mother. But she was a superficial, selfish woman, and sadly Paul had drawn the short straw with her.

'Spend it with me and Gran then,' she said, finishing off her margarita, her insides hit by a blast of tequila in the last dregs.

Paul grinned. 'I thought you'd never ask. I'd love to. Another round?'

Carver leaned back in his chair and squeezed his stress ball. Repeatedly. Until his knuckles turned pallid, his hand throbbed, and he found his mind zoning in on the uphill struggle he faced. He swivelled round and studied his wall, littered with facts, signposts, names, everything and anything possibly relevant to each murder; plastered with large, glossy prints of the victims – graphic, shocking, sickening to most, but not to Carver. The job had made him immune to the kind of atrocities that would give any normal, sane human being recurrent nightmares. It had to be that way. Otherwise, he'd go mad, let alone be able to get up and face the day.

His eyes rested on a map of London, marked with five red circles denoting the locations of each murder. Unlike many notorious serial killings, the murders weren't confined to a specific radius; two had been in the heart of the City, one closer to the West End, the last two in North London. The killer was like an octopus – prepared to stretch his tentacles in different directions, so long as the victims fitted certain criteria.

It wasn't just the killer who was stressing him out. He'd just come off the telephone with Rachel. Another rancorous conversation, in which she'd reminded him about his son's football game the next morning; that if he failed their son yet again, the poor boy would never forgive him, might well be mentally scarred for life and turn into one of the nutters he frequently put behind bars.

Carver had gritted his teeth throughout the more-or-less one-way discourse, resisting the urge to take petty swipes back at Rachel, mindful of Carl and the fact that he didn't want to lose what access he had to his boy by aggravating her further. He knew he wasn't the best father, that he'd let Daniel down too many times. But he also knew his son. Daniel was stronger than his drama queen mother gave him credit for. And, at the end of the day, *he* was Daniel's father, and Daniel knew how much he loved him – would give his life for him in a shot.

He looked at his watch: a little after 8 p.m. He was just thinking about wrapping up to leave when there was a knock on the door and in walked Sergeant Matthews. 'There's someone here to see you. Says they have information which may be relevant to the Scribe murders.'

Carver looked up, irritated by the phrase the sergeant had used to refer to the killer even though he knew it wasn't his fault. When Carver had briefed the press on Natasha Coleridge's murder, he'd used the term "inscribed" to illustrate the way in which "Tort" had been etched across her chest. The press had capitalised on this and christened the killer "The Scribe". Now the title was splashed across every front page, aired on every news channel, spreading like wildfire up and down the country.

In Carver's experience, serial killers craved attention and fame. And now the bloody press had dished out both to the latest lunatic on the loose on a gold-rimmed platter – a title sure to fuel the killer's thirst for blood. As usual, they'd made things worse, not better.

'Name?' Carver wanted more information before letting the stranger in. They'd already had umpteen people rocking up claiming to have information that could be helpful to the case. But the majority had been bonkers, or glory-seekers, or straight dead ends.

'Connor Dexter.'

Fortunately, this name rang a bell. Carver recalled that Dexter was an ex boyfriend of Sarah Morrell's, and one of the first people Drake had questioned following her murder. He'd been staying over at his fiancée's flat the night she was killed, a watertight alibi confirmed by the fiancée's flatmate.

Carver was intrigued to know why Dexter was back, voluntarily. He had to know something.

Five minutes later, they sat across from one another in an interview room. The overhead lights were blinding, the setting bland and deeply unfriendly. Perfect.

Dexter was smart, clean-cut, ridiculously good-looking. And, as

Carver noted from Drake's report, in the throes of a successful legal career. He found himself feeling quite envious of the lucky bastard.

Despite his looks and success, at that moment Dexter appeared about as confident as a four-year-old boy on his first day at primary school. He sat back in his chair, his eyes wide and fretful, his fingers nervously tapping the table as if he was high.

'How can I help you, Mr Dexter?'

Dexter spoke anxiously. 'I remembered something, something that might be relevant to Sarah's murder.'

'Something you failed to mention to my colleague, Detective Constable Drake, seven weeks ago?' Carver had no patience for people who held back – who wasted police time and hampered his investigations by failing to be honest from the outset.

'I only just remembered,' Dexter replied weakly. Carver didn't buy it for a second. His eyes were a sure giveaway. But he let it go. He didn't seem like a bad sort; he was just scared for his own skin, like most people.

'Okay, go on.'

The tapping continued. 'As you probably know, I dated Sarah from the beginning of April to around mid-June 2010.'

Carver nodded. 'And?'

'Something rather odd happened on our first date.'

'How do you mean?'

'We were having a drink in a bar in Bloomsbury. It was going really well until a woman – tall, slim, elegantly dressed, probably in her late thirties – walked up to our table and started having a massive go at Sarah.'

The adrenaline was there again. Carver leaned in. 'Who was she?'

'Elizabeth Stirling.'

This was big. 'What did she say?'

'She accused Sarah of sleeping with her husband, told her to stay away or she'd live to regret it.'

'And what was Sarah's reaction?'

'Sarah wasn't fazed in the slightest. Gave as good as she got, almost as if she was enjoying it. She accused Mrs Stirling of being cold and infertile, and insinuated that this was why the professor had strayed.

I'd never felt so uncomfortable in all my life. I realised then that Sarah was as hard as nails, that she and I were never going to work long-term. In a way, I found her more intimidating than Mrs Stirling. Ruthless, that's what she was.'

'And when Sarah said these things to Mrs Stirling, how did she react?'

'To give her her due, she handled herself very well. Remained dignified. But I could see the hurt in her eyes. And the anger.'

'Did you ever come across Mrs Stirling again?'

'No, never.'

'And did you or Sarah end your relationship?'

'It was kind of mutual.' Dexter briefly lowered his eyes to the floor then looked back up at Carver whose gaze hadn't left him. 'Sarah was a man-eater. She was very sexy and very sure of herself. Irresistible to most men. But she wasn't a keeper. She wasn't someone you could imagine sharing your life or having children with. Once we'd got over the sex, there wasn't much left. I guess it just fizzled out.'

'Why did you come here today, Mr Dexter? You say you only just remembered the encounter between Sarah and Mrs Stirling, but we both know that's not true. What you've just told me is something that would stick in a person's mind forever. Why did you hold back until now?'

Dexter held up his hands. 'Okay, you got me. I did hold back, and I'm sorry for that. But I guess I panicked. And I didn't want to get Mrs Stirling into trouble. She seemed like a decent woman, and I felt sorry for her. But now that some time has passed, and there've been four more murders, I didn't think it was right to keep it from you. Whoever's responsible can't be allowed to go on butchering innocent women the way they have.'

'I'd hardly call Sarah innocent, would you?'

'Sarah was a lot of things. She certainly wasn't the nicest person in the world, that's for damn sure. But she didn't deserve to die like that. And neither, I'm sure, did any of the others.'

'I agree with you there.' Carver sat back, then asked a question he'd gone over and over in his mind for the past fortnight. 'And tell me, Mr Dexter, do you consider Mrs Stirling to be capable of such atrocities?'

'I don't know, Chief Inspector. I don't know her well enough to speculate. But I do know that if someone had said some of the cruel, hateful things Sarah had said to Mrs Stirling to me, I'd be angry. Very angry.'

Chapter Twenty-Seven

'So, when will I get to meet Justin?'

Maddy and Paul left the shelter of Bow Road station for the glacial outside air. As Maddy spoke, a cloud of warm air trailed from her mouth. She plunged her hands into her coat pockets for extra warmth as they turned left in the direction of home. It had been a fun night, and for a few hours they'd been able to banish the murders from their minds.

After letting off steam about his mother, Paul had spent the rest of the evening gushing over his new boyfriend. Justin was American and worked as a graphic designer on the South Bank. In the bar, Paul had shown Maddy a photo they'd had taken together in a passport photo booth, arms around each other's necks, grinning inanely at the camera. Maddy could see the attraction. He was very much Paul's type. She hadn't seen him this happy in some time, and was glad for him. She only hoped Justin was for real, and didn't let Paul down, the way he'd been let down so many times in his life – by his parents, his mother especially, and by other men.

'Sadly, I'm guessing not till the New Year. He's flying back to the States for Christmas on Sunday. Got two weeks off in sunny Palm Springs, the lucky bastard.'

'He didn't ask you to join him?'

Paul laughed. 'Mads, we've only been dating a couple of months. I think it's a bit early to go on holiday together and meet the parents.'

'I don't know, whirlwind romances do happen, you know.' For a split second, Carver's face popped into Maddy's head. She quickly shook her mind free of it and picked up the pace. They'd only been outside a couple of minutes, but her toes were already numb. She dreamed of hot chocolate and buttered toast as an incentive to keep going.

They were only a few paces from home when Maddy's phone rang. She fished it out of her handbag. It was Carver. Her heart leapt. Even at 10.30 p.m. on a Friday, the man didn't rest, or worry about interrupting other people's leisure time. Or maybe he'd wanted to hear her voice? No, that was stupid. He certainly didn't view her that way. What was she, fifteen!

'Hello, DCI Carver.' Maddy glanced at Paul, who rolled his eyes in irritation. He kept his gaze on her as she listened intently to what Carver was saying.

'No, I don't see why he'd be lying. I hardly knew the guy, but he seemed decent enough. Probably the reason why he and Sarah didn't last.' She paused. 'No, I never met Mrs Stirling, so I really can't help you there. I don't blame her for being pissed off, though. That's evil, even by Sarah's standards.' Another pause. 'But would she really be capable of carrying out six murders single-handedly? I'm including Frank in that. Surely, it's Stirling who she'd want to take revenge against, not the women he slept with?'

Another pause, during which time they reached the front door of their building.

'No, I can't think of anyone else who'd bear a grudge against Professor Stirling. He was very popular, and I don't remember any students speaking ill of him. Sorry not to be of much help.' Paul turned the key in the door. 'Okay. Yes, have a good weekend too. Goodnight.'

Maddy followed Paul inside, luxuriating in the warmth of the centrally heated hall as she closed the door behind her. She felt the cold in her lungs and chest, and lightly stamped her feet up and down to get the sensation back in her toes.

'What the hell did he want?' Paul asked crossly as he began to trudge up the stairs to their flat. 'He shouldn't be calling you so late. It's bordering on harassment.'

‘Relax, will you?’ Maddy urged, trying to keep up. ‘He’s just doing his job. And he must be under a ton of pressure.’

They stopped outside their door. Paul turned to Maddy, said more gently, ‘True, I didn’t think of it like that.’ He opened the door, reached inside for the light, and flicked the switch. ‘But, as I’ve said before, I don’t want him putting you in jeo—’

He didn’t finish his sentence. His back to Maddy, he’d gone rigid. Slowly, he turned around to face her, but said nothing. He’d gone white.

‘What is it?’ Maddy asked nervously. Seeing that she wasn’t going to get a response, she eased herself past, Atticus appearing at her feet as she did so. ‘Hey, little guy.’ She briefly looked down with a loving smile, then up again.

And that’s when she understood Paul’s reaction. The living room door was open, and she could see directly into it. It looked like a tornado had ripped through it, the floor strewn with overturned furniture, books flung across the room from the bookshelf in the corner. The phone was off the hook, while a vase of flowers she’d arranged only yesterday had been knocked to the ground, water flooding the rug beneath it. Maddy shivered as she took in the carnage and realised a stranger had been in their flat.

Who was it? The killer? Some random burglar? Her heart prayed for the latter; her head told her otherwise.

As she continued to stare, she felt a hand on her shoulder. It made her start. ‘Sorry,’ Paul said. ‘Didn’t mean to scare you.’

‘Don’t be, I should have known it was you. I’m just a bit shaken up. Do you think it’s the killer?’

Paul shook his head. ‘I don’t know, but we need to check all the rooms, see if anything’s been taken, before we call the police.’

Maddy nodded and reluctantly made for her bedroom. The door was slightly ajar. She always shut it before leaving the flat. The intruder had been in there too.

She went in alone, while Paul checked his own room. As she’d feared, it was a mess. Her duvet and pillow were lying on the carpet, the white fluffy insides coating the carpet like a blanket of snow.

All her dressing table items were lying in disarray on the floor. Her chest of drawers had received similar treatment, her underwear and several carefully ironed shirts sprawled in a haphazard heap.

Her laptop, however, which aside from her mother's jewellery was the most expensive item she owned, didn't appear to have been moved.

Maddy felt violated. And then a worse thought struck her. In her bedside cabinet she kept a photo of her and her parents, taken six months before they died. Petrified that she might have lost it forever, she darted over to her bed and pulled the drawer open. *Thank God.* It was still there. Intact. She pulled it out, cradled it against her chest, willing it to give her strength.

After a minute or so, she kissed the photo and tucked it safely back inside the drawer. She then got down on her knees and fished under the bed for the safe where she kept her mother's jewellery. She breathed a sigh of relief when she felt the metal structure, pulled it out and saw that it was undamaged. She keyed in the code, just to check the contents were still inside, and exhaled once more when she saw nothing had been taken.

And then, looking up, she caught sight of her wardrobe. Had he been in there too – touching, smelling her clothes, tainting them with bloodstained hands?

Paul appeared as she made her way towards it. 'Christ,' he said, seeing the mess.

She stopped, turned to look at him. 'How's your room?'

'Pretty similar. Some of my records are damaged. Bastard. Luckily none of the classics. But nothing of real value's been taken. Laptop's still there. Strange, don't you think?'

'It would be if we were dealing with a straightforward burglary,' Maddy said. She gestured to the wardrobe. 'I need to check in there.' When she opened it, Maddy barely noticed that her clothes were still hanging just as she'd left them.

All she could focus on was the red lipstick scrawl on the inside door mirror:

You didn't listen to me. I warned you to stop helping Carver. If you do not, next time it won't be your home that's ripped apart. It will be something far more precious.

Carver scrutinised the message. Tried to understand how the killer could have known Maddy was still helping him. The only explanation was that he'd been watching them when they'd all been gathered at Natasha Coleridge's flat. That was the only time he and Maddy had come face-to-face since Emma Marsden's death.

He went over to Maddy, sitting on the edge of her bed. The room was still a tip, forensics going about their business. 'We need to take your phone. Check for bugs, any kind of tampering.'

'Okay, sure.' Maddy watched Carver pass her phone to a gangly CSO who carefully placed it in a clear sealed bag, as if it was a stick of dynamite. 'It's got all my contacts on it,' Maddy said. 'Will I get it back soon?'

'Don't worry, I'll make sure it's the first thing they look at.' Carver gave her a reassuring smile.

He'd got the call at 11.30. Having just walked through his front door, hungry and craving sleep.

Rather than call 999, and against Paul's advice, Maddy had insisted on calling Carver directly. It had pissed Paul off. He'd accused her of virtually spitting in the killer's face, of not taking his threat seriously. But then, his rant over, he'd tried to reason with her, pointing to the upheaval surrounding them, reminding her of the killer's clear warning that this was nothing compared to what would come next if she didn't do as he asked.

But Maddy was too sure of her instincts to be swayed. She trusted Carver. She'd struck a connection with him. He was the right person to call, and she didn't care what Paul or anyone else said.

No sooner had he heard her out, heard the alarm in her voice, than Carver had jumped in his car, calling Drake from the wheel and telling him to assemble a forensic team at Maddy's quick sharp.

Paul appeared with coffee and they moved to the kitchen, one of the few rooms left intact by the killer.

'Mr King,' Carver said, 'what time did you leave to meet Ms Kramer this afternoon?'

'Around 5.30. Maddy had called earlier to say she was kicking off work about then, and we agreed to meet at 6.45 at Jewel bar on Glasshouse Street. She said she was going to try and fit in a bit of Christmas shopping first.' Paul looked to Maddy for confirmation.

'Yes, that's right,' she nodded.

'As you were leaving the flat, did you notice anyone suspicious, either in the building, or outside on the street?'

Paul thought for a moment. Then shook his head. 'No, not that I can recall.'

'Please, think hard. It's vital that you play back every minute of this afternoon in your mind. Try and remember every step you took as you left the flat. Perhaps you let someone in the communal entrance? Someone you didn't know, but who claimed to be visiting a neighbour of yours. Perhaps you failed to close the door properly?'

Paul cupped his mug, his forehead knotting as he tried to think. 'I'm sorry,' he said, 'I really don't remember seeing anyone or anything unusual. Whoever it was must have been watching in secret, waiting for me to leave before getting in. And I definitely closed the door. I always make a point of checking it's locked.'

'How the hell did he get in then?' Maddy asked in exasperation. 'Or know that Paul was going out?'

'Ms Kramer...' It amused Maddy the way Carver continued to address her with careful formality; it may have been standard police procedure, but somehow it felt like they'd crossed that stage, so much had happened. '...we know this killer is highly intelligent and technically proficient. Breaking into your home isn't rocket science for someone like that.'

Maddy still wasn't happy. 'Okay, I get the breaking-in part. But was the killer just waiting around all day, hoping that Paul would go out at some point? If not, doesn't that mean it's someone we know? Someone familiar with our movements, who knows we live together, what we get up to?'

'Mads,' Paul cut in, 'we're young single people. The odds are pretty high that we'd both be out on a Friday night, particularly at this time of the year.'

Carver nodded. 'He's right, Ms Kramer.'

Maddy sagged back in her chair. 'I suppose so,' she grunted. But inside she wasn't convinced.

Carver got up. 'We'll speak to your neighbours and check the CCTV for anything suspicious.' He held Maddy's gaze, and she saw the compassion in his eyes. It comforted her – marginally, at least. 'For now, sit tight, and try and get some rest.'

'Thanks, but I can't see myself getting much rest.'

Paul wrapped his arm protectively around Maddy's waist. 'I'm nervous too, Mads. But at least we've got each other.'

Carver screeched to a halt at a red light. Watched a fox scamper across his line of vision, stopping to glance his way. It seemed to glower at him, opening its mouth wide to reveal razor-sharp teeth, its eyes glinting in the darkness, daring Carver to edge closer. *Come on, come closer, I dare you. You're no match for me*, it seemed to be saying.

Carver turned to Drake in the passenger seat.

'The killer's taunting us, Drake. Wants us to feel like we're making progress, only to shove it right back in our faces, the smug shit. Gets a kick out of it.'

'I don't think it can be the wife, sir, do you?'

'No,' Carver said as he pulled away and shifted into second from first. 'The only explanation would be if she's getting someone else to do the dirty work for her. But somehow I doubt it.'

'And Stirling?'

'That one continues to baffle me. I mean, we know he has a propensity to violence against women and was short on mummy love. Plus, he refused to tell us where he was the afternoon of Coleridge's murder.'

'*But*, sir?'

'*But*, his criminal record is squeaky clean. The man's in his forties, and we know from his wife that he's been a womaniser since his Oxford days, most probably before. Why start killing now? Why risk everything he's worked for? I mean, he could just be a very good actor, but he seems genuinely rattled. Most serial killers have the emotional age of an infant – incapable of connecting their crimes with the consequences, while some profess to have no memory at all of the murders. Something just doesn't fit where Stirling's concerned. The problem is, we have nothing else to go on.'

Saturday, 11 a.m. Maddy knew she shouldn't be doing this, but she couldn't help herself. The lack of progress frustrated her, while the break-in had been the last straw. Initially frightened by the killer's message, now she was just plain furious. She needed to face Stirling herself. Look into his eyes and demand the truth.

She didn't know if he'd be home. She just hoped that if he was, his wife wasn't. She knew she could have waited; stormed his office first thing Monday morning. But she couldn't hold off that long. She was too keyed up, despite barely getting any rest. It had gone 3 a.m. by the time forensics had finished up at her flat. And even the four hours' sleep she'd got after that had been scrappy.

She reached Stirling's front door, inhaled deeply and rang the bell. She waited a couple of minutes, her insides churning as she hovered from one foot to the other, but there was no answer.

'Damn,' she muttered. She tried again. Still nothing. Pissed off that she'd clearly had a wasted journey and no doubt faced another sleepless night ahead of her, she was about to leave when the door opened. It was Stirling.

At first, he looked at her with a perplexed expression, as if trying to put a name to a face. Then, recognition hit. 'I know you. You're Madeline Kramer. I used to teach you.'

He was still attractive. But now there was also a haggard look about him.

'Yes, that's right,' she said matter-of-factly. 'May I come in?'

Slight ambivalence, then, 'Of course.'

The wife is out, she has to be. He led her through to the living room.

'Please, take a seat. Can I get you something to drink?'

'No, thank you. I shan't be long.'

'So, what can I do for you?'

Maddy got to the point. 'Yesterday, my flat was turned upside down, while I was out.' She studied his face for a reaction.

'God, how terrible.' To his credit, he appeared genuinely shocked. 'Was much taken?'

'No, it was The Scribe – the scumbag who's been bumping off your ex-students. I've been helping DCI Carver with his investigation.' Her eyes searched Stirling's. She saw fear, rather than guilt.

'How do you know it was him?'

'He left me a message, warned me to stop helping the police. His second warning to me in fact. This is the first.' She held out her copy of the killer's letter to her. Stirling read it in silence, then looked up. He had the same look of fear.

'How awful. You must be terrified.'

'I was, at first. Now I'm just pissed off.'

Fear turned to discomfort. Stirling wriggled in his seat, still holding the letter. Maddy continued to glare at him. Then went for it.

'Is it you? Did you write that letter, ransack my flat, kill those women? I need you to tell me the truth.'

Her heart was in her mouth as she asked the question. If it was him, she knew she might not walk out of there alive. And even if she did, her days would surely be numbered.

Stirling leaned towards her, making her jolt. He kept his eyes on her as he said, 'No, it's not me.'

She'd been granted a momentary reprieve. Could breathe again. 'Why should I believe you?'

'Because I'm not a murderer. I'm no angel, you know that. Hell, I'm not afraid to admit it. But I'm not capable of murder; I have no motive to murder. And you must know that I don't resent you for turning me down that time when you were my student. But I don't blame you for thinking that's what the author of this letter is getting at. Somehow, I can't for the life of me think how he knows you turned me down.' He paused, then said again, 'I didn't write this, and I didn't murder those women.'

Maddy scanned the room. Saw the piano, the cello, the CD rack resting in the corner. He followed her gaze.

'It's not me,' he repeated with imploring eyes. 'Despite what little evidence they have may suggest.' Maddy returned his gaze and nodded. She was pretty sure he was telling the truth. 'Okay, thanks for seeing me.'

Stirling walked her to the front door. 'I want the police to find this maniac as much as you do.'

She smiled. 'That's good to hear.'

He opened the door, and she stepped outside.

'Goodbye, Madeline, and say hello to Paul for me. He's lucky to have a flatmate like you.'

He'd shut the door before Maddy had fully registered what he'd said. She stood stationary, his words ringing in her ears. Planting a seed of doubt.

How the hell did he know that she and Paul lived together?

'Idiot!' Stirling smacked his forehead with the palm of his hand as he lumbered upstairs.

He'd been doing so well. She'd believed him. He'd seen it in her eyes. And then he'd gone and ruined things. She was a smart girl, who didn't miss a thing. She would immediately wonder how he knew she and Paul King lived together. It wasn't something he'd have remembered from four years ago. And even if he had, which was a long shot, why would he have assumed they still lived together?

He'd slipped up and dug a hole for himself. The question was, how was he going to dig himself out of it?

'You shouldn't have put yourself in danger like that. It's not your job to question Stirling, it's mine.' Her phone pressed against her ear as she walked home from the station, Maddy let Carver have his say. She knew he'd be riled by her visiting Stirling, but she didn't want him hearing about it from Stirling himself. The last thing she wanted was to appear sneaky by going behind his back. She respected him, and she hoped the feeling was mutual.

‘I understand what you’re saying, but whether you like it or not, I’m in this. Deep. My best friend was murdered, and the same bastard ransacked my home and sent me two threatening messages. I can’t sleep, I can’t eat. I had to see Stirling face-to-face. Ask him point blank.’

There was a pause, and she heard Carver sigh. Finally, he said more gently, ‘And what did you think?’

‘I had thought he was telling the truth.’

‘Had?’

Maddy explained Stirling’s parting comment. ‘How could he have known that we live together? Even if he did by some remote chance remember that we moved in together at the end of our first year, why would he presume that we’re still flatmates?’

‘People assume things all the time.’

‘Hmm, maybe.’ Maddy wasn’t sold. ‘Has your team come back with anything?’

‘I was actually about to pick up the phone to you on that. Unfortunately, nothing suspicious was caught on CCTV. There was also no sign of tampering with your phone, and no fingerprints or DNA found in the flat aside from yours and Paul’s.’

‘You’re kidding!’ Maddy stopped cold. It was frustrating beyond belief. *How could that be?*

‘I’m sorry not to have better news. I’m having your phone couriered over to you as we speak.’

‘Okay, thanks. Keep me posted.’

‘I will. And no more playing detective. Not without me by your side. Is that clear?’

Maddy couldn’t stop a smile from creeping up.

‘Ms Kramer, are you listening?’

‘Yes, yes, I’m listening. I promise.’

Thankfully for Maddy, but unfortunately for Carver, he couldn’t see that she’d crossed her fingers behind her back.

Chapter Twenty-Eight

Christmas came and went with no more murders. It was now 29 December.

Carver waved and smiled at his son through his car window. Outwardly, he appeared serene. Inside, he was raging. Daniel had been staying over the last two days, and he'd just dropped him back at Rachel's. She'd been remarkably civil on the phone when they'd spoken on Boxing Day and she'd agreed, to Carver's surprise, that he could have Daniel for a couple of nights. They'd been to a West Ham game, made pizza, watched action movies back to back, kicked a ball around in the park. Carver had loved every second of it, and the tears in his son's eyes as they'd hugged each other goodbye had told him he had too. It was the best feeling in the world.

The terms of the custody arrangement were that he could have Daniel for one night a week only. Even then, Rachel usually made a fuss about how unsettling it was for their son. He should have known she was up to something. And now he knew what.

Fucking Carl had only gone and proposed to Rachel on Christmas Eve under the sodding mistletoe. *The cheesy bastard.* Naturally, she'd said yes. And now Carl would have every right to insist on Daniel calling him "Dad".

Rachel had dropped this bombshell as her ex was about to walk away from her doorstep, having instructed poor Daniel not to utter a word to his father while he was staying with him, because she had wanted to break the exciting news to him herself.

Carver drove away. His mind distracted, he nearly missed the lights turn red, and pulled up sharp. As he did, his phone rang inside his trouser pocket. With some effort, he extracted it and saw that it was the station. He quickly switched it to hands-free. 'Yes?' The lights changed, and he sped off.

'Sir, it's Drake.'

'Yes?' Carver repeated.

'I'm on duty today, sir, and I noticed something interesting that came in for you this morning.'

'What?' Carver asked less brusquely, his interest piqued. He knew Drake wouldn't be calling for nothing.

'A brown manila envelope with a typed label.'

Without signalling, Carver pulled in quickly to the side of the road, inciting the wrath of the white van driver behind him who gave a protracted honk of his horn, before shooting Carver an angry glare and the V-sign as he drove past. Carver took no notice, his mind absorbed by the implications of what Drake had just said.

'Open it,' he ordered.

'It's on your desk in your office. I'm on my way now.'

Carver sat restlessly as he listened to the sound of Drake's footsteps plod across the station floor, activity going on all around him. Then, sensing Drake had come to a standstill outside his office, he heard him open then close the door, blocking out the extraneous noise. This was followed by an envelope being opened, the rustle of paper being removed and unfolded.

And then the line went quiet. 'What is it, Drake? Tell me, for Christ's sake!'

'I'll read it to you, sir.'

Dear DCI Carver,

I trust you had a good Christmas and enjoyed spending some quality father and son time. There is nothing like the father-son bond, and I commend you for being such a devoted father, who clearly loves his son very much.

Carver froze. The killer had been watching him with Daniel and was now using this as ammunition – emotional blackmail to throw him off the scent, weaken his resolve.

I too have had time to rest and recuperate. And now that I am feeling refreshed, it is time to get back in the game. Are you ready to play, Chief Inspector? I hope so, because here's another riddle for you to solve:

"Competition is warfare. Mostly it is played by prescribed rules – there is a sort of Geneva Convention for competition – but it's thorough and often brutal." (Andrew S. Grove, New Yorker, Oct, 1997)

A qualified legal trooper, she works among the canaries. Sees the office from her bedroom window.

Get a move on, Chief Inspector. New Year's Eve is just around the corner. What better night than that to go out with a bang?

Silence.

'Sir? You still there, sir?'

'Still here, Drake. Canary Wharf?'

'That was my thinking. Are you coming in?'

'Yes. I'll call Kramer on the way. Meantime, brief the team. We don't have much time to figure this out.'

The killer gazed up at the second-floor decked balcony from the edge of the picturesque marina. It was a lovely spot, situated in a modern gated development in Limehouse, geared towards young, successful professionals wanting a convenient yet fashionable home to base themselves in.

It was amazing how anyone could just walk in, look around. It was going to be trickier getting into the block itself, but not insurmountable. It was astonishing how trusting neighbours could be; letting in strangers who claimed to be visiting friends without batting an eyelid.

Especially at this time of the year, what with goodwill to all men and all that sugary crap.

And who wouldn't trust the pleasant, respectable visitor standing by the waterside at that moment, holding a bouquet of flowers and wearing a friendly smile?

The target had momentarily appeared on the balcony, dressed in a powder-blue fleece dressing gown, cupping her hands around a mug, gazing out at the rows of pretty yachts resting peacefully on the water.

And then he had joined her. Surprised her from behind. Wrapped his arms around her waist, planted a warm kiss on her left cheek. And then she had turned around, wrapped her own arms around his neck, kissed him passionately on the mouth. And he had taken her hand, guided her back into the flat, before closing the sliding doors and shutting them away from the outside world.

The killer's eyes narrowed with envy. Then, sickened by what they were clearly about to get up to, channelled the anger brewing inside for a higher purpose.

The girl had today off, but she'd be back in the office tomorrow. No one ever did much work between Christmas and the New Year. So, unless you had a family, it was a waste of holiday. Much better to go in and pretend to work, illicitly scrolling the online sales, watching the clock until home time, which was usually no later than 3 p.m. during the holiday season.

Like so many others, she'd be back home early on New Year's Eve, the day after tomorrow, giving her plenty of time to get ready for the busiest party night of the year.

Only this year, she wouldn't be partying.

Her partying days were over.

'I knew it wouldn't be long before you called.' Maddy was lying on the sofa, feet dangling over the armrest, Atticus nestled in the small gap underneath. She muted the TV and sat up. Felt the tension, which had been simmering under a superficial veil of holiday cheer, return with a vengeance.

Just for a short time, she'd allowed herself to relax in the company of the two people she loved most – Paul and her grandmother – almost forgetting the darkness veiling her life. 'Somehow, I'd managed to push all that's happened to the back of my mind. I knew it was wishful thinking, though. The pattern is unfinished. There has to be more.'

Carver listened patiently, allowed her to vent the worry and fear he'd reignited in her with his call. Finally, he spoke.

'I'm sorry to break your holiday spirit, Ms Kramer, but I could really do with your help again. I understand that you might be reluctant after the break-in, but—'

'No, it's fine,' Maddy cut in. 'I keep picturing Coleridge's face. He's lost his only daughter, and I'm not sure he'll ever recover. I know all about loss. I know how much it hurts, how it changes you forever. We can't allow others to suffer like him and his family. We can't let the killer win.'

Carver was again blown away by Maddy's tenacity. In all his years on the force, he hadn't come across anyone like her. She wasn't a police officer, and yet she had so much courage; willing to stand up to a monster who'd murdered her best friend, threatened her life and violated her home. 'You're a brave young woman, Ms Kramer. Coleridge is lucky to have someone like you on his team. I'll text you the riddle now. Can you stay on the line?'

'Sure, I'm not doing much.'

It was true. Since getting back from her grandmother's the day before, she'd mostly lounged around the flat in her pyjamas, eating too much, watching too much TV. Paul had come back with her but wasn't around at night; he needed the extra money and was working every evening shift at the bar between the 27th and 31st.

Maddy waited anxiously for Carver's text to come through. When it did, she read it quickly first. Then again, more carefully.

'Well, figuring out where she works, and the subject, is pretty easy,' she finally said.

'Canary Wharf?'

'Yes, has to be. And I'm pretty certain the subject is EU.'

'European Union?'

'Uh-huh. Have you Googled this Andrew S. Grove guy?'

'Yes. He's a Hungarian-born American businessman, and the former CEO of Intel Corporation.'

'Ah, that makes even more sense then.'

'It does?'

'The killer talks about "competition". Although the quote's not specifically about competition law, it seems to be saying that competition between companies is a type of war, and therefore something which brings competition law into play. Competition is one of the main subjects we studied as part of the EU module on the GDL. It's all about maintaining market competition by regulating anti-competitive conduct by companies.'

'So how would that translate into practice? I mean in terms of how or where the murder might take place?'

Maddy thought for a while. She was on a roll, the challenge before her sweeping aside her initial gloom. Even so, she told herself not to rush, not if she wanted to get this right. 'So far, the victims have either worked in an area related to the subject inscribed – Sarah Morrell and Lisa Ryland – or in a building related to the subject – Emma Marsden – or they've been killed by a physical affliction related to the subject – Natasha Coleridge. They weren't all lawyers: Coleridge was still a student and Marsden a librarian. But as we know, they all attended the academy. And they were all taught by Professor Stirling.'

'So, you think we're looking at three different possibilities? Practice area, physical landmark or physical affliction?'

'That's my theory. As far as physical landmarks go, I guess it's possible the killer plans on striking in or around an EU-related attraction or site, but if we're right about location, I can't think of anything that falls under that category in Canary Wharf. As for physical afflictions, there's no disease or sickness related specifically to EU law I can think of.'

'Apart from the mental cruelty of being tied to the French and the Germans, of course?' Carver attempted to inject some humour into the conversation.

'Apart from that,' Maddy chuckled. He was funny as well as smart and attractive. *Don't go there.*

'So that leaves practice area?'

'Yes.' Neither spoke for a while until Maddy's cry of recognition nearly punctured a hole in Carver's eardrum. 'How could I have been so stupid!'

'What?'

'I've already mentioned it. Competition!'

'Still not following.'

'UK competition law is shaped by both UK and EU elements, and "competition" is an area of legal expertise offered particularly by the larger firms in the City and Canary Wharf. It can be a stand-alone department, or one element of an overarching department, for example, the Corporate department.'

'So you think the next victim is a competition lawyer?'

'That's my best guess. The killer calls her a *qualified* legal trooper, so she can't be a trainee.'

'Why trooper? What's he getting at there?' Carver asked the question more to himself, rather than to Maddy, not necessarily expecting her to have the answer. But she did.

'The killer's just continuing the same war terminology. He refers to competition as warfare. Hence, the victim is one of the "troops" engaged in this warfare. A legal trooper.'

Carver understood. 'Brilliant, Ms Kramer.'

Maddy grinned widely. She was glad Carver wasn't there in person to see it. She cleared her throat. 'That's all by the by. What we need to do is concentrate on potential victims who work in Canary Wharf-based firms.'

'Are there many of them?'

'Enough to make life difficult.'

'Damn. That's what I was afraid of. Once we have a list of names, we've then got to figure out where they live. It's the holiday season. They could be anywhere.'

'Let's take this one step at a time. Give me a couple of hours. I'll fire up my laptop and see which firms based at Canary Wharf have a competition department. I'll also try and put together a list of partners and associates who work in competition from the firms' websites. Some firms only list partners on their websites, in which case I'll need to go on to the Law Society database and try and locate the relevant names from there. As I said, the killer makes it clear this victim is qualified, so I think we can safely rule out trainees.'

'Great, I can't thank you enough, Ms Kramer. I'm heading to the office now. Text me once you have something.'

'I will. Maybe we won't be too late this time.'

'I hope so. But I can't help worrying the killer's got something else up his sleeve – something we haven't thought of.'

'We can only do our best.'

But that was exactly what Carver was secretly afraid of. He was afraid that their best wasn't going to be good enough.

Maddy spent the next two hours researching law firms based in and around Canary Wharf. There were lots. Four had competition departments. She was able to get the names of some competition associates and partners from the firms' websites. But as she'd suspected, not all of them listed their associates, so she was forced to go on to the Law Society's website to locate the remaining names. Once she had all the information she needed, she drew four columns on a piece of paper. She then wrote the name of each firm at the top of each column and listed every qualified lawyer who worked in the competition department of each underneath.

Taylor & Brant's competition department had six partners and four associates. Four were female.

Rider Freedman's had three partners and two associates. Two were female.

Cooper Bateman's had five partners and three associates. Three were female.

Jenson Mason's had six partners and five associates. Five were female.

All four firms were in the heart of Canary Wharf, either on Bank Street or Canada Square.

Fourteen women in total. Fourteen potential victims to track down and speak to. One of them was the killer's target, but which one?

Chapter Twenty-Nine

Carver's team spent the next twenty-four hours tracking down the fourteen women Maddy had found. Of them, six were partners, the rest associates. None of the partners had attended the academy, while four of the eight associates – all more senior than Maddy – had. Two of the partners were at their London homes, the other four on vacation. Although the killer had indicated that the next victim lived close to her office, and it seemed logical to focus on ex-academy students, Carver didn't take any chances. He sent officers to alert each partner and associate that they might be in danger and arranged for their protection until the New Year, planting teams in lookout stations to watch for anything suspicious.

The associates were easier to find. All eight lived east.

But all the time, Carver couldn't help thinking it was too easy. They were missing something, but he couldn't think what.

'I'm going to spend New Year's at Cara's if that's okay with you?'

30 December, 7 p.m. Maddy tore off a slice of the large pepperoni pizza she and Paul had ordered, continuing their run of unhealthy eating over the holiday season. In her mind, she pledged to get fit in the New Year. She could feel an extra inch at her sides. Usually, she swam or ran three or four times a week, but what with work, and becoming embroiled in Carver's investigation, she'd had neither the time nor the inclination.

'Yeah, course, why wouldn't it be? I'm only going to be working all bloody night at the bar. So, what time are you planning on heading to Cara's?'

'About sevenish. When does your shift start?'

'Six.'

'Will you remember to put some food and milk out for Atticus' breakfast when you get back? I don't want him going hungry, and I expect you'll be sleeping in.'

'That's for certain,' Paul said. 'Course, no problem.'

'Thanks. Not sure I'm going to be able to relax, though. Even at Cara's. I can't help thinking I've missed something. Carver's got men set up to guard all fourteen women tomorrow, but somehow it seems too easy.'

Paul put his beer down on the table then edged along the sofa closer to Maddy. He looked into her eyes, as if working up the courage to say something important. It made her anxious. 'Look, don't get freaked out or anything, but I think I was followed this morning.'

'What?' She sat up as straight as an arrow, alarm sweeping across her face. 'What makes you say that?'

'It was just a feeling I had. When I left the building, I saw this guy across the road. He was wearing a long leather coat and a baseball cap. It was raining hard, so I couldn't make out his face properly. But there was something suspicious about him. And then I saw him get into the same Tube as me, only a few carriages down. He definitely glanced in my direction, then quickly looked away as if he was worried I'd spotted him.'

'God. Do you think it could have been Stirling?'

'I really couldn't say,' Paul shrugged, a helpless look on his face.

'We have to tell Carver.'

'Hang on, that's not everything.'

Maddy's face fell. *And he's told me not to freak out?* 'How do you mean?'

Paul got up and disappeared from the room. Less than thirty seconds later, he reappeared, holding a piece of paper.

'What's that?'

'Read it.'

She took it from him and began to read:

Dear Paul,

I apologise for wrecking your flat, but the fact of the matter is I am growing sick and tired of your flatmate's meddling in my business. She doesn't seem to want to take my warnings seriously, so I thought maybe you could knock some sense into her? You seem like a nice guy, and I know you care for your best friend deeply.

I know you wouldn't want to see anything bad happen to her.

She's not like the others, and was never part of my plan, but I'm starting to have a change of heart. Don't make me take her life along with the others. My patience is wearing thin.

Stop her before it's too late.

For a while, Maddy didn't speak. She felt numb as her eyes wandered over the page. It was the same font and line spacing the killer had used in his letters to Carver and to her.

'We *have* to take this to Carver!' She finally came alive, waving the letter in the air. Her reaction amazed Paul. In her eyes, he saw resolve, rather than fear. He hadn't expected that.

'Do you reckon? Aren't you scared? Maddy, your life is in danger. Serious danger. It's all there in black and white. Somehow, the killer knows you're still helping Carver. You'll be next on the list if you don't stop. Please, I beg you. I just want you to think straight for a minute.'

'I am thinking straight, Paul. Whoever it is, I think, deep down, they're afraid – afraid we're getting close. Now, will you call Carver, or will I?'

Paul saw that she wasn't about to backtrack. If anything, she seemed more determined. There was no point arguing. She'd made up her mind and there was nothing he could do to stop her.

'I will,' he said resignedly. 'Do you have his number?'

Maddy grabbed her phone, dialled Carver's number, then passed it to Paul. 'You're doing the right thing. We can't let this lowlife get the better of us.'

Wednesday 31 December 2014, 9 a.m.

It had started to snow, and Carver was glad to be in the warmth of his office. He studied the five pieces of paper he'd laid out on his desk: the killer's three letters to him, plus his letters to Maddy Kramer and Paul King. The type of paper used was identical: everyday HP A4-sized. And as Maddy had pointed out on the phone earlier, the font and line spacing matched.

He buried his head in his hands, his temples throbbing. It was only 9 a.m., but he felt like a whisky to take the edge off. A dark, slippery slope he warned himself not to go down.

Focus! Focus!

He thought back to his conversation with Paul King the night before. It was obvious how much Maddy meant to him, and Carver had tried his best to assuage Paul's fears for her safety, while keeping his own fears buried. Because in his mind, Carver knew Maddy was placing herself in grave danger by continuing to help him. Short of placing her under the protection of an armed bodyguard 24/7, he had no way of guaranteeing her safety.

They just had to hope the killer got sloppy.

The killer stared at Atticus, faltering slightly, having worked up the resolve to go through with this unfortunate, but necessary, diversion in the plan. The cat had never done the killer any harm, was innocent in all of this. But like Frank, he was a tragic victim of circumstance.

'Come here, puss puss.' Atticus, sensing a warm cuddle, possibly some full-fat milk, walked obligingly towards the killer, who scooped him up, stroked his fur then, with closed eyes, plunged the knife into his pulsing side.

It didn't give the killer any pleasure, but Maddy Kramer had had enough warnings, and she had no one to blame but herself.

Maddy dived into the pool and immediately felt calmer. In the water, she was free, all the muscle tension and nervous energy floating away with each stroke, her mind less cluttered.

It was midday on New Year's Eve. She'd felt jumpy from the moment she woke up, worrying about the coming evening, whether her efforts to save the next victim had been good enough.

The pool was quiet, and it was heaven. She was a strong swimmer, having competed for her school, and she swam fifty lengths front crawl in under twenty minutes. Pushing herself harder with every length, even as she felt her thighs and arms begin to tire and burn. That was the way she was: she couldn't stand to admit defeat. She pushed herself to the limit, constantly, in everything she did. It was a strength and a weakness, because although it had brought her success, it was also draining. It meant she was never content, never satisfied with her lot in life, always striving for something bigger and better that surely had to be out there. That would surely make her happier.

Her swim over, she reluctantly got out of the pool. Her suit clung to her like a second skin as she stood under the tepid poolside shower to wash off the chlorine. She'd grab her stuff from the locker, quickly dry herself, then take a proper shower at home. The automated shower tailed off. She scrunched out the excess water from her hair and left the warmth of the pool area for the cooler temperature of the changing room. Shivering, she removed the locker key attached to the elastic band she'd fixed to her wrist and inserted it in the locker. She turned the key, opened the door, screamed, then passed out.

When she came around, two staff members were standing over her, looking concerned. As she took in her surroundings, she realised she was lying on a bed in the first aid room. They had wrapped a towel around her, but she was still freezing, with her damp hair and suit.

The side of her head pounded, making her wince. And then she remembered; felt an overwhelming terror, then grief. Atticus was gone. Her beautiful boy. Dead. A cut in his left side, giving off a grotesque odour. *How did the killer know about him? How?* It had to be Stirling. He knew where she and Paul lived. He'd broken in for a second time and killed her darling boy.

'I have to go,' she said, her eyes roaming the room as she tried to raise herself up. Her legs felt shaky, the pain in her head still intense, making her feel queasy. 'My cat,' she said, blinking back tears.

'It's okay, sweetheart, stay still for a while. We've called the paramedics to check you over.'

'I don't need checking over,' Maddy protested, on the verge of hysteria.

'You fell and banged your head. It's a precaution. We are obliged to make sure you're okay under health and safety regulations. Is there someone I can call?'

Maddy looked up at the man called Rob, according to his name badge. His face was caring, but his tone was firm. It was clear she had no choice but to wait and get checked out.

'Paul, my flatmate. His number's in my mobile, in my gym bag.' She glanced right, saw her bag propped up against the wall. Rob followed her gaze, went over to retrieve her phone. As he did, Maddy said, 'My cat, did you see him in the locker?' Tears rolled down her cheeks. 'Someone murdered him.'

'Shush,' Rob said. 'It's all taken care of.'

'What do you mean? I need to say goodbye. I need to bury him.' Maddy suddenly couldn't breathe. Was she having a panic attack? It felt like a mountain of bricks was crushing her chest.

'Calm down, love, you'll be able to bury your cat, don't worry. Just lie down for now and try and take some deep breaths. I'll call your friend.'

Two hours later, Paul guided Maddy into their flat. She still felt dazed, a little unsteady on her feet. And still unable to grasp her latest loss.

The paramedics had carried out various tests. She was in excellent shape, aside from her blood pressure being a little on the high side, but that was to be expected.

No sooner had Paul received Rob's call, than he dashed to Maddy's side. As Maddy had become more lucid, she'd asked if they could take Atticus home with them. She wanted to give him a proper burial, say goodbye.

But assuming The Scribe was to blame – and there wasn't any doubt in Maddy's mind that he was – Atticus was now a part of Carver's murder investigation and needed to be examined by forensics. She'd called Carver as the paramedics stuck twelve electrodes to her chest for a routine ECG. He'd come straight away, startled by the news, and informed Rob that his leisure centre would need to be temporarily closed so that a proper sweep of the premises could be carried out.

He'd reassured Maddy that his men were guarding the fourteen women, and that he'd do everything in his power to catch the killer before the New Year was in. But it didn't help much. Atticus' death had shaken her up badly, and she felt crushed by guilt.

Her beloved cat had never been part of the equation, but he'd ended up paying the price for her interference.

Chapter Thirty

At 3.55 on New Year's Eve, Bethany Williams trudged up the stairs to the third floor of her apartment building, inwardly cursing the maintenance men for not getting the lift back in order. Small-boned, she had delicate features and slender hips. But soon that would change. If she felt like this now, still trim and making her three sessions a week with her personal trainer, goodness knows how she'd feel in six months' time. No doubt fat, breathless, and unable to see her feet.

Although *he'd* disapproved of her decision to have the baby, it wasn't *his* decision to make. She was the one growing life inside her, and she knew that she could never bring it upon herself to willingly kill her baby. Yes, it should never have happened. But it had. And maybe it would end up being the best mistake she'd ever made.

Unlike *him*. He'd been a mistake. Even though she loved him. Couldn't resist seeing him, kissing him, making love to him. She'd known all along that he'd never leave his wife for her. Even now, pregnant with his child. He'd always been the same. For the entire eight years they'd known each other. Unable to resist his urges, moving from one girl to another, as if trying to fill a void. A void that no one, not even his wife, not even the woman carrying his longed-for baby, could fill. It was innate. As fixed as the moon in the sky.

She hadn't told anyone else yet, not even her best friend, Juliet. She was only just over the twelve-week mark, and it being her first pregnancy, wasn't yet showing. Luckily, she'd barely had any nausea, just the odd day here and there and a bit of heartburn, but nothing so bad as to attract attention. But tonight was going to be tricky. Juliet was having a house party, where the alcohol would be flowing and anyone not drinking would stick out like a sore thumb. Until now, she'd used work pressures, menstrual migraines and a tummy bug to avoid meeting up with her friends whenever booze was involved.

But she hadn't missed seeing in the New Year with Juliet since 2009. Getting out of it would arouse suspicion. Plus, knowing the man she loved would be spending the evening with his wife upset her. She didn't want to be home alone, drinking orange juice in front of Jools Holland; feeling sorry for herself. She needed company to take her mind off how complicated her life had become.

She turned the key in her door and felt for the switch inside. The thing she loved most about where she lived was that she felt secure. The gated system ensured she was never afraid that some lunatic might be lying in wait for her. She'd read so many stories in the press about people being attacked in their own homes. And now, more recently, the police were hunting a serial killer they were calling The Scribe. At first, she'd been frightened by reports that he appeared to be targeting ex and current female students at her former law school. But the father of her child had allayed her fears, told her to think sensibly. Hundreds of female students walked through the academy's doors each year. Bethany had been one of them – one of many – and that was getting on for nine years ago. Logically, it made no sense for the killer to target her. He told her she had more chance of being run over by a bus.

Her fears placated, Bethany had tried not to think any more of it. She focussed on her work, her friends and the life growing within her.

Once inside her flat, she removed her coat and gloves and headed straight for the open plan kitchen-diner. She grabbed the TV remote on her way and pointed it in the direction of the 46-inch plasma mounted on the far wall. A man's face immediately appeared. She recognised him. He was the detective leading the investigation into The Scribe murders. He was attractive. But he had a weary look about him as he warned the public to be vigilant, particularly as they had reason to believe another attack was imminent.

Bethany shuddered and switched channels. Some corny Christmas movie appeared. A much better alternative to the grim news. She flipped the switch on the kettle, turned on the radio and contemplated what to wear that evening. This time next year, if she hadn't lost the baby weight, she might not fit into one of her slinky dresses. She decided she might as well make the most of her wardrobe while she had the chance.

She turned around and saw two eyes looking at her, gleaming, like black jewels. She dropped the mug she was holding but scarcely heard it crash to the tiled floor, smashing to pieces around her feet. She attempted to scream but a gloved hand was suddenly there, preventing her. Aside from the eyes, the killer's face was masked by a balaclava. She made out a broad body sheathed in a long black leather coat and Nike trainers. They looked brand new. It was The Scribe. She was sure of it. She remembered reading about the Nike trainers in the press.

The killer gestured for her to be silent. She nodded, trembling. Slowly, the killer released her mouth, then took her by the arm, dragging her towards her bedroom. And that's when she heard classical music – closer and closer, louder and louder. And then, once inside her bedroom, she noticed a red MP3 player lying on her bedside table. It was playing Mozart's *Requiem*.

It reminded her of *him*.

She looked in horror at her bed. Rope cords were tied to each corner. The maniac was going to tie her up. *And then what?*

'Please, don't hurt me,' she begged. 'Why are you doing this? I'll give you money, just tell me how much.'

The killer didn't respond, and Bethany was suddenly beside herself with fear. She thought about the life inside her. Pressed one hand to her belly, felt her pelvis tighten. Even though she'd yet to meet him or her, she already felt a love like nothing she'd experienced before, and knew that she would do anything to protect her child.

She tried to wriggle free from her attacker's grasp, despite knowing it was hopeless. The killer was too strong, yanking her fiercely by the arm and throwing her onto the mattress, one hand pressed down on her belly, while the other tied a piece of rope around one of her wrists to the far right corner of the bed. Now, she had no chance of escape. The killer did the same with her other wrist and ankles, then used a pair of scissors to cut her clothes down to her black lace bra. Then the killer paused, eyeing her cleavage, before slowly cutting the join between both bra cups. She lay there, half-naked, like a human sacrifice. Her heart thumped with fear, everything that was her life flashing before her.

'Please, don't do this,' she pleaded, crazy with panic, tears streaming down her hot cheeks.

The killer worked quickly, methodically, as if engaged in a time-critical intellectual challenge. The leather gloves were removed, revealing slender fingers and neatly filed nails, which then reached into a black rucksack lying on the floor and pulled out a pair of latex gloves. The killer put them on, then delved into the rucksack once again.

Bethany's stomach lurched on seeing what was produced this time: a syringe and a clear solution in a glass phial. The killer expertly filled the syringe with the fluid, then leaned over her. She smelt a distinctive aftershave. Like James wore. Why did the killer not speak? She at least wanted to hear a voice.

At that moment, the love for her unborn baby superseded any fear for her own safety. 'Speak, you motherfucker!' she yelled. 'You cowardly piece of shit. Why don't you speak and show your face?'

She felt the sting of rubber across her cheek. Her violator leaned in closer, aiming the needle sideways underneath her left breast, pausing momentarily as it was lined up exactly where it needed to be, a faint pressure on her skin. And then she felt the needle go in, piercing her flesh, barely five seconds passing before it was removed.

'Why did you do that? What are you going to do to me?' she asked, her voice cracking.

She felt the urge to touch her chest but couldn't. It was as if her skin had gone numb. The killer placed the needle and phial in a polythene bag, before dropping it into the rucksack.

Bethany glanced at the clock on her bedside table. 4.14 p.m. The killer briefly disappeared from the room, then returned with something. Her phone. She watched the killer type something, before laying the phone on the bedside table. A text, an email? 'What were you typing on my phone?' she stammered.

She got no reply.

And then, with the killer's next move, Bethany knew what was coming. Her lover had been wrong. It didn't matter that she'd studied at the academy nine years ago. For some reason, she was on The Scribe's agenda.

The knife didn't look like any ordinary kitchen knife. It had a massive blade with a slightly curved tip. She needed to be sick, but her horizontal position prevented her. She heard the phone ring – recognised the ringtone she'd set for Juliet. She was probably calling to check what time she'd be over.

Knife gripped in one hand, the killer crawled onto the bed, knelt between Bethany's thighs, and towered over her. She saw eyes that were filled with hate and deadly intent. They slowly came closer. She couldn't help but lower her own and watch the gleaming blade slice through her skin. She felt no physical pain –only fear as the killer began to inscribe.

It wasn't a long word to carve. But that was the least of her worries. The worst was not knowing what came next. None of the victims so far had survived.

How did the killer plan to end her life? And the life of the child inside her?

Job done, the killer took a moment to gloat, before placing the soiled knife in a fresh polythene bag, then zipping it up inside the rucksack.

Rucksack slung over one shoulder, the killer walked towards the door, then hovered at the entrance, surveying Bethany with dispassionate eyes.

'You're leaving me like this?' she said. 'You're not going to kill me?'

A flicker of hope ran through her. Maybe the fucker had realised she was pregnant, had decided to take pity on her? She suddenly valued life more than ever. Saw that not being with *him* wasn't the end of the world, that there was so much she should be thankful for. Everyday things she'd taken for granted, sidelined as trivial, but which she now saw as beautiful and a blessing. She could live with being scarred for life if it meant she could go on living her life – be a mother.

She vaguely heard the door close and realised the killer had gone.

She started trembling, conscious that she'd wet herself, the insides of her thighs moist and warm. She wondered if Juliet would start to worry that she wasn't picking up and come over. She imagined this scenario, clung on to it, willing herself to be strong until she was found.

Ten minutes passed before the phone started to ring. Juliet again. Surely now, when she didn't answer, her friend would think something was wrong and come round? It wouldn't be long. She'd soon be—

What's that sound? A faint ticking, somewhere in the bedroom… somewhere to her left. She tried to lean her head that way, pricking her ear to see where it might be coming from. It was close, almost like it was under the bed.

The ticking grew more frantic, and then there was a deafening noise that sent a searing pain through her ears, and a pain through her stomach like nothing she'd felt before.

And then, after a couple of minutes, Bethany felt no more.

The bang was heard all around the apartment complex. And beyond. But it wasn't just the explosion that alerted neighbours and pedestrians. It was the shrill noise of Bethany Williams' smoke alarm that sent people flocking to her flat in Limehouse.

Carver was at the station when the call came through, his mind consumed by thoughts of Maddy. He'd never seen her look so scared, so fragile. He hoped she was doing okay, was strong enough to get over her ordeal. No one suspicious on camera had been caught entering the leisure centre, and the changing rooms weren't covered by CCTV. Forensics were still there, but he wasn't hopeful.

In the last half hour, he'd been liaising with officers stationed at secret hideouts monitoring the homes of the fourteen women, one of whom Maddy believed could be the killer's next victim.

But it was a pointless operation. Carver's heart plummeted when he listened to an officer recount the scene he and a colleague had been called to. Just as he'd feared, the killer had given them false hope, only to outwit them once again. This, his second kill of the day.

The victim – Bethany Williams – had been a former competition lawyer, five years qualified. But for the last year and a half she'd worked as an in-house lawyer at a leading global energy firm whose offices were situated on Bank Street in the heart of Canary Wharf.

...she works among the canaries. Sees the office from her bedroom window.

'Here we are. What you need is alcohol – lots of it.'

Cara came into the compact living room of her one-bedroom apartment, holding two champagne flutes. She handed one to Maddy.

Right now, Maddy felt more secure in Cara's gated community than she did in her own flat.

Yesterday, over the phone, before Atticus' death, they'd decided to have a quiet New Year. It seemed appropriate, in view of recent events, Paige's death particularly, and they had set themselves up for a night of DIY manicures, cocktails and ice cream. But now, still haunted by what happened after that, Maddy was no longer in the mood for such frivolity. She needed company, though. Paul had no choice but to work, and the last thing she wanted was to be alone in their flat. It had been the second time the killer had invaded her home, and it was almost as if she could feel his presence as she went from room to room. She'd also felt the stinging absence of Atticus, seeing his empty basket, food tray, stray hairs all around the flat.

Maddy took the flute gratefully, but her eyes were faraway. She had a sip.

It tasted good. Just what she needed, like Cara said. She simply couldn't switch off, relax. She kept wondering how Carver's stake-out operation was going; whether there'd been any sign of the killer; whether tonight the devil in human form might finally be caught and they could all breathe again.

The track on the radio faded out. It was just on seven, time for the hourly news:

'The body of a woman believed to have been in her early thirties was found this afternoon.'

Maddy straightened. Glancing nervously at Cara, she quickly placed her flute on the coffee table. 'Turn it up,' she said. Cara didn't hesitate. They listened to the announcer in dismal silence:

...following a loud explosion heard coming from a gated apartment complex in Limehouse. Police believe she may be the sixth victim of the serial killer police have been hunting since late October, known as The Scribe. They are again urging members of the public to come forward with any information that may be relevant to the murders.

'Turn it off,' Maddy said bleakly. Cara did as Maddy asked, then came and sat down beside her.

'You did your best,' she said, putting her arm around her friend. 'There's nothing more you could have done.'

Maddy turned to her, tears in her eyes. 'Yes, but how did the police not see the killer, or notice anything suspicious? It's just not possible that he could have walked right in and murdered her without being seen. There's only one explanation. It can't have been any of the women on my list.'

'But you thought you'd found every qualified competition lawyer who worked in the area, didn't you?'

'Yes, but obviously I missed something. I need to know what.' Maddy leapt up from the sofa, grabbed her phone, and dialled Carver's number. It went to voicemail. Frustrated, she didn't bother leaving a message, hung up, then tried again. This time, he answered.

'Ms Kramer, you've heard the news? I'm at the crime scene now. Fucker blew a hole in her stomach.' He sounded shattered.

'Jesus. I just can't believe it. It's like he's a ghost. Who was she?'

'She was a qualified competition lawyer as you predicted. But for the last eighteen months, she'd been working as an in-house lawyer at BP Global, whose offices are in Canary Wharf – which I can see from here, from her apartment balcony.'

'Fuck!' Maddy kicked herself inside for being so dumb, for not thinking outside the box – again. 'I can't believe I only focussed on law firms, on private-practice lawyers. It's all my fault.'

'No, it's not. Don't blame yourself. Look, I've got to go. Don't go anywhere tonight. Where are you? At home?'

'No, I'm at a friend's. After this afternoon, I couldn't face being alone in my flat with Paul working all night.'

'I don't blame you. Stay put. I'll keep you informed.'

'Just one thing,' Maddy managed to get in before Carver hung up. 'I'm guessing it was "EU" on her chest?'

'Yes.'

'Okay. Thank you. I won't hold you up any longer.'

The line went dead – exactly how Maddy felt inside.

Maddy spent the next thirty minutes on the phone to her grandmother and Paul. She needed to make sure they were both okay, her paranoia intensified by this latest tragedy. She didn't tell Rose about Atticus, or Bethany. She didn't want to spoil her New Year. It could wait until tomorrow.

Although the background noise at the bar was deafening, she'd managed a fifteen-minute conversation with Paul, thankful that he too was safe, and comforted by his calming assurances not to worry. In the morning, he'd come get her and they'd go home together.

The rest of the evening passed in a haze, Maddy's already deflated party mood reduced to nothing. She drank to numb her fear rather than celebrate the New Year, and by eleven she'd fallen asleep on Cara's spare bed, unable to welcome the start of 2015 when all she found herself doing was dreading the misery it might bring.

'We believe the killer set off the bomb remotely,' Dominic Avery, the crime-scene manager, explained to Carver as around half a dozen CSOs worked around them. 'The device was attached to the base of the bed.'

Carver cast his eyes around Bethany Williams' bedroom. The air was smoky, thick with dust and fumes, the walls stained black. 'What's your initial thinking?' he asked Grayson, who was bent over the body.

'My initial thinking is that she was alive when the killer carved into her chest. Looking at the neck and upper body, there are no signs of strangulation, or gunshot wounds that would have been fatal. And no lethal cuts to the abdomen or jugular.'

'Might she have died of a heart attack from the pain?'

'It's possible, but unlikely. Eventually, if there'd been no bomb, she would have bled to death of course. But come and see this.' He motioned for Carver to join him on the right side of the trashed bed, then bent down once again over Bethany. 'See this small wound here?' He pointed his index finger to a minor wound on the side of Bethany's left breast.

'Yes.'

'It looks like a needle incision. A fairly fresh one.'

'He injected her?'

'Quite possibly. With an anaesthetic.'

'Why bother?'

'Part of his sick game, no doubt. Once we bag up the body and perform a post-mortem, we'll know more.'

'Okay, thanks, Dr Grayson.' Carver was about to call Drake when his phone buzzed. He fished it out and saw that he had a text. From a number he didn't recognise.

He opened it up and stared at the message:

Sorry, I win, you lose. Again. Maybe you'll have better luck next time. Happy New Year, DCI Carver.

Carver's blood boiled. How the hell did the killer know his mobile number?

Chapter Thirty-One

A few hours before

Elizabeth Stirling studied her husband sitting across from her at the head of the dining table. It had just gone nine on New Year's Eve, and there were at least another three tiresome hours to get through.

She had to admit – he looked incredibly handsome in his black tux, clean-shaven, hair perfectly combed, flashing his famous smile at their dinner guests, the lot of them reminiscing about the good old days at Oxford, the unacceptable state of British politics, the unpredictable economy, the destructive effect of religious extremism, the latest legal developments...

Yawn, yawn, yawn. Elizabeth thought she might die of boredom. She chucked back her red wine in an attempt to block out the monotony of it all.

She didn't much like any of their guests – all wielding massive egos, authorities on everything from famine in Africa to world peace, deeply snobby and totally out of touch with the real world.

But unfortunately for Elizabeth, it had become something of a tradition for them to convene every year for dinner on New Year's Eve. Each couple took it in turn to host. This year, the burden had fallen on the Stirlings.

Lately, her philandering husband had been acting more suspiciously than usual. Although it was the Christmas break, she'd seen even less of him than she did during term time. No doubt spending the time screwing one of his trollops. Although, having said that, he definitely seemed bothered by something. Even with his dragon of a mother, he'd been short-tempered and unresponsive when she'd come over for Christmas lunch.

Something told her his preoccupied state was related to the murders, her hunch fortified by his strange behaviour earlier that evening.

He'd gone out just after 2 p.m., claiming he needed some exercise after all the Christmas excess. But when he returned home around 5.30, far from looking refreshed by his walk, he'd looked harassed. He'd avoided all eye contact with her, and barely spoke.

And then later, when they'd both been in the kitchen, arguing over which reds to put out on the table, he'd become noticeably anxious. The radio had been on, and they'd listened to the news of some girl's murder. She'd watched her husband go pale, before excusing himself to go to the bathroom. She'd followed him on tiptoe, put her ear to the door, heard him throw up. She'd realised then, without question, that the girl had meant something to him, and it had made her loathe him more.

Elizabeth didn't much like herself for it, but she found herself enjoying her husband's discomfort. And as she sat at the dining table and thought about what she'd popped in the post that morning to DCI Carver, it brought a smile to her face despite the dreary company.

She couldn't wait to see her husband's expression when the police came knocking. She still didn't think him capable of murder, but it was fun to try and make the police think that he was.

Friday 2 January 2015

Carver took the small jiffy bag from the postboy and looked at it curiously. He'd barely slept in seventy-two hours, existing on coffee and Pro Plus in the day, and consequently too wired to sleep at night. It was a vicious cycle. He could feel the weight of the bags under his slitty eyes, while every muscle in his body ached as if he'd run a marathon.

Tonight, he'd pop a pill. It was the only way. Without rest, he was no good to anyone. He'd go insane if he didn't shut his mind off from the case that was consuming his brain every waking hour of the day. His technical team was having no luck in tracing the text he'd received from the killer – it was likely, they said, that he had used an unregistered pay-as-you-go phone – and that dead end had only added to Carver's frustration and insomnia.

He ripped open the bag and peered inside. At first, he couldn't see anything. But then, looking more closely, he realised there was something lodged into the fold at the bottom. He reached down and pulled out a memory stick. There was no accompanying note, just the tiny device.

He looked at the handwritten scrawl on the envelope. Black ink, slanting, spidery, it was hard to tell if it was a man's or a woman's. Although the artistic nature of it made him veer towards it being female.

He was almost certain the killer hadn't sent the package, having typed every letter so far. Serial killers were creatures of habit: it would be both illogical and out of character to change the pattern now. More importantly, handwriting could be traced. The killer was too clever to take a chance like that.

Carver inserted the memory stick into his computer. After a few seconds, what then appeared on the screen shocked him to the core. It was Stirling. Lying on a bed, a young blonde straddling his torso, frantically screaming his name as she jigged up and down. It looked like they were in some cheap hotel room. The carpet was a drab dirty beige, the walls decorated with hideous brown and orange wallpaper, while the shoddy nylon curtains barely covered the window. It was the ultimate cliché.

The girl was probably in her early to mid-twenties, her long hair sheathing her back. Stirling's eyes were fixed on her breasts, which he fondled keenly. Carver couldn't quite make out the girl's face, and then, almost like she knew she was being watched, although he suspected she didn't, she turned her head towards the camera. Carver sat back in surprise. It was the latest victim: Bethany Williams. And the date read October 2006.

Every now and again, Stirling would glance at the camera, his eyes triumphant. It appeared that the twisted prick got a kick out of creating secret porno movies for his private gratification.

Once they'd finished having sex, the footage switched to Stirling with a different girl – young and attractive like Williams. As before, he intermittently glanced in the camera's direction, the action swelling to a loud climax.

And it kept going. One after the other. Occasionally, Stirling and the women engaged in kinky sex games. Carver had suspected Stirling was a sex addict, but he hadn't expected it to be quite on this scale.

He pressed the fast-forward button, wondering how long it went on for. But then, something caught his eye. It was the Morrell girl, several times, captured in different sexual positions with Stirling. But there was something about the way he looked at her that was different to the others. Almost a look of love. Maybe not love. Perhaps, infatuation? And there were no sex toys involved. Not only that, he tenderly caressed the side of her head as they had sex, something he didn't do with any of the others. Also allowed the camera to continue filming as they lay in each other's arms in bed. Sometimes enjoying a cigarette as they listened to classical music at Morrell's request.

It was clear that she had never been forced into anything. There was nothing timid or self-effacing about her. She knew what she was doing, and she seemed to be enjoying it. Until, that is, it came to a later rendezvous.

The date on the screen read 3rd April 2010. Carver watched as they went at it like rabbits as before. But then something happened that triggered alarm bells. Morrell told Stirling it was over between them, and he didn't take it well. He struck the back of his hand across her cheek, causing her to fall back onto the bed. She looked both shocked and repulsed, but then gathered herself, threatened to expose him if he did anything to jeopardise her career, before storming out.

There it was. Things had ended badly between them.

It made him wonder. Was Stirling's violent outburst towards Morrell a one-off, or a facet of his nature he couldn't contain – and which he also fulfilled and played out with meaningless gratuitous sex, and violent sex games?

Carver carried on watching, wondering if any of the other victims would make an appearance. They had to, surely?

And then Paige Summers came on screen. The sex was less violent. She seemed shyer than the others. It was obvious she'd been infatuated with Stirling, gazing at him with adoring eyes.

And then Carver reached the moment itself. He watched Paige tell Stirling she loved him. He'd coldly rejected her; put his hands around her neck when she'd continued to beg him not to end things. There was a genuine look of hurt on her face as opposed to the anger and revulsion he'd seen on Morrell's. It was almost pathetic, and he felt sorry for her.

There were many more girls, but neither Emma Marsden nor Lisa Ryland featured. Why was that? Maybe they'd been one-night stands or quickies in his office; who knew? Devereux had certainly been sure that Stirling had only ever had sex with Ryland the one time. Maybe there was another memory stick?

He carried on. Finally, he reached footage of something that knocked him for six. The camera was no longer focussed on some dingy hotel room, but a much more attractively furnished bedroom, with an impressive king-size bed. At the head of it was Stirling. At the foot, was Suzanne Carroll, performing oral sex on him.

Carver cursed under his breath. She'd lied about them only being friends. And now he was certain she'd lied to him about Stirling being with her the night of Lisa Ryland's murder.

He reluctantly watched the rest of the footage, just to make sure he didn't miss anything vital. He didn't. It was more of the same, and he felt sick to the stomach. When he got to the end, he briefed his Chief. Then he assembled his team for an urgent update.

Chapter Thirty-Two

Sunday 4 January 2015

On the first Sunday of the New Year, face hidden behind the latest edition of *Esquire*, snacking on granary toast and a blueberry smoothie, the killer sat at a table by the window of a popular café on Parsons Green Lane, a respectable, mainly residential, area, situated in the London borough of Hammersmith and Fulham.

Reports that the latest victim had been pregnant had been slightly disconcerting. It had to have been early days. She hadn't been showing. The killer took a moment to reflect on whether knowledge of the pregnancy would have made a difference. *Probably not. I've probably done the child a favour,* the killer thought. Saved the poor wretch from entering this sick world, replete with perverts and liars, mothers and fathers who didn't understand what it meant to be parents, who consciously and persistently neglected their children for the sake of satisfying their own self-serving desires. *What kind of a life is that?*

The killer continued to sit, observing the next and final victim from afar as she sipped her latte and tucked into her Eggs Florentine; poring over the *Sunday Times* and its unwieldy supplements like her world depended on it, spectacles perched precariously on the bridge of her unsightly nose as she – every now and again – wiped a smudge of bright yellow yolk from her repellent lips.

Her observer felt like clubbing her to death then and there. *The self-important, horse-faced bitch.* The killer couldn't believe she'd ever made partner; she was so needy and obsessed with a man she could never have. Then again, she was only a Trusts partner in some small-time firm in Putney. She hadn't exactly reached the top of the glamour stakes.

Suzanne Carroll was almost as abhorrent as the first victim. She'd die a fitting death. But not just yet. Not before her two-faced bastard of a lover was behind bars, and her pain would be racked up to the maximum.

Carver played back the footage for his team. The room fell silent as it ran. He didn't play all of it. Focussed on Bethany, Sarah, Paige and Suzanne.

When he'd finished, he pressed Pause. 'This clearly proves that Stirling has a predisposition towards violence against women, and that he was violent towards at least two of the victims while he was sleeping with them. This, together with his father's history of domestic abuse, makes him our strongest suspect. The problem is that he has alibis for the nights of Sarah's and Lisa's murders – from his wife, and from Suzanne Carroll. Carroll's alibi is, however, to be treated with caution because, while she categorically denied ever having had a sexual relationship with Stirling, this footage proves otherwise.'

'Sir, do we know who sent the recording?' Keel asked.

'No, we don't. Although I suspect it could be the wife. She's made it clear she has no love for her husband, despite providing him with an alibi for Morrell's murder. I think she may have been toying with him there – setting him up for a fall. She also told us he's been violent towards her in the past. The question is, do we have enough to bring him in for questioning?'

Just then, Drake, who he'd briefed before, burst in. 'We do now, sir!'

Carver gave him a puzzled look, also wondering whether his voice was so loud that Drake had heard him through the door. 'How so?'

'The forensics report on Williams came back. She had semen in her, and the same DNA was all over her flat.'

Carver's heart rate gathered speed. 'Any idea whose?'

'Stirling's, sir.'

'Jesus!'

'There's something else. They checked her phone log and email account. There were numerous emails between her and Stirling, dating all the way back to the summer. And here's the really interesting part. Williams emailed Stirling around 2 p.m. on New Year's Eve, asking him to meet her on Waterloo Bridge at 3 p.m.'

'Really? The post-mortem suggests she died anytime between 4.30 and 5.00. Waterloo Bridge isn't far from Limehouse. It's perfectly possible they went straight back to hers. None of the neighbours remember seeing her with another man?'

'No, sir, afraid not. It was New Year's Eve. People were either away or already getting hammered.'

'And her phone? Anything interesting there?'

'Yes, sir. She sent a text around 4.15 to her best friend, Juliet, saying she thought Stirling was going to kill her.'

Sunday, 5 p.m. Stirling frantically rummaged through his office drawers. He'd gone in that afternoon mainly to catch up on some paperwork before the start of the spring term.

But also to take his mind off things, and get away from Elizabeth. Although he'd tried not to show it, he'd been devastated by the news of Bethany's death – devastated and panicked. It was all too creepy, all too unreal. He'd only seen her two days before she died, and he was finally coming to terms with the fact that she'd decided to keep the baby.

She'd been adamant, and after the way he'd treated her, like the way he treated most of them, it wasn't his place to deny her that choice. Even though, when she'd first told him back in November, the same afternoon Natasha Coleridge was found murdered, he'd tried to convince her otherwise.

But as he'd driven home that afternoon, he'd found himself smiling. Finally, he was going to be a father. He'd deal with Elizabeth finding out if and when the time came, but at that moment he'd felt like the happiest man alive.

So, when Bethany had emailed around 2 p.m. on New Year's Eve asking him to meet her urgently on Waterloo Bridge at three, he'd gone without hesitation, fearing something was up with the baby, and giving

Elizabeth the excuse that he needed some exercise. He'd wanted to show her that he cared and would be there for her every step of the way.

But she never turned up. He'd waited for almost an hour. He'd called her mobile and landline but got no answer; tried her office, but by then everyone had left for the day. He should have been concerned. Instead, perhaps rather childishly, he'd been pissed off with her for dragging him out in the freezing cold for nothing. He should have gone straight home to Elizabeth, but instead, he'd walked for a while. His life was a mess and he'd wanted to clear his mind, pull himself together, before heading back to his loveless marriage.

But just a few hours later, as he'd listened, stunned, to the news of Bethany's death on the radio, his long-held dream of fatherhood had been shattered. And he'd felt racked with guilt for being angry with Bethany; for abandoning her and his unborn child when, had he gone to her, he might have been able to save her.

And now he was getting scared. All the girls had been his lovers, and none of his affairs had ended on good terms. Somehow, it felt like he was being set up. But by whom? Possibly some jealous boyfriend, or some girl he'd rejected in the past. The public was getting jittery, and the police were getting desperate. As far as he knew, he was the closest they had to a suspect, and he couldn't help wondering whether they were closing in for the kill.

They'd already spoken to his loose-tongued mother about his father's temper. And Elizabeth had done her utmost to rock the boat by revealing he'd hit her in the past. *God, how I regret my actions now.* With this in mind, as he prepped for a tutorial the following day, it occurred to him that he needed to destroy any evidence the police might use to prove his guilt.

He needed to destroy the memory stick. But it wasn't in the drawer where he always kept it. What with everything that had been going on lately, he'd neither had the time nor the inclination to look at it.

He couldn't understand it. He always kept it locked in the bottom right drawer, but it was nowhere to be found. He scratched his head in exasperation. No one had access to his key, which he always kept in the inside pocket of his briefcase. And he couldn't think who would guess to look in there.

He stopped short. Froze. Felt the colour drain from his face.

Except Elizabeth.

Drake took the wheel while Carver sat beside him in silence. He couldn't understand how he'd been so wrong about Stirling. He considered himself a good judge of character. So much of police work was as much about instinct as hard evidence, and Stirling hadn't planted that seed of suspicion in Carver's mind.

Granted, he was a clever man. But the killings had pointed to someone who was technically gifted – au fait with the mechanics of modern technology: CCTV, remote control bombs, hacking. He hadn't seen that in Stirling either.

But there was no arguing with the facts. The evidence was indisputable, as the Chief had pointed out: Stirling's DNA was inside Bethany Williams and all over her flat.

That was the miracle of modern science. A few years back, a female lecturer at the academy had been blindfolded and raped in her office late one night. All the male lecturers and students had been asked to give a sample of their DNA to eliminate them from enquiries. Stirling was one of them. A member of Grayson's team had searched the DNA from the semen found inside Williams on the Police National DNA Database and matched it with Stirling's.

But there was more startling evidence. Grayson had determined that Williams had been pregnant when she died. He'd conducted a pre-natal paternity test with DNA samples from the embryo, Williams and Stirling, and confirmed Stirling to be the father.

Had Stirling killed Williams to prevent word getting out that he'd got her pregnant? Had she threatened to name and shame him – reveal his infidelity to the world in the most embarrassing, humiliating way possible?

It would have tipped his wife over the edge and destroyed his professional reputation.

It was a perfectly plausible motive. Plus, Williams' last text had made it clear she feared Stirling was going to kill her.

But what of Sarah? Was that pure revenge for dumping him? Had she been an infatuation he couldn't shake off? And the others? Natasha? Had her rejection been too much of a knock to his ego? Was he trying to teach her a lesson? And then there was Paige, Lisa, Emma. What was his motive with them? Maybe they'd also pissed him off in some way, or threatened to expose him?

Or perhaps it went much deeper? Perhaps Stirling had had more of a difficult childhood than they'd realised. Was that the common link? Were the killings borne from an inbred hatred of women, nurtured by a cold mother and a violent father? Had Stirling himself been abused?

All these thoughts swam through Carver's head as they drove through the sleepy Sunday evening traffic along Gray's Inn Road, towards Stirling's house.

The hacker was nearly done. He'd watched Stirling leave his house just after one that afternoon. And now, at just gone five, he'd probably be on his way home.

He looked at the computer screen in front of him. Although physically it was his own computer, he was actually looking at Professor Stirling's documents. It had been so easy hacking into his machine over the last few months – just as he'd hacked into Bethany Williams' email account on New Year's Eve – gaining access to Stirling's emails, private documents and internet.

Once the police looked at his internet history, saw the surfeit of sickening sites Stirling had been on – indecent images of women, women being raped, abused, tortured in the most inhumane ways imaginable – Stirling would be mincemeat.

And it didn't matter that the document history of the item he was looking at right now would show it to have been created at 3 p.m. that afternoon. Stirling could just as easily have created it on his laptop at work. Luckily for this particular hacker, Stirling used a system that allowed users to upload and sync files to a cloud storage service, and then access them from a web browser or their local device. So, anything Stirling had created that afternoon at work on his laptop would automatically upload onto his home computer and vice versa.

When the police saw this, Stirling would be done for. They would stop hunting. And the killer would be free to put the final nail in the final coffin.

Stirling burst into his house, calling out his wife's name. 'Elizabeth, where are you, Elizabeth? I know you're here, and I know what you've done.'

No response. He marched angrily into the living room but stopped abruptly just inside the door. Elizabeth was there, sitting opposite Carver and Drake.

'Professor Stirling.' Carver stood up, walked towards him.

Stirling turned pasty. He looked at Elizabeth, who stayed where she was; silent, emotionless.

'Elizabeth, what have you done?' His voice was full of anguish.

'It's of your own making, James.' She remained still, but her eyes sparkled. He sensed her taking delight in his distress.

Carver came closer. 'Professor Stirling, we are placing you under arrest for the suspected murder of Bethany Williams—'

'What? You must be joking. This is insane!' Stirling backed away.

Carver edged nearer, as did Drake who produced a pair of handcuffs from his belt.

Carver continued to read Stirling his rights as Drake put the cuffs on.

Stirling had stopped listening, too stunned, too sick, too confused by the injustice of what was happening to him. They had the memory stick; he could tell from his wife's smug face. But that wasn't enough for the police to bring him in. What else did they have?

'What possible evidence can you have for this? I demand to know!' Stirling yelled as Carver and Drake dragged him towards the front door.

'Your semen was found inside Bethany Williams, and your DNA's all over her flat,' Carver replied. 'We know she was pregnant with your child. And we also know you met her on Waterloo Bridge at 3 p.m. on New Year's Eve. The same afternoon she was murdered. The same afternoon she sent a text to her best friend saying she thought you were going to kill her.'

'This is insane!' Stirling repeated. 'I'm being set up! The last time I saw her was 29 December. We had sex at her place…' a quick glance and he saw the stringy veins on Elizabeth's neck grow taut, '…and that's why you found my DNA. Sperm can survive for up to seventy-two hours, as I'm sure you know. It doesn't mean I killed her. I never met Bethany on New Year's Eve. I agreed to meet her, but she never turned up. Check her call history. You'll see several missed calls from me. Check mine, for God's sake!'

Stirling was telling the truth on that score. A member of Carver's team had flagged up several missed calls from him the afternoon Bethany died. But Carver couldn't ignore the DNA or Bethany's frightened text. Stirling could just as easily have dialled her number to make it appear he hadn't gone home with her that day.

'You didn't come home till after 5.30, James,' Elizabeth said, digging the knife in deeper.

'I know. I was angry, confused. I walked for an hour to clear my head before coming home.'

'Can anyone back you up?' Carver asked.

Stirling lowered his head, swallowed hard. 'No, I don't believe so.'

He caught the look on his wife's face. She was usually so good at hiding her feelings. But her facial muscles were twitching with hurt, humiliation and rage.

Her eyes steely, her head held high, she turned her back on her husband as he was led out of their home.

Chapter Thirty-Three

Friday 9 January 2015

It was 9 p.m. Five days on from Stirling's arrest. Maddy hadn't long been home. Dressed in joggers and an old sweater, she sat cross-legged in front of the TV watching Carver make a statement.

The CPS had decided there was enough evidence to charge Stirling with Bethany's murder, and he was currently being held on remand at Bishopsgate police station.

She'd first learned of his arrest on Monday. It had been plastered all over the TV and made the top story in all the papers, although for now, the exact nature of the evidence against him was being kept confidential. Keen to know whether any evidence had been found linking him to the other victims, Paige especially, she'd tried several times to contact Carver, but he'd been tied up and hadn't called her back.

Paul was working tonight. Although Cara had tried to tempt her with a drink after work, she'd declined. She'd had a heavy week. Clients had stirred from their holiday comas, and it was all systems go.

Although it continued to bug Maddy that Stirling somehow knew she and Paul still lived together, and she should have been relieved that the police had made an arrest, something didn't add up. Until Bethany, the killer had been exceptionally thorough. It seemed strange that after five perfectly executed murders, Stirling had slipped up so badly with this one. She didn't know what she was missing, but it was no doubt staring her in the face.

* * *

Suzanne Carroll couldn't watch any longer. She picked up the remote and switched off the TV. Then she walked to the kitchen, opened her fridge and grabbed the half-empty bottle of Chablis standing upright in the door. Her hands trembled as she poured herself a large glass, then swigged half of it on the spot. She was a wreck; physically and emotionally, her eyes red and swollen from all the crying she'd done since hearing of his arrest.

She didn't know how she was going to cope with her lover locked up. He was her world. No one had ever come close. Try as she might, she knew she could never love anyone the way she loved him – fiercely, passionately, all-consumingly.

She'd banished his angry outburst towards her last November to the back of her mind; forgiven this *minor* misdemeanour, just as she'd readily forgiven all his previous transgressions. No matter what he did, or how he treated her, she'd go to the ends of the world for him.

She'd been heartbroken to learn he'd fathered a child with Bethany Williams, a former student he'd taken a shine to some eight or nine years back, and with whom he'd recently rekindled a relationship after bumping into her by chance last summer.

She could cope with his meaningless affairs, which were just about the sex and nothing else, but the idea of Stirling having feelings for Bethany, as he had for Sarah, had filled her with an almost unbearable jealousy.

She'd been shocked at herself for secretly rejoicing in their murders, but now it seemed she was being punished for her wicked thoughts.

She paced the floor of her luxury flat, not knowing what to do with herself. She feared it wouldn't be long before the police came knocking on her door, demanding to know if she'd lied about being with Stirling the night of Lisa Ryland's murder.

She'd swear it to be the truth if she had to. She'd break every ethical code in the Solicitors' Code of Conduct she'd sworn to abide by if need be.

Cursing herself for not accepting a dinner invitation with an old client and his wife just to take her mind off things, she decided to do some work. It was a sad state of affairs – a well-off, successful woman in her forties with no company for herself on a Friday night, save a bottle of Chablis and her laptop – but there it was. She poured the rest of the wine into her glass and took it, together with her laptop, into the bedroom.

As she changed into some casual clothes, she decided to put on some music – something to remind her of him. She scrolled her finger down the CD stand tucked in the corner of the room and pulled out the CD he'd given her as a birthday present two years ago: *The Best of Beethoven*. She slumped down on the bed, then sat upright with her back glued to the headboard, placed her laptop on her outstretched legs, and fired it up.

A mountain of new emails, mostly work-related, had already accumulated since she'd left the office at six that evening. She wearily scrolled through them but stopped short when something interesting caught her eye.

An email headed: *I know JS is innocent.*

Her heart stopped, a myriad of thoughts rushing through her head. Was it sent by some crank – some sort of virus being circulated to all and sundry? It was possible, considering the national coverage James' arrest had generated. Or was it meant solely for her? She wouldn't know until she opened it. She shifted slightly, her eyes sweeping the room even though she was very much alone.

She examined the address: rellikeht@mai.co.uk

How odd. It makes no sense. Certainly not an address she'd seen before. Cagily, she double-clicked on the message:

Dear Suzanne,

I know James is a dear friend of yours, and like you, I am devastated by his arrest. He did not kill Bethany Williams. I know this because he was with me the afternoon she was murdered. He came to see me, in turmoil over Bethany's pregnancy, once more a little boy, unsure of the right thing to do.

The reason I haven't gone to the police with this information is because I am afraid to. Not long before James was arrested I received an anonymous letter in the post threatening my life if I provided him with an alibi. I believe that the letter was from the real killer. James knew about it and told me to do as the killer asked. Although I know it is cowardly of me not to have come forward, despite James' instructions, what you must understand is that I am old and alone. Rid of the husband who abused me for so many years, I am finally enjoying what I have left of life, and I am not ready to die yet. In short, I am afraid of what the killer will do to me if he finds out I've gone to the police. And I believe James knows this.

You are a smart, capable woman, and James has only ever had good things to say about you. You are his rock and I know that, together, we can find a way to set James free. Will you meet with me, Suzanne? It is too dangerous for you to come to my house. Both the police and the killer may be watching. It needs to be somewhere neutral, where we're unlikely to be followed.

You may know from James that I live close to Hampton Court Palace. Will you meet me in the centre of Hampton Court Maze on Monday at 3 p.m.?

I look forward to seeing you then.

Janis Stirling

Suzanne stared at the email. A mixture of relief, resentment and anger ran through her. James' mother was his alibi. But the selfish cow was too chicken to stand up to the killer. James had been right about her. Just as she'd put her own needs before her son's when he was a child, she was doing the same now that he was a grown man. Even when he was being accused of murder and potentially faced the rest of his life behind bars.

But that was by the by, an irritation she'd simply have to sweep aside. Ten minutes ago, she'd only seen a bleak future ahead of her with no James in her life. But now she'd been offered a glimmer of hope. She wasn't afraid of the killer.

And she'd do whatever it took to set her soulmate free.

Monday 12 January 2015

10.30 a.m. Stirling glowered at Elizabeth, sitting across the table from him in the cheerless visitors' room. Sparse, grey, airless. He was allowed three one-hour visits a week. She was his first.

The rest of the time he was locked up in a holding cell, around six feet by eight, with brick walls and one solid door that locked from the outside. The minimal furnishings inside the cell – a bed, a table and a chair – were equally heavy and anchored to the floor to avoid being broken or used as weapons. There was one stainless steel lavatory, a washbasin and a barred window covered by a flimsy curtain.

Stirling was surprised by his wife's visit. He'd half-expected never to see her again. But maybe she'd come to exult in his misery – locked away in dismal surroundings, for a crime he didn't commit. Although no one seemed to believe him.

'Come to crow, have we, Elizabeth? If so, you can leave now.'

'I can't say seeing you like this doesn't give me some satisfaction,' she said. 'Fathering a child with that girl was your cruellest blow yet, James.'

He saw the tears in her eyes.

Guilt rose up in him. 'It wasn't deliberate, Elizabeth,' he said softly. 'It just happened.'

'And that's supposed to make me feel better, is it? After all the affairs, the lying, the disgusting sex tape, I'm just meant to accept it?'

Stirling looked over at the watching guard. 'Shush, keep your voice down, will you?'

'Huh,' Elizabeth sniggered, 'there's no point worrying about your reputation now. There's nothing left to protect. We're way past that.'

Stirling swallowed hard. 'So why are you here?'

'I thought them taking you away and locking you up would make me feel better. But it doesn't. I still feel empty.' Her expression was sad, vacant.

Stirling leaned in, whispered, 'I didn't do it, Elizabeth. I swear I didn't.'

His eyes were sincere, and she believed him. For once. But she was finding it hard to care whether the truth came out or not. She'd wasted her life on a man who'd rejected, hit and humiliated her. Why would she help a man like that?

'I believe you, James. That's partly why I'm here. But you can't argue with evidence. Including proof in black and white of your violent behaviour towards women – more especially against two of the victims.'

'Yes, and whose fault is that?' Stirling barked. 'I saw your latest sculpture, Liz. Pretty warped, don't you think? When were you intending to give it to me? In here? After you'd grassed me up?'

'I wanted to make you suffer, James; to have a little fun, mess with your mind. Ruin the reputation you don't deserve. But I genuinely didn't think they'd find anything concrete to connect you with the murders.'

'Murder, Liz, not murders.'

'That's not true, James. What about those letters they found on your laptop? Your repulsive internet history? The riddles sent to DCI Carver, the letter sent to that girl and her flatmate?'

'Maddy Kramer?'

'That's the one.' Elizabeth looked away for a second then turned her gaze back. 'Was she another of your conquests?'

'No, she wasn't,' Stirling said firmly. 'But I think she might be able to help me.' He looked at her pleadingly. 'I know you don't owe me anything, Liz. And I probably deserve to lose my job, my reputation. But I don't deserve to rot in jail for a crime I didn't commit.'

She'd made him suffer enough. And deep down, she wasn't a cruel person. 'What is it you want me to do, James?'

'I've been doing a lot of thinking in here, and it's made me see things more clearly. I want you to contact Maddy Kramer. Convince her to hear you out.'

'Why her? Hear me out about what?'

'I believe she's the key to clearing my name. But first, listen.'

Chapter Thirty-Four

'Any ideas, Ms Kramer, because I feel like my head's hitting a brick wall.'

After Stirling's arrest, forensics had descended on his home and office like a flock of ravenous birds, picking at every nook and cranny for evidence, bagging up anything potentially interesting, including Stirling's laptop, home computer and printer.

It wasn't long before the computer forensic specialists had found all kinds of incriminating evidence.

Stirling's browser history had turned up various pornography. But that was by no means the worst of it. Stirling had been on sites which promoted violence towards women, sites which talked about methods of killing, how to murder undetected, methods of disabling CCTV, where to buy guns, how to make small bombs and so on.

And then there were the letters he'd written to Carver, Maddy and Paul, stored in his documents folder.

It was all there – damning, irrefutable evidence: Stirling was the murderer. An expert at covering his tracks, at playing the part of a bumbling professor – making fools of them all.

But Carver couldn't rest yet; not until he'd solved Stirling's last riddle, one he'd written and saved on his hard drive but hadn't yet got around to sending. The document history told Carver that Stirling had written it the previous Sunday afternoon, the day of his arrest, presumably in the privacy of his office.

It was now 3 p.m. on Monday 12 January. Three days after Stirling had been formally charged with Bethany's murder. Maddy had agreed to meet Carver for a quick coffee at Starbucks on London Wall. It was only half full, symptomatic of the usual post-Christmas lethargy, although the inhospitable weather didn't help. It had rained hard all morning, and now it was blowing a gale.

Maddy hadn't expected Carver to call. She was surprised by the level of excitement she'd felt on seeing his number come up on her phone. Was it the thrill of helping him with his investigation, or purely of seeing him again? Perhaps both? She couldn't be sure.

She stared down at the letter, which a member of Carver's team had printed out for him. Of all the riddles so far, this was the most cryptic, the hardest to decode.

Dear DCI Carver,

This is my last letter to you, and I intend to make it my best work yet. So far, you've not done brilliantly at solving my puzzles, despite the help of your beautiful legal eagle.

Better luck this time, although you'll be far too late to save my final victim. I killed her before I killed Bethany.

"Unrequited love does not die; it's only beaten down to a secret place where it hides, curled and wounded."

For years I placed my trust in certain people, Chief Inspector. People who had responsibilities towards me, people who I should have been able to count on. But my trust in those people was cruelly shattered. Obliterated forever. Like a broken mirror that can never be fixed.

She died in the trapezoid within the wilderness of yew where royalty have walked. There is only one way to find her. Make sure you take the right path.

Good luck, Chief Inspector. It gives me so much pleasure sending this to you, knowing that you'll never find her. Knowing that day after day, your mind will be tortured by not knowing where she is, and yet knowing she's somewhere out there.

Equity is not about justice for all, but only those who

deserve it. Those who do not deserve it should be treated accordingly.

That is fair, Chief Inspector.

That is Equity.

Maddy read the letter in silence three times before she looked up at Carver. 'She's dead already?'

'It would appear so.'

'This is the sickest one yet. I assume you've spoken to Stirling?'

'I have, but he won't talk. Or rather, he's adamant that he didn't write it, and therefore has nothing to say. He's been driven hard – hours of questioning. But hasn't broken once. Insists he had nothing to do with any of the murders, knows nothing about the letters, and that aside from watching a bit of porn every now and again, he's done nothing wrong. He claims he's been set up.'

'Do you believe him?'

'How can I? The evidence is overwhelming.'

Maddy held Carver's gaze. Despite what he said, she sensed he wasn't being entirely frank.

'But?'

Carver sat back and sighed. 'But it's still there…this little niggle at the back of my mind that keeps making me question: is he our man?'

'I know, I feel the same way. What if the real killer hacked into Stirling's system? Framed him that way? I mean, he's clearly computer-savvy; he managed to disable the CCTV at Channings.'

Carver smiled. She didn't miss much. 'Someone's looking into that possibility for me. I should hear back any time now. Stirling's DNA is our biggest problem.'

'I agree that complicates things.'

Carver gestured to the letter. 'For now we have to focus on this. I've Googled the saying about "unrequited love". It's by an author named Elle Newmark, from *The Book of Unholy Mischief*.'

'I wonder whose unrequited love the author of the letter – be it Stirling or not – is referring to? The killer's, or the next victim's?'

Carver shook his head. 'Your guess is as good as mine. Maybe both. Looking at this, do you have any ideas on victim or location? We know what the subject is – Equity – that's obvious. And all this talk of digging graves makes me suspect she's lying six feet under. But where? We need to find the body, Ms Kramer…before the press get wind of it.'

Maddy sipped her coffee, which was now almost cold. 'Can I borrow a pen?'

Carver produced a biro from his inside coat pocket, handed it to her, then watched her highlight certain words: "trust"; "unrequited love"; "trapezoid"; "wilderness"; "yew"; "royalty".

She looked back up at him. 'Okay, so as you said, the subject is Equity, so the victim must have some connection to Equity. At law school, the Equity module mainly consisted of learning about different types of trust, fiduciary relationships, rights and obligations.' She ran her fingers through her hair. 'Maybe the victim's a Trusts lawyer.'

Carver's back went rigid.

'What?'

'Suzanne Carroll. She's an old friend of Stirling's from Oxford…a Trusts partner at a firm in Putney. I questioned her a couple of days after Ryland was found. At the time she maintained they weren't lovers, but I saw them in action on Stirling's memory stick. Just before I arrested him. I'm certain she covered for him the night of Ryland's murder.'

He pulled out his phone, called Drake. 'Drake, call Suzanne Carroll's office, demand to speak to her now. If she's not in, find out where she is. If no one knows, find out when she was last seen.' He rang off.

'She's not been reported missing?' Maddy asked.

'Not as far as I know. Which makes me think, if she is the final victim, the killer's lying about having killed her before Bethany. She may well still be alive.'

'Which makes Stirling innocent.'

'Yes. Perhaps he got Carroll to cover for him because he got scared.' Carver glanced at his phone, his heart thumping at the thought of what

Drake was going to come back with. He looked up at Maddy. 'Let's get back to the riddle. What about location?'

'Well, the reference to royalty means it could be a palace or castle, I suppose.' She frowned. 'But then wilderness implies it's somewhere outside, maybe in a formal garden of some sort.'

'And what of this trapezoid thing? That's got to mean something, surely?'

'There's only one way to find out.' Maddy grabbed her iPhone lying on the table, went to the internet and typed in "trapezoid". The connection was slow. 'Come on,' she muttered. Finally, it loaded, and brought up over a million results. She read out the first. 'The trapezoid is a four-sided flat shape with straight sides that has a pair of opposite sides parallel. Called an isosceles trapezoid when the sides that aren't parallel are equal in length and both angles coming from a parallel side are equal.'

'Is that supposed to be helpful?' Carver joked.

'Hang on, don't be so impatient!' They shared a fleeting smile, before she looked back down and typed another search into her phone. Carver was still smiling inside, put in his place by his amateur sleuth. His *incredibly attractive* amateur sleuth. 'What are you typing in now?'

I must stop thinking like that, he told himself.

'Famous trapezoids.' This time there were over eight million results. But nothing helpful. 'There's only one thing for it, I'll just go for broke.'

Carver leaned forward, trying to read Maddy's next search upside down. 'Trapezoid, yew, wilderness'.

'Hmm, only 85,000 results. We're getting closer.' Maddy gave Carver a playful smile. It made him feel awkward – unusual for him. For a split second, he pondered why she had that effect on him.

Maddy cast her eyes down the list of results, hoping to spot something useful. And then she saw it. 'Yes!' she exclaimed – so loudly she attracted the attention of a nearby table. She felt herself flush, mouthed 'Sorry,' then turned her attention back to Carver, who was looking mildly amused.

'What is it?' he asked.

'Sixth entry down.' Maddy turned her phone around to give him a better look.

'Eight breathtaking garden mazes. Hampton Court.' Carver looked up. 'You think that's where she is?'

She didn't answer, clicked on the entry. 'Hampton Court Hedge Maze, to be precise.'

'Where royalty have walked,' Carver mumbled. Maddy read out excerpts from the entry.

> *'This popular trapezoid-shaped feature of landscape architecture in Surrey, England, has been delighting and disorienting visitors since the late 1600s… The third-of-an-acre maze with its seven-foot-tall yew hedge walls marked a departure from popular garden maze design. It was created with a multicursal, meaning multiple paths with numerous dead ends, instead of a unicursal, meaning single path, configuration, making it a pioneer of puzzle mazes… still one of the hottest outdoor attractions at Hampton Court Palace.'*

Maddy returned to the results page and clicked on another link. It brought up various photos of Hampton Court Maze. 'Look at the heading.' She turned her phone around again for Carver's benefit.

He read out the caption: '*Photos of the Hampton Court Maze in the Wilderness section of the Hampton Court Palace gardens.*'

He looked at Maddy and grinned. 'You're a genius, Ms Kramer.' Just then, Drake called.

After listening to what he had to say, Carver said, 'Okay, that's confirmed my suspicions. The real killer's still out there and plans to kill Carroll last. She may yet still be alive.' He glanced up at Maddy as he talked. 'Ms Kramer's worked out the location. Get a team of uniformed officers, CSOs and medics to Hampton Court Maze. Call ahead for someone to keep the gates open as it'll be closing round about now. You, come and get me now. I'm in Starbucks on London Wall. I reckon we can make it there in just under an hour, depending on traffic.' He hung up.

'Carroll wasn't in her office?' Maddy said.

'No, but she was in all morning. Left around one thirty. Didn't say where she was going.'

'So the killer did lie. She's not dead yet.'

'Let's hope that's true. Thank you, Ms Kramer.'

'No problem, I just pray you find her in time.'

Carver looked at his watch. 3.45 p.m. 'It's winter, the maze is probably closed by now, or about to.'

'I'm sure they'll make an exception for you.' Maddy's gaze lingered on Carver. He smiled; felt that awkwardness again.

'Can I keep this?' She gestured to the letter, rescuing him from his discomfort.

'Sure, it's only a copy. Any particular reason?'

'I'm not sure yet. It's a theory I have. One I've only just thought of.'

'Let me know if your theory comes to anything, won't you?'

'Don't worry. You'll be the first to know.'

Forty-five minutes earlier, 3 p.m.

Suzanne Carroll remembered running through Hampton Court Palace Hedge Maze – the most famous maze in the world – as a little girl, terrified of losing her parents, of not being able to find her way out. Back then, she'd found the narrow paths and seven-foot-high yew walls – designed and built for secret assignations – frightening rather than exciting. Now they were simply frustrating.

It had taken her three attempts to find her way to the centre on this occasion, cursing as she'd hit dead ends, or found herself back at the entrance again, having been fooled into believing she was nearly there.

It had been a dull, wet day, and with what little light there had been rapidly fading, and only forty-five minutes until closing time, she wasn't surprised to find herself alone at the centre of the maze. It was deathly quiet, not a soul in sight.

It had briefly stopped raining. But just then, she felt a faint spit. Suzanne wondered if Janis was on her way; whether the palace café was still open. There were also a few cafés the other side of Hampton Court Bridge. Perhaps they could grab a coffee and shelter in one of those while they talked? Surely, they'd be safe to chat privately there?

The rain became harder. Furious with herself for failing to pack an umbrella in her bag, she pressed herself up against the wooden trellis encircling the centre of the maze, praying that Janis would show up soon. She checked her iPhone for messages. Fifty had come through since she'd left the office just after one thirty, but she didn't bother to look at them in detail. She hadn't told anyone where she was going. Janis had made it plain that she wanted their meeting to remain private, and she'd readily respect that request if it meant finding a way to set James free.

'Hello, you all right there?'

Lost in her thoughts, Suzanne nearly jumped out of her skin at the unexpected interruption. A soft, husky voice. She looked up to see a nun standing there – tall, broad-shouldered, a little on the hefty side, although it was hard to tell for sure under the outfit. She had dark eyes and plain features.

'Are you waiting for someone?' The nun gave Suzanne a warm smile.

Before the nun's arrival, Suzanne had started to feel a little uncomfortable standing there, alone, the rain thrashing down around her.

But the presence of a disciple of God was a welcome comfort and allayed her sense of unease. Even so, she did wonder what the nun was doing there on such a miserable, wet day. She smiled back.

'Yes, an elderly lady, in her sixties. She's the mother of a good friend. She told me to meet her here. At three.' Suzanne glanced at her watch. It had just gone 3.10.

'You look cold,' the nun observed. She placed a hand on Suzanne's shoulder. 'I think I saw an old lady a little way back, looking rather lost. I know this place like the back of my hand. I often come here after praying in the royal chapel. I'll go try and find her for you. You know the maze shuts at 3.45?'

'Yes, I know. And that's very kind of you.' Suzanne was genuinely grateful. She was getting fed up of waiting in the cold, wet weather.

She didn't know if she'd ever find her way back to the centre if she went looking for Janis now.

'Wait here,' the nun said. 'Hopefully, your friend's just around the corner.'

Suzanne watched the nun disappear round the bend and heard the gentle shuffle of her footsteps fade away. She continued to lean against the trellis, her hands clasped together, her eyes shut tight as she said a prayer. She was by no means a pious person, but there was something about her encounter with the nun that brought out the religious in her. It was as if she'd been sent a guardian angel to help her. She lowered her head down to her clinched hands and said a prayer for James; that Janis held the key to his freedom, and that before long, they'd be together again.

After whispering 'Amen', she raised her head up. But not long enough to open her eyes and re-orientate herself with her surroundings. She felt the most searing pain across the top of her head, and then fell to the ground. She wasn't out cold, and through blurred eyes, she just about made out the face of her attacker. The nun. Standing over her, eyes wild and devilish, a wooden crucifix in her right hand, which was encased in a black leather glove.

'Wh-y?' she just about managed to get the word out, too dazed to say any more.

'Because you sicken me,' was all her attacker said before raising the cross high above Suzanne's head, then driving it down into her skull.

This time, everything went dark.

Chapter Thirty-Five

It was essential to be quick. There wasn't much time. She knew she was playing with fire, that anyone could appear at any moment. But that was part of the thrill; the thrill of committing the crime without being caught; of carrying out the most daring of murders, escaping capture by the skin of her teeth. It was a fitting end to her crusade. Although how she was going to carry on living, as if nothing had changed, she didn't know. Back to her tedious day-to-day existence, and her equally dull clients.

All except one, of course.

Taking lives had made her feel almost God-like. She'd never experienced such a supreme sense of power and control. It was addictive, and she was sorry it had come to an end with Suzanne. But it had always been the plan to follow a pattern, and the pattern was almost complete. She wasn't sure how, but she'd have to nurture her needs in some other way.

She grabbed her rucksack from behind the wrought-iron sculpture standing in the centre of the maze where she'd left it earlier and pulled out a pair of latex gloves; she quickly removed the leather pair and put them on, then delved back inside for her blade. Hauling her victim onto her back, she ripped open her coat, jacket and blouse until her white flesh was exposed. Suzanne was a heavy-set woman of forty-four, her skin a little looser, more damaged by time, than the others. The killer pressed the point of the blade into her chest, then started to carve.

As she did, she remembered all those times she'd gone hunting with her father. How she'd hated it: skinning those poor, defenceless foxes and rabbits; watching the blood drain out of them as her father looked on – always with critical eyes. He had cursed her for being too soft, for not being enough of a man about it; cursed her for not being the son he had wanted; what's more, for having turned out to be a girl, for being so damned unattractive – for being a constant disappointment. But all those years of practice had come in handy. She cut quickly, deftly, precisely.

Six letters, and then she'd have justice. If only her father had been alive. He'd have seen that she was more of a man than any son of his could have been; just as she'd proved to all those whores that there was more to life than good looks and being popular with men. That guile and brutality was what took a person far in life.

She heard voices, footsteps getting closer. Sprinting to the opposite hedge wall, she spied two groundsmen making their way to the centre. It was closing time, and they were checking that no one was left in the maze. *Fuck*. She'd got her timing wrong. She hadn't been quick enough. Now there was no time to push the body through the gap she'd found around the corner. A space in one of the yew walls of the maze big enough to squeeze a body through and dump among the foliage. She'd have to leave it where it was. The plan she'd spent so long fashioning was ruined.

She quickly grabbed the crucifix, along with her rucksack, and went back into the maze. She could feel her heart beating manically inside her chest as the voices grew closer still. She managed to gather her thoughts and found the same gap in the wall where she'd planned to leave Suzanne's body to rot. She squeezed herself through it, cutting her gloved hand on a sharp bramble as she did so. Blood trickled through the synthetic material. 'Shit,' she quietly cursed, licking it away.

She lay as still as possible, clutching her rucksack tight against her chest, trying to keep her breathing steady and quiet. She was still close enough to the centre of the maze to hear the men's voices. She began to count in her mind, thinking she'd be lucky if she got to five before they spotted the body: one, two, three – she was right.

'Jesus Christ,' one of them said. 'Call for an ambulance, Joe. There's a faint pulse, be quick.'

Fuck. Surely, he's mistaken? There's no way she could still be alive. She was sure there'd been no pulse after the second blow. She told herself to calm down. Even if she was alive, the force of the blow would surely have smashed her brain to a pulp, reduced her to a vegetative state. Plus, she was slowly bleeding to death.

'We don't have time to wait, we need to get her out of here,' the man named Joe replied. 'I'll make the call if you think you can carry her out.'

She heard groaning. Presumably the other man had lifted the body off the ground. 'Let's head for the first aid room and wait there for the ambulance and police.'

After a few seconds, the killer heard footsteps trail off. She was sweating profusely now, despite the arctic temperatures – sweat across the back of her neck, her brow, her lower back, her chest. When she was sure she was alone, she squeezed herself through the gap, back onto the narrow path, and stood up and swung her rucksack across her shoulder. She recalled that there was blood smeared all over the ground where Suzanne had lain. There was no time to go back and clean it up now. But in any case, she was safe. She'd been wearing gloves as usual, and they wouldn't find any trace of her DNA on Suzanne's body or in the area where she had fallen. And surely they wouldn't think to search the hole where she'd hidden and cut herself?

She prayed that the men had been too preoccupied with getting the body to the first aid room to think about closing the exit gate. As she ran through the maze, trying to keep her head and remember the exit route she'd memorised, eyes whizzing in all directions to make sure the coast was clear, she could already hear a siren approaching from somewhere in the distance. She blocked it out. Ran faster… faster and faster until she reached the exit. Thankfully, it was still open. She quickly peered her head out left and right, to make sure no one was watching, then strode purposefully through it, turned left onto the path and headed for the Lion Gates exit, only a short distance away. Having reached it, she slowed to a casual walk, ambled out of the grounds onto Hampton Court Road and headed for the nearest bus stop.

* * *

'What is it, Drake?' Carver drove kamikaze-style through the crawling traffic, siren blaring on top of the car.

Drake's phone was pressed against his ear. 'Thanks. Call me when you know more.' He hung up. Turned to Carver. 'A body's been found, sir.'

'Shit!' Carver banged the steering wheel.

'But she's still alive. Just. They've taken her to Kingston Hospital.'

'Yes!' Carver smacked the steering wheel again, this time triumphantly. 'Is it Carroll?'

'Just waiting on that.'

'So now we know for sure. Stirling's not our man. He can't be if the victim was only attacked this afternoon.'

'But what about the evidence, sir?'

'He's being framed, Drake. We know he was seeing Williams, but so did the killer, it seems. We also know that the killer's technically gifted. He must have hacked into Stirling's account and written the letters remotely. Call Turner in computer forensics for an update. We need to find out ASAP if I'm right about that.'

Drake's phone rang. He answered it. 'Okay, thanks,' he said, then rang off. 'You were right, sir. The seventh victim is Suzanne Carroll.'

Carver pictured the riddle in his mind. *Unrequited love.* He realised what it meant. She'd covered for Stirling the night of Lisa Ryland's murder. She loved him, but she wasn't loved back in the same way.

The killer had framed Stirling, but why? And what had been the plan with Carroll? To conceal her within the walls of the maze on the premise that she would never be found? His final, cruellest kill yet – knowing that Stirling would never be able to lead them to Suzanne simply because he didn't do it. And why wouldn't the world believe that Stirling was responsible for this murder, just as he'd been responsible for Bethany's, for all the others?

'And her chest? Was it obvious what he'd written?'

'Yes. It was—'

'Equity.'

'Yes, sir. Her head had been smashed with something heavy.

Groundsmen found her around 3.40, lying in the centre of the maze. They claimed to have seen nothing and no one suspicious, only a nun, who'd been praying in the royal chapel.'

'We'll have to wait and see if she comes round. If her head's been smashed, there's a good chance she'll be in a coma. Even worse, she'll be a vegetable. Meantime, get forensics all over the maze and surrounding area. This is the first time the killer's let his guard slip. We can't afford to miss anything.'

Chapter Thirty-Six

Maddy couldn't open her front door fast enough. She flung off her coat, kicked off her heels and raced into her bedroom. Paul was home. She heard the shower going, the radio blaring over it.

Ever since her meeting with Carver, she'd been desperate to get home. But the world of corporate law was almost as cut-throat as the serial killer she was hunting, and she'd had several work matters to deal with before she was able to leave the office without raising any eyebrows.

She rummaged through the pile of papers stacked on her desk until she found it: a copy of the killer's letter to her. Carver's forensic team had the original. She laid it out flat on the desk. Then set the copy of the killer's latest riddle next to it.

She was right! The letter to her had faint lines running across the page, whereas the killer's latest riddle, printed out by Carver's team, didn't. She needed another comparison. Paul's letter. He must surely still have it?

The radio stopped playing. She darted outside, waiting for Paul to emerge from the bathroom. Steam seeped out into the corridor as he did so, a towel wrapped around his waist.

'Hi, you okay?' he said.

'Do you have a copy of the letter the killer sent you?'

Paul frowned. 'From Stirling, you mean? Er, yes, maybe, why?'

'Can you look for it please? I need to see it.'

'Er, sure. Can I just put some clothes on first?' There was a slight tetchiness to his voice. Maddy felt bad for jumping on him with her demands before he'd even had a chance to dress.

'Yes, of course. Go for it. I'll be in my bedroom.'

A few minutes later, Paul appeared at her door, dressed and holding a piece of paper. He handed it to her. 'Here it is. What's all this about?'

Maddy took it off him. 'Thanks,' she said, then placed it on the desk next to the other letters.

'I'm right!'

'Right about what?'

'Come take a look at this.'

Paul went over, peering at the letters over Maddy's shoulder.

'Do you see?'

'No.'

Maddy pointed to the letters mailed directly to her and Paul. 'Both of these have faint lines running across the page. Whereas this one, the killer's latest riddle, which was printed out by Carver's team, doesn't.'

'So, you're saying Stirling's printer produced these funny lines when he printed out his letters?'

'Yes. If it was Stirling of course. I'm betting the police have his printer.'

'What do you mean *if* it was Stirling? They have DNA evidence. And he wouldn't necessarily have used his home printer. He might have used one at work. Or anywhere, in fact.'

'That's true. But at least the police can test his home and work printers. If there's a match with the letters, we'll know for sure it's him. If not, it introduces an element of doubt.'

'Has something happened today? Something you're not telling me.'

Maddy told him about her earlier meeting with Carver.

'But that sounds like she's already dead. That Stirling murdered her before they arrested him.'

'Agreed. But if it's Carroll, as Carver thinks, he can't have done, because she was only seen this morning. Have you listened to the news recently? I've no idea if a body's been found or not.'

'No, I haven't. I've been out pretty much all day. I went to visit my mother.'

‘Really?’ Maddy stopped short. She took in Paul’s face. He looked a little off-colour. ‘How did that go?’

‘Awful. She texted me, saying she really needed to talk, and I thought I’d better go, seeing as I didn’t see her over Christmas.’

‘Is she still with Philip?’

‘Unfortunately, yes.’

Maddy heard her phone ring from the hallway. She dashed to answer it. It was Carver.

‘What did you find?’ she asked anxiously.

‘She’s alive. Just.’

‘What? Who? You mean Carroll?’

‘Yes, I was right about her. And you were right about the location. Some groundsmen found her lying in the centre of Hampton Court Maze, bleeding and barely conscious, “Equity” carved into her chest. She’d also been hit hard over the head. They took her to Kingston Hospital. She’s in a coma.’

‘So it’s not Stirling?’ Maddy looked up at Paul, who appeared flabbergasted.

‘Well, he’s certainly not responsible for this attack. Unless he’s in it with someone.’

‘Do you think that’s possible?’

‘Anything’s possible. But I think not on this occasion. The most plausible explanation is that he’s being set up.’

‘Why do you think the killer left her like that?’

‘Maybe he thought she was dead. Or didn’t have time to hide the body when he heard the groundsmen approaching, so took off and hid. Apparently, they were quick to carry her out of the maze to the first aid room. It’s possible, in that short time frame, that he was able to hide from sight until they’d gone, at which point he fled the scene. The riddle made it clear we weren’t supposed to find her. I think he meant to hide her body somewhere in the maze, so we’d have no way of knowing whether or not it was Stirling, but obviously the plan didn’t work out.’

Paul cocked his head at Maddy. ‘What’s he saying?’ he mouthed. She raised her finger up as if to say, ‘One minute.’

'Let's pray she wakes up,' she said. 'I'm glad you called because I have a theory to run by you.'

'Oh yes?'

'I compared the letters the killer sent to me and Paul with his last letter to you which your team printed out.'

'And?'

'The letters to me and Paul have several faint lines running across the page, which I think indicates a printing error. The one printed by your team does not. You should check the killer's letters to you to see if they have the same marks.'

'Great spot, Ms Kramer, I will. And I'll get one of my team to check Stirling's home and work printers again.'

'It may be that he used a totally random printer, but with this latest development, it seems unlikely. He can't be the killer. Do we know why Carroll was in the maze?'

'No. We've spoken to her office and she didn't tell anyone where she was going. Her work calendar just said "private meeting". It may be that the killer contacted her, pretending to be someone else. We're unlikely to know if that's the case until she wakes up. Although her phone log and emails may prove helpful.'

Carver promised to keep Maddy posted, then rang off.

'They found another victim?' Paul asked.

Maddy filled Paul in. 'Stirling's innocent; I knew it,' she said.

Paul shook his head. 'I don't buy it. It's him, it has to be. There's too much bloody evidence.'

Maddy narrowed her eyes at Paul. 'This has really got to you. You seem determined for it to be Stirling. Why?'

'Can you blame me? He slept with all the dead girls. Got one pregnant. Has a violent temper. He's not exactly a victim in all of this.'

'Point taken. But he still doesn't deserve to spend the rest of his life in jail for a crime he didn't commit.'

'Okay.' Paul held up his hands. 'Let's agree to disagree.'

Maddy's phone rang. It was a number she didn't recognise. 'Hello?' she said gingerly as Paul disappeared into the kitchen.

‘Ms Kramer, this is Elizabeth Stirling.’ Maddy nearly fell back in shock. Stirling’s wife was the last person she’d expected to hear from. ‘Ms Kramer? Are you there?’

Maddy sat down on the edge of the sofa. ‘Yes, yes, I’m still here. Just surprised to hear from you.’

‘That’s understandable. I can’t actually believe I’m making this call myself.’

‘How did you get my number?’

‘That’s not important. What’s important is that, for all his faults – and believe me, he has many – I believe James is innocent. He’s not a murderer. He’s not capable of it.’

‘How do you know that?’

‘I know my husband, Ms Kramer.’

‘I’m sure that’s what the loved ones of most serial killers have said in the past. And they couldn’t have been more wrong.’

‘James believes he’s being framed. He thinks you’re in the best position to help catch the real killer.’

‘And why’s that?’

‘Because he believes the killer is your flatmate – Paul King.’

Maddy stiffened. Looked towards the kitchen. Paul hadn’t yet re-emerged. ‘That’s crazy,’ she laughed.

‘My husband doesn’t think so.’

Maddy tried to remain calm. She spoke in hushed tones. ‘Forgive my bluntness, but quite frankly, the idea is both absurd and slanderous. Your husband’s clutching at straws. Paul is the kindest, most loving, caring man I know. There’s just no way he’s a murderer, let alone a serial killer.’

‘To quote you, Ms Kramer, I’m sure that’s what the loved ones of most serial killers have said in the past, and they couldn’t have been more wrong.’

There was an ear-splitting silence. Part of Maddy was livid, so violently insulted by the idea that her best friend might be a murderer, she was tempted to put the phone down.

But her curious side had the edge. She needed to hear Elizabeth out.

‘Go on, I’m listening.’

Friday 11 December 2009

'Ah, Paul, please come in.'

It wasn't the first time Paul King had been in Professor Stirling's office. Since starting at the academy three months ago, he'd been struggling with some elements of the course, and they'd met for extra study sessions two or three times a week for the last two months. None of the other students knew, not even Paul's best friend at the academy – Maddy Kramer. Neither she, nor any of the others, knew about Stirling's long-standing friendship with Paul's parents.

Stirling had known Paul since he was a baby. Paul's father, George, and mother, Evelyn, had been at Oxford with him, and after graduating, Stirling had trained and briefly practised with George at the same law firm. While Stirling had missed academia, and quickly went into teaching, George had gone on to become a top corporate lawyer at one of the most prestigious firms in the City. From the outset, he'd instructed Paul and Stirling not to publicise their friendship at the academy. As a child, Paul, a shy, somewhat reclusive little boy, had frequently been bullied by other less fortunate kids who resented his privileged background. George, dismayed by his son's sexuality, was desperate for him to thrive and fit in at the academy. The last thing he wanted was him getting aggro from his peers who might, should they learn of the Kings' and the Stirlings' special connection, accuse Paul of receiving preferential treatment.

Still, Stirling had always had a soft spot for Paul, and he didn't like seeing him struggle. He saw no harm in helping him, so long as he did it discreetly.

As well as being patient and understanding, Stirling was highly intuitive. He knew about Paul's sexuality from George, but it couldn't have been more obvious than on that first day Paul set foot in his lecture hall.

Sitting along the same row as Sarah Morrell, Paige Summers and Madeline Kramer, Paul hadn't looked at these stunning women the way other young men in the room had looked at them. Or, indeed, the way Stirling himself had looked at them.

Stirling knew George was ashamed of his son's homosexuality, and that he'd pushed Paul –who'd do anything to please his father – into law as a means of making up for what he saw as a deep flaw in his only child's genetic make-up.

When George died suddenly of a heart attack, three months into the course, Stirling saw how hard his death had hit Paul; he was a sensitive young man, who, like Stirling himself, had worshipped his father, and resented his shallow mother. A woman who only ever had time for herself, a woman who had palmed her son off to nannies, after-school clubs and holiday camps, rather than give him the time, love and devotion a boy needs from his mother – a mother who, unknowingly, had made her son resentful and distrustful of women.

Professor Stirling had called Paul to his study that day, two weeks after George's death, not to go over a piece of work, but to check that he was doing okay; that he wasn't about to throw himself off a bridge. He wanted to show Paul that he was there for him as a shoulder to lean on; that he didn't judge him on his character or sexuality; that he understood how affected he'd been by his mother's cold indifference.

In so many ways they were similar. But as far as one fundamental aspect was concerned, they were very different.

Paul walked into Stirling's study and closed the door behind him. He flopped down onto a chair and buried his head in his hands. 'I just can't stop thinking about him – wonder if it was me who made him ill, caused his stress levels to soar.' He looked up, locked eyes with Stirling. 'You know, because I'm not how he'd imagined me to be.'

Stirling pulled his chair closer to Paul. Then put an arm around his shoulder.

'Don't be daft,' he said gently. 'Don't you dare tell her this, but if anyone sent him to an early grave, it was your mother. I know he was a workaholic, but he loved her, and that should have been enough for her. She shouldn't have slept with other men. He didn't deserve that.' He sighed, at the same time marvelling at his own hypocrisy. 'Women can be so cold, so vindictive. Sometimes, I think my life would be far less complicated if I was like you. I'm sure you have it much easier, Paul.' Stirling chuckled lightly to himself, clutching Paul's hand as a gesture of warmth and reassurance.

But Paul had taken it to mean so much more. From his early youth, he'd been secretly smitten with Stirling; captivated not only by his good looks, but also his humour and intelligence, and the way he always took an interest in him. A part of Paul had died with his father, but when he was with Stirling – mature, kind, understanding – he almost felt whole again. He looked at Stirling's hand, locked around his. The sensation was tantalising – both in the way it comforted him and aroused him. He looked up at his idol, holding his gaze, then leaned in and kissed him on the mouth. It was so quick, so unexpected, Stirling hadn't had time to avoid it, but no sooner had their mouths connected than he backed away in horror, wiping his mouth with the back of his hand in disgust. He scraped back his chair and stood up, distancing himself from his confused, desperate student.

'I... I thought,' Paul began, getting up from his chair.

'You thought what exactly?' Stirling edged back further, his face contorted with anger and revulsion.

Paul remained rooted to the spot. 'I thought we had a connection. We're from similar upbringings, and we understand each other. I thought we could be good for each other.'

'We are nothing like each other!' Stirling's eyes were gleaming with rage. 'I am no faggot! I love women, okay? They may irritate me, drive me mad at times, but I love everything about them, and I have never in my life contemplated being with a man. The very thought makes me sick! Your father was right: I should never have called you here. You ever try anything like that again, and I will have you kicked off the course, do you hear me?'

Paul felt violently sick. But he was also angry. He'd been angry for so many years: angry with God for making him the way he was; angry with his mother for never being there; angry with his father for never accepting him for what he was, and then for dying. And now he was angry with Stirling.

'I hear you. But I also know things about you. I know you've been fucking that uptight bitch, Sarah. What do you suppose would happen if word got out?'

Stirling came closer, squared up to Paul, their noses almost touching.

'That is none of your business. If you so much as utter one word, I'll make a complaint against you for sexual harassment. And then your father's good name will be forever tainted by a son who not only lacked a proper set of

balls but couldn't keep them in his trousers when it came to straight-up, heterosexual men.' He paused. 'My silence for yours. Do we have a deal?'

Paul hesitated, then nodded slowly. 'Fine. We have a deal.'

'Good.' Stirling walked over to the door and gripped the handle. 'Now, please leave. From now on, your tutorials will be with Professor Everly.'

'What will you tell him?'

'I'll think of something. Please go.' Stirling opened the door.

Paul picked up his rucksack and walked towards the door, pausing to face Stirling. 'You can't be allowed to treat people the way you do. One day, you'll get what's coming to you.' Stirling didn't budge. He gestured with his bespectacled eyes towards the open door.

Paul left. His heart crushed, his pride wounded, his mind contemplating revenge.

The present

'You still there, Ms Kramer?'

Maddy had lost her voice. Listening to Elizabeth Stirling's explanation of what had happened between Paul and her husband, it was almost as if she hadn't heard right. She was Paul's best friend, and yet he had never intimated, either when they were at the academy together, or since, that he'd had feelings for Stirling, or mentioned any falling-out between them. And she certainly hadn't known about his father's friendship with Stirling.

'Yes, I'm still here.' Maddy got up from the sofa. 'But how do I know your husband's telling the truth?' She knew she was asking out of desperation, but that was the point; she was desperate for it not to be true. How could she cope with the knowledge that she'd been living with a murderer all this time; a serial killer who had viciously murdered one of her best friends; who had deceived her and lied to her face?

'He's not lying, Ms Kramer. Why would he make up something like that? It's too outrageous a story for my husband to fabricate. The idea of any gay fling between him and a student getting out would break him. So, the fact that he's told me all of this makes me certain it's true.'

Maddy thought back to her earlier conversation with Paul. The way he'd seemed determined to prove Stirling's guilt, desperate even. She edged back and, almost in slow motion, sank down on the sofa.

'You need to get this information to the police, Ms Kramer. They're more likely to take you seriously than me or James. My husband is convinced his system's been hacked – that that's how your flatmate wrote those letters and made all those disgusting websites show up on his internet history. Please, Ms Kramer. Help him.'

Shit. Paul was back, chewing a piece of toast. He locked eyes with Maddy, and her palms were suddenly clammy. She managed a smile. 'Yes, of course, Gran. I'll look into that for you.'

'Ah, I see, he's there,' Elizabeth said.

'Yes, Gran.' Maddy smiled another fake smile, her heart pounding. 'Look, got to go now, but I'll call you later when I've found it. Bye!'

She put down the phone without giving Elizabeth the chance to respond.

Paul gave her a circuitous look, and she tried not to shiver. She didn't know for sure that he was guilty – after all, just because he and Stirling fell out didn't mean he killed those women – but she was suddenly looking at him with very different eyes. 'Something up with your gran?' he asked.

Think quickly!

'She wants me to find a heated blanket for her on the internet, that's all.'

'Oh, okay. Let me know if you need any help. You know I'm a whizz on the web.' He grinned broadly.

'Yes, yes, I know. Thanks.' *The letters, the internet, the CCTV!* She headed for the door. 'I'd better start looking now, in fact. She sounded pretty desperate for it.'

'Sure, go for it. I'm off out in a minute. Meeting Justin for a drink.'

Maddy inwardly sighed with relief. But at the same time, she wondered if that's where he was really headed. 'Okay, great. Have a good time.'

Her legs felt heavy as she walked towards her bedroom. Once inside, she closed the door. She wanted to lock it, but she never normally did, and it might make Paul suspicious. She opened her laptop and turned it on. As she waited for it to power up, she told herself to calm down and think logically. All she had was the Stirlings' word. *Why should I trust them?* Stirling had been charged with murder; he was desperate. People would no doubt go to any lengths to escape life imprisonment – to be free.

And yes, perhaps Paul did have a crush on Stirling, perhaps he did try it on, go a step too far, only to be flatly rejected. *But does that make him hunger for revenge so badly it turns him into a killer?* People said things in the heat of the moment all the time. But they mostly never acted on their threats: they cooled down and forgot about it – that was human nature.

She told herself not to jump to any conclusions before she had the facts.

She'd wait until she heard Paul leave, and then she'd do what she knew she must if she wanted to find out the truth.

Chapter Thirty-Seven

Friday 25 June 2010

'What are you staring at?'

Sarah Morrell was plastered. It had been a gruelling sober fortnight of revision and exams. No sleep, no social life. What most students in the room really needed was their beds. But the adrenaline was still hurtling through their veins, egging them on for a night of partying at the end-of-year summer bash.

Sarah had watched Stirling leer all over Lisa Ryland with a mixture of jealousy and disgust. She'd recently split with Connor Dexter who'd turned out to be dull and gutless following the incident with Elizabeth Stirling, and for once, she found herself short of male attention. With few female friends at the academy to speak of, she had decided to get very drunk before pouncing on some equally smashed red-blooded male.

She'd barely noticed Paul King standing at the bar next to her, sipping a beer and eyeing her with disgust.

'Nothing.'

'Oh, come on, I saw the look. Don't tell me you've still got it in for me?'

'Got it in for you?' He wrinkled his brow. 'And why would I have it in for you?'

Sarah necked the rest of her vodka, then laughed facetiously. 'Because I fucked the dishy college professor, and you didn't get to.' She held his gaze, a look of triumph in her own.

Paul felt his face burn with shame.

'Oh, I'm sorry. Was it meant to be a secret?' Sarah cooed. 'You know how people let things slip between the sheets. Pillow talk and all that.' She leaned in closer, so that he could smell her perfume, her breath. It sickened him. 'The very day you made a pass at Stirling, he gave me the best fuck of my life. You rattled his manhood, Paul, with your filthy, queer ways, but your undoing was my gain. It was a night I shall never forget. In fact, after that night, the sex never quite lived up to expectations, and I grew bored with him.' She turned her gaze towards Stirling who'd just disappeared into the crowd, Lisa Ryland a few steps behind. 'And now it appears he's got his dick inside another girl.' Another pause as she turned back to Paul. 'Why, Paul, you've gone quite pale,' she said with mock concern. 'Can I get you some water?'

Paul was consumed with rage. He felt like he was going to explode. Sarah's words, together with seeing Stirling go off with his latest tart, had brought him to boiling point. But somehow, he managed to rein in his temper. 'You are a cold, selfish bitch,' he replied, 'who cares for nothing and nobody but yourself.' He edged a little closer. 'The world would be a better place without vixens like you shitting all over it.'

He saw the flash of alarm in her eyes, but she quickly brushed it off.

'Sure, whatever, I'm sure that would suit your kind very well, but thankfully you're in the minority. Now, if you'll excuse me.'

He watched her strut off like the prima donna she was. Although he'd done well to control the anger that had been steadily growing in him over the last six months, he didn't know how much longer he could restrain himself. He needed another outlet, something to take his mind off things. So far, he'd filled it with his writing, but he needed something more – something human to soak up his anger and resentment.

Maddy Kramer had asked if he wanted to flat-share once the lease at her current place ran out. She was the exception to most women he'd known over the years – kind and considerate, not one to flutter her eyelashes and drop her knickers at the first hint of male attention. Even Paige, who considered him a friend, was a slut, swooning all over

Stirling like some pathetic teenager. It made him sick, and he was sure she'd banged him too.

But Maddy and he were kindred spirits. She was an orphan, while he might as well have been one.

He'd move in with her, and she would act as a check on his urges.

The present

As soon as she heard the front door close, Maddy emerged from her bedroom, laptop wedged under her right armpit, phone clutched in her left hand. She was alone, but she couldn't help looking around nervously. Seeing that the coast was clear, she headed towards Paul's bedroom door across from hers. Her heart briefly sank when it occurred to her that he might have locked it. Thankfully, when she turned the handle, it opened.

She crept in like a crafty cat, conscious of her own movements, every noise – however small – she made. The room was tidy, as Paul always kept it. His laptop was closed, resting on his desk, his printer on a stand to the left of it. She had no idea what his password was and didn't want to waste time trying to crack it; in doing so, she might possibly alert him to her efforts.

She pushed the laptop to one side to make room for hers, which she then opened to see the Word document she'd just created, headed *Please don't let it be him.*

She grabbed the loose cable running from the printer and inserted it into one of the USB ports at the side of her laptop. Then she pressed Print. As the printer groaned into action, it felt like an eternity waiting for the page to emerge. Print job complete, she hesitated to pick up the single sheet of paper. Her heart was pumping so furiously it hurt, her hand trembling as it hovered over the potentially damning evidence.

Come on, Mads, get a grip. You've come this far, now see it through for pity's sake.

She slid the piece of paper off the printer tray, then slowly turned it over. It was blemish-free. It didn't match the letters printed and mailed by the killer.

She was overcome with relief. But also with guilt for doubting Paul. For very nearly betraying her best friend to the police.

She'd been so foolish. The Stirlings had tried to lure her into their ugly, deceitful trap and she hated herself for ever trusting them.

Chapter Thirty-Eight

'Any improvement?' Carver looked up hopefully at Drake, back from Kingston Hospital. It was nearly 9 p.m. and he had just tested Maddy's theory about the killer having used a faulty printer.

It appeared she was right. The killer's first three letters to him had the same faint lines running across the page as his letters to her and Paul King, in stark contrast to his last letter – printed out by a member of Carver's forensic team – which was clean.

Now he was waiting to hear back from Jim Turner, head of computer forensics, as to whether copy from Stirling's home or work printers displayed the same marks. He was sure they wouldn't, because he was now certain Stirling wasn't the killer.

'Afraid not, sir. Doctors aren't sure she'll ever wake up.'

'Damn!' She's our bloody answer. She needs to wake up and tell us who or what she saw.'

'Forensics are examining her personal items, including her personal mobile and work phones. Maybe they'll help us determine how she came to be in Hampton Court Maze on a wet Monday afternoon.'

'Let's hope so.' Carver's phone rang. 'Yes?' A pause. 'I'll be there right away.'

It was Drake's turn to look expectant. 'Something's come up, sir?'

'Copy from Stirling's home and office printers comes out clean. It also looks like his PC's been hacked.' He jumped up from his chair and made for the door. 'We've got the wrong man, Drake. Trouble is, I still don't have a bloody clue who the right man is.'

* * *

Maddy sank down into the bath, still racked with guilt.

She chastised herself for getting sucked in by Elizabeth Stirling's bullshit story. Paul had been her citadel for nearly four years; the brother she never had, with whom she'd shared so many special memories. *How could I ever have doubted him? I've been so gullible.* It was preposterous when she thought about it. And the fact that the Stirlings had been prepared to cook up such a malicious scheme to frame an innocent man for a series of despicable crimes he didn't commit, dissolved any shred of sympathy she might otherwise have had for Professor Stirling.

The attempted murder of Suzanne Carroll that afternoon might well put Stirling's guilt into question, but he and his wife were far from innocent as far as Maddy was concerned.

'Tell me what you've got.'

Carver waited for Jim Turner to explain. Turner was in his late thirties but looked at least ten years older. A thin, wiry man, he had a slight stoop and sallow skin suggestive of someone who spent most of his time indoors. In front of him was Stirling's home computer and laptop.

'We ran an anti-malicious software program for traces of any Trojans.'

'Trojans? You mean some sort of hidden virus?'

'Yes. Disguised as something normal or desirable, which a user unwittingly installs.'

'Go on.'

'It appears that around the end of last September, Stirling's system was infected by a remote administration tool.'

The man is brilliant but incapable of speaking in English.

'What does that mean exactly?'

'It's a malicious program that runs invisibly on the host PC and permits the hacker to connect to and control it, as if they had actual physical access to it. They can monitor a user's activity, manage files, install additional software and control the entire system, including any present application or hardware device. They can also modify essential system settings, turn off or restart a computer, et cetera.'

'How might Stirling's PC have become infected like that?'

'Any number of ways. The most likely is that Stirling opened a bogus email which appeared legitimate on the surface. Or got given an infected floppy disk or CD-ROM which, when inserted, unleashed the malicious software and gave the hacker unfettered access to his PC.'

'And Stirling wouldn't have picked up on this?'

'It seems the hacker also installed a software package known as a "rootkit" – something which modifies the host's operating system so that the virus is hidden from the owner. Also, more practically, if the hacker operated at night, Stirling wouldn't have been aware that someone else was controlling his PC. Hackers tend to work between 6 p.m. and 8 a.m.'

'Bring up Stirling's letters. Let's see what time they were created.'

Turner navigated his way to a file hidden within Stirling's documents folder. All but the last letter, which Carver already knew had been written the afternoon Stirling was arrested, had been created between 7 and 11 p.m.

'So, whoever's been controlling Stirling's server could have browsed all those dodgy websites?'

'Yes. He could have done anything.'

'If Stirling had noticed something wasn't right with his system, what might have alerted him?'

'Password changes, the cursor moving by itself, new toolbars, that sort of thing.'

'We need to have a word with Stirling.' Carver turned to Drake.

'There's something else,' Turner said.

'What?'

'We've picked up the same malicious software on Bethany Williams' system.'

Carver's face brightened. He glanced again at Drake. 'If that's the case, the killer could easily have written the email from Williams to Stirling, asking him to meet her at Waterloo Bridge.'

He turned back to Turner. 'Are you able to decipher whether it's from the same source?'

'We're working on that. The hacker's very good at hiding his tracks.'

Turner walked over to another table and removed an iPhone from a clear plastic bag. He came back over, appeared to search for something on the device, then showed the screen to Carver. 'This is Suzanne Carroll's phone.'

Carver looked at the screen, displaying an email from Janis Stirling to Carroll on Friday 9 January at 9.15 p.m. Drake leaned over Carver's shoulder to get a closer look.

'She was meeting Stirling's mother?' Drake said.

'No,' Carver shook his head. 'It's the same hacker, I suspect. The killer – who's also managed to infiltrate Janis Stirling's system. That email address is odd, though.' He peered at it: 'rellikeht@mai.co.uk,' he said slowly. 'Holy fuck. The little shit.'

'What is it?' Turner asked expectantly.

'Read it backwards, Drake.'

Drake studied the address. Then he saw it. 'Bloody hell, sir – it says "i-am-the-killer".'

'Arrogant son of a bitch. We need to get someone over to Janis Stirling's place. Drake, tell Keel I want her to go because she's dealt with Janis before. Turner, I'd like you to go along with Keel. Run the anti-virus software on Mrs Stirling's computer and report back as soon as you have something.'

'Yes, sir.'

'Drake, let's go see Stirling.'

Carver and Drake waited for the guard to open the door, then walked into the interview room. Stirling was already there. Dressed in the standard grey prison uniform, sitting behind a rectangular table, shoulders slouched, a broken man. Gone was the charming smile, the twinkle in his eye, his normally smooth face now covered with stubble.

'Hello, Professor Stirling,' Carver said, pulling back a chair and parking himself in it. With new leads to go on, he'd forgotten how tired he was. He knew Stirling was innocent, the victim of a cruel, masterfully planned deception. And yet he still had no way of definitively proving it. He was still no closer to unveiling the identity of the real killer.

'Hello, DCI Carver.' Stirling's voice was flat.

'Professor Stirling, we have reason to believe your computer has been infected with a virus which allowed the hacker to control it.'

Stirling's eyes were suddenly alive, a glimmer of hope filtering through them. He leaned forward, elbows resting on the table. 'Since when?'

'Since the end of September. Professor, do you remember seeing anything suspicious on your computer…some strange message, virus warning, some sign it was being tampered with?'

Stirling thought for a while. Then he remembered something. 'That Sunday, when I was in my office, a few hours before you arrested me, I'd mostly been working on paper. I'm old-fashioned like that – still prepare all my tutorials by hand, then get my secretary to type them up. I've got a tutorials folder stored in my documents file. When I went back to look at an old tutorial from last year, my mouse wouldn't do what I wanted it to do. It was sort of moving by itself.'

'Can you put a time on that?'

Stirling sighed, made a puffy sound. 'God, I don't know, around 2.30, 3-ish, I should think.'

Carver retrieved a piece of paper from his inside pocket. It was a printout of the document history of Stirling's letters to him, Maddy and Paul, listing the date and time each was created. The last one was dated 4 January 2015, created at 2.40 p.m.

'Do you remember seeing or opening anything dodgy, Professor Stirling, towards the end of September? Either an email, or a CD-ROM you might have received. Alternatively, did you ever speak with anyone on the phone, someone who claimed to work for your internet service provider and asked you to confirm specific security questions? Think, Professor Stirling. This could be the key to your freedom.'

Stirling pondered the question for a moment. Then recognition engulfed his face. 'Jesus Christ.'

'What is it?'

'One afternoon, I think it may have been the last Monday in September, a CD-ROM had been left on my desk. It had the standard academy logo and was labelled "Draft Information Evening Guide 25

January 2015 for final approval". Essentially, it was an open evening for prospective students.'

'Go on.'

'All the tutors are expected to attend, me especially, being the Head of Contract. I always have a say over the look and content of the guide before it's finalised.'

'Had you any idea who left it?'

'No, but I assumed it was my secretary or someone in the press department. I didn't think to check, and automatically inserted it into my hard drive.'

'And was it what you'd expected?'

'No, all that was on it was the academy logo. Nothing else.'

'And what did you do then?'

'I spent some time clicking various buttons, inserting it and reinserting it, wondering if I was doing something wrong.'

'Then what?'

'Nothing happened, so I rang my secretary. She said she knew nothing about it. She spoke to the press department for me, and neither did they.'

'What then?'

Stirling shook his head. 'I was stupid. I should have looked into it further, found out who was responsible, but I didn't. I tossed the CD in the bin and thought nothing more of it.' He lowered his eyes, then looked up again. 'Until now.'

Carver held his gaze. 'I believe you are innocent, Professor Stirling, but the fact remains that your DNA was all over Bethany Williams' flat, and the killer's letters were created on your PC.'

'But you know it's been infected. You know I didn't create them.'

'Yes, but until I know who did, I can't let you go. Right now, my men are trying to track the software to the source. But it's not easy. It takes time.' He paused. 'There's another reason why I want to keep you in here for now, and if you'll allow me to explain, I think you'll agree it's a credible one.'

'Go on.'

'We need the killer to still feel like he's in control. We don't want to give him any reason to suppose we're onto him.'

Stirling nodded, then appeared to hesitate, as if weighing up whether to divulge what was obviously on his mind.

'What is it, Professor?' Carver asked. 'Is there something you're not telling us? If you think you know something that could be helpful to our investigation, to your cause, you need to tell me, however embarrassed or ashamed you might be to reveal it. Your freedom depends on it. A killer is out there, and he needs to be caught. The pattern is complete, but who knows whether or not he's done?' At that moment, Carver thought of Maddy. He quickly banished her from his mind. 'He may well strike again. Other lives may be at stake.'

Stirling looked at both men, a look of resignation in his eyes. 'Okay, you're right. I have a theory – something I explained to my wife when she came to visit, and which I asked her to relay to Madeline Kramer.'

Carver straightened in surprise. 'Madeline Kramer? What's she got to do with it?'

'Listen, and you'll find out.'

Carver wearily stepped into his hallway at just gone 1 a.m. He switched on the light, then tossed his keys and some loose change on the ledge. Without bothering to remove his jacket, he went straight to the kitchen, grabbed a tumbler from a tall cupboard and reached for the single malt on the side. He filled two-thirds of the glass, before downing half en route to his tiny living room where he crashed onto the tired-looking settee. It had seen better days – a bit like Carver.

Stirling's story had been so unexpected; at first, he'd wanted to laugh in his face. The idea that Maddy Kramer's flatmate might have something to do with the murders was ludicrous. Paul King was a decent, down-to-earth guy who'd been nothing but helpful with their enquiries. What's more, he was Kramer's best friend, had been close to Paige Summers; and the idea of him threatening Kramer, killing her cat, not to mention ransacking their own apartment was nonsensical.

But he couldn't ignore it. Paul was a former student at the academy who, as Stirling had pointed out, had a difficult relationship with his mother. And, assuming Stirling had been telling the truth about the incident in his office, had been in love with, and rejected by, the man being framed for the murder of six women, and the attempted murder of one. Not to mention the unfortunate security guard.

He had to follow it up. But for now, he was deadbeat. He'd drink his single malt, and then he'd sleep.

Chapter Thirty-Nine

Tuesday 13 January 2015

Maddy opened her eyes. Turned and gazed at the clock. 9 a.m. She'd woken late. Shockingly late for a work day.

It was gone 3 a.m. before she'd finally drifted off to sleep, too restless to switch off, her mind spinning with recent events, her emotions in turmoil.

And even as she slept, it hadn't been a deep, peaceful sleep; faces appearing in her dreams: the victims, Paul, Carver, Rose, and Stirling locked in a prison cell, protesting his innocence. At one point, she'd woken up in a cold sweat, relieved to know she'd just been dreaming but still haunted by the realness of her dreams.

She sat up, rubbed the sleep from her eyes as she flung off her duvet, and swung her bare legs off the bed and onto the floor. She'd never done it before, and her conscience certainly wasn't okay with it, but she decided to pull a sickie. She was knackered, mentally and physically. She couldn't face people today. She needed time to herself.

She wondered if Paul was up. She'd only just crawled into bed when she heard him come through the front door around 11.45. She'd popped her head out to say hello, but he'd been in a foul mood. He'd had a row with Justin and didn't want to talk about it. He did briefly mention having to visit his mother again today. Apparently, she had something important to tell him she didn't want to say over the phone. Why she couldn't have told him when he'd gone round earlier, Maddy couldn't figure out.

'Fuck knows what it's about,' Paul had grumbled before disappearing into his bedroom without so much as a goodnight. Maddy had returned to hers, unable to settle herself, half-expecting Paul to crash out of his at any moment, demanding to know why she'd been snooping around his belongings, even though she was certain she'd left things exactly as she'd found them.

As she opened her bedroom door, she vaguely heard the radio playing in the kitchen, the clitter-clatter of crockery. She walked towards the noise, the music gradually becoming louder.

Paul was at the sink, washing a bowl. He must have heard her approach as he turned around before she had the chance to speak.

'Morning, not like you to sleep in till gone nine. You do realise it's a work day?' He looked both amused and concerned. *At least he appears to be in a better mood this morning.*

'Yeah, I know. I just couldn't drop off last night.' Maddy felt the skin under her eyes sag. 'I'm pulling a sickie.'

Paul looked at her in amazement. 'You sure you're not actually sick?' he grinned. 'I would never have thought it of you.'

She watched him swivel back round to rinse the bowl before stacking it on the dish rack. When he was done, he turned to face her again, wiping his hands with a tea towel. 'Something's up, I can tell. Maybe I can help?'

For a moment, Maddy was sorely tempted to tell him about her conversation with Elizabeth Stirling. But her instinct said otherwise. There was no point upsetting him. Even if there had been an incident between him and Stirling, she didn't want to embarrass him further by bringing the subject up. *Why rehash an old memory he clearly wants to forget, and has deliberately avoided telling me about in five years of friendship?*

She shook her head. 'Just one of those nights, that's all.' She stretched out her arms, gave a big yawn. 'Want a coffee? I need one badly.'

'Er, no, thanks.' Paul gave her a quick peck on the cheek as he dashed past and out the door. 'Got to finish proofing the last two chapters of my book, then be at my mother's by midday,' he called out over his shoulder, 'and I'm already running behind schedule.'

12.30 p.m. Carver tapped his right knee incessantly, willing the thick traffic ahead to disperse at his touch, like Moses parting the Red Sea. 'You know I hate taking liberties, Drake,' he said, having finally lost all patience, 'but put the damn siren on. We need to get there. Fast.'

Twenty minutes earlier, the officer guarding Suzanne Carroll's hospital room had called to say she'd woken from her coma and was able to talk. At first, she'd been confused. But as her thoughts had become clearer, and she'd realised where she was, and what had brought her there, her confusion had quickly turned to fear. She'd muttered something about Stirling's mother, and a nun in the chapel, lashing her arms about wildly before the doctor treating her was forced to administer a low-dose sedative. She'd fallen asleep, but the officer didn't think it would be too long before she woke up.

Just as Drake pulled into a space at Kingston Hospital, Carver's phone rang. It was Jim Turner. He and Keel had headed over to Janis Stirling's place first thing that morning to question her about Suzanne Carroll and examine her computer.

'Carver here.'

'Sir, as we'd suspected, Janis Stirling didn't contact Carroll asking to meet up at Hampton Court Maze. Although she remembers her from Stirling's Oxford days, they've not crossed paths in some time.'

'Did you find anything suspect on her machine?'

'Yes, sir. Picked up the same virus we found on Williams' and Stirling's machines when I ran the scan.'

'What did she say when you told her? Did she have any idea?'

'Not at first. Not until I probed.'

'And?'

'She said that around a week ago, a man called, claiming to work for BT, her internet service provider. He told her she was due an upgrade on her system but needed her to confirm her username and password.'

'Christ. And she believed him?'

'She's an elderly woman, sir. This kind of thing happens fairly frequently.'

Carver leaned back against the headrest. 'Yes, I suppose that's true. Find out if she keeps her phone records. We might be able to trace the call to a specific location. And try and get her to remember the date and approximate time of the call.'

'Yes, sir.'

'Are you any closer to narrowing down the source of the virus?'

'My team are working on it round the clock, sir. I'll let you know as soon as I have anything.'

'Good.' Carver hung up, relayed the latest to Drake, then got out of the car. As they walked towards the hospital entrance, he barely noticed a young nun brush past him.

'Bloody hell!' Maddy had just stepped into the shower when she heard the phone ring. She was tempted to leave it. But her grandmother was always at the back of her mind. *What if she's had a fall, needs my help?* She'd never forgive herself if something terrible happened to Rose, all because she'd been too lazy to answer the phone.

She hopped out, shivering as she wrapped a towel around herself, and dashed barefoot into the living room. The phone rang off just as she was about to pick it up. Typical! She was about to dial 1471 to see who'd called when it rang again. She answered immediately.

'Hello.'

'Madeline?'

She knew that voice. It was Paul's mother, Evelyn.

'Evelyn? How are you?'

'I'm very well, thank you. I just wondered if my son's there?'

Maddy frowned in surprise. She eyed the wall clock: 12.30. Paul had left for Evelyn's fifty minutes ago. 'But he's with you, isn't he?' she asked. At the same time, a feeling of dread pervaded her as she imagined something terrible had happened to Paul en route to Evelyn's. The killings had curbed her usual optimism; made her fear the worst.

Evelyn chuckled. 'Me? What on earth would make you think that? I've not seen Paul since the start of last summer.'

Maddy took a step back, sat trance-like on the sofa. 'But, but he said he saw you yesterday.'

Silence. Then, 'I'm afraid my son's been lying to you, Madeline. We had a major falling-out in early June. After I told him I was marrying Philip.' Another shock. Maddy couldn't speak. 'He didn't tell you?'

'No, he didn't.'

'He accused me of being a selfish tramp, who'd driven his father to an early grave and should never have been allowed to bring a child into this world. I was devastated, told him to get out. Philip and I married in Lake Como in August. It was a beautiful day, but my one regret is that my only child wasn't there to share in my happiness.' A pause. Maddy thought she heard Evelyn dragging on a cigarette. 'I take it he's not told you any of this?'

'No,' Maddy said faintly.

'I wasn't the best mother, I'll grant Paul that. But I'm guessing he's never told you that George wasn't the best husband. Fact is, he changed as soon as we were married – went as cold as stone. He was married to his work, rather than to me. Plus, he had a temper. When I complained to him that we never did anything together, that I was lonely, he would fly off the handle. Tell me I was ungrateful. That if I didn't shut my mouth, I'd be out on the streets.'

'Paul's never mentioned any of that,' Maddy said. *Just like he's never mentioned his feelings for Stirling.*

'No, I bet he hasn't. Paul worshipped his father. He was devastated by his death. I know that, deep down, no matter what he says about me, he blames himself. Thinks he broke his father's heart when he told him he was gay.'

'And did he?'

Another lull. 'Yes, I'm afraid he did. We always knew Paul was different, right from an early age. He was a strange little boy, locked in his own world. He didn't make friends easily, kept himself to himself. In fact, when I think about it, you're the closest friend he's ever had.'

Neither spoke for a while, until Maddy broke the hush. 'What made you pick up the phone to Paul now?'

'It's been seven months, it's the New Year. I thought it was about time one of us got in touch. Plus, one of my friends saw him having a drink with his therapist yesterday evening.'

'His therapist?' If Maddy hadn't been sitting down, she might have fallen over in shock. Why had Paul told her he'd met Justin for a drink the night before – even fabricating some row?

'Yes, Marcia Devereux. You must have known her. She was in your year at the academy.'

'Marcia Devereux,' Maddy mumbled, still in shock. Lisa's friend, the one who found her body. Shy, always sitting at the back, afraid to speak. Not the best-looking girl in the year, although there was nothing wrong with that.

'You remember her?'

'Yes, yes, I do. But Paul and Marcia weren't friends as far as I know. And she left after the first year.'

'You're right, I don't think they were friends at the academy. They met, quite by chance, about a year ago. Paul didn't go into much detail, but from what I could gather, Marcia decided law wasn't for her and, as you said, left after the first year. She trained as a clinical psychologist, psychology having been her undergraduate degree. Last year, Paul decided he needed to see a therapist, and it turned out to be Marcia. Small world, isn't it? I'm surprised you didn't know.'

'Yes, so am I,' Maddy said vacantly. 'I had no idea he was depressed.'

'As I said, Paul's wasn't an easy childhood. My son has a lot of issues. And his father's death crushed him.' Another drag. 'It's a nasty business about James Stirling. George and I were good friends with him and Elizabeth once. Did Paul tell you?'

'Yes, I'd heard that.' Maddy skirted the truth.

'We lost touch after George died. It's not for want of me trying, but for some strange reason, the Stirlings went cold on me. If truth be told, I felt rather let down, as I'm sure Paul did. But I have to say, I'm shocked by James' arrest. I'd like to think I know him pretty well, and so I'm finding it hard to believe he's a murderer.'

'Yes, I think we all are.'

'What does Paul make of it?'

'He thinks Stirling's guilt is beyond doubt.'

'Well, judging by the news reports, I can't argue with that. But my son's attitude surprises me. I always thought he was rather fond of James. Will you let him know I called?'

'Yes, of course.'

Maddy hung up. How could she not have known that Paul was seeing a therapist? Why had he hidden something so huge from her?

What else is he hiding?

Chapter Forty

'She's dead, sir.'

'Dead? How's that fucking possible? She'd only just bloody woken up!'

Carver glared at PC Benson, the officer on duty, attempting to prise a credible explanation out of him. They'd arrived at Suzanne Carroll's hospital room to find an army of doctors and nurses fluttering around her bed, frantically trying to keep their patient alive. She'd gone into cardiac arrest out of the blue, and after numerous attempts to shock her heart into action, they'd called it a day. Time of death: 12.45 p.m.

'I don't know, sir. I was here all the time.'

'You were here all the time?' Carver eyed Benson sceptically. They were stood in Carroll's room, the door wide open.

'Yes, sir.' Benson bit his lip, his itinerant eyes betraying a guilty conscience. 'Aside for about five minutes, when I gave her and the nun a bit of time.'

'What nun?' Just then, Carver had a flashback: a brush of shoulders as he'd reached the hospital entrance. Black cloth, black trainers. And hadn't the groundsmen at Hampton Court mentioned there'd been a nun wandering the maze?

'From Carroll's church. She came to visit. Almost like she'd sensed Carroll mumbling for her when she first woke up. Ironic really. I needed to relieve myself and I didn't see the harm. I was only away five minutes.'

'Ironic!' Carver bawled, attracting an audience of frowny nurses and shocked patients in the corridor. 'It's not bloody ironic, it's why she's dead, you bloody moron! Do you remember what she looked like?'

Benson looked at Drake for help but got none. 'You think the nun killed her?'

'I think the nun was no goddamn nun!' More stunned looks and grimaces all round. Drake could make out a bulging vein running across Carver's forehead.

'Jesus,' Benson mouthed. 'She was around five-ten, dark eyes, rather large nose. Late twenties, early thirties I should say. Quite a heavy-set lady. Looked like she could take care of herself, certainly not a dainty thing.' He leaned closer, whispered, 'Or much of a looker. Not surprised she went for the profession she did. Let's just say, you wouldn't expect many blokes knocking on her door.'

Carver was about to have a heart attack himself when a doctor appeared. 'Who's in charge here?' he asked calmly, although his face told a different story.

'I am,' Carver said. 'Do we know what killed her?'

'Potassium cyanide. God only knows how it happened. It was injected in the upper arm.'

Carver glared again at Benson. 'I think I have some idea.' He looked up at the ceiling. 'Do you have CCTV in this ward?'

'Yes.'

'I need to look at the footage.'

'Now?'

'Yes, now!'

'I don't understand it,' the security guard said. Carver and Drake stood looking over his bulky shoulders at the TV monitor. The screen was blank.

'You say all the wards have cameras?' Carver asked.

'Yes.'

The guard rewound the tape, tried again. There was no footage of the ICU ward between 11.30 and 12.30.

'She disabled it before entering the building.' Carver turned to Drake. 'Like she did at Channing & Barton before killing Frank and Sarah.' He was still struggling with the idea that all this time, they'd been hunting a woman.

'What about reception?' Drake asked.

The security guard shifted his chair across to face a different screen, displaying the main reception area. He pressed Play on the tape, then Rewind. Carver leaned in closer, scrutinising the image. And then he saw it – the back of the nun. A surprisingly broad figure, dressed in a black tunic, head lowered, walking out of the main entrance. From behind, if it wasn't for the veil, you certainly wouldn't have been able to tell it was a woman.

'We need Benson to give a full description to a sketch artist. Give him a copy of this image too. It's clear she got to Carroll, but as a matter of routine, all hospital staff and patients will need to be questioned. Check the visitors' log as well. We're so close, Drake.'

'I can't believe the killer's female,' Drake said. 'All this time I just assumed we were after a man.'

'I know, Drake. It's easy to make assumptions. But by all accounts, we don't appear to be dealing with a delicate wallflower. Judging by Benson's description, and the fact that, save for Carroll, the victims have generally been of slim build, I'm betting she didn't have too much trouble overpowering them. She knows we're onto her. For the first time, she's on the back foot, and we need to bring her to heel.'

'How's your mother?'

Paul walked into the living room, slung his bag on the floor, then bent over to kiss Maddy on the cheek. She pretended to casually flick through a magazine, despite not being able to relax since Evelyn King's call.

'The usual.'

Why the fuck are you lying? she wanted to scream. Instead, she said, 'How so?'

'Oh, you know, full of herself. She and Philip are having problems. Apparently, he doesn't pay her enough attention. In truth, I reckon she's just getting bored of him. Planning on husband number three.'

'Husband number three?' Maddy sat up, looked Paul straight in the eye. 'I didn't know she was married to number two.'

He cleared his throat. 'Didn't you? Er, yeah, she did it on the quiet a couple of months back. Some registry office in Putney. Couldn't bring myself to go.'

More lies. One after the other. *What's he playing at? What's he hiding?*

Maddy got up. Placed a hand on his shoulder. 'You know you can tell me anything, don't you? I'm always here for you. I won't judge you in any way.'

Paul laughed uneasily. 'What are you saying, Mads? You're making me nervous. I'm fine. Really, I am.'

'Okay,' she said. 'I just wanted you to know that.'

'DCI Carver, it's Dominic Avery.'

Carver had been waiting anxiously for Avery to get back to him with his report from the maze. The killer had failed to finish the job there. It was the first chink in her perfectly executed plan. Maybe this time she'd left something incriminating.

'Yes, Avery?'

'We've found something.'

Carver shifted in his seat. 'What is it?'

'Blood. On one of the hedge walls of the maze. Near the centre. There was a rather large gap there. Large enough for someone to hide. We also found traces of sweat.'

'Sweat? At this time of the year. Who sweats in January?'

'I don't know, Chief Inspector. Maybe a killer about to be caught?'

Carver considered this. Avery was right. The killer had still been inside when the groundsmen had entered the maze. With no time to lose, she'd hidden within the space Avery had described until they'd gone. Perhaps cutting herself on a thorn as she'd scrambled to get in, or out.

'You still there, Chief Inspector?'

Carver stirred from his thoughts. 'Yes, sorry, still here.'

'There's something else.'

'Yes?'

'The DNA was female.'

'I see.'

'You don't sound surprised.'

'I'm not. Had you heard Carroll's dead?'

'Yes, one of my team informed me half an hour ago.'

Carver told Avery about the nun who'd visited Carroll moments before she was found dead.

'So you think it could be *her* DNA?'

'Almost certainly. Have you run a check on the system yet?'

'No. I wanted to speak to you first.'

'Do it and get back to me ASAP.'

'Did you speak to Maddy Kramer about Paul King?'

Tuesday, 5 p.m. Carver sat across from Stirling. He looked different. Whereas yesterday his eyes had been dead, now they showed signs of life. They had lit up as soon as Carver had entered the room.

'Not yet.'

Stirling frowned. The light had quickly been extinguished. 'Why?'

'Because events took over.'

'What events?'

'Suzanne Carroll died this morning.'

Stirling opened his mouth to speak, but nothing came out.

'Do you need some water?' Carver asked.

'No, I…I don't understand. I thought she was stable.'

'She was. In fact, early this morning she woke up, and I was on my way to question her when it happened.'

'What happened exactly?'

Carver noticed Stirling's eyes were glistening. He had clearly cared for Carroll. 'She was injected with potassium cyanide and suffered a massive heart attack.'

Stirling placed his hand over his mouth, then let it drift up to cover his eyes. His body started to shake, then came the sound of sobbing.

A few seconds of uncomfortable silence went by. Finally, Stirling came up for air. 'Why haven't you questioned Paul? You know all about his background. He's punishing me for rejecting him. And he's punishing all those women for sleeping with me. Because I slept with *them*, not him. He hates women. He had an unhappy childhood. Blames his mother for not being there for him, for making a fool out of his father, for sending him to an early grave. What's more, he's not lived up to his father's reputation. A failed lawyer, a failure at life. I'm telling you, he's sick in the head and he sees this as a way of making his mark on the world, of winning at something for once.'

Carver saw the frustration on Stirling's face. He looked at him earnestly. 'Professor, I understand your need to find the person responsible. Your reputation and your marriage are both in ruins, and you are hurting. You're desperate to get out of here, to make someone pay. But we're ninety-nine per cent certain the killer's female.'

Stirling's mouth fell open. Looking confused, he swallowed hard. 'Female?'

Carver nodded and explained. 'Professor, I need you to think. Is there anyone else, any woman you can think of, who might bear a grudge against you?'

Stirling smiled wryly. 'Chief Inspector, you know I've not got the best record with women. I've treated a lot of women badly over the years. Including my wife. I have a problem, an addiction, I'm not shy to admit it now. Plus, I do have temper issues, as you've seen for yourself on the recording. There could be any number of women who might want to get back at me. And now it appears I am paying the price.'

His honesty was admirable. It was amazing what truths came out of men's mouths when they were inside; no job, no marriage, no cloak to hide behind; just a man in prison clothes, suddenly craving the freedom he'd once taken for granted.

'I appreciate all that, Professor Stirling. But think.'

Stirling ran his hands through his hair, then fingered his stubble distractedly as he thought. He seemed a different man to when Carver had first met him. It was hard to believe that was less than three months ago. Finally, he shook his head. 'I told you, I don't know. There have been so many women over the years.'

'What about larger women?'

'Larger women?'

'Yes. Have you ever slept with a larger woman? Suzanne's killer was on the bulky side. With short dark hair, dark eyes. Does that make a difference?'

The wry smile was there again. 'Another thing I'm ashamed to admit is that I'm deeply shallow when it comes to women. I like them slim and pretty. I don't notice the plain, overweight ones.'

'I see.' Having started to feel some sympathy for Stirling, on hearing this latest confession, Carver felt he probably deserved everything he got. If only Rachel had been there to witness his admission, maybe she'd realise her ex hadn't been that bad after all. 'But what about Suzanne? She didn't exactly fit into that category.'

'No, she didn't. Suzanne was the exception, though. She was incredibly bright and witty. She made me laugh. She was a good friend. All these qualities drew me to her. She knew I could never be true to her, but she accepted that. We knew we could always rely on each other when the chips were down. We were each other's rock, I suppose.' He lowered his head to the floor. 'I didn't deserve her.'

'Touching,' Carver muttered.

The door opened. It was Drake. 'Sir.'

Carver sprang up from his chair and went over to him. 'What is it?'

'Turner's team has managed to trace the virus to the same internet service provider, Virgin Media, somewhere in the Hyde Park area.'

'That's good news. They can't narrow it down further?'

'Not yet.'

'What about the phone call made to Janis Stirling? Did a number show up on her statement?'

'The number was withheld. BT won't trace the call without authorisation from us.'

'So, what are you waiting for? Give them authorisation!'

'Yes, sir.'

Chapter Forty-One

The killer woke early. She'd slept little, and even then, it had been patchy. It wasn't just the howling wind and relentless rain battering her bedroom window that had caused her to toss and turn all night: it was the feeling that she was losing control; that the roles of hunter and hunted had been reversed; that Carver smelled blood and was coming for her.

Until Suzanne, it had all been going so well; despite Maddy Kramer's interference. She'd planned things to perfection, and her success had been exhilarating. A bit like her favourite classical composition of all time: Beethoven's *Symphony No. 5*. His greatest piece of work as far as she was concerned. Like the great master himself, she had decided to seize fate by the throat, become a master in her own right, transform herself from a tragic, pitiful, uninspiring figure to a triumphant, venerable, talked-about one. How she'd delighted in her nickname: The Scribe. She was famous, feared, utterly fabulous.

So unlike her life to date: dull, unremarkable. As a child, she'd spent so much of her time trying to please her hard-hearted father who had abused her from the age of three, perhaps as punishment for not being the boy he'd craved; telling her she was so unattractive, she might as well have been male.

And then there was her beautiful, fickle mother, who'd stopped taking any interest in her only child when it became clear that looks would never be her forte. She'd had no more use for her then, preferring to lavish her attention on her stunning five-year-old niece – the spoilt little brat.

It had made her resentful of beauty; caused her to believe that it distorted people's perspectives; made them lose all sense of what was important; blinded them to the person behind the mask. Instead of dressing her Barbie dolls in pretty outfits, brushing their hair and painting their nails, she'd stick pins in them, twist their long blonde locks around their necks, deface their perfect faces with clown expressions, scratch their chests with the sparkly hair grips her mother had forced her to wear, but which she had loathed. Her mother had taken her to a child psychologist, but she had been as sweet as candy in his sessions, and he'd quickly surmised it was just a phase she was going through; that it would soon pass. The mutilation of Barbie dolls stopped when she was granted her wish to have cello lessons, and her mother soon forgot it had ever happened.

After that, she'd spent most of her academic life trying to please her father and fit in wherever she went. But she'd never quite managed it. At school, she'd been bullied and teased by both sexes; at college, it was only the fat, desperate geeky boys who'd wanted to shag her; at uni, she'd retreated further into her shell – consumed by her studies and her love of classical music, fascinated by the complexities of the human mind, desperate to make sense of people, to understand what made them tick, what made them think the way they did, act the way they did. She would play her cello at night, alone in her university bedroom, while those around her got intoxicated with drink and drugs and had lots of sex. People could be so shameless, so disgusting, and it sickened her.

She'd enrolled on the law conversion course at the academy because her lawyer father had insisted that psychology was not a proper profession. He'd indulged it as a first degree, but that was all it had been to him: an indulgence. He'd refused to finance the necessary postgraduate training for his daughter to become a clinical psychologist and had insisted that she get her act together, grow a spine and enrol at the academy. Resenting every second of her time there, she'd found herself mostly surrounded by women who made her feel inadequate, and young men who never gave her a second look.

And then there was the handsome, charismatic professor, whom she'd developed a crush on from the first day. But who had humiliated her at the most public event of the academic year, through one of his many whores. And laughed about her behind her back with another.

But life took a turn for the better when her mother called at the end of her first year to say that her father had died of a brain haemorrhage. She'd felt not an ounce of sorrow, just relief. And it had provided her with the chance to escape. After a few weeks of playing the grieving daughter, she'd gone to her mother, asking for the money to finance a postgraduate degree in psychology. Her mother didn't care what her daughter did so long as she kept quiet and left her alone. She let her have the money, and three years later, the killer was a certified psychologist.

But her time at the academy hadn't been completely wasted. It had given her a brilliant idea, and it had led her to her partner in crime. It had inspired her to carry out a spate of murders so chilling, so brilliant, her genius would be forever etched in history. She was The Scribe, and she would no longer be the plain, dull girl in the background. She would have the last laugh.

But Marcia Devereux blamed herself for choosing such an ambitious setting for her last kill. She'd grown cocky, and now she was paying the price. The problem was, the more she'd killed and got away with it, the more she'd wanted to push herself.

And she had wanted Suzanne to die spectacularly, because she couldn't understand how someone like her – a fellow stout, plain spinster – had managed to stay in Stirling's bed for so many years. The others had all been stereotypes: slim, beautiful heartbreakers; perfect women in the eyes of most men – the antithesis of her.

She couldn't fathom this. Psychologically, it made no sense.

Wednesday 10 February 2010

'Why do you hang out with her? She's so dull. Got the personality of a goldfish and, aside from her peculiarly well-manicured hands and nails, the looks of a bullfrog. She's holding you back.'

Sarah Morrell was sitting at a table in the far corner of the academy's student canteen, along with Lisa Ryland, Paige Summers and Madeline Kramer. The table was strewn with annotated legal textbooks, A4 pads and several pens. Professor Stirling had split his tutor group into two groups of four for his latest assignment: a mock negotiation which both sides were to carry out in class as if they were two sets of lawyers thrashing out the terms of a legal contract in a meeting room.

Sarah had kicked off by making her usual malicious comments, saying it was the clever hotties versus the struggling misfits, and that it didn't take a genius to work out whose team Stirling would be keeping his eye on. While Paige and Lisa didn't like Sarah's remarks, they were intimidated by her, and felt it safer to keep quiet. But Maddy wasn't one to take anything lying down. It was bad enough being forced to work with Sarah, but the day she let Sarah get away with bad-mouthing those who'd done her no wrong, was the day when hell would freeze over as far as she was concerned.

'Just because Marcia's not the smartest, or textbook beautiful, doesn't give you the right to talk down about her. Does it, Lisa?'

Maddy turned to Lisa and widened her eyes. 'Er, no,' Lisa replied half-heartedly. 'But Marcia's not *really* my friend. We happened to sit next to each other on the first day, and I sort of got lumbered with her from then on. I don't think she's ever had any real friends…'

'Hmm, I'm not surprised,' Sarah sniped.

'And,' Lisa said, looking at Maddy almost apologetically, 'I kind of took pity on her. In truth, she's a bit of a pain – so clingy. I wish she'd leave me alone sometimes; find someone more like her to hang out with.'

'Why don't you just tell her that? Or ignore her,' Paige suggested. 'If you let her down enough times, she'll get the message.'

Maddy looked at Paige crossly. 'I can't believe you. How can you be so heartless? Poor girl, she's done nothing to any of you. You should all be ashamed of yourselves.'

'Oh, please, pass the sick bag,' Sarah yawned. 'Let's get on with this, shall we? I wish I'd fucking never said anything, particularly with you around.' She rolled her eyes at Maddy. 'Mother fucking Teresa. We all know you hang out with misfits.'

'What misfits?'

'Paul King.'

'Paul?'

'Yes, P-a-u-l,' Sarah mocked. 'We all know he's as gay as they come.'

'So what?' Maddy couldn't believe she'd heard right. She tried not to explode.

'I've got nothing against gays per se. But he's so bloody obvious, eyeing up all the blokes on the course. Plus, I've seen the way he looks at Stirling. He's got the hots for him, big time.' She shuddered. 'He gives me the creeps. Seems to have it in for women. Once, in the lecture room, I caught him staring right at me. His eyes were mad, like he wanted to kill me.'

'Don't be so bloody ridiculous.' Maddy looked around the table for support.

'Yeah, Sarah,' Paige said. 'I mean, I'm with you on Marcia, she's a bit odd, but Paul's a really nice guy. I consider him a friend, and you need to cut him some slack.'

'Whatever,' Sarah shrugged her shoulders. 'Anyway, let's stop wasting our time on those losers and get on with this. I don't just want to win; I want to slaughter them.'

The four girls put their conversation, and all thoughts of Marcia and Paul, to the back of their minds and knuckled down to the task Professor Stirling had set them. In fact, it was a conversation they soon forgot and never spoke of again.

But it was a conversation the person sitting at a table the other side of the paper-thin wall would never forget; a conversation which had felt like a knife being plunged into her heart, causing her immeasurable pain and humiliation; a conversation which had enraged her, made her think back to all those airhead Barbie dolls whose chests she'd ripped apart with every morsel of hate and envy running through her veins.

A conversation forever engraved on Marcia Devereux's mind, and which she later relayed to the person whose help she needed to make sure those women never hurt women like her again.

Or tempt men like the professor again.

Or live to bear children who'd behave just like them, all over again. The vicious circle of victimisation had to be stopped.

Wednesday 14 January 2015

Wednesday morning. It was only 7 a.m. but Marcia had been up for hours. She picked up the phone, dialled the number from memory. After six rings, it went through to voicemail. *Damn.* She left a message, her voice uncharacteristically fraught. 'We need to get rid of the evidence. Quickly. I'll be at the base from 10 a.m. Meet me there as soon as you can. And text me to say you got this and that you're coming.'

Everything needed to be destroyed: the hard drive, the printer, the phone, any tangible evidence that could possibly link them to the murders.

Maddy listened to the message, then hung up, trying to make sense of what she'd heard.

She'd felt guilty about faking a sickie the day before and had risen at 6.30 a.m. with the intention of being in her office by eight. She'd been making a coffee when Paul's phone had started to ring. There wasn't a peep from his room. He'd worked a late shift at the bar the night before, and so the sound of his all-too-familiar ringtone was not something she'd expected to hear at seven in the morning, shattering the silence.

It had been coming from the hallway, and she'd gone to answer it, thinking he must have left it there by mistake when he'd got in. She'd also been curious to know who could be ringing at this early hour and had feared it could only have been bad news.

Having followed its ring to where it was lying flat on the hall table, she'd hesitated to answer when she saw from the caller ID that it was "Marcia". By the time she'd finally picked it up, it was too late, and the caller had rung off.

Her conversation with Evelyn still fresh in her mind, Maddy had naturally assumed it was Marcia Devereux, Paul's therapist, and the same strange girl who'd been in their tutor group at the academy. She knew it was wrong to listen to the message, but curiosity had overwhelmed her. There was so much Paul hadn't told her, and he'd been acting so strange and overly secretive of late.

And now, having heard Marcia's message, Maddy was filled with alarm as she recalled Carver's text of yesterday afternoon, informing her of Carroll's death.

What did Marcia mean by "evidence"?

Carver had explained how Carroll had suffered a massive heart attack in hospital, that he believed the killer had got to her, and that he was now almost certain the killer was female, the last person to have seen her alive being a woman dressed as a nun. Almost certainly it was the same nun spotted in Hampton Court Maze shortly before Carroll was attacked. He'd told Maddy that for now, the police were keeping this information quiet, not wanting to alert the killer to the fact that they were onto her. Maddy had promised not to breathe a word to anyone – not even Paul.

As she stood there, her conversation with Elizabeth Stirling came back to haunt her, as did Evelyn's revelation about Paul needing therapy – the fact that he'd been a lonely little boy, resenting his mother, broken by his father's death.

And why did he lie to me about his mother's marriage, about going to meet her? About meeting Justin for a drink?

The truth was too hideous to contemplate: that Paul might somehow be mixed up in the murders after all, responsible for ransacking their flat, killing Atticus.

It just can't be true...can it?

Still holding Paul's phone, she tried to calm herself down, pacing the floor, willing herself to think rationally. Marcia might have been talking about something else. *It's possible, isn't it?* She racked her brain, trying to come up with a plausible explanation when a voice stopped her dead in her tracks.

'Why are you holding my phone?'

Her heart stopped on hearing Paul's voice. She looked up to see him standing there in his pyjama bottoms. She felt like a thief in the night caught red-handed, his eyes torpedoing through her.

'Because it rang,' she said. 'I got up at six, planning to head to the office early. I was making a coffee in the kitchen when I heard it ring. I was surprised. You almost always keep it by your bed.'

He looked grumpy, distracted.

'I was knackered last night. Must have left it there by mistake.' Another brutal stare. 'You didn't think to bring it to me?' His tone was harsh, accusatory.

'I would have done but it rang off before I had the chance to reach it.'

'Is there a message?'

Maddy felt her face flush. 'I don't know.'

Paul continued to glare at her like a human lie detector. 'You don't know?'

She swallowed hard. The room was suddenly caving in on her. 'Why are you staring at me like that? What is this, the third degree?' She gave an uneasy laugh, then walked towards him, offered up the phone, trying to stop her hand from shaking. She hadn't saved the message, but neither had she deleted it. She prayed it wouldn't be obvious that she'd listened to it already, but she was conscious of the symbol that popped up to say there was a voicemail, along with the call history.

Paul's gaze softened as he took it from her. 'Sorry, it was a late night as I said. Plus, my mother really got to me yesterday.' He leaned in and kissed her. For the first time, his kiss felt artificial.

'That's okay,' she smiled. 'Well, I think I'll go make myself some breakfast.'

She left Paul standing in the hallway, not feeling the least bit hungry as she made her way to the kitchen.

Chapter Forty-Two

Carver was dead to the world when a loud thumping on his front door woke him. For a moment, he wasn't quite sure of his bearings. He'd spent so little time at home lately, it was as if he'd woken up in a strange environment. It didn't help that he'd drunk too much last night. He couldn't remember the last time he'd been able to fall asleep naturally, without the aid of alcohol, pills or punishing exercise. It had probably been the first few months of Daniel's life, when he'd shared the bottle feeds with Rachel, and it hadn't taken much to make him doze off while the most precious thing that had sprung from their relationship lay contentedly in his arms.

He turned his head a fraction, but even that small movement hurt. He pressed his palm against his temple but it did no good.

More incessant thumping was this time accompanied by a voice. 'Sir, you in there?' Carver squinted at the bedside clock: 10 a.m. He hadn't meant to sleep that long. Then again, he'd never meant to drink that much. More thumping. *God, that boy can be annoyingly keen at times.*

He realised he was freezing. Looking down, he saw that he'd not actually made it under the covers. Dressed in nothing but his vest and boxers, no wonder he was cold. It was nearly mid-January and his heating had been up the creek since late December. He simply hadn't had time to get it fixed.

'Coming,' he called out gruffly. It took every effort to haul himself off the bed, throw on the trousers he'd worn yesterday, stagger out of the room and open the door.

Drake was one of the most tactful young officers Carver had come across, but even he couldn't disguise his dismay on seeing the state of his superior. 'You okay, sir?'

'Me?' Carver said in surprise. 'Yes, why shouldn't I be? What you got? I thought you were about to break the bloody door down. It's a wonder the neighbours aren't out here complaining.'

'Sorry, sir, but we've got a trace on the call made to Janis Stirling. To a block of flats on the Edgware Road. Seems to be the same area the hacker operated in.'

Carver felt re-energised. Quickly forgot about his raging hangover. 'That's probably because the hacker made the call, Drake. Give me ten minutes to get myself sorted, check my messages. In the meantime, get a uniformed team on standby in the area. I don't want to call them in until we've checked it out for ourselves. It's vital we don't alert the killer. But they need to be ready all the same. This could be it, Drake, and I'm not taking any chances.'

One hour earlier

'Off out?'

Two hours on from their uncomfortable encounter, Maddy caught Paul at the front door, coat on, rucksack slung over his left shoulder.

He looked around in surprise. 'Er, yes. My mother's. Why are you still here? Thought you were going in early. It's just after nine.'

And the lies keep on coming. Maddy ignored his question.

'You've gone from not seeing her since last year, to three days in a row? Is she ill or something?' She fixed her gaze on Paul, goading him to spout yet more lies.

He gave a heavy sigh. 'Yes, you're spot on. She's not been well at all, actually. I didn't want to bother you with it, what with all that's been happening. Doctors aren't sure what's wrong with her. They're doing all the tests, but it's frustrating.'

Incredible! Who is this person standing in front of me?

'Yes, it must be. Why the sudden concern for someone you can't stand – someone who's made your life a misery over the years?'

It was a reasonable question to ask, but her tone was interrogative, rather than curious. Their roles had been reversed from earlier; this time it was Maddy's glare that drilled through Paul.

He laughed uneasily. 'What can I say? Blood is thicker than water. She is my mother after all.'

Their eyes remained glued on one another, neither willing to yield. But in the end, it was Maddy who relented. If she pressed the point, it would look suspicious. *Hell, I've probably overstepped the mark already.* She softened her gaze. 'Yeah, that's true. I can understand that. Well, give her my best, won't you?'

'Will do.' Looking relieved, Paul smiled nervously back, then walked out the door.

No sooner had he left than Maddy grabbed her handbag, phone and flat keys, slung on her raincoat, and slipped out the door, closing it gently behind her. Work could wait. Besides, it might look suspicious if she went back as right as rain the day after she'd supposedly been at death's door.

She had to be quick. She heard the communal entrance door slam shut, then raced down the stairs two at a time, nearly tripping and falling flat on her face in the process. Her heart raced as she reached the door, turned the knob and pushed it open. Out on the street she glanced right to see Paul turn the corner onto Whitechapel Road. Bow Road was the nearest Tube to the right. But he went left, in the direction of Mile End station.

She pulled her hood over her head and started to follow him, terrified he'd look back at any moment and see her. If he did, she'd just say she was heading into work, and fancied walking the extra bit to get a direct Central Line Tube from Mile End to Liverpool Street.

London was waking up. By the time she reached Mile End station, the traffic along Whitechapel Road was moving at a snail's pace, and the commuters were arriving in droves. She had to use every scrap of concentration to keep track of Paul. He was a fast walker with a longer leg stride, and she found herself running every so often to keep up with him.

Oyster card at the ready, she held back at the entrance, waiting for him to go through the gates before doing the same, tracing his path to the westbound platform towards West Ruislip. *Where the hell is he going?* She prayed she could keep enough distance between them so that he didn't spot her, but at the same time, not so much that she lost sight of him.

She lingered at the top of the stairs leading down to the platform, waiting for him to find a spot in front of a carriage. She'd stay there until the Tube arrived, wait for him to board, then hurtle down the stairs and jump on herself.

It was a six-minute wait. She noticed him check his watch every so often, glancing around anxiously, as if concerned someone might be watching.

She decided to text Carver. She had no idea where she was going, but her instinct told her to let him know she might be onto something, and that if her intuition was right, she might be in grave danger.

> *I think Paul might somehow be involved in the murders. He's gone to meet Marcia Devereux. She left a message on his phone about destroying evidence. She's Paul's therapist. I think you interviewed her after she found Lisa. I'm following him now, but to where I don't know. Hope to text you with more info when I can. MK*

The Tube pulled up at the station just as she pressed Send. She started down the stairs, camouflaging herself behind a lofty teenager who didn't appear to be in any hurry, earphones on, seemingly immune to the world around him. Just as Paul stepped onto a carriage, he glanced up right. *Shit.* She quickly ducked her head back in behind the boy, her heart burning as she prayed Paul hadn't spotted her. She willed him to hurry up and board properly, fearing that she was going to miss her chance to get on. She had no choice but to sneak a peek around the boy to see if Paul was on board. Her pulse racing, she took a furtive peep. She couldn't see him. He must have boarded, and he couldn't have seen her. *Thank God.* She raced down the stairs as the doors were about to shut, and just made it onto the adjacent carriage, the sliding doors nearly slicing through her left ankle as she did so.

It was the tail end of rush hour and still busy. For once, she was grateful to be squashed up against the door, barely able to breathe. She clung onto a handrail as the Tube ploughed its way west, picking up passengers at every stop. At the same time, she desperately tried not to lose sight of Paul, who'd miraculously managed to get a seat. Rucksack resting on his lap, earphones on, he kept his head down the whole way.

The Tube driver was a particularly mad one, swinging the Tube this way and that as if he was competing at Silverstone. Finally, as the Tube approached Marble Arch, Paul got up and moved towards the nearest exit. Maddy's pulse quickened as she realised she needed to get off, keep pace with him, and yet, at the same time, not let him see her.

She mumbled her apologies to her fellow passengers as she shuffled herself into position facing the door, primed like a gazelle to get off. But she wasn't the only one. There were hundreds like her, looking to disembark at one of London's prime tourist hotspots. She had no choice. She became one of those commuters she slated every day, rudely shoving her way off the carriage, attracting angry glares all round as she stepped onto the platform and craned her neck to keep sight of Paul. She spotted his head in the masses and started to follow him – up the stairs from the platform level to the escalator.

About twenty heads separated them on the escalator. The ticket hall was bustling with activity when she reached the top. She fought her way through the crowds, sprinted through the exit gates and kept her eye on Paul as he took the stairs up and out of the station. She waited until he'd reached the top step, then jogged up the twenty or so steps herself. He turned right out of the station, and she followed, this time more closely. There were hordes of people, and it was far easier to lose herself in the crowds here than it had been at Mile End. He didn't stay on Oxford Street for long, taking a right onto Edgware Road. For Maddy, it brought back memories of her days at the academy; when they'd go clubbing around Oxford Street, end up at some dodgy kebab house at 4 a.m., hankering after grease to mop up the booze. Happy, carefree days.

There was no other road like it in London: Little Beirut, or Little Cairo, as it was more affectionately known. Whatever the day, whatever the weather, Edgware Road never slept, wall to wall with traffic and a diverse array of sounds, smells and cultures.

She continued to follow Paul, ducking out of view every now and again when he occasionally looked back over his shoulder. She was still wearing her hood and felt confident he hadn't spotted her. *Otherwise, he'd have turned around and confronted me, surely?*

They were about halfway between Marble Arch and Edgware Road Tube stations when Paul crossed over the road, then turned left onto a side street. Maddy held back a few seconds before doing the same. The street led onto Park West – a smaller side street housing a vast block of serviced apartments on either side, connected by a covered walkway. She watched from a distance as Paul crossed over to the main entrance, pressed the buzzer and appeared to talk to someone over the intercom. *Marcia?* Within seconds, he pushed open the door and entered the building, disappearing from sight.

Now came the tricky part. She'd done well to get this far without alerting him, but how the hell was she going to get into the building? She looked around, hoping to spot a resident or visitor, but there was no one about. It was a long shot, but there was no harm in trying. She tore across the road and up to the front entrance. Looked at the list of names to the side of the door. She didn't recognise any of them, while one of the buzzers was nameless. She tentatively tried the door. She couldn't believe it. It was open. *How can Paul have failed to close it?* It didn't matter. The fact was – she was in.

Inside, an aroma of spices greeted her: cardamom, cumin, nutmeg. Given the area, she wasn't surprised. There was a lift to her immediate left. It looked in sore need of repair. There was also a set of stairs. She was suddenly at a loss. She didn't have a clue which apartment Paul had gone into. She thought about ringing Carver, letting him know where she'd ended up, that she'd lost Paul, needed help with next steps. But then, just as she reached in her pocket for her phone, she heard music.

It was coming from above and must have been turned up very loud for her to hear it from the ground floor. Or perhaps it was coming from one of the first-floor apartments, and therefore in close range? Slowly, she made her way up the stairs, letting her ears lead her in the direction of the music. She was right: it *was* coming from the first floor. She exited the stairs and found herself on a long, brown-carpeted corridor. The music to her left was getting louder. She knew that piece. It was unmistakable: Beethoven's *Symphony No. 5.* – loud and dramatic.

She turned left, walked the length of the corridor, stopping at the last apartment on the right. The door was ajar. Her chest burned. This was all too easy. *Am I being led into a trap?* Her head told her to run for her life, call the police. But her fearless side willed her to see it through.

She cautiously pressed her hand against the door and pushed it open. It led her into a studio apartment with a worn beige carpet, a basic kitchenette to her immediate left and a threadbare two-seater sofa in the centre. But she barely noticed these, or any of the furnishings at first, her line of vision immediately captured by the newspaper cuttings and photographs pinned to the off-white walls.

Photos of the seven victims – of Carver and Drake, Stirling and his wife, and the most chilling of all as far as Maddy was concerned, a photo of herself. All had been taken without any of the subjects' knowledge – at work, on the street, in a public building and, in her case, at home as she sat curled up on the living room sofa, watching television, stroking Atticus.

She ventured closer. Saw that the newspaper cuttings included in-depth reports of each murder, interviews with the victims' families, friends and work colleagues, press statements made by Carver and others in his team, leads and updates on the case, feature centre spreads analysing the minds of pathological serial killers.

Maddy could scarcely believe what she was seeing. Her stomach reeled as she scanned the walls, almost breathless with fear.

At the far end of the room there was a table propped up against the wall, a chair tucked under it. On top of the table was a laptop. The cover was up, and the machine appeared to be turned on, whirring steadily. Clearly, someone had been using it recently, and that knowledge made Maddy's heart gallop even faster. The source of the music was also resting on the table, to the right of the laptop. A sleek red MP3 player, so tiny it was hard to believe the strength and range of sound coming from it.

To the left, lying on a smaller table, was a printer, and nestled in the far right corner of the room was a two-door wardrobe.

It was warm in the studio, but Maddy couldn't help shivering as she looked around and surveyed the scene, trying to get her head around it. *Run, run.* But a burgeoning curiosity propelled her further into the room. She walked over to the wardrobe, opened it tentatively. Inside were two knee-length leather jackets, three pairs of leather gloves, a box of latex gloves and two pairs of black Nike trainers. One pair of trainers looked brand new, as if they hadn't been worn outside. There was also a nun's habit. On the floor of the wardrobe there was a bottle of heavy-duty hairspray, a manicure set and a shallow crate holding a pistol, some rope, separate bottles of Paul Smith aftershave, chloroform, propofol and potassium cyanide, and a clear plastic bag containing several hypodermic syringes.

Was she looking at some kind of uniform, disguise, belonging to the killer?

Leather was wipe-clean, resistant to loose fibres; gloves would hide any trace of DNA or fingerprints; hairspray would prevent any unwanted hairs from falling onto the victim or the surrounding crime scene; Nike trainers were fast, sleek, noiseless, including a new pair to wear inside, leaving no footprints, while nail clippers would avoid nails catching skin or other fibres.

And the items in the crate? All were weapons and instruments to help facilitate the killer's vile design.

Maddy walked back over to the printer, which was on, and opened the tray. It was loaded with paper. She pressed Print, waiting with her heart in her mouth as the machine droned into action and did its job. A single sheet of paper slid out the bottom. She picked it up. What she saw made her heart beat even faster.

The page had faint streaks running across it. Just like the letters she and Carver had received. Just like the letter Paul had no doubt written to himself.

It said: *You shouldn't have come.*

She started to edge backwards, panic rising in her as she reached inside her pocket for her phone. She wondered if Carver had seen her message. Whether he had or not, she needed to call him. *Now.* She pulled her phone out, went to her contacts list.

'Put the phone away, Maddy.'

She knew that voice. She lived with that voice. It was the voice of a friend. *But why does he now sound like the enemy?*

Slowly, she turned around. Paul was standing there. He had a coldness in his eyes she'd never seen before.

'Paul, what have you done?' Her voice was weak, choked with fear. 'All this time, it was you.'

'You shouldn't have followed me, Maddy.'

'You saw me?'

'Yes, I'm afraid you'd make a lousy snoop. I spotted you at the top of the stairs at Mile End station. Did you think I'd left the front door open by accident?'

'Why didn't you confront me until now?'

'Because I had to let you come. I know you listened to that message. You think I wouldn't have noticed that you'd dialled voicemail? That I had a missed call from Marcia?'

'I…I thought it might have been urgent.'

'You shouldn't stick your nose into other people's business, Maddy. That's when you get yourself into trouble.' He took a step closer, and she retreated in fear. 'You were warned not to help Carver, but you just wouldn't listen. Not even after I killed your bloody cat.'

Tears flooded Maddy's eyes. 'You're an animal. You knew what Atticus meant to me, how could you?'

'I hated that cat, Maddy.' His tone was cruel, his eyes laced with scorn. 'I only put up with it because I cared for you.'

'How did you avoid being spotted on CCTV at the leisure centre?'

Behind him, the door swung open. Standing there was a tall, well-built woman, with short dark hair, jet-black eyes and a nose that swamped the rest of her face. It was not an attractive face by any means, not helped by the resentment imprinted on it. She was wearing a brown mac, secured with a belt which only seemed to accentuate her wide girth.

Although it had been more than four years since she'd last seen her, Maddy knew instantly who it was: Marcia Devereux.

'I put the ugly mug in your locker. I expect the police weren't looking for a large, unattractive woman dressed in tracksuit bottoms and a hooded anorak. And as you probably know, there's no CCTV in the changing rooms.' Her smug grin made Maddy's flesh crawl. 'There's nowhere to run, I'm afraid.' Her tone was unnervingly calm.

'You're going to kill me too?' Fear almost suffocated Maddy. She knew she shouldn't be surprised but hearing as much from the killer standing before her was terrifying. She turned to Paul, looked him in the eye, praying he'd see sense. 'How can you be a part of this? I thought we were best friends. You saved my life once. How can you possibly want to kill me now?'

She thought she spotted the tiniest flicker of guilt, of doubt. But still he didn't relent. Maybe it was an illusion, what she'd wanted to see. 'It doesn't give me pleasure in having to hurt you, Maddy. We never intended to hurt you. We never had a problem with you. But you meddled, and now you know too much. You've brought this on yourself. We have no choice.'

Maddy was scared senseless, but she was also raging inside. Furious for being lied to by the person she'd loved as a brother – the one person she'd never in her wildest imagination have thought capable of such vicious disregard for human life. She was going to die, she realised that, but she wasn't going to die without a fight; without knowing the whole truth, what had brought him to this point, how he and Marcia had managed to pull it off.

She turned her gaze on Marcia, her eyes blistering with contempt. 'You evil bitch. You corrupted Paul; you made him do all this. Tell me, how? How could you possibly have convinced him to be a part of something so sick?'

Marcia didn't respond. Just stood there with the same smug look on her face. Maddy turned back to Paul. Tried to reason with him again. 'How could you? Paige was your friend.'

He laughed. 'She was no friend. She was a pathetic, gullible slut like the rest of them. Like my darling mother, using her looks to fuck men nearly twice her age.'

'You mean Stirling?'

Paul glanced at Marcia, as if seeking her permission. 'Go on, tell her,' she said. 'She might as well know the truth; she's not going anywhere.'

Paul nodded, then faced Maddy square on. 'Stirling was a good friend of my father's. They were at Oxford together, and he's known me since I was born. My parents used to socialise regularly with the Stirlings.'

Maddy knew all this from Elizabeth Stirling, but she didn't let on. She pretended to look shocked. 'Why did you keep all that quiet?'

'Because I didn't want it to look like I was getting special treatment. And neither did my father, who instructed Stirling to keep it a secret. You see, I was bullied as a child, even as a teenager, and my father didn't want me to suffer the same fate at law school. He wanted me to succeed – make it up to him for being gay. But the fact is, I struggled in my first few months at the academy, and Stirling offered to help me, probably because of his friendship with Dad, although I was dumb enough to think he cared for me. He'd invite me to his office for private tutorials on subjects I was finding difficult to get to grips with, and he pretended to be concerned for me when Dad died. I was so grateful, and I loved him. I'd been in love with him for a long time, and I would have done anything for him. But he led me on. Always putting his arm around me, hugging me as if he felt the same way. I really thought he loved me. But he cast me off like some animal.' Paul's tone was vengeful. Maddy saw the hate in his eyes, and it scared her. 'He said the cruellest things. Made me feel like a pariah. And then I found out he'd slept with my mother while they were at university together – when Mum and Dad were already dating. My good-for-nothing prostitute of a mother, who never took any interest in me. Who was never a mother to me. Who spent all her time cheating on my father, screwing any man who cared to look her way. And then it came to me: women like her needed to be stopped. The academy was full of them: Sarah, Paige, Lisa. They needed to be taught a lesson. Flaunting their looks to get what they wanted. Not a second's thought given to anyone else's feelings. Bitching about those they considered beneath them. Stabbing them in the back.'

Paul glanced at Marcia, a look of recognition passing between them, then he turned back to Maddy. 'And Stirling also needed to be brought down a peg. He had a mother like mine. I thought he understood, that we had a connection, that he was different. But he's just as bad as all those whores; worse, in fact. A disgusting, filthy sex addict who treats love like nothing more than a flimsy piece of paper; something he takes freely then rips apart as if it had meant nothing to him. He needed to be taught a lesson. He needed to pay, to suffer. And fortunately for us, he dug his own grave by being the sex maniac he is. And by letting me into his childhood – a childhood deprived of a mother's love, scarred by memories of an abusive father.' He chuckled lightly. 'Everyone knows the saying: like father, like son. And then there were his other hobbies that proved useful. Anyone who knows Stirling knows how much he loves classical music; all those CDs proudly on display in his office, his house. Not to mention the fact that he actively encourages his students to listen to it. Little clues left here and there just to spark DCI Carver's interest. Although, to be fair, we hadn't anticipated extra help from Mrs Stirling. That sex tape was a real bonus, the icing on the cake. And Stirling leaving his DNA all over Bethany Williams' flat, even better, inside her, was the cherry. You see, we'd been keeping a close eye on his comings and goings for some time. We knew he'd been screwing Williams since the summer. We knew he'd visited her in her apartment on 29 December. Once again, his inability to keep his dick zipped up proved to be his downfall.'

Maddy was dumbstruck. *How have I never picked up on any of this?*

She'd lived with Paul, day in, day out, for four years. She'd been so blind. 'Did you kill those women, Paul?' she asked.

'No, he didn't,' Marcia said. 'It was me. Every time.' She looked down at her frame. 'You see, sometimes it pays to be an unattractive, stocky woman. But I wouldn't have been able to pull it off without Paul's help.' Her tone was victorious, and then she smiled. It was a crazy smile – *Jokerish*. The woman was completely insane.

'How so?'

'Ever noticed Paul is a whizz with computers?' Another manic grin. 'He's also very articulate, very creative. You must know that. After all, he is a writer.'

Maddy started to understand, the pieces of the jigsaw finally coming together in her mind. 'It was you who turned off the CCTV at Channings?' Paul's self-satisfied smile said it all. 'You hacked into Stirling's system. And Williams' too. That's how you got Stirling to Waterloo Bridge to make it seem like he'd been with her the afternoon she was murdered. You wrote the letters to Carver, to me, to yourself. You littered Stirling's internet history with repulsive websites.'

Paul sniggered. 'The internet sites weren't all me. Stirling's internet history wasn't exactly squeaky clean before I played with it.'

'So what? That proves nothing!' Maddy yelled. 'I'm damn sure he's not into websites showing women being tied up and beaten black and blue, is he?'

'No. That was all me.' He sounded so pleased with himself, and it sickened Maddy. It was hard to believe he was the same person she'd spent Christmas with at her grandmother's only a couple of weeks ago. She'd been living with a lie.

'And it was you who trashed our flat? Wrote that message on my wardrobe mirror? Made up that bullshit story that you were being followed?'

Paul nodded. 'I told you, we didn't want to hurt you. But you had to be stopped. It's a shame you didn't listen, Maddy. If you had, you wouldn't be here, and your beloved Atticus would still be alive.'

'Paul was my fix-it man,' Marcia announced proudly, placing her hand on his shoulder. 'He even rented this studio for us. I couldn't have done it without him.' Her face was a canvas of bitterness and hatred.

'That's how you knew where Sarah and Paige would be the night you murdered them,' Maddy said. 'From Paul. Who knew from me. And Emma Marsden? How did you know she'd be walking through St James's Park that night?'

'A little bird told me.' Marcia smiled at Paul. 'We'd been watching her for a while. She'd often cut through the park. But that night, a certain fictitious tourist happened to be standing in Parliament Square, taking photos, when darling sweet Emma left work for the night. One quick phone call to me and the rest, as they say, is history.'

'And the bomb that ripped open Bethany's stomach? How did you manage that?'

'Ever heard of YouTube?' Marcia asked. 'It's amazing what you can learn on there. All sorts of helpful DIY tips, including how to make bombs, pick a lock. It also gives you a lot of information about buying pistols and silencers, although they're generally much easier to get hold of.'

'And what about Suzanne? How did that pan out?'

'Paul hacked into Janis Stirling's system for me, after the old bag helpfully provided him with her username and password over the phone.'

'Why would she do that?'

'He pretended to be a charming BT advisor, and offered her a much better package than her current one. How could she turn that down?'

'Go on.'

'Once he'd hacked into Janis' system, Paul sent an email to Suzanne pretending to be Janis, asking Suzanne to meet her at Hampton Court Maze on the pretence that she had information proving Stirling's innocence.' Marcia hissed. 'That woman was so gullible, so desperate to please Stirling, I knew she'd fall for it.'

'But you slipped up, Marcia, didn't you?' Maddy said, looking to unsettle her.

It did the trick. Marcia became flustered, not expecting this challenge to her euphoric rant. 'The last location was slightly ambitious, even for me. I got my timing wrong, that's all. But I took care of it, and the bitch is dead. They're all dead, and the syllabus is complete.'

'Why, Marcia? What the hell had any of those women done to you?'

'The same thing that's been done to me all my life. You see, Maddy, I was never wanted as a child. My father was intellectually brilliant, but he was also a cold, violent man, who'd only ever wanted a son. He never me showed any affection. He hunted regularly, engaged in dangerous sports, gambled, drank to excess and played out his sick sexual urges in all sorts of ways – with hookers, and on me from the age of three. I hated him. I would have killed him, but I took more pleasure in watching him suffer when I set fire to his beloved horse.' She chuckled to herself. 'You should have seen the tortured look on his face: it was priceless. He made me go hunting with him. I hated every minute of it. And I resented the way he treated his fucking horse and dogs better than he treated me.' Another pause. 'He taught me one thing, though: how to use a knife, skin my kill. I have to say, it came in handy.' She took a breather, her eyes gleaming with excitement. She seemed physically aroused by her atrocities. For the first time, Maddy noticed her hands. Unlike the rest of her, they were slim and smooth, with long, graceful fingers and shaped, clipped nails. It was as if she took tremendous care of them – the only part of her she was proud to show off.

Marcia wasn't finished. 'And my mother…' she let out a scornful laugh, '…wasn't much better. She was exceptionally beautiful, while I turned out to be the runt, the ugly duckling who failed to turn into a swan. Not what she'd expected or hoped for, unlike her darling niece, Gracie, with her cherub-like features and fucking Shirley Temple curls. I used to scratch the chests of my Barbie dolls with my hair grips, all the time imagining it was Gracie's chest I was cutting.'

Maddy felt nauseated. She swallowed hard, trying to steady her nerves. 'Is that supposed to make me feel sorry for you? After what you've done? After you've murdered and butchered those women?'

'No, I don't want pity. I want respect.'

'Respect?'

'Yes. They all deserved to die. All seven are symbolic of what's wrong with this life, this world – what's been wrong since the beginning of creation. You know, I don't think Adam and Eve is a made-up story. It has to be true – the truest thing in the Bible – because what it's about surrounds us, has been with us throughout time, history. All this bullshit about women being oppressed is just plain wrong. It's beautiful women who are in control, who upset the order of things. Poisonous, cut-throat, scheming women, who manipulate men, treat them like their puppets. Take Sarah and Stirling for example. Sure, he had his eye on her from the start. She didn't exactly have to hunt him down. But she certainly didn't play hard to get either. She used him, without any thought for his wife, his reputation, and she got him to wield his influence in the City to bag her a training contract. Then…' she clicked her fingers, '… just like that, she dropped him. Do you think he would have done the same for me? The plain Jane who he barely noticed was in the room? Who he deliberately ignored and made to feel like shit.'

'You can't blame Sarah for being attractive,' Maddy retorted, desperately trying to play for time, her eyes darting around the room for an escape route, a weapon, anything. In her heart, she knew it was futile. The door was locked. There was no way out. It was two against one, and she could only pray for a miracle.

'No, I can't. But I can blame her for making a fool of me; for laughing and jeering at me behind my back; for taking pleasure in hurting my feelings; in mocking the fat one, the ugly one, the boring one. I heard the four of you that day in the canteen. You, Sarah, Lisa and Paige. You were all supposed to be preparing for a mock negotiation. Instead, Sarah slagged me off. And Paul. She taunted Lisa for being my friend, ridiculed Paul for his sexuality. Until then, I thought Lisa was my friend. I was waiting for her to stick up for me. But she betrayed me, sold me out to that ruthless she-devil of all people, made a mockery of our friendship, as if it meant nothing. But I never forgot. She was my easiest kill, you know – even gave me a key to her flat. You should have seen the look on her face, the Judas. It was priceless. And Paige was the same – Perfect Paige who wouldn't say boo to a goose but who screwed Stirling as well. And then Lisa dropped her knickers for him at the end-of-year party. No sense of self-respect, no shame – no thought for anyone but themselves.'

Maddy remembered the conversation in the canteen. Remembered being disappointed in Paige at the time – for being weak; for stooping to Sarah's level.

'But you stayed friends with Lisa all this time. Why did you wait till now?'

'Like Paul, I tried to contain my anger, my thirst for revenge. But it was always there, stewing, desperate to get out. And then, when I met Paul, I realised it was possible. The right moment had arrived, and I had a brother-in-arms to help me fulfil my vision. You know what they say, two heads are better than one.' She gave another terrifying smile.

'You didn't even know the last four victims. Why kill them?'

Marcia sighed. 'That was all rather random.' She walked over to the wardrobe, opened it, bent down and picked up the rope lying in the crate. She then gave it to Paul and gestured with her eyes towards Maddy. Paul stepped forward, grabbed Maddy by the wrists and dragged her across the floor to the chair. He pushed her down on the seat, yanked her arms behind her, and tied her wrists to the back of the chair, so tight, she could feel the cord already cutting into her flesh.

She looked up at him pleadingly, hoping he'd see sense, that she could reach the Paul she knew. But he looked at her blankly, and she realised she was seeing the real Paul now. Like his mother had said, he'd been a strange, reclusive little boy; and strange, reclusive little boys often grew up to be deeply troubled men.

Marcia came closer. 'Give her the full story, Paul,' she directed. 'There's no harm in that. She'll be dead soon anyway.'

Paul nodded. 'After Stirling rejected me, he became my obsession. I followed him regularly, day and night, more so after we left the academy. A part of me wanted to kill him – kill all his whores. It was indescribable, like nothing I'd felt before: an insatiable urge. I moved in with you because I believed you'd act as a check on my urges. You were the only good thing that came out of my time at the academy. You were different from the rest of them. You rejected Stirling, and you made me believe that women could be beautiful and decent. And so I was content with just watching him; watching him leave the office or his house to go and meet his sluts in shady hotel rooms – Emma, Bethany, or in the case of Suzanne, her own flat. But the urge was still there, and the longer I let it go unfulfilled, the stronger it got.'

'There must have been other women in four years. Why not murder them all? Why stop at seven?'

Marcia shook her head as if she was addressing a naive child. 'It's not just about killing for the sake of it, Maddy. Paul and I wanted to make a statement; prove our worth in this shitty world. We were considered second-rate to the likes of you and Sarah at the academy. And we've not been as *successful* in our careers. How then are we to make an everlasting impression on this fallen planet? By carrying out a brilliant, perfectly planned series of murders, targeting women we could match up to an area of law we studied at the academy; throwing the law back in their faces, and in Stirling's; devising brilliant riddles to test, confuse and drive DCI Carver and his team to distraction – riddles that even you were too late to solve.'

'What about Natasha?' Maddy ignored Marcia's arrogant response. 'She was only in her first year at the academy. What made you target her?'

'That was purely by chance. In fact, we'd intended to take a break from our plan until the New Year, let Carver sweat. But after I'd dealt with Emma, I headed for Piccadilly where I was meeting a friend for drinks. A strong drink is just what's needed after a kill. And that's when I saw Stirling go into Duke's Hotel with Natasha. I could immediately tell she was like the rest of them: a conceited little slut who thought she had the world at her fingertips. Later that night, I Googled her. Found out whose daughter she was. I bet she thought she had it all – a rich successful daddy, brains, beauty, a training contract waiting for her, a horny professor wanting to fuck her.'

Maddy shook her head in disgust. 'You're the one who needs a bloody therapist. You think I feel sorry for either of you?' She looked from Marcia to Paul. 'You think your crappy childhoods, your cold mothers, justify what you've done? I lost my parents to a drunk driver at the age of nine. But I'm able to do what any sane person does. I keep my rage, my inner demons locked up. I see sense, I know the difference between right and wrong. Both of you have done what you've done for one reason only.'

'Oh, and what's that?'

'You're both fucking insane.'

Before Maddy had time to think, she felt the full force of Marcia's hand across her cheek. Her neck jarred as she winced in pain, momentarily giddy. But Maddy wasn't finished talking yet. She needed the full story. 'And how did you both come to dream up your sick little plan?' She looked directly at Paul. She had to hear it from him.

'For three and a half years, I fought my urges, channelled my anger into my writing, focussed on our friendship, on meeting new men. But it was always there, needling me. I knew I needed to speak to someone, to vent my anger. So I made an appointment to see a therapist in Aldgate.'

'Marcia,' Maddy whispered.

'Yes. I didn't know it would be her until I turned up. We immediately remembered each other from the academy. And, as it turned out, when I told her about my life, the way Stirling had shunned me, made me feel so loathsome that I wanted to kill myself, the way Sarah had talked down to me so viciously, I discovered that she understood me far better than I could ever have hoped for – far better than anyone, even you, could have done. We shared a common bond, a common aim.'

'To murder innocent women?'

'When will you get it into your thick head?' Marcia raged. 'They're not innocent. None of them were innocent!' She chuckled. 'You should have seen the look on Sarah's face when she realised her time was up, that her looks and brains weren't going to save her this time. For the first time in my life, I called the shots. I dominated Sarah, I dominated all of them, and they were powerless to fight back.'

'And you think you're going to get away with this? By killing me? If I can discover the truth, Carver will. You slipped up with Suzanne. You may have got to her in hospital, but Carver knows it's not Stirling.

And he knows the killer's female. They found your DNA in the maze, and the back of you was captured on CCTV at Kingston Hospital. It's only a matter of time before he figures it all out.' She looked directly at Paul. 'You can't hide forever.'

'We'll take our chances,' Marcia answered for Paul, who suddenly looked panicked by Maddy's revelation. 'It's time, Paul. Do it, now.'

'Paul, I'm not lying. Carver knows it's not Stirling and he'll be coming for you both. But there's a chance your case will be treated with leniency if you back down now and help me.'

'She's bluffing,' Marcia said. 'She's making it all up to save her own skin. They've got nothing to connect us to the murders. I made sure of that.'

'You can't do this.' Maddy still tried to get through to Paul. 'You saved my life once, and now you're going to take it? We've been friends for so long, shared so many happy memories. We spent Christmas together, for God's sake. Think about my grandmother. Think about what it'll do to her.'

She saw the hesitation in his eyes. Unlike Marcia, Paul had some good in him, despite what he'd done. He'd been doing okay until he met Marcia, but he was the apprentice she'd been seeking all her life. She'd brainwashed him, manipulated his urges to fit her own designs. If only he'd opened up to her about Stirling, she might have been able to help. 'You don't have to do this, Paul. You can help make things right by letting me go. What about Justin?'

'There is no Justin,' Paul snapped. 'I made him up to throw you off guard. I thought you'd have realised that by now.'

'But what about the photo of you two together?'

'The wonders of Photoshop,' he smiled.

'Told you,' Marcia smirked. 'A whizz with computers.'

'Paul, it doesn't have to end this way,' Maddy persisted.

'Don't listen to her,' Marcia said. 'She doesn't get us. She may have lost her parents, but she had the same cosy upbringing as the rest of them. If you let her go, she'll go straight to the police. Do it, now.'

Paul suddenly looked like a confused little boy. His eyes flitted from Marcia to Maddy as he stood there, immobile.

'For fuck's sake, *I'll* do it,' Marcia growled. She went over to the wardrobe and gathered up the nun's habit, leather jackets, trainers and gloves, then dropped them on the floor in the centre of the room, about a metre and a half away from Maddy. 'Move,' she instructed Paul. He edged backwards, his eyes fixed nervously on Maddy as Marcia went over to the kitchen and reached into a cupboard for something.

When she returned, Maddy saw that she was holding a plastic can of petrol. Realising what Marcia planned on doing, Maddy was suddenly paralysed with fear.

Marcia unscrewed the lid, then doused the pile of clothes and shoes with the fluid. It released a potent smell, exacerbating Maddy's nausea. Marcia reached into her pocket, pulled out a lighter, and flicked the switch. She looked around the room, then directly at Paul. 'This place has served us well. But once I throw this lighter on the ground, no one will ever know. Any evidence will be reduced to dust, including you, Maddy.'

'That's where you're wrong!'

Maddy looked up. It was Carver, Drake just behind him. Carver briefly held her gaze, and at that moment she saw more than a policeman doing his job, protecting a citizen; she saw the feeling in his eyes and realised that he genuinely cared about her.

Carver focussed back on Marcia, who spun round in alarm. 'Police! Put that out and put your hands up. We know everything. The game's up, and there's nowhere to run. You are under arrest.'

Surprise and disbelief swamped Marcia's face. Carver aimed his gun at her, while Drake kept his on Paul. She glanced at Paul, saw his resigned expression. 'It's over, Marcia,' he said, putting his hands up. 'I don't regret it. Stirling's a worthless piece of shit, and he deserved to suffer. As did all his whores.'

'No, it's not over.' Marcia smiled at Paul, stepped onto the petrol-soaked clothes, raised the lighter above her head and dropped it onto her hair.

'No!' Paul cried out.

Flames immediately erupted – devouring Marcia's body. Maddy watched in horror as the screaming burning figure flailed around wildly. And then, without warning, Paul lunged into Marcia, trying to drag her from the flames. But the fire was too strong, and now his own arm was alight.

'Paul, stop, you're on fire!' Maddy shrieked. The heat was unbearable, burning her skin, her eyes, her throat as she coughed and spluttered, trying desperately to wriggle free. She could no longer see Carver and Drake, her vision hindered by Marcia's burning body. But there was still enough of a gap around the edge of the room to squeeze through. She heard Carver yell at Drake to get Paul away from Marcia and evacuate the building. Then came the sound of a kitchen drawer being opened. As she began to lose consciousness, Maddy just made out the faint outline of a figure approaching her. It was Carver, shielding his head behind the inside of his elbow as he came around the back of her. She felt a sharp tugging, then her arms were suddenly free, hanging limp from lack of circulation.

'Come on,' he urged, lifting Maddy up from the chair and into his arms. 'We need to get out, now.'

Outside, in the distance, Maddy heard sirens approaching. Her head felt foggy with the smoke, but somehow, she managed to keep awake as Carver sidestepped the edge of the scattering flames. They made it to the door, heard the heavy trudge of footsteps coming up the stairs before a cavalcade of firemen appeared. 'Anyone still in there, sir?' one of them asked.

Carver looked back over his shoulder, panting heavily, his eyes squinting through the thick smoke. 'No one that can be rescued now. Just put the damn thing out.'

Outside the blazing building, it was like a war zone. Hundreds of people out on the street – stunned residents, curious passers-by, policemen, firemen, nosy reporters quick off the mark. Carver carried Maddy to one of two ambulances parked across the road. A paramedic immediately dashed towards them with a wheelchair as they approached. 'Here, see to it that she's well taken care of,' Carver instructed him. As he lowered Maddy down into the chair, they held each other's gaze.

'Thank you,' Maddy whispered. Carver didn't reply, just smiled at her with his eyes.

He broke his gaze from her to address the paramedic again. 'She's inhaled a lot of fumes.'

'What happened to Paul?' Maddy desperately searched the sea of faces.

'I don't know. I'll find Drake.'

But Drake found him first. 'Sir.' His jacket was missing and, like Carver and Maddy, he looked like he'd been mining coal.

'I'll be back.' Carver gently squeezed Maddy's shoulder, then gestured for Drake to follow him a little distance away.

Although she didn't know it yet, he was certain Maddy was in shock. He didn't want her hearing bad news first-hand if that was what Drake had come to tell him.

'What of King?'

'He's alive. I managed to put the flames out with my jacket before getting him out. But it looks like he's suffered third-degree burns to the right side of his face, along with his right arm and leg, trying to pull Devereux away. He's already been taken to St Mary's.'

'Okay, keep a police guard stationed at all times.'

'Yes, sir.'

Carver placed his hand on Drake's shoulder. 'And well done, son. You're going to make a great inspector one day. Maybe even Chief. Thank you. I'm proud of you.'

Drake was overwhelmed. 'Thank you, sir. That means a lot. It's been a pleasure working with you.'

Carver gave him a droll smile. 'Don't say it like it's the last time, Drake. Next time I find myself hunting down a pair of psychopathic serial killers, you'll be the first to know.'

Drake grinned. 'Thank you, sir. I think that's the best compliment I've ever received.'

'I mean it.' Carver's eyes creased up at the sides. 'But don't tell anyone. I don't want word spreading that I'm getting soft in my old age. That'll never do.'

'No, sir,' Drake grinned again, 'you have my word, my lips are sealed.'

Chapter Forty-Three

Friday 25 June 2010

'You're not jealous, are you?'

Marcia hadn't noticed Sarah Morrell approach. The party was drawing to a close, and it had come to that point in the evening when the music slowed and the loved-up couples took to the dance floor, while the unloved stood around watching uncomfortably, wishing they'd left earlier, wondering how they could escape without it looking patently obvious why.

Marcia turned to look at the biggest bitch in the year. Sarah was plastered, her eyes glazed and bloodshot, yet spiked with the same vindictiveness they always held.

'No, why would I be?'

Sarah looked Marcia up and down, made a spitting sound. 'Have you looked in the mirror lately?'

A switch flicked on inside Marcia, but somehow she maintained her cool on the outside, even when Sarah continued her spiteful tirade: 'I mean, you could have made an effort, for tonight at least. But you're never going to get laid if you dress like a middle-aged spinster and don't lose at least thirty pounds.' She leaned in closer, whispered in Marcia's ear. 'And you'd be wise to doll yourself up a bit for other reasons, you know.'

'Oh yes, and why's that?'

'Because while I was still shagging Stirling, he told me that you'd never make it as a lawyer, that you lacked the brains and the guts to succeed in such a tough, intellectually demanding profession.' She sighed wearily. 'But the poor sod didn't have the heart to tell you. Shame really. I always feel honesty is the best policy.'

Marcia thought back to her childhood, substituted Sarah's face for one of her Barbie dolls and mentally stuck pins in it. That felt good. Now she could respond to her comment. 'I'm glad you feel honesty is the best policy, Sarah, because I'm going to be honest with you right now. You might be beautiful on the outside, but you're actually one of the ugliest, most despicable human beings on this planet. You have no friends, no steady boyfriend, and you were so unsure of your own worth when you started here with no job in the bag, that you felt the need to fuck a professor to get a training contract.' She edged closer to Sarah, their noses almost touching. 'Your life will amount to nothing, you mark my words. You will get your come-uppance. And when you do, I'll be watching, having the last laugh, enjoying every minute of your pain and suffering.'

For once, Sarah Morrell was lost for words, never expecting a response like that from a girl she took delight in treating like a second-class citizen.

It was a response which triggered the making of Marcia Devereux – and the undoing of Sarah Morrell.

The present

Stirling walked through his front door, a free man and yet not really free. He'd lost everything: his job, his reputation, the life he had known.

Although his name had been cleared, it would forever be tainted – tainted by his arrest, by the fact that his lust for women and casual sex was now public knowledge, by the fact that he'd fathered a child by one of his students, and by the fact that he had been hated enough to be framed for murder by two deranged young people, who'd nearly succeeded in sending him to prison for the rest of his life.

And now, looking at the suitcases lined up in the hallway, he realised he had lost one more thing: his wife. As he continued to stare at the cases, Elizabeth appeared. She looked beautiful. She was beautiful. And it had taken him nearly three weeks behind bars to realise this. Looking at her now, he realised how selfish and stupid he'd been. It was useless begging her to give him another chance. But he'd give it one last shot all the same.

'Please don't go. I can change. Give me another chance.'

She stared at him with dispassionate eyes. She regretted sending the memory stick to Carver, and she was glad her husband was free. But she couldn't live like this anymore. She could never trust him again, no matter what he said. It was far too late for that; too much had happened. Being separated from him was what she'd needed. In that time, she'd realised she was stronger than she'd thought. She could do this. She was only forty-four. She could make a new life for herself. She could start again.

'No, James. I think you know as well as I do that we're well beyond that point. I should never have put up with your affairs for as long as I did. Particularly with no children to hold us together. I was weak. But now I feel stronger. I managed without you before we met, and I can do it again.'

He said nothing. There was no use protesting. He could see that her mind was made up. He respected her for it, and he wished her well. 'Where will you go?' he asked.

'I'm going to stay with Pamela for a while.'

'As in Pamela who lives in New York?'

'Yes. We've always kept in touch. She was a good friend at Oxford. She knows what's been going on and has offered me refuge while I sort my head out. No one will know me there. It's just the sort of anonymity I crave right now.'

The telephone rang. Elizabeth answered it. 'Yes, thank you, I'll be out in a minute.' She put down the receiver, looked at her husband. 'My taxi's here.'

Stirling took up her cases, followed her outside, and loaded them into the boot of the taxi. They paused to share one last moment with each other on the pavement.

'I'm sorry I was such a rotten husband,' Stirling said, his eyes filled with genuine regret. 'You deserved so much better.'

'You need help, James. Make sure you get it. I wish you well.' She kissed him tenderly on the cheek. It was the warmest kiss he'd received from Elizabeth in a long time.

And then she got into the taxi and was gone. And he was glad he'd never told her about the biggest regret in his life – the secret he'd carried around with him for twenty-three years; the secret that most certainly would have killed her.

And yet, at the same time, it was something that might have prevented all this ghastly mess from happening.

Carver was feeling more human again. He'd slept for seven hours straight without the aid of whisky or pills and was enjoying an early morning session in the gym. Sparring with his mate, Lionel, who was pleased to see his friend sober and back in the ring after a three-month absence and looking more like himself, if not a little out of shape.

Paul King was still under police guard in hospital. He'd suffered third-degree burns and was receiving various treatments. Doctors treating him said he still wasn't fit for questioning, and so until then, Carver was making the most of a well-earned hour to himself.

He bounced around the stretched canvas floor like his son's space hopper, jabbing right hooks at Lionel who avoided his punches with deft slips demonstrating a keen eye and years of practice.

'You're on fire today, Jake.'

'I tell you, Li, it's amazing what a bit of sleep does for you. And, of course, cracking a multiple murder investigation.'

Lionel kept his eye on the target. 'Yes, I can imagine.'

Just then, a familiar face caught Carver's eye. He lost concentration, and Lionel took his chance, knocking his friend to the floor. They were both wearing helmets, so it didn't take long for Carver to recover. Still on his backside, he shook his head in disgust, then looked up angrily at the person he blamed for letting his guard slip.

'What the hell do you want, Drake? I came here to escape. And yet you're following me around like some puppy. Am I going to regret giving you that compliment?'

Drake felt the full force of four eyes drilling through him. Lionel was a big bald man who wouldn't have looked out of place on the WWF team, and Drake couldn't work out whether his stern expression was a show for Carver's benefit, or whether he really wasn't someone you wanted to get on the wrong side of. But then, Lionel's face broke out into a broad grin.

'Aw, give the lad a break, Jake, won't you?' He removed his gloves, offered Drake a sweaty palm. 'I'm Lionel, and I've heard a lot about you. Sounds like my crabby friend here wouldn't have solved that case without your help. Just ignore him. He's more hot air than substance.'

Drake shook his hand and managed a smile. Then Lionel left them to it.

Carver removed his helmet, revealing a mass of damp hair, loose strands clinging to his forehead. 'What is it, Drake? I assume you've not come here to take up boxing?'

'No, sir. Paul King's condition is stable, and yesterday we obtained his fingerprints and a DNA sample.'

'Yes, I should hope so. It's standard police procedure. And? You're obviously going somewhere with this.' Carver wondered what the hell Drake was going to say next.

'And his DNA matched Stirling's.'

Carver's jaw dropped. 'You're messing with me, right?'

'No, sir. I'm deadly serious.'

'Are you saying Stirling is King's father?'

'It would appear so, sir.'

'Does King know?'

'I don't know, sir. Clearly, it would go to motive. I mean, if he did know, and Stirling had wanted nothing to do with him, that might have driven him to help Devereux – by framing his real father for the murders, I mean.'

Carver shook his head. 'That doesn't fit with what Stirling's maintained all along. He said Paul was in love with him and wanted revenge against him for spurning his advances. He said Paul hated all those women for having what he couldn't, and that his hatred of women stemmed from his childhood, the way his mother had ignored him and cheated on his father.'

'So maybe he doesn't know?'

'Maybe not. The question is, does Stirling?'

Chapter Forty-Four

'Yes, I know that Paul King is my son.'

Carver and Drake sat across from Stirling in his living room. There was a sad, empty feel to the place. Despite it being bigger and far more lavishly decorated, now it reminded Carver more of his own home. It was missing something – a woman's touch; her scent.

He noticed Elizabeth's cello was gone, the vase on the mantelpiece which had always been filled with fresh flowers was empty, and there was no music. The only sound was the sound of silence.

'How long have you known?'

'Since he was three.'

Carver was gobsmacked. 'And you didn't think to tell us?' he said, trying not to lose his temper. 'You know that counts as perverting the course of justice?'

Stirling sighed. He looked dead on his feet. The bags under his eyes protruded like purple pufferfish. 'I told you I thought Paul was somehow involved. That he was trying to frame me.'

'Yes, because of what happened in your study, after he made a pass at you.'

'Whether or not I told you he was my son would have made no difference. He'd already helped murder those women. The deed was done. His brain isn't right. He needs to be locked up. For life.'

Carver knew what Stirling said was probably true. But as a father, he couldn't understand how he could have kept something so important from his flesh and blood; how he could have lived his life knowing there was a piece of him out there; how he could have ratted on his own son, despite what he had done.

'I know what you're thinking, Chief Inspector,' Stirling said. 'You're wondering how I could possibly have held back and not told Paul; that had I told him, it might have made a difference; that he might not have helped that crazy woman do all those horrific things.'

Carver was silent. He had a feeling Stirling had more to say. He was right. 'I had a brief affair with Paul's mother, Evelyn, at Oxford, during our third year. I was only twenty-one, and it was just before I met Elizabeth. She and George, Paul's father, had been seeing each other for nearly two years when it happened. In fact, they'd just become engaged. She was very beautiful, and I'm not sure why she allowed herself to be tied down to George so early. He was a good man back then, but very English, a man who always crossed his t's and dotted his i's. Boring, some might say. I'm guessing the main attraction was that he came from a very rich family and could offer Evelyn the extravagant lifestyle she craved. Unlike me, who, although I've done okay for myself, found City life too stressful. I've always been an academic, and I guess that's what Elizabeth and I had in common, aside from the music.' Stirling took a sip of water. 'George went home one weekend. Evelyn and I were at a house party, wasted as was often the case, and we succumbed. It happened two more times, I think. And then we called it a day. She was going to marry George, and she didn't want to risk him finding out.'

'So, I take it one of those three occasions resulted in Paul?' Carver said.

'Yes. But she didn't tell me until just after Paul's third birthday. Naturally, George assumed something had gone wrong with their birth control. He did the right thing, brought the wedding forward, married her before she started to show – although a lot of people talked, that's for sure.'

'So why did she tell you?'

'George and I remained good friends after Oxford. I worked with him briefly in the City, at the same firm. We'd have dinner parties, mix with the same crowd, see each other at Christmas and family birthdays, et cetera. Including Paul's third birthday. You know how parents always make such a fuss of their kids' birthdays.'

Carver nodded, for a split second remembering how he'd helped his son blow out the candle on a Thomas the Tank birthday cake Rachel had spent nearly three hours making for his first birthday. Happy times.

'It was the summer.' Stirling woke Carver from his fleeting daydream. 'A heatwave, in fact. George and Evelyn threw a garden party for Paul. All the kids were in their swimwear, and I remember Paul was dressed in these pirate swimming trunks. He had long hair for a boy, past his neck. I remember Evelyn saying she wanted to keep it that way for as long as she could get away with it. At one point, when Paul was splashing around in the paddling pool, he lost his balance, fell over, and started to cry. As usual, his parents were busy with friends and didn't appear to notice. And I seem to recall the nanny had the day off. I went to help Paul. Lifted him out of the pool, dried his legs off with one of the towels laid out for the kids, then his hair. And that's when I saw it: a stork bite – the same as me.' Stirling swivelled round. He pulled down the back of his jumper to reveal a flat, salmon-coloured birthmark on the back of his neck.

'My heart almost stopped when I saw it. I confronted Evelyn a few days later, and she had no choice but to admit it was true. It was hard, but I agreed to keep my mouth shut. Elizabeth and I were only just married, and it would have killed her. And it would have destroyed George and Evelyn's marriage. I tried to take an interest in Paul whenever I could. I was delighted when he came to study at the academy, although George didn't want any of the students to know about our connection. Paul had been bullied at school by kids who envied his privileged upbringing; also, because he was a bit of a loner. George didn't want that to happen at law school. Although I respected his decision, when I saw that Paul was struggling with the course, I couldn't just turn a blind eye and not help him. As a father, I wanted him to succeed and couldn't bear to see him suffer. The same was true when George died.'

'And you had no idea he had feelings for you?' Carver asked. 'Sexual feelings?'

'No.' Stirling shook his head emphatically. He got up from his chair, moved decisively across the room. 'No idea at all. I knew he was gay. I'd spent several evenings discussing this with George over a bottle of whisky. He really did love Paul, and it had devastated him. Secretly, it devastated me. But it had never crossed my mind that Paul saw me in that way. I thought he viewed me as "fun Uncle James". I was shocked, repulsed, when he tried it on...because I knew the truth...I knew he was my son. But I also couldn't tell him why. Too much time had passed. There was my reputation to think about, and Elizabeth. Not being able to have children broke her. For her to suddenly learn that on top of my affairs, I had a grown-up son – I couldn't do that to her. And so, I had no choice but to cut myself off from him – from the entire family. It was painful, but there was no other way. I kept my eye on him from afar, though. I knew he still lived with Maddy Kramer and had given up on law; that he'd self-published a couple of books and worked in a bar.'

'But you were ready to commit yourself to your baby with Bethany Williams.'

Stirling came back over and sat down. He buried his head in his hands, talked down into the darkness of his palms. 'Yes, yes I was. Four years had passed since I turned Paul away. My marriage had deteriorated even further, and I realised I had real feelings for Bethany, that she actually meant something to me. I wanted to do the right thing, and she agreed to keep my identity a secret. No one was to know – not Elizabeth, not even her mother or best friend, Juliet. At least, not for a long time.' He took a breath, his eyes moist with tears. 'For a while, I thought I'd finally been given the chance to be the person I wanted to be, what my father never was, what I never got to be to Paul – a loving father.'

'Are you going to tell Paul the truth?'

'What's the point? He's ruined his life, and I've ruined mine. What use can come of him knowing now?'

'At least he'll know why you turned him away.'

Stirling shook his head. 'No, I don't want to go down that route, not when there's no future, for either of us.'

Carver and Drake left Stirling to himself. A man who had once had everything – but who was now alone.

Now, the man who had once had it all, had nothing.

Carver parked up at the station, his hands still gripping the wheel, as if the physical act alone allowed him to focus. They'd driven back from Stirling's house in silence. Finally, he said what was on his mind. 'Sentimentality aside, we need to bring the subject up with King. Stirling may not have told him, but someone might have done. Obviously *after* he tried it on with Stirling in his office. He might be deranged, but I'm certain he's not *that* sick.' He took a deep breath. 'We need to know if he knew. It goes to motive.'

'Do you want me to speak to him, sir? He might open up to me, being a similar age.'

Carver eyeballed Drake. 'What are you saying? That I'm old and unapproachable?' He looked furious, and for a moment Drake thought he'd undone all the goodwill built up between them. But then Carver grinned. 'S'okay, son, I'm only joking. Thanks for the offer, but I can only think of one person he'd be likely to open up to. I just hope she's willing to do me this one last favour.'

Chapter Forty-Five

'I don't want to see him.' Maddy didn't smile, bat an eyelid, or move a muscle. Carver felt awkward, impotent. He realised he had a lot more convincing to do.

It was 11 a.m. on Saturday, three days on from the day Maddy had nearly died. A freakishly warm January morning, with hardly a cloud in the bright blue sky. Maddy sat next to Carver on a bench, overlooking the Embankment. The sun was intense, and she found herself squinting as she watched a riverboat cause a ripple of waves as it meandered its way down the Thames. Beyond the boat, and above Embankment Bridge, the London Eye turned steadily, its movement so slow it was almost imperceptible to the human eye, while above it, a British Airways jumbo jet gradually gained height, leaving a trail of thin, wispy smoke as it disappeared for a few seconds into a rare fluffy cloud.

Maddy would have given anything to be on that plane right now.

In view of her traumatic experience, and key role in capturing those responsible for his daughter's death, Coleridge had insisted that she take at least a week's paid leave. She'd been both surprised and grateful, half-expecting him to fire her on the spot after discovering she'd been living with one of the culprits, despite having no inkling as to what Paul was up to.

She certainly wasn't ready to return to work so soon, to brush off what had happened as if it was some minor triviality. In truth, she wasn't sure she could ever go back to Channing & Barton – the scene of the first murder, a murder her flatmate had played a star role in. For the last two and a half months, she'd discussed the murders with her colleagues, secretaries, even the cleaning staff, speculating who it could be, whether they were safe from the killer's clutches, where or when the killer might strike again.

And now it turned out that she'd been best friends with the person who'd helped facilitate those murders. That he'd been right under her nose. How could she show her face to those people again? Most of them had been amazing, sending supportive emails, leaving compassionate voicemails. But the questions would always be there, lurking under the surface water of pleasantries, every day she walked the firm's corridors: How did you not see? How could you not have known? How could you have been friends with that psychopath?

'I understand how you feel, Ms Kramer,' Carver said, 'but I need your help. I truly believe he'll open up to you.'

'Like he opened up to me about hating Stirling, about hating Paige, about planning a string of murders?'

Maddy's tone was resentful. It was the first time Carver had heard her talk like that. Until now, he'd seen the scared, the plucky, the inquisitive side of her, but never the embittered side. He hoped it was a passing phase, that she would come through it. She was an intelligent, beautiful, brave young woman, and she deserved the chance to be happy. It was too soon for someone so young to become so disillusioned with life. He was too shy to tell her, and in any case, it wasn't appropriate, but he'd come to care for her – deeply. He didn't want her to change; he wanted her to continue being Maddy.

He'd yet to tell her that Stirling was Paul's real father. All he'd asked was whether she'd be willing to visit him in hospital, his hope being that Paul might confide in Maddy of his own accord. But seeing her reticence, Carver knew it was time. He had no choice.

'James Stirling is Paul's real father.'

Maddy gave Carver the same open-mouthed expression he'd given Drake after hearing the news.

'What?' she finally spoke. 'How do you know?'

'Their DNA matched, and Stirling confirmed it.'

'He knew?' Maddy said in disbelief.

'Yes.' Carver told her about his conversation with Stirling.

'So, you want me to find out if Paul knew this before he helped Marcia commit murder?'

'Yes, we need the full story, Ms Kramer. Was he motivated purely by lust for Stirling and a deep-rooted hatred of women? Or, did he decide to help Marcia after learning the truth about his real father, hell-bent on taking revenge against Stirling for never telling him the truth? For, as far as he was concerned, never wanting to be a father to him? Perhaps he imagined that Stirling, like George King, was ashamed of him being gay.' He took a breath. 'Don't get me wrong, Paul King is clearly not right in the head. I'm certain neither you nor I would consider helping someone commit a series of horrific murders under similar circumstances. But the jury will need to hear everything and may have more sympathy with option two.'

Maddy sat back, pressed her head against the back of the bench. Almost oblivious to the constant stream of traffic behind her, the passing droves of tourists, everyday life still going on around her as if the world she had known and loved hadn't come crashing down on her. She turned her gaze to Carver. 'Why do you care if the jury has sympathy for Paul? You've got your man. Now it's up to the CPS and Paul's defence counsel to try the case, and the jury to reach a verdict.'

Carver didn't answer at once. Then he told her. 'I guess because I'm a father. Because I, for one, can't ever imagine hiding the fact that I am his flesh and blood from my son. If finding out about his real father is what motivated Paul, there's a small part of me that has some sympathy for him. It will sort of make sense. And maybe we can prove that Devereux manipulated his anger to her advantage. After all, he didn't physically commit any of the murders. Once Paul is well enough, he'll be taken to a police station and questioned. After that, and once all the evidence has been collected, including your statement, it will be my duty to write to the CPS detailing the circumstances surrounding the case, and provide them with all kinds of written evidence. So, you see, Ms Kramer, I'm still very much involved in the case. What I send the

CPS will impact on how they decide to proceed against Paul.' Carver paused, his expression suddenly stern. 'But if he never knew the truth, and it turns out he's just another mentally unstable cold-blooded killer, with a sick fetish for slaughtering young women because of his shitty childhood, then I'll do everything I can to make sure the CPS lock Paul King away for life and throw away the key.'

Monday 19 January 2015

'I never expected to see you again.'

'The feeling's mutual.'

'So why are you here?'

Maddy sat down on a chair next to Paul's bed. When the ambulance had brought him to St Mary's in Paddington, the entire right side of his face and body had been burned to a crisp. The damage was so extensive, it had penetrated through every layer of his skin, but at the time had caused him no pain because the nerve endings had been destroyed. He'd undergone a number of procedures, having dead skin and tissue removed from the burned area, and had also received several treatments, including intravenous electrolytes, antibiotics and various pain medications. And that afternoon he was due to have skin graft surgery, a procedure which would hopefully speed up the healing process and reduce the amount of time he needed to be in hospital.

It was hot in the room, as was so often typical of hospitals, but especially so in the case of burn victims, whose damaged skin prevents them from effectively regulating body temperature. Maddy found herself perspiring under her coat and quickly removed it, along with her cardigan. She briefly glanced up at Carver watching through the window. He gave her a barely visible nod of encouragement before she turned her attention back to Paul.

Half of him was covered in bandages, including his right eye. She had therefore deliberately sat on the good side of him, making eye contact with his left. The eyes were the window to the soul, and if she was going to get the truth from him, she needed to see at least one of them.

'Because I'm curious, I guess. Curious to know whether you're just plain insane, or whether there's some deeper issue at work here. I mean, you blame what you've done on your mother, on Stirling for rejecting you, on the fact that women like your mother need to be taught a lesson. But I want to know if there's something else? Something that tipped you over the edge. If there is, I might be able to help.'

'Water, my mouth is dry.' Paul gestured to a plastic cup lying on his bedside table.

Maddy nodded, put the cup to his mouth, then watched him take slow, painful sips.

'Enough,' he said.

'So?' Maddy persisted.

'How could you possibly help me?' Paul's speech was laboured, every word an effort.

'Well, there's a chance of your sentence being reduced if your defence counsel can prove temporary insanity.'

She saw the briefest spark in Paul's good eye. 'How would they be able to do that?' he asked.

'They'd need to prove something happened which caused you to lose all reasoning, so that you failed to comprehend the nature and quality of the crimes you committed.' She paused. 'What I mean is, did something else motivate you – something that made you feel seriously wronged, and therefore justified in framing Stirling? After all, if the jury can be convinced that your main aim was to frame Stirling for murder, rather than kill those women – which is what Marcia did with her own two hands after all, you just helped facilitate that – it might help you.'

Again, she studied Paul's reaction. Instead of sadness, regret, she saw his brain going into overdrive. He'd realised what this meant – that there was a potential way out – and right now he was desperately trying to think of one. And at that moment, she knew. Knew for certain that Paul had no idea Stirling was his real father, and that the murders he'd helped Marcia commit were driven by something biological – a defect in him that had always been there, simmering at the surface until Marcia helped bring it to boiling point.

'You can help me, Maddy,' he said excitedly, his good eye flickering with a madness that made Maddy's stomach turn. 'You're a great lawyer. You can think something up, invent some argument to get my sentence reduced. I know you can. You've always been there for me. Not like my mother. Not like Paige, all the other bitches. They deserved what they got. But you're like a diamond in the rough. It's Stirling who deserves to rot in jail, not me. I was so much better for him than those promiscuous whores.'

She didn't answer. Her friend was insane, but he'd also known exactly what he was doing. His guilt was unequivocal, and she hoped, for darling Paige's sake, that he'd be locked up for a very long time.

She left without saying another word, closing the door behind her.

THE END

THE LUME & JOFFE BOOKS STORY

Lume Books was founded by Matthew Lynn, one of the true pioneers of independent publishing. In 2023 Lume Books was acquired by Joffe Books and now its story continues as part of the Joffe Books family of companies.

Joffe Books began in 2014 when Jasper agreed to publish his mum's much-rejected romance novel and it became a bestseller.

Since then we've grown into the largest independent publisher in the UK. We're extremely proud to publish some of the very best writers in the world, including Joy Ellis, Faith Martin, Caro Ramsay, Helen Forrester, Simon Brett and Robert Goddard. Everyone at Joffe Books loves reading and we never forget that it all begins with the magic of an author telling a story.

We are proud to publish talented first-time authors, as well as established writers whose books we love introducing to a new generation of readers.

We won Trade Publisher of the Year at the Independent Publishing Awards in 2023. We have been shortlisted for Independent Publisher of the Year at the British Book Awards for the last four years, and were shortlisted for the Diversity and Inclusivity Award at the 2022 Independent Publishing Awards. In 2023 we were shortlisted for Publisher of the Year at the RNA Industry Awards.

We built this company with your help, and we love to hear from you, so please email us about absolutely anything bookish at feedback@joffe-books.com

If you want to receive free books every Friday and hear about all our new releases, join our mailing list here.

And when you tell your friends about us, just remember: it's pronounced Joffe as in coffee or toffee!

Printed in Great Britain
by Amazon

55169193R00200